GAMAN
SHINASAI

GAMAN SHINASAI

DARRELL WEIDNER

VANTAGE PRESS
New York

This is a work of fiction. Any similarity between the names, characters, and places in this book and any persons, living or dead, is purely coincidental.

FIRST EDITION

All rights reserved, including the right of reproduction in whole or in part in any form.

Copyright © 2005 by Darrell Weidner

Published by Vantage Press, Inc.
419 Park Ave. South, New York, NY 10016

Manufactured in the United States of America
ISBN: 0-533-14889-8

Library of Congress Catalog Card No.: 2004091580

0 9 8 7 6 5 4 3 2 1

For Hazel . . . cause for my love of reading,

for Tracy, Jeff, Ryan, Brittany, Tatum . . . my life,

and finally, for Sara (Sweetie) . . . my passion.

> He shall wipe every tear from their eyes, and there shall be no more death or mourning, or crying out or pain.
>
> —*(Revelations 21:1–5)*

Prologue

Singapore . . . thirty-eight years ago

DIMLY LIGHTED STREET lamps dotted the narrow cobblestone road. The stench from garbage and urine littering the roadway settled itself in the misty air, violating each breath taken.

Several slump-shouldered figures, visible here and there, stumbled along with occasional assistance from the decaying two and three-story buildings that bordered each side of the road for approximately eight hundred meters until abruptly ending at the polluted bay.

No one was in a hurry. None took notice of the other. The light rain was annoying.

These unfortunate creatures of fate and choices made, having satisfied their habits and having freed themselves from reality for another night, now sought refuge in doorways . . . for rest.

Once a flourishing merchandising trade quarter, the sagging structures, with their rotted boarded windows, were now warehouses and shelters for drug users and drunkards . . . and for private meetings that required discretion away from scrutiny of government authorities. Here, the dark waters of the bay had produced many soulless humans. Local police paid little attention.

In the shadow of a doorway, hidden from anyone who might be searching, a man stood holding a small figure. The man was not Asian. He was tall . . . over six feet. Though slender, his moves would be deadly if the wrong person approached.

The child tried but was unable to hold back tears. The man softly whispered into the boy's ear, "Gaman Shinasai." The man allowed himself no tears.

Ten meters away, another figure in an unseen doorway watched as the man turned to the small Asian woman who stood at his side facing him.

The man placed the child into her arms.

She understood the man's pain.

The woman, barely five feet tall, looked up at him and, with her eyes and a nod, acknowledged what was expected of her.

She moved from the safety of the doorway onto the road, and with her light shawl shielded the small face from the rain. After thirty steps she quickened her pace. Her head remained straight while her eyes continued scanning side to side searching for movement.

The woman was cautious but moved quickly without drawing attention. The child was held close . . . the woman would die before allowing harm to her small companion.

Several hours passed and two figures appeared at the crossroads of a paved highway and a mud-filled road that led inland. The drizzling rain seemed to have subsided, the air seemed warmer . . . the inner feeling of assurance changed the weather. The woman and two-year-old boy would be safe. She would fulfill her promise.

She paused as she turned to gaze, for the last time, at the distant skyline. She would never see the man again. She remembered . . . Gaman Shinasai!

The woman lightly tugged the small hand she held. "Come, we begin."

* * *

Brentwood, California . . . twenty-five years ago

The boy flinched and his head jerked slightly from the sound of the heavy metal door slamming shut with the ringing of steel banging against steel. Now it was quiet. The room was dark. The only light came from a small flickering flame surrounded by a one-inch dark-red glass candle holder fastened to the center of one of the four bare walls of the tiny room. This wall was opposite the door. Above the light was a small crucifix whose shadowy figure seemed to move as the dancing flame spoke to it. The boy, barely four years old, trembled. *What next?*

His eyes adjusted to the faintly lit room and he noticed a small sleeping cot set against the wall that was adjacent and to the right of the wall with the door. Except for the crucifix the room was washed like a water color of a dim red glow. A small pillow, with what appeared to be a white pillowcase buffed with the pale red tint, rested at the head of the cot. The boy could see a white or grey sheet, also bathed in the reddish tint, neatly covering the small bed that was also partially covered by a dark, maybe indigo or ebony, blanket.

The boy was not alone. Two soldiers stood quietly at parade rest against the bare wall adjacent to the door. Each carried a holstered sidearm. Finally, the boy saw them.

He felt disoriented and frightened, and he began to remember. *Two soldiers ran into my room at my house and took me. The airplane ... I was on an airplane ... a long time. I slept a lot. I landed in pretty lights in the airplane. The soldiers ran when they carried me to a big black car. The car was dark inside ... I couldn't see out. The soldiers picked me up and carried me from the car, and they ran with me to this place. Why? Where's my mother? Where is she? ... Where is she?*

* * *

Washington, D.C. ... *two years ago*

As he held the phone to his ear, the soft buzzing sounded a third time, intruding on the silence.

It was 11:30 P.M., Sunday.

The fourth buzzing sound was interrupted when a calm voice quietly answered. "Yes?"

"Mr. President," the caller's hushed voice acknowledged. "This is Warren Turner."

"Hello, Warren." The president always called him by his first name even though Turner was twelve years the president's elder.

The president spoke softly in his usual quiet and deliberate manner, "I understand we're ready."

Turner was sitting in his favorite deep-cushioned easychair as he listened to the most powerful man in the world. A small desk lamp provided barely enough light to reveal a generous, yet comfortable study. The fragrance of Turner's special blend lingered from his spent pipe which now rested lifeless on the small lamp table next to him.

Two walls adjacent to one another contained floor-to-ceiling bookshelves. A third wall displayed a small fireplace where once-burning logs were now red smoldering coals that suggested the past warmth of a January fire.

As he sat staring through the large picture window, Turner saw the lights of the nation's capital twelve miles away. This Virginia hillside view was part of his reward for the forty-three years he had served his country.

"Mr. President. I've been advised by *Jericho,* who just returned from the *'Garden,'* that plans are almost complete, and are expected to hit us in less than twenty-four months. We don't know what it is yet, but *Jericho* said it would be devastating . . . and could cause another damn global war."

Turner paused for a few seconds before continuing, "I'm afraid it will be biological, Mr. President."

The president knew Turner was referring to the "Garden of Eden" . . . code name for the Middle East.

"All preparations of phase one were completed eleven months ago," Turner's voice sounded a trace of hesitation. "We'll begin the initial contact and phase two of 'Operation Gardenstone' tomorrow."

There was a momentary silence before the president spoke, "I understand your reservations." He was sincere. "What you're being asked to do is violate a trust. Your country will always be indebted to you."

After another somber moment of silence, Turner heard the president's sympathetic voice, "Goodnight, Warren."

"Goodnight, Mr. President." Turner heard the phone disconnect.

The room was still. For several minutes he held the receiver in his lap and stared at the night. Warren Turner loved his country. But did he have the right to break a promise he had made many years ago to someone whose friendship had meant more to him than his own life? Did he now have the right to destroy someone else's life?

He replaced the receiver on the side table next to him and sank back in his chair. The dimly lit office shielded him from the view of anyone outside.

As his tired eyes fixed on the distant lights, he thought about tomorrow.

After a few lingering moments, Warren Turner, professor of International Relations at Georgetown, slowly rose and turned off the lamp.

Present Day

1

EVERY NOW AND then I seize a glimpse of the March sun, a planetary reddish-orange ball in the sky just moments ago, as it begins settling itself behind the southern end of the White Tank Mountains that lie a few miles west of Luke Air Force Base some twenty miles away. And then, just seconds after it completely dispositions itself out of sight, the cloudless sky freezes a bright orange to pale blue to grey as it furthers itself from the western horizon.

Aware of the late model green Chevrolet minding itself several cars back—something I've become quite accustomed to over the past two years—I wheel my disgustingly expensive Porsche convertible around the corner of Glendale Avenue and sail north up Seventh Street.

For the first time in months, it seems, a slight ripple of a smile births itself like a long forgotten ocean wave caressing the sands of a tempered beach at dusk. I slowly inhale and hold for a few seconds while my eyes briefly close, and finally, though reluctantly, I exhale slowly, still savoring the smile lifting me up to heaven. The sweet perfume-like fragrance from this year's early-blooming orange blossoms subtly spreads its flavor throughout the melody of the wind. The Valley's remarkably warm and dry winter has induced the blossoms out weeks earlier than usual.

I try to ignore the throbbing pain just below the back of my neck where it feels as if it's been sliced open with a surgeon's scalpel, and then the opening surgically closed within the past hour.

This incessant pain first made its unwelcome breed present about three years ago beginning with a delicate nagging warning that was, then, slightly more than just an irritable aggravation domiciling itself between my shoulders. It's now advanced itself to the point of becoming almost unbearable at times. Aspirin and other pain killers are no longer capable of amending its unsolicited behavior.

Because of all the world turning itself upside down in my life three years ago, I know well that stress feeds the pain. So I exist with its thorny manner and try to relax muscles that run across my shoulders and along the base of my neck.

When this occurs I attempt repeatedly to try to concentrate on other things, letting my mind strike other times, other places. Hue had always told me, *"When experiencing physical pain, let your mind be somewhere else . . . a different time . . . a different place."*

I grimace now with disgust and frustration as I massage the back of my neck with my right hand and tell myself it's not always that simple.

While my jet black sports car roars across the small bridge over the Arizona Canal that flows beneath Seventh Street halfway between Northern and Dunlap Avenues, I secure a glimpse of the unusually fast flowing water. My thoughts transpose as I try to blot out the pain and begin recalling how the canals came to be.

Only about thirty to forty feet across, they meander more than twelve hundred miles throughout the valley, and have a normal depth of about five to eight feet. Below the surface, upon which I sometimes notice a steel blue effervescent glaze not unlike I imagine the ice cold northern seas to be, the flow can be more rapid and quite treacherous as opposed to the slow current that is normally visible on the surface.

Nowadays, these canals are used primarily as a water supply to valley municipalities for their utilities customers as well as for irrigation for farming and lawns for older residential areas, and for serious thinking joggers racing along the soft powdery dirt banks that border each side.

Through the rearview mirror, my eyes transiently lock on the canal bridge as it rapidly grows smaller in the distance until trailing vehicles finally block my view.

As I reflect on the canals, I'm reminded of the earliest known settlers to Arizona . . . the Native Americans who were, in history books, called the Hohokam Indians (meaning "those who vanished").

They were in Arizona from 30 A.D. until about 1450 A.D. At one time, almost twenty-five thousand of them found themselves inhabiting what is now the state of Arizona. They were the only humans living there at the time.

I can't help but think that they were out of their sun-deranged minds to ever have come to this desolate hell on earth that seems, somehow, to lure one, once here, to the point of never wishing to leave. And yet, while conceiving in my own mind that they were just plain idiots, I bear this unmistakable sense of envy, and I'm forced to respect their tenacious gifts of patience, providence, and endurance—especially endurance.

In order to survive, they had built a network of irrigation ditches that allowed them to divert water from what is now called the *Salt River* that flowed east to west across the Valley carrying melted snow from mountains that resided in the eastern part of the state. Many of those irrigation ditches are still in use today.

With that thought in mind, I sometimes find myself wondering, not optimistically, if anything built *today* will still be used fifteen hundred years from *now*.

Approaching Dunlap Avenue, I gun the Porsche around a slow-moving pickup and again the orange blossoms penetrate my senses with forlorn, almost unidentifiable, memories dating back to years long past when I courted my wife. This sweet fragrance takes me to her shoulder, where my head lies, where my face, my lips, lightly brush the softness of her neck, and I melt in her raptured scent . . . no other like it in the world.

Another razor sharp pain steals across my shoulders and I can't help grimacing and attempt to abort recognition of the throbbing at the base of my neck. I visualize Hue telling me about the first white settlers who came to Arizona, after having endured numerous obstacles that life parceled mercilessly upon them for months upon months as they traversed mountains and wastelands, and, then, eventually hauled citrus trees to this hellhole that were expected to grow.

I have often scolded myself for having been far too hasty to prejudge them to be too ignorant to know better. What arrogance, though! To think that this place, barely befitted for cactus, rattlesnakes and Gila monsters, could produce thousands and thousands of acres of orchards filled with orange, lemon and grapefruit trees. I know that those western pioneers had more balls than I'll ever have, I remind myself as my right hand repeatedly clutches at the back of my neck.

Every year, when the orange blossoms first make their presence, usually in midMarch, they remind me of when I, at the age of three, was first brought to the Valley of the Sun thirty-seven years ago.

Hue and I were sitting together in the back seat of a taxi driving along Van Buren after having landed at Sky Harbor's small airport just a few minutes earlier.

At first, when I detected the sweet fragrance drifting through the opened windows, I thought it was perfume that Hue was wearing ... until she remarked about the sweet flowery scent dancing through the taxi's windows, wondering aloud what it was.

The driver turned his head back toward her with a twinkle in his eye, it seemed, and a wide grin, and proudly proclaimed that the fragrance was from the orange blossoms. As he spoke, he acted as if he were part of this natural phenomenon, as if he had invented this enticing bouquet and was letting us visitors know that his valley was full of wonderful things.

At that time, the Valley of the Sun was saturated with citrus orchards. Today, urban growth has almost eliminated them.

My Porsche begins crawling along barely ten miles an hour as traffic has snarled itself into a slow moving parade of helpless metal machines of movement with nowhere to go. Hue was right, having my mind somewhere else *does* help. The painful throbbing between my shoulders has subsided somewhat.

I can still recall times when, as a boy, Hue would tell me about the history of the Sonoran Desert and Arizona. She was an avid reader, and the history of the Valley was an insatiable passion for her, resulting in countless numbers of times that I would tag along with her visiting local libraries.

I spent many happy hours listening to her soft voice intriguing me with stories about the people who had roamed Arizona over the centuries and had survived in spite of the multitudes of harshness that life wielded in unforgiving portions that could force one to curse one's God on a regular regimen, and wonder why in hell there was any kind of reasonable thinking by one's Creator that would allow such abuse.

Now, I keep a small covered wagon model on a credenza in my office to remind me that the *so-called* asperities I face today don't begin to compare with what those poor souls braved. I came upon the covered wagon years ago in a quaint tourist shop in the small Mexican village of *Puerto Penasco* that is commonly referred to by Arizona "Anglos" as *Rocky Point.*

The village sits on the northeastern shore of the Gulf of California about a hundred forty miles south of Phoenix, of which about sixty miles are south of the Arizona-Mexico border. My former old beat-up '63 Corvair's speedometer verified this on numerous trips that Hue and I took to the small fishing village for picking up inexpensive fresh shrimp . . . huge jumbo-blue shrimp, the kind that can't be bought anywhere in the valley.

My mouth waters even now as I imagine chomping into one of those ice cold jumbo-blues dipped in cool red shrimp sauce. I haven't been to *Rocky Point* in almost twenty-five years. I miss Hue.

I can still visualize her sitting at the top of North Mountain or Piestewa Peak after the two of us had climbed one of those mountains, and we'd sit for hours while she would tell her stories about the history of Arizona. She read everything she could get her hands on, and I too learned to love this land and its history.

She was particularly interested in the Spaniards, the Conquistadores, who in the mid 1500s first came to the Sonoran Desert, which included what is now northwestern Mexico and much of Arizona and New Mexico.

The Conquistadores dreamed of finding treasures of gold, and saving souls. They found more souls than gold. I sometimes wonder what those so-called explorers thought when they first encountered the Native American inhabitants who were not only physically attractive, but highly intelligent and possessing of a childlike innocence. The *true* treasures of the new world... whose way of life was changed forever by those *cultured* Europeans.

The traffic jam has mysteriously taken flight, and so my fancy Porsche races past Mountain View, and my thoughts wander from history to the present as the pleasant cool breeze, filtered by the dry desert air, races through my hair and caresses my face that bears a light tan due to my almost-daily climbs along mountain trails in the late evenings just before dusk. I honestly believe, as I deem others throughout the world most likely judge of their own beloved lands, that the sunsets I feel privileged to observe from these peaks cannot possibly be more beautiful, more spectacular, anywhere else.

Now, as I round the curve up Seventh, my most common, almost constant and nagging memory of the past takes hold. Who would have ever guessed, after everything that happened, that three years later I'd be driving a car like this. I smile big at that and can say to myself now, *What the hell!*

But, I still bear an uninvited pain that won't allow me to forget. Julia and I lost our home and almost everything else. She tried her best to hide her feelings. But I knew she'd been disappointed, her dreams shattered... and I, alone, was to blame.

I had everything—almost everything—well thought out, calculated down to the penny. Now, I know I never should have taken such a risk. *Foresight is a wretched slave subservient to hindsight and both should be stricken from existence,* I found myself constantly pondering while I searched for excuses for my failure, and prayed to God I would be awarded some remarkable insight from this inversion on my life.

As I've done almost every day for the past three years, I think about the months of depression and the self doubts about my competence as an accountant. Before that, nothing ever seemed to bother me, like I had invisible armor to battle trivial setbacks... I was always able to tell myself, *The raft-rides through the rapids are too short... forget the bouncing and bruises... clean out your pants later, Michael Everest... enjoy!* But this was no small defeat. Hue used to admonish me that I didn't take life seriously enough. Well, without hesitation at any level of thought, I can honestly declare that I'm taking the events of the past three years seriously . . . very seriously.

I recall it as if it were yesterday, how my clients lost confidence in me. Most of them had been with me since the first year I had begun practicing on my own ten years ago. It didn't take long for word to get out about my failed investment. Just like tumbling dominos, all those clients who invested with me, one by one, told me they needed a change . . . needed fresh input for their financial and tax planning . . . *nothing personal, of course.*

Now, as I cruise by the entrance to North Mountain Park, the pain retakes possession of my shoulders and becomes even more intense as it shoots through the base of my neck like a burning sting similar to an electrical shock. Again, without conception, I grab at it with my right hand and massage the ache.

The sky has now lost its watercolor tones and merged into a greyish blue, and still remains cloudless. Because of the closeness of North Mountain, I'm no longer able to see the horizon above the White Tank Mountains, where, if I were now at the top of North Mountain, I'd be able to observe the bright orange glow hidden behind and above the western mountains from what would appear to be a mammoth fire roaring out of control on the other side of the White Tanks. But, in reality, only a mirage.

Seventh Street is loaded with hikers and joggers walking and running along the side of the road, most headed for the entrance to the paved road that winds upward with a good incline for almost a mile until reaching the top of North Mountain.

I climb it about four or five times a week. The transcendent view at the top seems to inspire me to wish upon myself the ability to take flight and soar across from mountaintop to mountaintop during the day. At night, the magic of shadows flowing downward in enchanting disclosures are like mystical illusions as I gaze out across the black valley floor suffused with golden tints from street lights strewn out like a blanket that seems to go on forever . . . Glendale, Peoria and Sun City to the west; Moon Valley to the north; Scottsdale in the east; Tempe, Mesa, Chandler, Gilbert and Ahawatuki in the southeast, interrupted only by midtown and downtown Phoenix high rises and a few scattered lesser clusters of mountains, and then spreading all the way to South Mountain. Most of the valley can be seen from the summit. I can honestly say, without apology, I dearly love this Valley.

The mild weather has brought out a lot more joggers than ususal. As I approach the incline on Seventh Street, I continue trying to focus my attention on other things, even unpleasant things.

I still analyze, as I've done countless times during the past three years, what went wrong. A real estate project developing condos should have made me and more than a dozen of my clients very wealthy.

But, two of my clients, Campbell and Worthington, both normally quite reliable and predictable, backed out just one day before the expected closing of escrow on nineteen hundred acres. One day before!

Time isn't right, Campbell had said.

Worthington had apologized, *I'm just not comfortable with this.*

Now the sky shades to indigo blue as the glow from the sun finally vanishes, and my dark Porsche begins the ascent up Seventh Street away from the lights of the Phoenix skyline.

As often I have tried, I continue to be unsuccessful at erasing the memory of Campbell and Worthington . . . loyal clients as well as good friends. It wasn't like them, not their texture at all.

More than half of my clients and I had already contributed almost ten million dollars as a down payment, and I know that all of those clients, aside from losing confidence in *me*, survived the loss. But Julia and I were financially and emotionally dismantled.

That financial loss was nothing compared to the mess I'm in now. Julia would kill me if she knew, I warn myself as my sports car finally touches the summit of Seventh and begins the descent into Moon Valley.

The green Chevrolet still confines itself a short distance behind, and I'm able to see the lone passenger in the Chevy occasionally glance at the driver whose eyes seem fixed straight ahead . . . at me. Neither appear to be speaking. Two late-model pickups and a Jeep Cherokee separate the Chevrolet from my Porsche on the three lane street.

Several minutes pass as I approach Thunderbird Road and obey the green left-turn arrow, and then accelerate west for about a half mile before slowing, signaling right, and coasting through the entrance of Moon Valley Country Club Estates, a wealthy cluster of large ranch-style homes, sequestered from one another by a sprawling green belt that is part of a private golf course that roams throughout the upper-class subdivision.

On a few occasions I have played the golf course with clients who live there . . . *ex-clients*, I remind myself.

After several blocks, I skew the Porsche right onto a narrow-winding lane lined with the well-spaced homes. Dampness from the watering of freshly cut lawns fuses in the air with the aroma of the orange blossoms.

Another half mile later, I slow and glide to the side of the lane. I'm the last to arrive.

2

"THAT'S GAME and set," Walter Barron yells as he strolls toward the opposite side of the net. "That's two in a row for me. C'mon, Jack, it's time you won a set."

Assistant Phoenix Police Chief Walter Barron takes these matches more seriously than the rest of us. Walter's about five-foot-eleven with a stocky, muscular build. He always wears the latest style of brand-name tennis apparel that always seems to my judgement to be a size too small.

Ever since I've known Walter, I have established in my own mind that Walter leans heavily, more so than most, on the side of being quite meticulous when it comes to his appearance. One supporting circumstance relative to my thinking, is, for one thing, Walter always makes sure his shirt is firmly tucked inside his tennis shorts, never to venture out.

Walter Barron appears to be five or six years younger than his forty-one years, and, by anyone's standards, I firmly believe, is considered to be an exceptionally good-looking man. I've been told by many who know, that Walter is well liked and highly respected not only by the chief of police, but more importantly to Walter, by his peers and the police officers on the streets. He's the odds on favorite to be the next chief.

Since his tight-fitting tennis outfits always seem to be a little out of place on a tennis court these days where loose-fitting attire is more *in,* I find myself harboring mischievous thoughts of ridicule, though no evil intended, but simply for my own self entertainment or self amusement. And, obviously, I have no desire to shatter my best friend's perception, distorted though it may be, of himself.

Besides, I naughtily grin to myself, no harm no foul. *Anyway, there's hardly ever anyone else around the secluded tennis court for Walter to embarrass the rest of us,* I chuckle to myself as I sense a tinge of light-humored deception just thinking that.

In contrast to Walter Barron, I always wear a loose-fitting T-shirt, two sizes too large and hanging outside my loose-fitting baggy tennis shorts that barely brush my knees. I guess I'm definitely not the one to criticize Walter. I can't help smiling again at that thought.

"You enjoy that feeling for now, Barron," Ted Mills jokes. "You've got Jack to hold up now. We're gonna kick your ass. C'mon, Michael, let's do some bad shit."

Ted Mills is another assistant chief in the Phoenix Police Department. He and Walter first met at the police academy, and then began working together as patrol officers almost twenty years ago. They became instant friends . . . and competitors.

Mills dresses like a jogger, a badly dressed jogger in my way of inspection, or, for that matter, any way anyone else with common sense would view it. Mills always wears tight, faded blue or yellow T-shirts that tuck into his snug-fitting ugly-red silk running shorts with knee-high white socks.

I chuckle to myself again thinking that Mills' shoes belong on a running track or on a cross country course and are unarguably out of place on any tennis court. However, I've never felt the urge, though, to advise him of my view on that subject.

Mills, also forty-one years old, same as Walter, can pass for twenty-five with a boyish face that conceals what I have already decided is an extremely intelligent mind that drives this police department administrator. I have heard that Ted, like Walter, is also highly respected by his subordinates and peers.

Mills is several inches shorter than Walter but is just as muscular. The two of them still workout together with weights three or four times a week, a ritual they began together at the beginning of their careers. I, in contrast, see myself as lean and mean.

In my mind, the two professional lawmen, together on a tennis court, look about as out of place as a tourist at the Grand Canyon wearing a picture of the Canyon on his beige T-shirt and bright leprechaun-green Bermuda shorts with knee-high black socks and white Converse basketball shoes, with a camera dangling around his neck. Hue and I actually saw that spectacle once.

That being the case, however, every Wednesday evening, Walter Barron, I sense, sees himself as one of those slender and lithe hard bodies, stroking, sliding, slamming and sweating on this court surrounded by huge dark-green olive trees that reach up into the sky and encircle the court.

With their dark leaves constantly swaying in the amalgam of the night light and the shadows, like a stadium crowd, to and fro from the winds sweeping across the valley, they procreate the jam-packed stadium that is not unlike, Walter probably imagines, the old dark-green Stadium Court at Wimbledon.

Walter Barron experiences Wimbledon every Wednesday evening. There are times though, I am certain, he wishes he had taken a tennis lesson or two.

Then there's Jack Hopkins. Jack is also an assistant chief. He's fifteen years older than the others, and has been a Phoenix cop six years longer.

If Walter's and Ted's appearances are comical, Jack is a traveling show. I can never comprehend in my own way of thinking about how certain laws of gravity can be so totally rebuked and ignored by those faded-purple Suns basketball shorts, two sizes too large, hanging to Jack's knees, that stay in place on his five-foot-ten-inch lanky thin frame. And, at least one and sometimes both of Jack's almost knee-high white tube socks always take flight to his ankles by the end of the first set.

As if Jack's appearance is not hysterical enough, when combining it with his tennis style, I often find myself, when totally lacking control of any sort, practically rolling on the ground dying from laughter. It doesn't take a brain surgeon to recognize, with little study of the matter, that Jack is definitely not as athletically inclined as his two younger police brothers.

Even if dressed in a tux, I find myself imagining that Jack Hopkins would still look as if he had just come in from riding a horse on the range.

I stroll past Jack as we exchange sides, and the older man utters an apology that is actually quite serious, "I'm not playing worth diddly-shit tonight, Michael. I just cost you a set."

"I won't be able to sleep tonight, Jack, thanks to you," I joke.

Walter Barron and I were high school classmates, and I was best man at Walter's wedding nineteen years ago. Our tennis foursome has played together for almost six years, and tries to play every Wednesday evening.

It gives me a much needed distraction to that maddening and always lingering pain constantly hovering just below the back of my neck. But, recently, more often than I care to admit, someone has to fill in for me because of my unavoidable traveling the past two years.

I am the only one of the foursome who plays serious tennis outside our group. After having been a latecomer to the game, just eight years ago, I've somehow managed, for the past three years, to achieve a USTA singles ranking of sixth in the thirty-five-and-over age group in the Southwest Sectional which consists of Arizona, New Mexico and Southwestern Texas.

As I await Walter's serve, I can't help wondering what my tennis buddy police officers would think if they knew what I, the boring accountant, am involved in up to my red-lined ass.

"I can't believe the great one just messed up," Walter yells as he blasts a lucky shot past me.

The tennis court nestles in a green belt sculptured by small rolling hills with plentifully placed mature olive trees, Arizona pines, grapefruit trees and assorted evergreen shrubs noted for their year-round green foliage. Expensive condominiums surround this park-like setting that is only accessible by a single lane passing by the west side of the court.

Contrary to traditional and thoughtful planning, the court runs east-west lengthwise. In Arizona it's more common for a tennis court to run north-south in order to reduce the time that the sun can interfere with play. Almost all the tennis clubs in the valley are set up with the north-south layout.

But, valley builders, when developing subdivisions, normally lay out the tennis courts wherever they'll fit, with little thought of the rising and falling of the sun. I noticed it the first time I stepped onto this court.

The sun is no problem now for us four tennis soldiers. It exhaled behind the western mountains over an hour ago allowing the night to harbor itself into every crevice in the valley. And none of our foursome notices the empty, green Chevrolet parked alongside the lane.

3

EVEN BEFORE ANSWERING the telephone in the family room, Marlene Manucci knows as well as anything that her husband will be leaving for the evening and possibly for the entire night.

It's just past eight thirty.

"Okay, I'll be there in twenty minutes. Give the location again." Detective Lieutenant Joseph Manucci doesn't need to write it down.

"Sorry, hon, it's another girl," he swears under his breath.

As he drives toward the Salt River bottom that courses east-west through south Phoenix, Manucci slowly shakes his head and dreads what he's about to see . . . what he's about to investigate. *Thank God for Marlene.* Manucci knows in his soul how lucky and blessed he is to have someone like her as his wife. She's an emergency room nurse; that's where they met, twenty-seven years ago.

Manucci had brought his bleeding partner to the hospital after Manucci, his partner, a rugged Irishman transplanted from New Jersey, and eight other Phoenix patrol officers had broken up a brawl outside the Capri Lounge on East Van Buren.

Along East Van Buren from Sixteenth Street all the way up to Fortieth Street prostitutes of both sexes congregated to parade their merchandise. Manucci thought about how, depending on how one looked at it, their endeavor was somewhat rewarding. Most were able to feed their five-thousand-dollar-a-month habits, and those smarter ones were able to become upper middle class citizens within a few years. And Manucci knew that the relentless watch, interference and harassment by the Phoenix Police Department was like nothing more than a moth being scatted away with a flick of a hand to these entrepreneurs and their pimps.

The Capri was located between Sixteenth and Twenty-fourth Streets. At that time mostly urban cowboys and cowgirls danced to the new-sounding country music that could be heard blaring out across Van Buren seven nights a week. Even though there were quite a few prodigious bouncers mingled among the crowd, the police department was still called upon to break up fights almost every night.

Anyway, Manucci's partner had been smashed over the head with a half-full Jack Daniels bottle, and St. Lukes Hospital was just up the street. With blood dripping down both sides of his face, the impaired police officer looked worse than he was to Manucci. Even though the bottle broke, Manucci's associate suffered only superficial wounds just above his forehead. He lost a little blood, but other than that was back on the street with Manucci the next night.

This gorgeous brunette nurse pampered his partner as soon as Manucci brought him into the emergency room. And, patrol officer Joseph Manucci almost forgot his partner was there when his less than manageable eyes reposed on Marlene.

The rest is history. Manucci, being the cautious type, dated her for four years before he popped the question.

She understands as much about the rotten side of this world as I, Manucci opines to his way of thinking as he turns south onto Sixteenth Street. He disparately wishes at that moment that he was home in bed and clinging tightly to her now . . . forgetting the rest of the world. *At least I've got her instead of a bottle.*

It's easy to find. Four marked patrol cars are parked along the side of the road with their emergency lights quietly flashing in the darkness, creating a fortuitous scene that if observed from a short distance calls out that an unusual and unhappy ambiance has befallen those silent beings moving here and there.

Manucci climbs from his car and attempts the descent. His stubby legs straighten and bend as he awkwardly maneuvers down the sandy embankment of the dry riverbed, occasionally losing his balance . . . and composure.

Once on somewhat level ground, his legs straighten for good and he is again the man in charge.

"She's over here, Lieutenant," one of the uniforms motions to him.

Manucci guesses the temperature's about sixty-five degrees, and the wind has begun to swirl with little dust devils blindly skirting aimlessly in unpredictable directions and projecting minute particles of sand around just enough to irritate his already somber mind, but not enough to hamper the undesirable task at hand.

Two spotlights illuminate the area, and Manucci, squinting to keep dust out of his eyes, sees the body of the young girl some twenty feet away, lying on her back . . . eyes closed as if she's asleep. A greyish-blue blanket covers all but her face.

The officer continues speaking, "Appears to be the same as the others, Lieutenant. Looks like she could be a college student like them . . . shot through the left side of the head."

She looks so peaceful, Manucci despondently considers to himself as he trudges through the sand at his feet and approaches her. He feels a chill run down the back of his neck that then pounds and punches an area between his shoulders.

He reminds himself that he's been investigating these murders for over three years. Tonight's grim scene is the sixteenth that he has had to reconnoiter during that time. At first, one every few months, and now more frequently—one almost every month.

All were students at Arizona State or at one of the local community colleges, all between the ages of eighteen and twenty-four.

Manucci is baffled as to why their conditions are all the same before dying. They were all dehydrated almost to the point of death before they were raped. Semen from the same three males is in the mouth and vaginal areas.

Normally a calm and gentle man Manucci judges himself to be, he gazes at the young girl lying there, and momentarily loses control as anger and frustration rim past the boundaries of reason, and he half-yells out to no one in particular, "This is bullshit! I've been in this department over thirty fuckin' years and I've never seen shit like this. We've got to find these goddamn sons-of-bitches . . . and we are going to find them . . . now!"

After his explosive eruption Manucci immediately becomes aware of his outburst and it is clear in his thinking at that moment, that the officers and crime scene investigators are observing him become someone whom they are not accustomed to seeing, and he at once wishes his fit had engaged a quiet tone in nature, or, better yet, not happened at all. He knows this behavior isn't appropriate around his fellow cops. *But, damnit! Who ARE these monsters?* he pleads to himself.

As he relaxes his shoulders and begins to walk over to get a closer look at the dead girl, one of the uniforms yells from a patrol car up by the road, "LIEUTENANT, CODE THREE . . . THREE DOWN!"

Manucci's powerful legs move like pistons as he scrambles up the slippery embankment, his hands assisting him as the officer continues yelling from above, "THREE BRASS GUNNED DOWN IN MOON VALLEY WHILE THEY WERE PLAYING TENNIS."

The officer runs alongside Manucci as he races to his car. "They're at John C. Lincoln at North Mountain."

Manucci's grey three-year-old unmarked four-door Chevrolet squeals away as he floors the throttle without really thinking about what he's doing.

Then his mind speeds itself to catch up to where he really is at the moment, and, that done, now in control again, he recalls playing tennis in Moon Valley a few times . . . on Wednesdays.

Today is Wednesday.

Heading up Central Avenue, Manucci reins in the cruise control of the Lumina to five over the limit. He scoots past Indian School Road, then Camelback Road, no siren, no emergency lights. The adrenaline rush subsides while his somber mind conjures up images of the three chiefs. He trained them at the academy.

He crosses Bethany Home Road, Glendale Avenue a mile later, then another mile and Northern Avenue's history . . . one mile to go.

4

"H . . . HELLO!" JULIA Everest labors to catch her breath as she grabs the phone in the family room. She had just opened the door leading from the garage into the kitchen when she heard the first ring. "No, I . . . I just walked in," she struggles to say as she swallows and takes a few deep breaths while listening to her best friend's frantic voice.

"It's all over the news!" Tess cries, "Six people were shot. Some were police. They were playing tennis. Is Michael playing tonight?"

Julia had just left Tess, less than a half hour ago, in the parking lot of Arizona State University West in Glendale where she and Tess are both political science professors, and where they had just finished instructing their night classes.

Stunned, she barely listens as Tess's frantic voice continues to ramble over the phone line. Julia's eyes subconsciously search for Michael's face in the portrait placed on the entertainment center against the opposite wall of the large family room. Next to it is a twelve-inch LLADRO figurine depicting a male tennis player posing as if ready to smash a serve. Julia scrutinizes the server who is wearing a white long-sleeve collar-shirt and long white pants, not unlike those worn back in the twenties and thirties. Times that Julia imagines were much simpler.

She remembers Michael opening this Christmas gift from her just over two months ago. She can still see the surprised grin and flash of excitement on his face.

He had noticed the porcelain figurine in the window of a boutique when Julia and he were strolling together through *Fashion Square Mall* in Scottsdale on a Friday evening just a few weeks before Christmas.

Predictably, for Christmas, Julia would normally buy Michael clothes such as dress shirts, sweaters, maybe an expensive jacket of some kind . . . things like that. She was excited when she purchased the figurine, and knew he would be pleased.

She feels a lump in her throat, and her thoughts dissolve as she hears her friend's voice again, "Julia, is Michael playing tonight?"

"I believe so . . . I don't know for sure." Julia's mind is now nothing more than a wonder in absolute confusion that borders subdued hysteria as she continues saying to her friend, "I'll try to find out." She pauses briefly, then asks Tess, "Are you at home? Okay, I'll call you."

Julia replaces the receiver on the wall and consents to allow her arms to fall listlessly at her side. She stands motionless. Her eyes fix on Piestewa Peak framed by the sliding doors leading to the back patio.

She thinks about how Michael has kept his promise to make it up to her for the loss of their home. That was almost three years ago, ages ago . . . but not so long ago that the pain has yet been extinguished sufficiently to be forgotten by either of them.

She blamed him, though she never told him. She knows he unmercifully scourged himself in his soul-searching for them losing everything they possessed except the few items allowed them by the bankruptcy trustee.

And now, with a bittersweet taste manifesting in her dry mouth, Julia warms herself, but only briefly, with the thought that they will soon be moving from this rented house to their new home being built a fourth of the way up the Peak less than a mile away that unveils in almost every room a titillating sight that magnetizes and freezes the vista of the Phoenix lights.

She glances again at Michael's portrait and reflects about them beginning to walk the surrounding hills just a few months ago, after so many, far too many, wasted years of distance between them.

Everything is perfect now, she tells herself as she, with some effort, calmly picks up her purse and slowly walks toward the door while wiping moisture from her eyes with a tissue that she pulled from her purse. As if in a daze, she reasons to herself, *I should go to the hospital.*

5

JULIA DOESN'T KNOW any police officers other than those who play tennis with her husband, and she's acquainted only with Walter Barron's wife.

It takes her twelve minutes to reach John C. Lincoln Hospital-North Mountain. Since it's the nearest one to Moon Valley, she believes the injured officers will most likely be there.

When she maneuvers into the parking lot, a dozen or so uniformed police officers are outside the emergency entrance. From what Julia can tell, they're not just loitering around. Five or six of them are carrying rifles that look like machine guns to her. She feels the knots in her stomach as she turns off the ignition and climbs out of the Lexus.

She's a little surprised that she isn't questioned or stopped by the police officers as she finds her way into the emergency room lobby where dozens of reporters and television news people are trying to get answers. Everyone seems to be talking at once.

The unmistakable hospital odor, so familiar to her from so many years ago, quickly fills her breathing. She detests the all too familiar scent . . . the smell of death. She will never forget it.

Until back then she had never been inside a hospital. She came to Good Samaritan every day for five months and watched her "Papa" die the slow death as the cancer from the copper mines strangled his lungs. She watched the once-proud man helplessly gasp for breath for those five long months.

Now, the spoors inside the hospital flaunt the odors, the reminders of that agonizing pain that her father so courageously accepted. And since then, Julia has not been inside a hospital for eleven years—until now.

She begins maneuvering her way toward the crowded admitting counter and is just a few feet away when a casually dressed youthful looking man enters the lobby from a door behind the admitting clerk. Julia sees that he's accompanied by two uniformed police officers.

Reporters begin yelling questions at him all at the same time before he's forced to raise his hands for a few seconds and the room calms itself.

"I'm sorry," he begins, "you'll have to wait until someone from the department comes down. We don't know any more than you at this time. The chief of police is up there now with the injured officers."

Then, Julia watches the man disappear through the door that quickly closes behind him as she hears the chorus of voices in the lobby rise to a crescendo pitch even louder than before as everyone searches for answers.

Julia finally manages to reach the admitting clerk. The noise and confusion in the lobby make it difficult to hear. Her voice cracking, she yells at the clerk, "I'M MRS. MICHAEL EVEREST. HE WAS WITH THE INJURED OFFICERS. WHERE IS HE? IS HE ALL RIGHT?"

Julia sees tears reflecting kaleidoscope images from the corners of her eyes. *Michael would be disappointed,* she admonishes herself. She needs someone now. The clerk will do.

"JUST A MINUTE!" the clerk yells above the noise. "WHAT'S THAT NAME?"

Julia stares into the eyes of the middle-aged woman, and realizes with no recognizable hope whatsoever that admitting probably does not even have the names of the officers who were wounded, much less the name of her husband.

But Julia cries out Michael's name to the lady anyway. The clerk tactfully confirms Julia's thoughts.

Turning away, Julia gently brushes the tips of her fingers just below her eyes, gently wiping tears that trail down over her high cheek bones, praying to herself, *Oh God, dear God, please . . . please. . . .*

She slowly maneuvers through the throng of reporters and finds a vacant spot and braces her shoulder against a wall. At that moment, her senses, being less than acceptable but not yet totally withdrawn, tell her that her trembling knees are forewarning her legs that they are about to involuntarily buckle.

I've got to be strong. Michael would want me to be strong. She dabs her eyes again, this time with a paper tissue.

Standing there in the lobby, she recalls the counseling sessions that she and Michael began taking together six weeks ago. How she and Michael have finally begun talking more to one another . . . getting closer to one another. She thinks about how in love she is with him. *It can't be too late for us . . . not now,* she half cries.

Her thoughts abruptly return to the chaos around her when a rather obese man bumps into her trying to position himself closer to the front of the crowd of reporters, and almost knocks her to the floor. He aplogizes.

About forty minutes pass. Julia maneuvers closer to the admitting counter herself, and watches and waits with the others. She finds that there's not so much talking now. Another hour passes. The clock on the lobby wall reads ten fifty. Reporters and police officers still pack the lobby.

After a while longer, Julia listens to speculating on what happened as, she surmises, reporters begin to recognize the antsyness in their underdrawers.

"Is it a conspiracy?"

"Mafia?"

"Gangs?"

Suddenly, their meaningless questions and observations are muted when a door opens behind the admitting desk, and the young hospital spokesman reappears with a tall heavyset man. In his late fifties, Julia absentmindedly guesses.

The younger man speaks loudly as the lobby becomes quiet. "This is Major Dantley. He'll brief you about what we know."

Major Dantley has a deep voice that cracks at times as he undertakes to speak louder than normal, glancing occasionally at a yellow legal pad he holds.

"This evening three off-duty police officers were engaged in a game of tennis near the residence of one of the officers. At approximately eight-thirty P.M. they were attacked by three or more assailants with automatic weapons. One of the officers was mortally wounded and pronounced dead on arrival."

The sudden announcement of death stills the crowded billet of journalists for just a microsecond before mumbling among themselves takes flight and drones as one sound filling the air and overriding what positive energy may have existed in the overcrowded room. Julia feels the air lose its merit and her mouth disengages itself from any moisture whatsoever when she hears the words. Her chest instinctively holds in air as she momentarily aches from the chills racing through her that do not bring gentleness nor the benefit of warmth soothing to her, but, instead, carry with them a final outcome that is up to no good.

The recurring dream comes to her now. The dream that has haunted her ever since that day when she was just a child.

The rag doll approaches directly towards her, flying end over end through the air with its arms and legs helplessly flipping and flopping . . . its eyes staring at Julia until it bounds into her face.

The thought forces her instinctively to flinch from the dream, and, like a reflex, she flings her arms up to protect herself from the turbid doll.

Suddenly, she realizes where she is, and sees Major Dantley . . . her arms still raised as a shield.

The major stops for a few seconds and clears his throat before continuing. "The other two officers are now in surgery with numerous gunshot wounds that have been described by doctors as life threatening."

For a few seconds, mumbling voices give away the shock arising from the crowded lobby.

Julia can see the younger spokesman raise both of his hands gesturing for quiet.

The sounds hush and Major Dantley continues, "Bodies of three suspected assailants were found at the scene of the attack. They appear to have been killed as a result of gunshot wounds."

Julia swallows hard as her disengaged heart instantly searches for refuge on its own without her beckoning and finds route to her stomach. No sound comes from her lips as her soul pleads, *What about Michael?*

She is well aware of the nature of the vulgar taste in her mouth and knows well that it is forewarning her senses to take guard against the main assemblage of vomit that will closely follow as she hears Major Dantley finish his statement. "All names are being withheld until we contact families of the victims. That's all we have at this time."

"MAJOR, WERE THE INJURED OFFICERS POLICE BRASS?" One of the television reporters yells out.

"I'm sorry, I can't tell you anything more at this time," the major answers.

Then the younger spokesman quickly ushers him from the lobby.

All the reporters scramble for exits, and Julia approaches near the admitting clerk again. Her hands and shoulders tremble, and tears form again, and, as she speaks, her voice cracks, "My husband was playing tennis with the injured officers. His name is Michael Everest. Is he here?"

"I'm sorry, Mrs. Everest, we still don't know their names."

"Is there anyone I could speak with?" Julia asks as she flavors tears trailing down her cheeks and finding their way to her lips.

"Please, honey, just wait and I'll try to get someone to help," Julia hears the sympathetic clerk say to her as the clerk picks up the constantly ringing telephone.

6

"SI, SEÑOR ORASCO," the fidgeting caller in a phone booth at First Avenue and Polk in downtown Phoenix speaks nervously in Spanish. "Our objective was accomplished. However, there were complications."

The caller wipes his forehead with a handkerchief as he awaits the reaction.

"Complicaciones?" the threatening voice at the other end questions.

"Unfortunately, Señor Orasco, several police officers were accidently wounded and our two friends did not survive. But they carried no identification and it will be very difficult for the police to discover who they are."

Orasco's calm but angry toned voice is spark clear to the caller, "I believe you are quite aware ... that none of this business is ever to be traced to Baldarrama ... or to me. Do you understand?"

At that moment, the caller clearly senses from the unpleasant chills running down the back of his neck and not stopping at his shoulders that Rodrigo Lara Orasco wants to hang him by his balls. And, not atypical under the circumstances, the caller feels the cheeks of his ass impulsively pucker to an unfamiliar tightened state of affairs.

"I want ... I demand you see to it," the threatening voice continues through the telephone's receiver.

"Si, Señor Orasco. I assure you there will be no problems for you or Señor Baldarrama." The telephone goes dead in the caller's ear.

"And fuck you too, Señor Shithead," the drug lord's informer bellows out loud as he slams down the receiver and stomps from the booth.

The caller is determined; he will not be intimidated, although he knows he must be cautious with this powerful and dangerous South American prick.

The informer climbs into his new Maxima. *I better check out the hospital.* The informer wasn't comfortable with what happened. *Those fuckin' cops . . . what the fuck were they doin there? The rest of em' are gonna be pissed and its gonna get fuckin' hot in the valley for a while.* He heads up Central Avenue towards John C. Lincoln.

After he motors a few miles, he smiles to himself. *My man, soon you'll be in Cancun spending all the money these Latin shits have paid you. When you go south, their information pipeline goes south. Fuck 'em all!*

He smiles another wide grin as he fancies the white beaches, chilled margaritas . . . and, of course . . . señoritas.

7

THE SOUTH AMERICAN drug lord snaps tight his cellular and pronounces with an inflection that even startles himself, "I'll kill that untrustworthy piece of rat shit with my bare hands." Rodrigo Lara Orasco can barely control his anger. "AVILLA, BRING ME A SCOTCH . . . NOW!" he screams in his native Spanish.

Lara Orasco then flips open his phone and dials . . . area code Washington, D.C.

"Hello," the Senator's familiar voice answers in a tone that sounds less than calm. As if he were expecting—and dreading—the call.

There is little trace of a Spanish accent as Orasco, calmer after taking several large swallows of the scotch that Avilla promptly delivered to his boss, speaks in English to the powerful Washington politician on the other end of the line, "Senator Graves, I received word that the Phoenix obstacle has just been successfully consummated. I expect the transaction in your fine city to be finished no later than Monday."

"Yes, Señor Orasco," the senator's shaky voice answers, and then Lara Orasco clearly hears the politician cough slightly before clearing his easily detected troubled voice, "I promise that everything here will be completed in five days."

"Excellent!" Orasco sounds in control, "I will notify our friends to the east. They will complete the European transactions also on Monday. A 'New World Order' is about to begin." The drug lord smiles as he seals shut his cellular phone, ending the call.

As he gazes out through the large veranda doors overlooking the Mediterranean Sea, Rodrigo Lara Orasco has one more call to make. *I want her brought here.*

He dials . . . Scottsdale, Arizona, USA.

8

IT'S ALMOST TEN-THIRTY P.M. by the time Joseph Manucci pulls into the parking lot of John C. Lincoln Hospital, which lies about a quarter mile south of North Mountain Park in north central Phoenix.

As he approaches the emergency entrance doors some of the uniforms, with whom he's familiar, acknowledge him with a quiet hello or a slight wave of the hand. Manucci notes to himself that the mood outside the emergency entrance is indisputably sedate. There's none of the usual chatter.

When he enters through the automatic sliding doors, he's approached immediately by Detective Sergeant Robb Winters who is one of Manucci's men.

"Hi, Lieutenant," Winters is somber and Manucci feels uneasy as he is obviously being scrutinized at that moment by his right-hand man who bears a look of sympathy in every corner of his face. "Chief Barron was DOA, Lieutenant," Winters tells

Manucci. And then quickly adds, "Ted Mills and Jack Hopkins are still in surgery and we've got three dead civilians." Manucci knows that Robb isn't aware that Manucci has more than just a passing acquaintance with the chiefs. Robb Winters' words hit Manucci like a pendulum-swinging steel beam slamming into his chest, and he stops in his tracks as if the blow stuns him beyond any recognition of pain other than numbness.

He knows he's investigated hundreds of deaths, accidents, suicides ... murders, many of them gruesome. At times like these, he realizes that whenever it hits close to you, with someone you know, those other anterior deaths don't matter, they don't insulate you, they don't reward you with a protective barrier against the misery of seeing one of your own associates or one of your friends losing their lives.

He stares at Robb, and like a reflex, Manucci's jaws tighten, his lips purse together as his eye's clinch shut and his head tilts downward as if he's trying to block the blows from Robb's words.

What really hits Joseph Manucci, something he realizes at that moment, and normally not recognizable at other times, something he and his associates often forget, is the fact that there are still the living who must bear the pain of losing a loved one. And now, he is one of those survivors ... one of those mourners. Now, he is one of those suffering lamenters being told dispirited words, distressed truths ... that are final!

And it isn't only the information that Manucci has just been given that strikes him, but rather, it's Robb's matter-of-fact business tone, like he's just doing his job, going through the motions, very professional ... like cops do. "Chief Barron was DOA."

Walter Barron is dead! He's gone! Joseph hears over and over again and again as these coarse words plant themselves in repetitive tones and seem to invite no reprieve from their grating message.

After a brief moment, Manucci sighs, gathers himself and heads to an exit sign leading out of the lobby and down a hallway.

"We don't know what the hell happened," Robb continues as he noticeably attempts to keep up with Manucci's quick strides.

"Where are the civilians?" Manucci asks as he continues walking with a mission toward the elevators.

"They're in a lower level morgue. C'mon we can use the elevator in the back," Robb says as he places his hand on Manucci's shoulder.

Robb always knows what's on my mind, even before I do, Manucci muses to himself. He reminds himself that the two of them have worked together for the past eight years, and Manucci knows that he trusts no one more than Robb Winters. As the morgue attendant pulls back each of the covers respectfully concealing death, Manucci doesn't recognize the three civilians . . . two Latinos and an Anglo.

"None of 'em have I.D., Lieutenant," Robb chimes in. "Lab's running prints now and we're checking out two cars found at the scene. One's a rental, and the other one looks like it's stolen.

"The Anglo had a bundle of hundreds in his pants pocket . . . two thousand bucks, all rolled up in a nice package." Robb is thorough.

Manucci heads back to the elevator. "I'm going to Moon Valley. Let me know as soon as you get a make. Good work, Robb," Joseph quietly remarks to his associate.

9

AS MANUCCI'S CHEVY angles past the entrance to North Mountain Park and reaches the summit of Seventh Street he can see the lights of Phoenix reflected in his rear view mirror.

A beautiful sight, He sighs with that bittersweet thought. *A dead girl, a dead police officer . . . maybe two more.* Joseph sniffs the orange blossoms through the open window . . . *A lovely night.* His eyes slide away from the rearview mirror and his head slowly rotates from side to side in disbelief. His sad eyes now focus on the quiet, lazy lights of Moon Valley spread out below as he begins the winding descent.

As his well-used Lumina pulls up in the lane on the west side of the tennis court, Manucci sees two men in civilian clothes spraying water from two separate hoses as the court is being cleansed from the massacre that perpetrated itself there just two hours earlier. He doesn't know either man. It seems a little unusual to him that the tennis court is being washed down so quickly.

He climbs from his car and is promptly approached by a Phoenix police detective with whom Manucci is vaguely familiar.

"Looks like they didn't waste any time cleaning this up," Manucci says to the detective as if an answer to his statement requires an explanation.

"Yeah, Lieutenant, the whole area's been checked," the detective says as he follows Manucci toward the tennis court.

Manucci feels dampness in the air from the water on the court. He knows enough to guess that the court surface isn't cement, but, due to his total unfamiliarity with matters of tennis court planning and construction, has no inclination to even attempt to speculate what the material is made of.

Whatever it is, it's causing the humidity to rise, he considers to himself irritably, then wonders why in hell that fact matters. He and the detective, a sergeant, he seems to recall, continue their stroll around the perimeter of the court.

"Chief Mills was found in the back of the court on the other side," the man tells Manucci as he raises his arm and motions toward the center of the court on the opposite side of the net. "Chief Barron was found on this side along with Chief Hopkins, right there by the net." The detective subtly points toward the near side of the net. "It looks like they didn't know what hit 'em."

As Manucci surveys the scene he continues walking slowly around the court with his guide while the detective continues briefing him. "The two Latinos were found about forty feet apart down that little embankment over there on the side of the court near those bushes." The detective points toward the clump of bushes and olive trees that surround the south side of the court just behind a white metal patio table and four matching chairs.

As Manucci and the detective approach Manucci's car, the detective says as he gestures toward the lane, "The Anglo was found by the road."

"Thanks, detective," Manucci says as he settles into his car and closes the door. He watches the man return to the others waiting by a car, apparently satisfied that they have cleared the court of any reminders of the night's carnage. None of them are Manucci's detectives.

10

JOSEPH SQUARES HIMSELF in his car seat while studying the flooded tennis court and surveying the surrounding green belt. He thinks about it again. It crossed his mind at the hospital morgue, but something, he can't remember what, interrupted him at the time.

He calls dispatch on his mobile to get an address . . . his vehicle doesn't carry the computer that the marked Phoenix patrol cars now have—the computer that can give him the address with just the push of a few buttons. Manucci loathes computers.

As he waits, he wonders how Ted Mills and Jack Hopkins are doing, and thoughts provoke images of the girl in the dry Salt River bottom.

After a few minutes, the mobile phone interrupts his thoughts. Just as the dispatcher gives him the address, the tennis court instantaneously flickers to a darkness that, of its own nature . . . at this place, bears no resemblance to life anywhere near. It's just after eleven thirty.

Manucci heads for Piestewa Peak . . . *it takes four to play,* he tells himself.

11

AFTER DRIVING AIMLESSLY around for a few hours, I finally park the Porsche on a side street about two blocks from my office. I glance at the time displayed on the car's digital clock that reads eleven forty, just before I compress my eyes shut and lean forward cushioning my forehead with my grimy hands tightly gripping the steering wheel.

I feel dried sweat mixed with dirt on my face and hands, my face believes it's on fire . . . and my throbbing head seeks sympathy as it seems to be bracing itself for the explosion which it is now convinced is surely about to occur in the depths of its most central place, and, of course, the ever-present fiery stabbing stings between my shoulders feel like lightning repeatedly striking, absent letup whatsoever from any manner of kindliness.

I try recalling what happened . . . how, in God's name, it happened!

* * *

The four of us had just changed sides when all of a sudden we heard short bursts of what sounded like machine gun fire coming from an area west of the tennis court. I didn't see anything at first as my three friends and I glanced toward the lane. Walter Barron and Jack Hopkins were on the side of the court nearest the lane, and I saw both of them instinctively dive, at the same time, to the ground. At the time, I didn't know if Ted Mills had dropped to the ground or not because I was already running toward the patio table at the side of the court.

A split second later, as I was running, I glanced back and saw two men appear, running from the lane toward the tennis court and spraying it with bursts from their automatics.

I heard metal slamming into the court and spitting into the surrounding trees as I threw myself down the small embankment, rolled several times, and then scrambled into a clump of shrubs alongside the court.

I heard a voice yell in Spanish, directing the other to circle the court. "Go that way! *Gaman* is over there."

From behind the bushes, I could see the man motion to where I had tried to hide myself, so, without hesitating, I quickly scrambled away from the first group of shrubs past several olive trees and hid in a clump of bushes . . . and waited.

I could see my tennis bag lying on the patio table some thirty feet away with my Glock 226 semiautomatic tucked comfortably—and unfortunatly—inside the bag. I couldn't suppress a brief shiver because I felt like I couldn't breathe for a few seconds. It was as if my body had frozen and refused to allow all foreign objects to enter. I inventoried myself, checking to see if I'd been hit. Touching a few sore spots revealed . . . no blood. I must have banged myself when I dove down the embankment, I assured myself.

The natural act of swallowing decided to shroud itself, so I lapped my tongue around inside my mouth searching for moisture that was now obviously taking the position of its most stubborn stage and refusing to appear in any noticeable lot.

My heart had found its own purpose as it raced out of control toward I knew not where, and I was afraid the killers could hear it pounding. Panic barreled through my chest, and I thought about Hue.

I remembered her always reminding me to relax. *Slowly, one deep breath . . . hold for two seconds, then slowly exhale,* she would say. *Repeat again. Relax your shoulders. Drive fear from your thoughts . . . forget all fear . . . relax.*

I breathed in slowly, held it and counted to two, then slowly exhaled . . . then repeated. It didn't help.

Right then, I wished I had continued going to the dojos. Even though I still performed my Kata—hand movement strikes and kicks—faithfully every day, it had been more than fifteen years since I had sparred in a dojo. I've only done it once before! I dejectedly reminded myself. Jesus, help me! I'm going to die!

My thoughts raced back twenty-five years.

Although I had had some intense sparring matches in the dojos thousands of times, my skills had never before been seriously tested with regard the deadly Shorin Ryu Kata, Mai Thai *and* Ju-Jutsu *that Hue had taught me as I grew up.*

Then, one day it happened during my sophomore year at St. Mary's High School.

The boy known as Corto was only five-foot-two-inches tall and weighed about a hundred twenty pounds. I had seen him at school and had the impression that he was quiet and not a troublemaker. Because the boy was two years older, I had never met him before.

That day, I had just walked three blocks from school on Third Street when I saw, half a block away, three hulking bully-looking types—probably in their early twenties—leap from an old car on a side street and grab Corto.

I felt the tension mounting inside like a river roaring out of control and sucking me in as I picked up my pace toward them. I didn't have time to think about what I was doing as I hustled forward, I just reacted.

The largest man was facing Corto and had placed a hand on each of Corto's shoulders and began pushing him and yelling in Spanish. I couldn't understand what the man was saying. But, from a block away, I could tell the man was not very happy with Corto.

Luckily, none of them noticed me until I was less than ten feet away.

The leader with his hands still on Corto and still yelling, began pushing harder against him, all the while screaming louder and louder into the small boy's face.

Then, all of a sudden, I felt everyone notice me all at the same time. I saw that the leader only glanced at me, and all I was to him, probably, was a skinny kid with glasses, and so the large man just looked away and continued his rampage.

Three minutes later Corto and I collapsed behind an old broken-down house seven or eight blocks away, both of us gasping for breath.

Corto, when he was able to breathe easier and could talk, promised, at my insistence including the threat of bodily harm, that he would never tell anyone how I, in less than five seconds, had left the three shitheads on the ground and in obvious pain.

At that moment I felt like a "badass," and it felt pretty good, even though I was still trembling like an aged leaf that was being teased by a sturdy autumn breeze and was about to make its final plunge from its master tree.

Sitting there with a fellow high school student behind that old house, I wondered why I had held back and had hurt the three pricks only enough for me and my new friend to escape. I was fairly certain, though, that two of them would never father children.

As I sat there, more relaxed now in that moment of macho glory, leaning against the old boarded-up house, I recalled Hue's words to me several years earlier.

"You are very good, Michael," she had said. "You practice your Kata faithfully. You have mastered the techniques. You have sparred well at all of the dojos where I have taken you.

"But, you will be weak to all opponents. Why? Because you cannot fix your eyes on their existence and see them as the enemy. Your soul possesses too much compassion . . . too much tenderness.

"You are like a young pup full of energy, eager to explore, content to chase the fox. But, once you have caught it, you cannot look into its eyes and destroy it."

12

MY THOUGHTS OF the past were suddenly jolted back to reality when I heard twigs snapping as the assassin crept closer.

I'm going to die . . . Holy Jesus, help me! That pleading prayer kept flitting through every web of conscious deliberation that my mind was capable of assembling at that instant. My mouth was still too dry to swallow, and I kept opening and closing my fists, trying to stop my hands from shaking.

I thought about Hue . . . *"Lose anger . . . lose fear . . . you 'will' relax."* I didn't feel like a badass now.

The killer stopped, and faced so that I was to the man's left less than eight feet away.

I relaxed my shoulders and barely flexed my calves and forearms while I tried to breathe in a normal cadence as I sidestepped forward. I felt my body sliding toward the intruder from my crouched position . . . like I had done in the dojos.

Just as the startled assassin tried to turn toward me, I felt my body instantly lock like granite . . . I was nowhere else. I could feel my energy and strength centered in my *ki* as I forcefully exhaled at the instant my right backhand-forearm tore into the front of the killer's neck, crushing the man's Adam's apple.

I heard the impact, like the muffled crunching sound of the smashing of a dead locust that had been dried out by the sun after it had attached itself to a tree trunk.

The man's reflexes took over. Instantly, he dropped his rifle and grasped hopelessly at his crushed throat with both hands and let out a barely audible groan that sounded like a combination of a gagging sound and a cough.

The impact caused the man's upper body to lurch backwards allowing me to smash the palm of my flexed left hand upward into the killer's groin.

As the dying man's upper body instantly pitched forward, my right-hand forearm hammered a deadly blow to the base of the poor man's skull. The assassin had no time to cry out as he dropped instantly.

With my chest heaving uncontrollably as I struggled for air, I froze for a few seconds while my hands and forearms remained flexed. My legs were still coiled for another assault if necessary. From the time I slid toward the killer until now, I'd had no time to think at all. Everything happened in an instant, and my actions were based solely on instinct and reflexes that my subconscious mind, by the grace of God, had not forgotten.

I finally relaxed my arms and shoulders and released the tension in my legs momentarily as I stood looking down at the back of the man lying motionless on the ground.

When the killer had fallen, the right side of his face had landed in the soft dirt. The lights from the tennis court filtered through the trees and bushes allowing me to see the dead man's opened left eye staring straight ahead . . . at nothing, and I suddenly began tasting vomit trickling up into my mouth.

The rest of the man's body was in shadows, but I was still able to see that the killer had crumpled downward still reaching for his throat, causing his arms and hands to come to rest beneath his body which had been prevented from rolling on its side because it had fallen against the bottom of the trunk of an olive tree.

For another three or four seconds, I just stood there staring . . . staring at the man whose life I, Michael Everest, had just ended.

After a few seconds I believed I was at least partially recovered from the shock. The realization that I was still in danger seemed to prompt me back to an awareness of surroundings. I took a slow deep breath and exhaled, then grabbed the dead man's rifle from the ground and slid into the shadows of the brush.

"Zalo! Donde Esta? (Where are you?)," I heard the second killer, about seventy feet away at the west end of the court, call out to his partner.

Lying on my stomach with the rifle cradled in my forearms, I inched my way toward the remaining assassin.

When I was about ten or twelve feet away, I saw the man in an open area with only his lower body hidden by shadows.

I brought the dead man's automatic up, clutching it firmly, and aimed at the assailant, and then fired a short burst that tore across the man's chest, knocking him out of the shadows into the light illuminating from the tennis court, and instantly producing crimson-red-appearing splotches that spurted out upon impact all across his beige shirt.

I heard him gasp, breathing out, just once and then saw his helpless body fall back and slump silently to the ground.

I became aware that I was breathing heavily as I stood momentarily over the bloody corpse while light from the tennis court lurked through openings in the brush to allow me to witness the second killer's closed eyes that I knew now were nothing more than useless earthly matter. The sound of the distant sirens, which I had not been aware of before, now pierced my ears.

As I ran around to the south side of the tennis court and started up the embankment, I could smell death from the first assassin whose body I had just run past. And, for the first time, I was aware of the burnt smell of cordite imbuing the air from the spent weapons.

When I reached the height of the tennis court, I saw the three police officers reposed in total silence on the court that bore blemishes displaying caricatures formed with black-appearing blood that fraudulently suggested at first glance that they were mere blankets upon which my friends lay.

At first, without my mind actually grasping yet the whole of what had just taken place, I started toward them, but, hearing the sirens getting closer, quickly decided there was nothing I could do. And, at that instant, I knew child innocence, what little I may still have possessed after forty years of life . . . would never again find my heart.

Before heading to the lane, I rushed over to the table and chairs on the side of the court and grabbed my racquet and tennis bag and ran to the Porsche.

As I drove away, the repugnant smell of death still lingered in my breathing.

13

JOSEPH MANUCCI HESITATES for a few seconds and stares up at the mountain rising twenty-six-hundred feet above him. It appears to be a towering black silhouette against the silvery moonlit sky.

To Joseph Manucci, the mountain radiates a mystical presence . . . as if it has arms flowing down its shadowy slopes all the way to its base, embracing, even protecting, the homes nestled below. He feels the quiet. It's like the energy around him has slowed time.

As he walks along the sidewalk, he pauses for a moment, and a sense of peace seems to engulf him.

In the past, whenever he had ever driven by Piestewa Peak, he had never really paid much attention to its overpowering dominance, especially at night.

It appears different now as he walks from the street up the walkway to the large residence. He thinks to himself that it's probably because he's never been this close other than when he was inside his car racing along Lincoln Drive.

The Peak seems to him to be less than two blocks away. *But, in reality, it's probably at least half a mile or more,* he guesses. Right now, he feels about the size of an ant.

The amber light next to the front door guides him up the walkway leading to the home. Even though it's nearing midnight, he sees dim rays of light trickling out through windows that reveal closed shades or shutters.

He rings the doorbell.

The door is slowly pulled open, but only halfway, by a woman dressed in a beige sports shirt and navy-blue slacks. Manucci presumes she's Mrs. Everest.

"Hi! I'm sorry to bother you so late. I'm Lieutenant Manucci with the Phoenix Police Department." He holds up his badge. "May I speak with Michael Everest?"

"He isn't here," Julia Everest says as her stare seems to transfix Manucci. She has one hand still holding onto the inside doorknob, so the door still remains only half open. "I don't know where he is."

Manucci doesn't know it, but as she tells him this, her mind flashes back and she remembers the dead man at the hospital whose body a police officer took her to identify.

She swallows hard now as she recalls how dry her throat felt as she prepared to look at the corpse . . . her husband's corpse, lying on a metal table in the hospital's morgue. She had fleetingly lost control as she let out a cry of relief when the technician drew back the white sheet revealing the lifeless pale face. It wasn't Michael!

Manucci looks, aware that he's staring and not wanting to look away, at this strikingly beautiful woman. *Slim, about five foot three, dark hair that's been cut just above her shoulders*

... beautiful olive skin and dark-brown eyes ... sensuous ... very sensuous. The kind of woman that causes countries to war against one another. Manucci is tired. "Are you Mrs. Everest?"

"Yes." He senses her uneasiness as he notices her keeping the door half closed.

"Can you tell me the last time you saw your husband?"

"This morning before he left for his office," she tells him. Manucci is looking at her and her eyes continue staring at his ... her glare doesn't waver.

He looks at her a few seconds longer, then looks down at his feet, shuffles them and looks back at her before asking, "Mrs. Everest, have you heard about the shootings in Moon Valley tonight?"

"Yes." Manucci notices her wavering and at the same time feels her scrutinizing him. Then he catches her eyes flinching several times, and she opens the door all the way. "Please ... come in."

Manucci sits uncomfortably, in mind only, in a luxurious wingback chair opposite the generously oversized sofa where he observes Julia Everest sitting with her hands in her lap. A long expensive-looking dark-wood coffee table separates them.

Manucci's no expert, but he senses that the furniture in the clearly quite formal room is considerably more expensive than he can ever afford. He and Marlene occasionally look at furniture like that ... and dreaming is as close to it as they'll ever get. "Was your husband playing tennis tonight with the police officers, Mrs. Everest?"

"I think so ... I'm not sure, but I think so. I have no idea where he is. I don't know why he hasn't called or come home. He's usually home by ten o'clock. Maybe someone there took him." As she rambles those words, she isn't looking at Manucci.

He watches as her eyes are fixed on her hands, which she nervously massages together in her lap, and he realizes she wonders why she said that.

"Why would anyone take Michael?" she asks barely audible as an afterthought and Manucci surveys her as she looks up at him as if wanting an answer.

He tries to be sympathetic, "I'm sorry Mrs. Everest. I don't know why this happened tonight. Please call me if you hear from your husband." He stands, leans over and lays his card on the coffee table. "I'll see myself out."

He takes several steps toward the entry way, then stops and turns back toward the woman still sitting on the couch. "Could you give me your husband's office address? I'd like to talk to someone there in the morning."

14

AS HE OPENS the car door, Manucci feels drained . . . his energy totally dispelled. To Joseph, it's not an infrequent befalling the past few years. He briefly gazes up at the Peak with eyes that march to a subtle cadence of melancholy and reminds himself, *Tomorrow's going to be a long day . . . time to go home.*

His tired hand turns the ignition and the loyal Chevy's engine flows to life. As he positions the grey sedan into drive, the loathsome vision of the girl lying on the dry Salt River bottom forges itself into his remembrances . . . he had forgotten for a while.

15

IN THE DARK, I have difficulty seeing and stumble on one of the legs of a heavy visitor's chair and swear to myself as I step past the secretary's desk before feeling my way to my private office which is in the rear of the large suite.

They're going to kill me . . . Jesus, they're going to kill me, keeps grating its ghostly message in my head over and over as I seek shelter in the windowless bathroom adjacent to my office. I snap the door shut before switching on the light.

As I glance into the mirror, I shriek as my sweaty and defiled reflection jolts me. I feel like I'm looking at death . . . at a stranger. I can hardly believe I was part of what happened just a few hours earlier.

After several frozen seconds, able to look no more at my sorry image, I turn away from the mirror. At first, I consider showering, and then expeditiously quell the thought. "I have to get out of here," I tell himself. "I know they'll come here. Where the hell is Julia?" I feverishly interrogate myself. I tried to call her four times during the past two hours.

While I tug open the bathroom's closet door and grab the small suitcase and snap it open before dropping it on the bathroom floor, I capture my hands trembling. Then my entire body begins to shake almost uncontrollably and renders no hint as to how it might stop. My psyche seems to disposition itself to a blank mold, and yet, at the same time, I feel the same mind hurtling itself into an uncontrolled fit as if every thought I have ever possessed rifles through my consciousness . . . everything too muddled to make any sense.

Without even thinking about it further, I grab my toothbrush and toothpaste from the medicine cabinet along with an electric razor, aftershave and deodorant, wrap the toothbrush in a paper tissue and shove everything into a side pocket of the suitcase.

Then, still without even stopping to think twice about what I'm doing, I snatch up several sweatshirts, a few pairs of denim slacks and some slipover collar shirts and stuff it all into the suitcase along with five or six pairs of ankle-length sports socks and a similar number of underwear before slamming the suitcase closed.

My reasoning finds no justice of any vestige and continues its useless term while refusing to tell my will where the hell I can go . . . or for how long. I do recognize, however, that what lies ahead for me at that moment is no more than the steps I will soon take out through the doorway of my office. After that,

I bear no thoughts of the future that comfort me in any welcomed fashion.

After wiping my face with a wet towel for a few minutes, and then drying myself with another, I change into a pair of blue denims and a clean T-shirt and slip on a dark-green pullover sweatshirt along with black tennis shoes. I try tying one of the shoes and, after several futile attempts, finally get it right.

"Where should I go? Where the hell should I go?" I feverishly plead to myself aloud as my now recognizable thoughts have stirred up speed as if they are in perpetual motion ready to fling my soul, without any purposeful sense whatever, into space, and words keep rattling out. I know I *must* get to Sotello . . . "I can't use the phone here . . . what the hell should I do? They're going to kill me."

With my back braced against the wall, I suddenly feel weightless and my legs seem to buckle and I slowly slide down to the floor resting on my buttocks and rolling my head side to side in disbelief at the nature of the happenings carried on in such deadly portions over such a lean period of time. "They're dead! They're all dead! I killed them," I sough to myself with a sense of desperation and frustration that has found even the most minute areas of my mind and body on which to feast, the likes of which I have never before imagined possible.

My mind keeps seeing Walter and the others just lying there in the "black" blood . . . not moving. *I killed them!*

I don't realize how long I sit there. Time seems to have vacated any intent toward movement with any degree of normal cadence, and now my mind keeps drawing her in. *She's the only one I can call . . . no one knows about her.* And I honestly believe it's for no other reason that allows me to even *think* about contacting her. And *that* makes me shudder as I selfishly consider *using* her again. Only this time, I will be aware of it.

After a while longer, I raise myself and slowly pick up the suitcase and, before turning out the light, aimlessly glance around checking to see if I'm forgetting anything.

Finally, I pull open the bathroom door and listen guardedly for any foreign sounds before precariously advancing toward the reception area. I remind myself, in a whisper, "I can't use my cellular or call from here, they'll know."

16

AFTER STEPPING PAST the front door of my office suite—the only entrance it has—I begin walking, half running, in the direction of the Porsche that sits in an all night supermarket's parking lot a few blocks away. All the while, I have this dark feeling—maybe too much imagination I tell myself—that they, whoever "they" are, are lurking in the shadows all around me and are ready to rip my body apart. But as I reach my car my eyes see no one . . . and I'm still alive.

As I climb into the Porsche, half of my consciousness wrestles with whether or not I should dare draw her into this nightmare, while the other half of my brain begins reflecting on those who have been a part of the past two years of what I now tell myself has been nothing less than a deadly game . . . only it's not a game anymore.

As I shift the Porsche into drive, my thoughts recreate what I have lived and what others have later told me that lead to this day that now may well be my last.

It all really began on a cool day in June in California . . . three years before I was actually spawned into this monstrous whirlpool two years ago and swept helplessly to a point where there is no going back.

Five Years Ago

17

Westwood, California . . .

FATHER JOSHUA STONE gathered up the six volleyballs one by one and dropped them into the string-net bag. As he slung it over his shoulder, the chilling rain began pouring down even harder.

Several of the boys had already taken down the volleyball net and were racing toward the storage room. As boys always did, they were laughing as they ran for cover while tugging on the net trying to make one another fall on the slippery playground . . . there were three of them.

"HEY, GUYS," the priest yelled across the field, "BE CAREFUL. YOU'LL TEAR OUR NET." He chuckled to himself as he said it.

The twenty-five-year-old diocesan priest was convinced they weren't listening to him. He smiled as he watched the thirteen-year-olds giggling as they disappeared around the corner of the school building to a world only young virgin optimism can know.

The downpour had already soaked through the Dodgers' baseball cap that was now plastered to Father Stone's drenched head, and the ragged sweatshirt with the University of Michigan Wolverine logo boldly brandished on the front was sopping wet and clung to his body as he gingerly trotted across the slick playground, in many places barren of grass of any standing texture that had now begun turning to mud.

He glanced at his watch . . . three-thirty. *I might as well head for home,* he thought as he looked up at the bleak sky.

Father Joshua Stone had been temporarily assigned to St. Thomas the Apostle Catholic Church, in Westwood, for the past two months. He had just celebrated his First Mass three months ago, one week after his ordination.

Excitement and anticipation still coursed through him as it had when he had lain prone in the cathedral, vowing his life to humility, chastity, obedience, and vowing to serve all of his brothers and sisters in the name of God the Father, Son and Holy Spirit.

At the ordination Mass, Bishop Adolfo Carbajal had reminded Deacon Joshua Stone and two of his fellow Deacon classmates that they were about to become chosen apostles of Jesus. The bishop reminded them that they, like all living souls, would never take another single breath without the Holy Spirit touching their hearts . . . Joshua strongly believed this.

That was the happiest day of his life.

18

IT TOOK LESS than six seconds for Father Stone to open his car door and slush the thirty-five feet to and up the five steps onto the front porch that ran three fourths of the way across the front of the house. The yard had already flooded up to his ankles, so his heretofore dirty white tennis shoes were soaked.

The rain had not let up. He would surprise Uncle Dit and Aunt Kotsie. They weren't expecting him for another hour and a half.

Joshua was about to ring the doorbell. The first warning was the screen door ajar and the closed front door. At this time of day Aunt Kotsie normally would have locked the screen door because she would leave the front door open to let in the late cool breeze. It seemed briefly odd to Joshua, but not of any consequence . . . he just passed it off as oversight . . . and entered.

He froze.

Lying on the living room floor near the hallway leading to the back of the small compact house he could see his Uncle Dit sprawled on his back with a tiny dark crimson splotch on the right side of his forehead. Blood trickled out of the opening, slowly finding its way down his uncle's right cheek and dribbling onto a purple appearing puddle on the light sugar-brown carpet.

A faint sound came from the T.V. A crowd roar...the Dodgers were on.

Joshua stood there and just stared. Then he heard Aunt Kotsie's scream, "NOOOO!" And then two repeated sounds, like a BB pump-gun being shot, coming from the kitchen.

Without any thought at all, he instinctively lightly flexed his knees and then, quietly, but swiftly, glided sideways, like a cat ready to pounce, toward the dining room swinging-door leading to the kitchen.

Joshua still had not fully comprehended what had happened when no sooner had he reached the side of the door, it slammed outward toward him and a large muscular man charged through not expecting Joshua's left forearm to be extended across and flying into the man's Adam's apple. The killer's feet went out from under him and he crashed to the floor on his back.

Before the assassin could regain his breathing, Joshua's left foot instantly side kicked the man's raised head, crushing his left temple. The killer grunted out his last breath and his head dropped to the carpet.

Joshua stood over him for only a second, then jumped through the kitchen door, screaming, "AUNT KOTSIE!" He saw a small dark-maroon hole in her forehead and another in the front of her throat as she lay on the kitchen floor on her back, her arms flung outward, her blank eyes staring at the ceiling. The dark liquid oozed from the wounds down onto the white tile.

Joshua sank to the floor and couldn't stop the tears flooding his eyes. He pulled his knees to his face and wrapped his arms around his bent legs, and rocked his body back and forth, moaning and, finally, wailing and screaming incoherently.

He lost track of time. When he finally stirred, he sat there, his eyes gazing at his aunt's motionless body. His eyes trailed to one of her well-used navy-blue tennis shoes that had fallen off and lay next to her. Then he saw the other one, still on her foot. Joshua just stared at the shoe on her foot.

He thought about when she had put it on that morning. *What was she thinking about as she laced the shoe. Was she happy, was she thinking about her chores for the day? Would she even have imagined, then, that she would never again take off her shoe, nor ever put it on again.* More tears.

19

"HERE, JOSHUA, DRINK this," he heard Bishop Adolfo Carbajal softly say as the bishop stood over him and offered a small glass of bourbon.

Joshua Stone was sitting on a sofa in the Bishop's dark study and was leaning forward with his elbows resting on his thighs while his fingertips massaged his forehead. His eyes felt puffy and he recognized dry tears that had settled there as he gazed downward toward the shadowy floor. He was barely aware of the dim table lamp at the end of the sofa providing the only light in the large room. At that moment, Joshua didn't want to see anything. He didn't want to see or think about anything at all.

Without taking his eyes from the floor, he reached up with his right hand and graciously took the glass from the Bishop without drinking from it, and quietly said, "Thank you, Father."

Minutes passed . . . neither spoke. They were alone, just the two of them. The bishop had found his way to one of his reclining chairs opposite the sofa and had also poured a warm bourbon for himself.

Finally, Adolfo Carbajal heard Joshua mumble something inaudible.

"I'm sorry, Joshua, I didn't hear you."

Joshua looked up at the bishop, his friend, his mentor, and proclaimed, this time louder, almost as if a plea, "I'm not sorry. I feel . . . no remorse. I feel . . . I feel no remorse for that man. I'm glad I killed him. I hate him."

The bishop sat there, staring at the young priest. Adolfo Carbajal loved Joshua like a son. He felt the pain too. Dimitrus and Konstantina Stone, Joshua's Uncle Dit and Aunt Kotsie, were the dearest friends that Carbajal had. That was the reason why they had been chosen to be Joshua's adoptive parents.

Joshua placed his glass on the small table where the lamp was positioned and stood, his arms folded across his chest, and stared down at his mentor. "Father," he cried, "I can't go on! I'm no longer a priest. I'm not sorry for what I did. I want to kill him over and over. Why? . . . Why? Why did this happen?" he cried even louder, slumping down onto the sofa, his hands gripping each side of his face as tears flowed down his cheeks.

For a few minutes Adolfo Carbajal continued sitting and observing his young priest . . . until Joshua finally became still. Then the bishop rose from his chair and slowly walked over to the small bar in the corner of the room. With his back to Joshua, he faced the bar and slowly poured more bourbon into his own empty glass.

Without turning around, the popular auxiliary bishop of Los Angeles spoke, "Do you remember when you were brought to me, Joshua?" Adolfo didn't wait for the young priest to reply. "You were four years old."

The bishop turned toward Joshua, his young protege, and returned to his chair. "I was a priest here at Saint Sebastian. Neither I, nor Dimitrus nor Konstantina have ever told you what I am about to tell you.

"Your father was Harold Mitlak. His Catholic Lebanese parents, your grandparents, came to the United States six years before your father was born. Harry, as your father was called by his friends, was a member of the Central Intelligence Agency. He was killed in Iran twenty-five years ago, just three weeks after you were born.

"Your mother was Sabrina Mitlak. Her parents were French and came to the United States three years before she was born. And you were born in the United States, but your mother left the CIA and took you to France to hide soon after she had received word that your father had been killed.

"For four years you and your mother lived with her cousins in a small village called Espalion on the Lot River in central France. She thought the two of you would be safe from the terrorists who had killed your father. She was murdered the day you were brought to me here at the rectory.

"To this day, we don't know how they found the two of you. She had always been extremely cautious when she corresponded with Konstantina and Dimitrus."

As he listened, Joshua's focus shifted from the dead man he had killed. He sat forward on the sofa, his forearms resting on his thighs while he stared intently at the bishop.

Adolfo Carbajal continued his story, "As soon as Sabrina, your mother, became aware that the two of you were in danger, she was able to hide you and make arrangements with your cousins to sneak you to the embassy in Paris. A few days later you were taken by the French military to one of their Air Force bases and flown to me by the United States military.

"We were told of your mother's death before you arrived at the rectory here at Saint Sebastian.

"Your Aunt Kotsie's parents were also Lebanese, the same as you father's parents. She was born here in the States, and spoke English, French and all of the Arabic dialects.

"Your Uncle Dit's parents were Dutch, and he was born in the United States in the same year as Aunt Kotsie. In addition to English, French and the Arabic dialects, he also spoke Dutch, German and Spanish. That's why you're fluent in all of those languages, Joshua.

"Dimitrus and Konstantina became your immediate guardians and gave you their last name, which they had chosen for themselves. Naturally, we were able to skip the normal red tape with the guardianship."

Joshua rose and went over to the bar to refill his glass, to the rim this time. Then he returned to the sofa. He could hardly believe what he was hearing. He took a long sip of the bourbon and scowled as it stung his throat. He had always been told that his parents had been killed in an airplane crash. And now . . . this.

After Joshua had settled onto the sofa again, the bishop continued, "As you probably have guessed, Dimitrus and Konstantina were also CIA. They worked with your mother and father until your father was killed. After that, they no longer wanted any part of the killing, so they chose to quit the agency at the same time that your mother took you to France. They never saw your mother again."

Bishop Adolfo Carbajal paused momentarily and moved uneasily in his chair. Finally, he stood up while staring at his young priest. After a moment of contemplation, he let out a deep breath and his voice cracked as he told Joshua, "I too was a member of the Central Intelligence Agency."

Carbajal stood there overwhelmed with guilt. He knew he possessed no armor for his shame in front of the man he loved like a son. The culpability that Adolfo Carbajal had harbored within his own tortured soul, all those years, branded him as being just as responsible as the terrorists for the deaths of those Joshua loved and could have loved. Their business had been his business. Adolfo Carbajal felt like he had deserted his friends because he had chosen not to kill again.

"But," interrupted Joshua, "you're a priest. You were a priest when I came to you. I don't understand."

The bishop slowly stepped over to his desk and unlocked a drawer. He pulled it open and lifted out a large manilla envelope. Then he loosened the single binder at the top, and carefully removed its contents. He looked up at Joshua, and laid the empty envelope on his desk before slowly walking over to the couch and handing photographs to the young priest.

Joshua's unsteady hands took the three black and white photos from Carbajal. The lamp's soft light next to the sofa elucidated enough lighting for Joshua to easily view them.

The first one revealed a closeup, taken maybe ten feet away, Joshua estimated, of a dark-haired man, very handsome Joshua thought. The young man appeared to be in his late twenties. He was sitting on the ground and leaning back on his hands with his legs stretched out on what looked like grass, with lots of trees in the background. Probably a park, Joshua guessed. The man wore a loose-fitting light-colored T-shirt and dark Bermuda shorts of a color the black and white was incapable of defining. The young man wore no shoes.

Sitting next to him, leaning back on one arm with legs folded together on one side, was a strikingly attractive light-haired girl, in her twenties, Joshua guessed. She wore a light-colored short-sleeve top with a small collar, and some kind of dark-colored shorts that seemed to end about midway of her thighs. Joshua couldn't tell for sure since she was sitting.

"Those are your parents, Joshua," Adolfo softly told him.

Joshua sat there, his eyes locked on the photograph. He felt chills inching from his shoulders to the back of his neck. His eyes bristled with moisture.

Adolfo placed his hand on Joshua's shoulder and felt the energy between Joshua and himself. He sensed, in a most intense and overpowering presence that actually produced chills ordering themselves down the back of his own neck and through his shoulders, that the two of them, together, the sole survivors, sharing the photograph, would at that moment have their lives changed forever . . . one now to be the teacher, and the other now to be the student.

Joshua finally placed the photograph beneath the other two and looked at the second one, which appeared as if it had been taken at the same place as the first one. It included his mother and father, and, he guessed, Aunt Kotsie, Uncle Dit and Adolfo Carbajal.

"As was the first one, this was taken three years before you were born, Joshua," Adolfo, in his normal soft tone, related. "I had just resigned from the agency."

The third photograph displayed a small child, maybe two or three years old. He appeared to Joshua to have very light olive skin and soft, dark eyes and thick black hair. His lips were full and complimented his high cheek bones. Only his upper torso showed. Adolfo exclaimed the obvious, "That is you, Joshua . . . when you were almost three. It was taken in France."

The two of them sat quietly for a while before Joshua broke the silence, "Why did you stop, Father?" Joshua had always called Adolfo Carbajal, Father, even after Carbajal had become a Prince of the Church when the title of Monsignor was bestowed upon him . . . the highest official "title" of the Roman Catholic Church except for the Pope. Joshua is quite aware that Bishops and Cardinals are not titles but clearly quite prestigious administrative positions in the hierarchy of the Church. Only in the presence of others would Joshua speak to or about Adolfo Carbajal, as he rightfully should, as "Bishop Carbajal" or "Excellency."

"I've tried to answer that question many times, Joshua. I just seemed to have evolved slowly toward my intended vocation. Nothing was really going on at the time for any of us. I had been getting the call in my head. And then one day, I decided that I would rather serve than deceive and destroy.

"For a long time afterwards, I missed it. I missed the others. Then, when your mother died and you were brought to me, I knew that Dimitrus and Konstantina, who were living in Los Angeles, would welcome you into their home. They wanted, very much, to raise you as their own. They loved you as if you *were* their own."

"I know, Father."

Joshua paced the floor a few times while Adolfo sat in his chair. Finally, Joshua stopped, faced the bishop, and asked, "What do I do now?"

"I believe you should visit the Casa in the desert. Take five or six weeks, or as long as you need . . . and pray, Joshua! Then you will know what you are to do."

He *did* go to the Casa . . . in the Arizona desert. And during the next two and a half years, unmercifully tormented, Joshua Stone prayed to his God, and discovered what he was to do . . . what he *must* do.

20

Krems, Austria . . .

THE UNFORGIVING LATE-SEPTEMBER north wind swept bitterly cold gusts across the small square, causing mustard-yellow paper napkins to flutter violently as the weight of the glass plates held them fast to the small circular black wrought iron tables that were set along each side of the sidewalk in two rows of six outside the quite popular pastry shoppe on the banks of the Danube River, near where the northwestern portion of the Wachau Valley began.

All tables were occupied as they always were that time of year between eight and ten thirty each morning, Saturdays and Sundays included. Today was Tuesday.

The topaz-blue sky was accentuated by frosty-white baby clouds thickly scattered and racing across from one horizon to another.

This quaint village, a few miles east of Vienna, moored to its sister village, Stein, was one of the dozen or so small towns clustered along the beautiful and well known river winding through the Wachau.

Tourists were drawn to the region's Baroque style of architecture so prevalent throughout the valley. They did not, however, confine their visits to sightseeing. They also came to savor the strong smooth espressos and the famous poppy-seed cake, oven fresh, redolent, crowned with a subtle breath of warm chocolate and topped with freshly made whipped cream, equaling the finest pastries in all of Europe. Almost all of the shoppe's patrons, who sat at the tables, had, for warmth, at least one hand tucked deep inside their heavy mackinaws that were prudently buttoned up all the way.

Except to munch a bite or to sip from their espresso cups, all of the diners' chins were also tucked snugly down into the raised collars of their heavy coats for refuge from the glacial wind gusts that refused to let up.

Sitting alone at one of the tables in the row on the outside edge of the sidewalk was a tall, lean visitor with medium-length sandy-red hair that fluttered sharply in the wind, probably an American.

He shivered from the freezing air thrashing mercilessly across his face while he attempted to sip the strong espresso that he carefully held with both hands at times in order to prevent it from spilling all over the table.

Any type of coffee was quite foreign to him. It was not his normal choice of drink. He preferred orange juice and good ol'

American milk. Neither had been available. However, considering the circumstances, he eagerly welcomed its warmth as the coal-black brew coated the inner lining of his throat.

He had difficulty combating the wind gusts that relentlessly disturbed the American paperback novel that he held with his left hand. He had no idea what the first page of the book revealed, nor did he care. He had purchased it only about half an hour earlier from inside the pastry shoppe where he had not even scanned the back cover as a person might normally do. It just happened to be the first one he saw on the book rack.

The tall American, about six feet, occasionally glanced up at the sky, and then casually perused across the rows of tables and the square leading to the edge of the river. His concern was four tables away in the same row he himself had occupied for the past twenty-five minutes.

After three days of having observed the habits from a distance, the American had made sure that he had arrived before the man from the Middle East.

After another thirty minutes passed, the black-bearded Arab with the matching matted hair, folded his French newspaper, rose from his table and began walking down the sidewalk away from the hazel eyes that closely followed him.

Let him go, the observer thought. *I know which streets he chooses, to take his exercise. No need to hurry . . . patience . . . patience. That's what they taught me.*

21

AS IT SHOULD have, at a time like this for most normal men, the American's right hand did not tremble at all as he loosely gripped the compact pistol just enough to reassure himself that it was still there. It was the weapon most preferred by Israeli

Mossad agents . . . the highly popular .22–caliber Beretta semi-automatic pistol. And the American had it well hidden deep inside the right pocket of his mackinaw.

He had left the pastry shoppe fifteen minutes ago. Now he saw his opportunity, just like they had taught him. He was now only twenty feet away from where Yehiham Alkam, the notorious Hamas bombmaker, had stopped to view small electric trains that were in a storefront window display.

The American approached in a normal stride, and slowly removed the compact pistol from his mackinaw, all the while trying to conceal it down at his side.

He continued until he was approximately six feet from the bearded man who was also well known as a Palestinian terrorist who had masterminded many suicide attacks that had killed scores of Israelis.

Alkam, sensing the approaching man, slowly turned his head toward the assassin who promptly raised the pistol and lightly squeezed twice.

Both reports spit through the center of the terrorist's forehead just above his gaping eyes, creating two small splotches of bright red liquid that instantly transformed to dark maroon as more began oozing from the holes.

The man's mouth opened wide and he crashed backward through the display window, his upper torso landing inside the display case on its back leaving the legs and feet dangling down not quite touching the sidewalk.

The assassin looked up and down the street. No one was within fifty yards of him. Wind gusts were still strong and still very cold.

He pulled up the collar of his mackinaw, and calmly walked over and removed one of the dead man's shoes and left it lying on the sidewalk next to the body. Then he walked away, never looking back, and finally disappeared down a side street.

22

HE SECURED THE second suitcase and lowered it from the bed to the floor alongside the other. He had already paid for the room in advance for five days, but, he had only needed four.

However, as his intense training had taught him, he had to have patience, and consequently, had appropriately chosen to remain a guest of the hotel one more day. He wished to have no suspicion of the recent murder in the street directed his way. He was just an American tourist who still had to visit the Krems Weinstadt museum, which housed a superb collection of Gothic, Renaissance and Baroque paintings and wood sculptors.

As he opened the door to his room and proceeded down the hallway toting his two suitcases, the assassin stared ahead. He felt nothing . . . no sorrow, no remorse. His revenge had only scarcely been satisfied. This was the first . . . for the man known as *Jericho*.

* * *

Washington, D.C. . . . two days later

It seemed to Warren Turner to be unusually cold for an autumn evening in the nation's capital. He gazed out the window of his small office on Georgetown's campus. The sun had disappeared an hour ago. The lighted campus walkways outside allowed him to observe the leaves still brandishing their dark greens and appearing to mock the looming winter as they danced in the brisk wind that huffed with vengeance from the east.

Schools had already been in session for several weeks, and, vacations over, government activity bristled. Elections awaited around the corner, just over a month away. Optimism seemed to be contagious. Everyone seemed to move with more gusto . . . the hot humid summer having passed with no sad regret by anyone with even half common sense.

Professor Turner had just finished a lecture to one of his graduate classes, but, before leaving for his Virginia hillside home, was anxious to check his e-mail.

He sat at his small desk...waiting. He had already switched on the personal computer. He still had his overcoat on since he knew he would not be there long.

Once it was ready, Turner logged on to the Internet and went directly to his messages. His blood pressure advanced slightly when he saw there was a message from Cardinal. Turner punched in to read, and stared at the message.

JERICHO HOME. DELIVERY POSITIVE.
CARDINAL

After briefly reflecting on the message, he deleted it and punched in the following:

ACKNOWLEDGE. HAVE ANOTHER JOURNEY
... NEED COMPLETION NOVEMBER.
ITINERARY AVAILABLE.
T.

Then he fingered the proper keys to send the message to cardinal@car.com.

Verifying that it was sent, he deleted it before quickly reviewing his four other incoming e-mail messages that could be dealt with later. Then he logged off and placed several sheets of paper into his briefcase before rising from his desk while sad reflections overthrew all other thoughts and wrestled their way into the fore of his thinking... *Possibly a sorrowful day for a mother... a wife is probably weeping, and there may be children who are crying. Sad... so sad.*

Warren Turner's face was tight and his lips curled as he clutched his briefcase and locked the door to his office and slowly walked down the brightly lit hallway as students scrambling to get to their evening classes brushed past him. *Where will it all end?*

23

"MR. EVEREST, I'M Catherine Steele," she said as she extended her hand while approaching me as I stood in the waiting room clutching my briefcase.

"Nice to meet you," I said as I lightly accepted her hand.

I knew that Catherine Steele was a litigation attorney for the Internal Revenue Service, and that she represented the government in tax disputes. Her adversaries included attorneys and certified public accountants licensed to practice before the federal tax court.

She led me back toward her office on the twelfth floor of the Central Trust Towers located in the midtown business district on Central Avenue.

As I followed her I had this disconcerted feeling as if I had met her before. I felt like the air around me and extending through the entire office suite had come to a standstill, and for some reason not discernable in my thoughts I felt a knot in my stomach.

At that instant I felt like I had suffered a great loss in a past life, and this stranger was a reminder. It was an odd unexplainable feeling that I had never consciously struck before. What seemed even more strange about it, was that I honestly knew I had never before laid eyes on this woman.

As I sat opposite Catherine Steele's desk explaining my client's position I felt that she was listening, but, at the same time, appeared to be distracted by something. I sensed that she was involuntarily scrutinizing me, but not just as her newest adversary.

I wondered how I knew this. I couldn't explain it, though I knew it as if she had told me herself. And I didn't have a clue why I was feeling this, for I had met with numerous female government agents before, and had found several of the ladies just as attractive as this one, but not possessing a certain, almost unidentifiable softness radiating from their eyes in a similar vector as commanded by Catherine Steele.

Time set its own swift pace of passage, it seemed, and, for a while, I found myself somehow forgetting that unexplainable feeling that had found presence in my thinking when I had first met Catherine Steele, and before I realized it, we had reached the stage of the meeting where I was summarizing my client's position.

And all the while, I was trying to avoid looking directly at the government agent as much as possible without her thinking I was hampered by lack of proper intelligence or that I was some feebleminded introvert whose eyes were flittering aimlessly like a drunken fly swooping unremittingly around the room.

When we had finished, I stood, and, without daring to look directly at her, attempted somehow, remarkably well in my opinion, to concentrate on placing my papers in my briefcase as calmly as I was able to summon my usually quite acceptable professional demeanor. However, having been somewhat subjective in judgement of my own activities at the time, I had no way of gauging Catherine Steele's evaluation of my ineptness if any was actually manifested. That done, I glanced down at her for a split second and said, "Thank you, Ms. Steele. I'll get the information to you within the next two weeks if that's all right."

"Yes, that will be fine," she said as she rose from her chair and reached out her hand. As I took it, and only for a quite brief second, it felt chilled to mine, which felt embarrassingly hot, and I swore I felt her trembling.

Then I barely glanced at her and smiled briefly before turning and hurrying out of her office into the long hallway that led to the reception area. I was eager to escape this abysmal feeling, this yearning, that had seeded itself throughout my entire body, and yet, still, I didn't want to leave her office at all. As I stationed myself in the vacant elevator and watched the door slide closed, I found myself wondering if my appearance would cause even a subliminal interruption to her thoughts that day.

24

THE MEETING WAS over and Catherine Steele ached in an unlabeled fashion she couldn't identify. It was as if the day had ended . . . and yet it had just begun.

Often, during the remainder of the morning, she found it difficult to concentrate on other cases as her thoughts kept drifting to Michael Everest.

Early thirties, she thought as she sat straight up in her chair with her forearms resting on her desk. *Tall . . . looks athletic.*

She could still see his soft blue eyes that the natural light, wafting through her outside window, seemed to have intensified. She pictured his tanned face sitting across from her. *This is "one" accountant who doesn't live in his office all day*, she decided.

Catherine remembered nervously shifting around in her chair, trying to concentrate on what Michael Everest was saying. *He was all business,* she thought, n*ot only in conversation, but in his eye contact, no flirtatious glances.*

She reflected on male attorneys and accountants she had met during the past sixteen months that she had been in Phoenix. She had yet to meet one who had not flirted with her . . . until now. She felt a glimmer of rejection, and that was not the way she wanted her day to begin. And then her heart missed a beat as she thought about the simple gold band on Michael Everest's left hand.

Catherine leaned back in her chair and thought about when she had reached her hand out for him to shake just before he left. She remembered it trembling as she felt the warmth of his.

Here I am . . . twenty-seven years old, from the huge metropolis of Helena, Montana, a sophisticated woman of the world, she facetiously smiled to herself. *Why didn't Michael Everest fall at my feet?*

For a while Catherine sat staring out the window at South Mountain in the distance. Dark grey clouds hovered over the entire range of mountains all the way to the Estrellas southwest of Phoenix.

Determined that she would get some work done, she finally reached for a file that needed to be reviewed for her next meeting.

After a half hour or so, as she leafed through pages in the file, she thought about when, during her sophomore year in high school, she had begun dating Ronnie Swanson. He was a year older than she. He was sophisticated, it had seemed to her at the time.

She smiled again to herself at that overstated thought when all of a sudden, without warning, her daydreaming was interrupted when she was startled by quarter-size raindrops pelting her window. She glanced up and saw lightning bolts slithering across the dark murky sky over the distant mountain ranges, and then heard the cracking of thunder.

As she watched the rain battering the window from the sweeping storm, Catherine thought about when she had been elected captain of the cheerleading squad, the first junior with that honor at Capital High in Helena.

I could put that on my resume for Michael Everest, she beamed to herself.

She smiled as she glanced at the picture of the twins sitting on the corner of her desk next to a Jack O' Lantern, which was the smaller of two that the twins had helped—or thought they had helped—her carve two evenings ago.

Catherine thought about how great everyone had been . . . her mom and dad, her friends, schoolmates, and especially her high school teachers. She had only missed two weeks of school. The twins had been born just three weeks before she graduated.

She never saw Ronnie again after he left Helena that August before her senior year had started, and he never saw the twins.

Mom and Dad had been incredible, Catherine thought. *All the times they had been just a phone call away while I attended law school, after three hard years at Carroll College in Helena. They gave up so much for me.*

She missed them now.

She recalled how her small scholarship and a few small grants, alone, had not been enough to support her and the twins. So her mom and dad would send what they jokingly called childcare funding to her every week. Every Monday, she would discover that a Wells Fargo Bank deposit had been made the previous Friday by someone in Helena, Montana. It wasn't much, and Catherine knew they really hadn't had the money to spare, but it had kept her from having to send the twins home to stay with her parents.

She recalled stepping out of the terminal at Phoenix Sky Harbor International Airport that first time in the middle of June just sixteen months ago. She thought she had entered hell.

She recalled thinking how glad she had been that the twins had stayed with her mom and dad until she had become settled. She remembered thinking that she thought her babies would have burned up in the desert if she had brought them with her then.

Kellie, the secretary, interrupted Catherine, "Your next appointment is here. Who was that in your office this morning? Seemed, to me, he took a lot longer than he should have," Kellie joked.

Catherine just smiled at her.

25

A WEEK HAD PASSED since my first meeting with Catherine Steele. I had just called her office and was waiting for her to get on the line.

"This is Catherine speaking." She sounded very professional, almost too formal, it seemed to me after hearing her voice . . . it was a nice one.

"This is Michael Everest," I announced. "I have the information you requested for Doctor Chapin. I was wondering if it will be all right if I mail it to you today? If you have any questions, you could call me."

"Yes, that'll be fine. I'll review everything and get back to you," her voice still sounded straightforward, very professional. I don't think I made much of an impression on her.

Then, out of nowhere, I felt a tinge of that same contingent aura I had experienced in her office the first time I met with her. So, I said to her, "Thank you . . . Bye!" And then, not waiting for her response, I promptly hung up the receiver, and found myself, with a quiet bank of discomfort, reflecting to myself about my own melancholic solitude idling inside me. *Because I feel abandoned and lonely, can I dare and am I allowed without sin to marvel about this woman . . . and let her haunt my dreams? And wonder . . . wonder what type of man would be loved by a woman like Catherine Steele?*

Sitting there with the phone still held at her ear, Catherine mused for a few seconds over how depressing a dial tone could be. She recalled how she had hated to hang up when her mom and dad had called long distance every Saturday evening while she was in law school. She had felt a little guilty the times when she had kept them on the phone longer than she knew she should have.

And now, she knew she didn't want to let Michael Everest go. She sat staring out the window . . . it was raining again. *Just like it was when Michael Everest was here that first time,* she recalled. She felt a hopeless void clawing at her insides.

Why does this man make me tremble? Why do I have this yearning? Catherine didn't understand nor was she capable of placing this foreign longing that found its uninvited breed attaching to her every conscious thought. She understood one thing though . . . Michael Everest was affecting her in a way she had never experienced before.

And he had given no indication of interest in me beyond that of his client, she thought as she rose from her chair and walked over to inspect the rain. *He hardly looked at me at all the entire time he was here, and in those instances when his eyes captured mine it was as if air would hold itself in frozen flight and refuse to allow me to breath it.*

What kind of man is this who's capable of changing the air? What cut of man is this who effortlessly suffocates my breathing with nothing more than a glance in my direction?

Catherine's fingertips lightly brushed the condensation of moisture that had formed on the inside of the window as the spray-like rain drops gently lighted against the outside.

The sun had just set and the sky was blanketed from horizon to horizon with a low hanging cloud cover that held the illumination of a somewhat bright pale-grey because of the valley's floor of lights reflecting off of it.

Catherine looked out at the pictorial lights of the downtown skyline three miles south. The rain made everything look like a celebration as the spirited lights reflected off of Central Avenue and the adjoining drenched streets below. And her thoughts were prisoner to this man's being as she thought, *In one day that began with no extraordinary promises construed nor expected, I've been reduced to less than a semblance of my strength by a total stranger.*

And I'm completely powerless at rationalizing this confusing veneer of unknown and unsettling excitement that seems to smother me. What will happen with this potent force to which I have found myself marked? I feel as if I've been completely devoured and helplessly wielded to the mercy of God knows what . . . and hopeless, under any dimension of dreams.

"My God! He's married," Catherine caught herself bluttering out, almost loud enough for her secretary to hear.

As she picked up her coat she told herself that she would be too busy to think about Michael Everest during the next few weeks and she would forget him.

26

Karpathos, a small Greek island . . .

RICHARD DUMAS STEPPED out of the shower and grabbed the emerald green bath towel and briskly dried himself before wrapping it around his waist. Then he reached up and swept back his soaked sun-bleached golden-brown hair into a ponytail that brushed just below the back of his neck. He held it there and secured it with a small elastic tie.

After shaving and splashing on a dash of Calvin Klein *Obsession* aftershave, he pulled on a nondescript dark-green collar shirt with sleeves running to his elbows and allowed it to hang loosely over his beige shorts that brushed his knees. The medium-brown leather Johnston & Murphy Passport loafers, no socks, finished the visitor from France.

The hotel's restaurant overlooked the adjacent white beach that gracefully embraced the steady waves rolling in from the blue-grey November waters of the Mediterranean Sea.

Except for the tiny island of Kassos, Karpathos was the most southern of the Dodecanese Islands of Greece. In Greek, Dodecanese meant, "twelve islands," but there were actually fifteen, or as many as eighteen islands, depending on which guidebook was looked at, Dumas had been told.

The city of Karpathos, which lay in the southeastern part of the island of the same name, was about forty miles southwest of Rhodes, the better known and largest of these Greek islands.

Rhodes, once a Greek island, which had become a Turkish possession for the past four centuries, was given to Italy as a result of the First World War, and became a popular holiday playground for Dictator Mussolini. In 1947 its ownership had finally been returned to Greece, which was fine with Richard Dumas.

The Frenchman saw that the inside area of dining tables was filled to capacity, and was told that nothing would be available until ten thirty in the evening . . . more than two hours away.

The outside patio offered better possibilities, he was further advised by the maitre d', if he would be so inclined as to check that out.

That choice didn't seem promising to Dumas either. Not only were all the dining tables taken, but the outside bar area was overrun with men and women whose bodies were already elbow to elbow and four and five deep to the bar, from what he could see.

There were more ladies than gentlemen, the Frenchman judged. And, he mused, all of both sexes were most likely dedicated to the pursuit of adventure and maybe that *one* chance of meeting a soul mate . . . or, if not that fortunate, at least a damn good time. Whatever, they would feel no pain until the sun rose, he concluded.

Richard Dumas, however, harbored no such fantasies for himself because *that* was not his cut in this life. His hazel eyes scanned across the crowded patio toward the beach. From where he stood, seeing nothing of interest, his eyes wandered again inside the main restaurant. There he spotted what he was searching for.

Now, Richard Dumas, French tourist, had to find *his* soulmate. It would not be difficult. He knew he was easily the most attractive looking male anywhere in sight, and genuinely knew that his thinking truly lacked arrogance of any measured order . . . just a fact that shared little importance with his vanity. And, as he could easily tell, most of the female eyes were directed toward him anyway. He simply . . . just had to choose.

The twenty-eight-year-old Frenchman . . . that's what his passport read . . . focused on a brown-haired beauty, he guessed from Italy or Greece, who stood about fifteen feet from him near the outside bar where he knew he could be seen, and wished to be seen, from anywhere inside the restaurant.

As he inched toward her he noticed the air had chilled as it allowed itself to be fetched along in the form of a slight breeze coasting in from the sea. He had already noticed the moonless black sky filled with what seemed like millions of bright sparkling diamonds.

It reminded him of a mountain trek he had taken alone on the Mogollan Rim one summer in central Arizona several years ago. It was where he had found this calling.

The thought made him melancholy for a brief moment as he continued gazing upward.

Until . . . until he heard her voice, excited, yet soft, "Hi!"

He lowered his eyes to her, his head still tilted back. He smiled and his head slowly joined the rest of him as his gaze took in the most beautiful crystalline brown eyes he had ever seen. "Hi!" he said.

"They're spectacular, aren't they?" she laughingly remarked in English as she admired the dark heavens and their array of sparkling lights above the island, and then, just as quickly, directed her gaze at him.

"Yes," he breathed out, in English with a strong French accent. "But, they don't have an exclusive on spectacular." Richard Dumas startled himself, but he truly meant every word as he scanned her face.

She blushed, he could tell. "I'm Ellen . . . Ellen Hisker."

"I'm Richard Dumas. My friends call me Rick." He reached out.

Ellen firmly accepted his hand, "Nice to meet you, Rick."

As she released it, she looked at him and asked, "What is Rick Dumas doing out here by himself. Or, is he waiting for someone?" Her English accent was Italian, or Spanish, he thought.

Now *he* blushed, took in a deep breath, looked away from her for a few seconds, and then returned her stare. "I was wondering the same about you." She had a beautiful tan that was not just recently acquired, he thought. She was about five foot seven, incredible body, and undeniably, the most attractive woman he had ever laid eyes on.

After the most exhilarating next four hours that Richard Dumas had ever encountered, he found himself wishing, dreaming that the night would never end.

They had drank some, probably more than either should have. They had talked and talked, and laughed together, more than Dumas had done of either . . . in years. They had danced with one another all evening, and had a delicious dinner of clams, lobster and fresh vegetables, and warm fresh breads. They had held hands while they strolled along the white sandy beach, letting the chilled titillating waves rush across their bare feet.

Dumas knew his night's escapade had been successful. He was sure of that, without really knowing. Everyone at the restaurant saw them dancing and sharing the evening together.

Is this what it feels like to fall in love? If not, then that feeling must rise all the way to heaven's gate, he pondered as he lay on his pillow and daydreamed—or night dreamed—about holding her hand when they had walked.

He recalled that they had finished the evening with just a fleeting good-night kiss, and a "Maybe I'll see you tomorrow," she had whispered before closing the door to her suite.

It struck Dumas as he lay there. He had not chosen her . . . she had chosen him. He smiled as his head seemed to spin, and he drifted off.

Ellen Hisker sank into the plush pillow. She closed her eyes and smiled as she thought about the all too brief yet sensuous kiss that tasted so sweet and delicious. For, at that moment, she had felt like she wanted to be his love slave forever.

As warm blood raced through her veins, she urgently wished that she could surrender to what her body ached for . . . craved.

She had done her job. He had not chosen her . . . she had chosen him. But, he had left his mark. She shuddered and tightly clutched her pillows and tried to sleep.

27

THE SUN BARELY filtered through the drawn drapes leading to the balcony. Dumas lay there in the darkened room staring at the white ceiling. Her face was centered directly in front of his view. Her image smiled, and he blinked and she was gone.

He glanced at the clock on the nightstand and reached over and snatched the phone on the side table and asked, in French, for her room. It was ten-forty-seven in the morning.

"I am sorry, monsieur," the female voice answered in perfect French, "Ms. Hisker has checked out of the hotel."

The warm sun was already high overhead in the cloudless blue sky by the time Dumas entered the hotel restaurant. All of the scattered forty or fifty tables with their brilliant white cloths draped over them were occupied, but he was able to clearly see the entire dining area without any difficulty. There was no sign of her.

He stepped out onto the patio that was less crowded. She was nowhere in sight. Dumas felt a lump in his throat. His stomach fluttered with an emptiness that was foreign to him . . . a distant and desolate longing that even the warm breeze seemed to carry.

Later, he decided on a pastry along with cold sheep's milk from Greece for breakfast, and occasionally found himself searching the crowd for her. By the time he had finished, he concluded that it was just a fun night . . . that had ended. *Time to take your party favors and go home,* he bitterly decreed to himself.

28

TWO MORE DAYS passed before Richard Dumas had decided on how to complete his assignment.

It was Friday afternoon, and he had just finished lunch. The sky was clear except for huge grey and white clouds along the eastern horizon, and the breeze was of a cool and kindly nature in attitude. He wore a blue long-sleeve Polo shirt rolled up to his elbows that hung outside his full length khakis. His feet were bare inside his white canvas tennis shoes.

Dumas, now the hunter, had observed his prey commit the same mortal sin that everyone on holiday relegates themselves to if they hang around in one place more than a day or so. They develop a habit. It's like an infant, out of the womb, in foreign surroundings. The young child just can't seem to break away from that womb . . . from familiar surroundings. And so, the same is said for most vacationers. They seem to bind themselves to certain places, familiar places, comfortable surroundings . . . the same routine, even for murderers on holiday.

Even so, Richard Dumas had been told that this prey was dangerous, for this man was also an assassin, a very good one. His name was Akram Rabahm, and he was Libyan and maintained his safe house in that country. He acted only on behalf of his own country or nations friendly to Libya. His hits included nine highly ranked diplomats from Western Europe and two potential presidents of two South American countries.

Dumas had been told that Rabahm had millions of dollars at his disposal and his network included spies all over the world, many of them simple hotel employees at many resorts in Europe and South America. He paid them well.

Dumas knew there were, most likely, many spies there . . . or Akram Rabahm would not feel so at ease and reckless. Dumas suspected that the killer had, at least, two or three bodyguards protecting him.

He had the time down. It was the only way to do it. And so, there he was, dressed as a hotel porter, and even working from the kitchen and bar, providing room service. He was a trainee, he had told the supervisor when he had reported for his evening job shift at six o'clock. It was a very busy time for the supervisor who could not even verify that hotel management had sent the newcomer.

Dumas had easily removed the fake ponytail and had changed the color of his hair to a dark brown while his eyes remained hazel, thanks to the contact lens.

During the next five hours, he performed admirably and had made almost two hundred fifty Euro dollars in tips, providing room service throughout the hotel. He had even made three deliveries to the eighth floor. And, yes, there were two bodyguards stationed outside his target's room. Dumas had nodded his head and courteously smiled each time he passed them. They even nodded back. They knew him now . . . their mistake.

It was just after eleven and he was now expecting the call. Champagne and lamb delicacies with warm bread and olive oil were to be delivered to room 801 at precisely eleven twenty.

It wasn't difficult to time his pace with the other dozen or so porters so that he would happen to be the one who would make the delivery. No one gave it a second thought.

Dumas swallowed hard, took in a slow deep breath and then just as slowly exhaled as the elevator door slid open. He stepped out and began wheeling the service tray down the long hallway corridor toward the two bodyguards. Both were Eastern European or Russian, he guessed. When he approached them, he expected they would let him enter since they, obviously, would remember him . . . he hoped.

In French, he told them he had room service for suite 801. First, one of them briskly searched him from shoulder to ankle, and then the same bodyguard asked him to remove the cover to the mobile serving unit.

Dumas was glad he had taped the .22–caliber pistol to the underside of the cover because the men examined even the bottom of the mobile cart. Had they considered to look at the underside of the cover which he had lifted off of the service tray and delicately tilted away from them, Dumas would have had to kill them both.

The men didn't enter the room with him because Rabahm had a guest, whom, it turned out to be, had been one of the young male porters who, earlier, had worked alongside Dumas for a few hours.

The former porter, who sat on a large and luxurious cream-colored sofa alongside the suite's guest, was no longer in uniform. He now wore a white bathrobe as did Mr. Rabahm.

Per instructions from Rabahm, spoken in French, Dumas placed the mobile service tray at one end of the long, white marble coffee table that sat about eighteen inches in front of the sofa.

Dumas wasn't one to linger. Once the service tray was in place, he lifted the cover with his left hand and snapped the

Beretta from the underside of the tray's cover with his right, took two quick steps toward Rabahm, and two quick bursts pierced the center of the Libyan's forehead just above his eyes. The custom-made silencer, only one-half inch in length, prevented any sound traveling more than ten to fifteen feet.

Then, before the dead man's lover could react, Dumas stepped up and over the coffee table and snapped his opened hand into the side of the boy's face. The boy fell over on the sofa and was left with only a broken jaw. When he saw that the former porter was out cold Dumas breathed a sigh of relief because he had not had to kill the boy.

He stood motionless for a few seconds, staring at the dead man's feet. The man wore no shoes.

Dumas then walked into the bedroom and opened the closet door. He reached down and picked up a black leather dress shoe, carried it into the living room and dropped it next to Rabahm's body.

Then he tucked the lightweight pistol into the front of his pants and shielded the weapon with the white coat, which he wore loosely out over his pants. He was ready.

He opened the door of the luxury suite, said good evening in French to the bodyguards and walked in a normal step down to the elevators. *Jericho* would have to leave before morning.

* * *

Virginia . . . four days later

Warren Turner's eyes were intent as he studied the monitor screen glaring in his face. He had not turned on any of the three lamps in his study.

Finally, he looked out through the huge window facing northeast and saw low, dark clouds towering overhead. The Capitol wasn't visible that freezing-cold early December morning. The central heating system had just kicked on. Though he couldn't hear it, Turner felt the light air movement brushing his face. He glanced again at the screen.

JERICHO HOME. GOOD TRIP.
CARDINAL

The International Relations Academic deleted the message and sent one of his own.

ACKNOWLEDGE. WISH SIGHTSEEING TRIP
TO GARDEN. NEED DECEMBER. NO
DELIVERY REQUIRED. ITINERARY AVAIL.
T.

Turner typed in the e-mail address, cardinal@car.com, sent it before deleting, then let out a long sigh and sat back in his executive chair. *It's probably going to snow,* he thought as he regarded the threatening clouds.

29

THE YOUNG WOMAN with the medium-length brown hair, in her mid-twenties, wore a beige blouse along with a conservative dark brown business suit that appropriately complimented her slim figure and revealed just enough of her beautiful long legs to make it interesting.

She felt just a twinge of nervous anticipation as she sat appropriately straight with one brown *Bandolino* pump properly crossed over the other on the thick carpet in one of the two occupied leather-cushioned visitors chairs in front of the huge dark-stained oak executive desk. It had to be at least eight feet long, she judged, and at least four feet wide.

Before being seated, she had taken in the rest of the large study that was just as imposing, including the cozy fireplace with the faint crackling fire, and the very large floor-to-ceiling window looking out across the Virginia hills. She swore she had glimpsed a view of the Capitol many miles away . . . through that mammoth window that was now to her back.

Lora Parks had just been introduced to the highly regarded and highly respected Warren Turner, for whom, unbeknownst to her, she had performed an assignment six weeks before. It was her first field assignment since joining the agency nineteen months ago, and had been filtered down through the normal ranks at Langley until reaching her field supervisor.

No big deal, she had thought . . . until about two minutes ago, when the powerful political figure himself had informed her that she had been personally selected by him.

Turner had been impressed by her file, especially her language-learning talents. Her extraordinary good looks quite apparent from her photograph had been impressive to the influential statesman. But, it was her determined, yet soft, eyes that stirred Warren. Now, sitting across from her, he realized that the flattering photograph fell far short of doing justice to this lady.

Lora was still in a small state of shock and uneasiness ever since she had been quickly summoned just two hours ago to go directly to Turner's private estate. She had been working out at her Aikido dojo near her condo in Reston, Virginia when her cellular had beckoned her. Now, she felt just a little intimidated even for a rich girl from Chicago whose father was a wealthy shipping magnate on the Great Lakes. Normally, no one intimidated Lora Parks, she reminded herself.

After having already picked up a Bachelor's Degree from Ohio State, and a Masters from Columbia, both in Arabic languages, with a minor in French, Lora had just spent sixteen of the past nineteen months at Camp Peary. She had received high marks for everything to which she had been introduced.

And, having the extraordinary ability to learn fluent Spanish with such ease at Camp Peary earned her instant "star" status at *The Farm*—the name commonly used for the Central Intelligence Agency's training facility at Williamsburg, Virginia.

In a very short period of time, Lora had also picked up passable Italian, and was making headway on her Greek. Next, she told herself, she was going to learn Japanese.

"Ms. Parks," Warren Turner politely addressed her, "we appreciate you meeting with us on such short notice." Lora quickly learned that Professor Turner did not waste time getting to the point. "Mr. Palmer and I wish to discuss with you, whether or not you would have any difficulty working closely with the agent you recently assisted in the Mediterranean."

The statement . . . question, or whatever, caught her off guard, and she uncomfortably shuffled in her chair. Her reaction, she was sure, was not unnoticed by the two professionals. She became instantly aware that she was blushing and quickly tried to recover without any hesitation, responding with a simple and professional sounding, "No, sir, I would have no problem at all."

Lora recalled with an inner smile . . . that warm, and, oh so brief, kiss. She had thought about it many times since. Even found herself experiencing several wet dreams over it. Rick Dumas . . . she mulled his name over in her mind. After that night she thought she would never see him again.

David Palmer occupied the second visitor's chair. He was on assignment from the National Security Council as a personal assistant to Warren Turner, Lora was told. *In his early thirties,* she guessed. His hair was brown and cut military style, *nice high cheek bones with a handsome square chin.* He wasn't a big man . . . lean, maybe five ten, some hundred-sixty pounds, Lora judged. *Could probably kill me in a microsecond if he chose to do so. He looks like he's in excellent physical shape . . . too good a shape to just be a grunt.*

"Well, good, then that's agreed," David Palmer remarked as he moved his chair closer to the front of Warren Turner's spit-shined desk and established a work area by sliding a few knick-knacks out of the way and placing an opened manilla file folder on it. He then declared, "Now, I would like to tell both of you a little about Richard . . . Rick Dumas."

Turner, it seemed to Lora, didn't blink an eye at his special assistant's measures of reshuffling the top of the statesman's desk, and making room for his papers. Obviously, Lora speculated, Palmer and Turner were quite at ease with one another. They've been together a long time, she decided.

Lora was an attentive audience as David Palmer began his recitation, "His real name is Joshua Stone. He's twenty-seven years old. Two years ago Mr. Stone began his training with the agency, and he's been in the high speed lane ever since.

"Before coming to us he spent seven months in the mountains up on the Mogollan Rim in Arizona and down in the Sonoran Desert along with a modern day mountain man by the name of Bill Marshall, who, we discovered, is a big game hunting guide up on the Mogollon Rim around Payson, Arizona.

"Marshall is considered by every professional guide we were able to talk to, to be as good as any there ever were."

Palmer continued reading from the file and glanced up ever so often at Turner or Lora, "Stone learned survival skills in high mountain terrain under both winter and summer conditions, as well as in the desert during the deadly hot summer months. On several occasions he tracked lions and a grizzly. Actually had them cornered in his sights, but, once he had them, he walked away without the kill."

Lora felt the hair stand on the back of her neck when she heard this. *Well, Mr. Dumas . . . or, rather, Mr. Stone, you're quite a trooper!*

Palmer's mild yet firm voice resumed the expose, "From there Joshua Stone went to Camp Peary for nine months, receiving extensive intelligence training from the agency. Then, after six months dividing his time between a Green Beret unit at Fort Bragg and a Navy SEAL team at Coronado, he spent another five months with Delta Force at Fort Bragg."

Palmer paused and took several sips of coffee from a blue-and-white China teacup while Lora shifted in her seat. Warren Turner was sitting back, appearing quite relaxed in what Lora decided was a very expensive, dark-brown leather executive chair that appeared to be padded quite comfortably.

Turner's personal assistant, all business, carefully placed his cup on the matching saucer and continued reading the dossier, "Stone is highly trained in terrorism counteraction, political warfare indoctrination, special warfare intelligence and other covert operations, all of which his instructors felt would be of value to him.

"This guy's been through it all," Palmer didn't let up, "including scuba and parachute training, and he's rated as 'expert' by both the Army and Navy at using pistols and rifles. They say he can, with a small .22–caliber pistol, light a match fifteen feet away in a flash of an eye with one shot, from starting with his hand holding the weapon at his side. They say *that* .22 is like an extension of his hand, and he just points."

Palmer paused while Turner and Lora sat there waiting for more. Lora facetiously chuckled to herself, *It seems Mr. Stone is overtrained. I do believe I've met my match.* She crossed her legs.

Palmer turned over a sheet of paper and resumed, "As a child, Stone was taught by his aunt and uncle to speak fluently in English, French, Dutch, German, Spanish, and the Arabic languages. He was also taught several different styles of martial arts by his uncle.

"Naturally, at Fort Bragg, Stone trained in Jerry Peterson's **SCARS** fighting system, which is taught to our military's 'Special Forces'. He's certified at the instructor level. In other words, he's a bad dude, and he's already served with distinction."

Palmer cleared his throat, closed the file folder, glanced at Turner, then at Lora, and concluded by saying, "His code name is *Jericho*."

30

BEFORE THE MEETING with Warren Turner and David Palmer had ended, Lora was instructed by Turner to more or less sit and wait for his call. He had suggested that she needed to research, for the next week or so, the religious habits and traditions of the Middle East. She was now assigned exclusively to Turner, no intermediary supervisors. Soon she would be on assignment with *Jericho*.

As she drove away from the gated entrance to Warren Turner's estate in her new Infiniti Qx4, black with gold trim and all the goodies—a belated graduation present to herself—she remained curious and apprehensive about Rick Dumas, or rather, about Joshua Stone.

It seemed eerily quiet to Lora all of a sudden as she sat in the luxurious utility vehicle and regarded the silent snowflakes impetuously, yet gently, settling themselves on her front windshield while she waited for the red light to change. She saw no other vehicles.

Well, Lora Parks . . . she reflected, *you wanted exciting, you wanted fast. Guess what? You're jetting now!*

The light changed and Lora steered left and headed for home. She wondered, *Is Joshua Stone anything like Richard Dumas?*

31

THE MAN'S FOREARMS rested on the edge of the grey metal desk. His receding hairline allowed the overhead flourescent bulbs to glow luminously on his glossy forehead. His eyes squinted above his fleshy cheeks to prevent smoke entering from the cigarette dangling in his mouth as he slowly turned over pages in the manila folder. The folder contained approximately thirty written pages as well as several photographs.

Stan Dodd was in his late fifties. His thinning white hair was combed back emphasizing the opposite desired effect of that hairline marching upward and toward the rear.

His five-foot-eight-inch frame didn't justify the two hundred thirty-five pounds he carried due to his weakness for machaca enchiladas, shredded beef tacos and chili burritos, especially the ones with red and green hot chili peppers from New Mexico. The recent Christmas and New Years celebrating festivities at his sister's didn't help matters either.

For the past six years, Dodd had been Agent-in-Charge of the Phoenix office of the Drug Enforcement Administration. He had spent his entire career in Phoenix except for a three-year assignment in San Diego eleven years ago.

On the opposite side of Stan Dodd's desk, Henry Sotello leaned back in the barely padded grey metal armchair, guiding Dodd through the file. "He speaks fluent Spanish . . . learned from his father-in-law who died nine years ago."

Dodd kept leafing through the file as Sotello continued, "Has an accounting practice out on East Indian School Road, nothing fancy . . . filed bankruptcy eight months ago because of some bad investments."

"Some of his clients lost their asses, but none of them went after him . . . seemed a little unusual to me. Nowadays everybody wants to sue their lawyers and accountants."

"He'd have to be nuts not to go for this, especially after losing everything," Dodd mumbled through his cigarette just loud enough for Sotello to hear as Dodd continued turning pages in the folder.

"I've got an appointment set up this afternoon if you say, Go! Stan." Henry Sotello was eager to get started.

"Henry, you and I, and two local chiefs are the only ones who know about this," Dodd remarked as he closed the manila folder. "We've got to keep the lid locked tight as a daughter's chastity belt on this one. Apparently, some bigwigs in D.C. have given us no choice . . . they want *him*.

"You're to be his only contact, Henry, and no one else in this office is to know. You can give him my name, too. Washington has given him the code name, *Gaman*." Dodd coughed a few times from the cigarette still dangling from his mouth.

"Dammit, Stan, I keep telling you those things are gonna' kill ya," Sotello declared as he rose from his chair and smacked his lips together in a smile at Dodd. He eagerly snatched up the file that Stan Dodd had just read, and headed out of his boss's private office door. Henry wanted some fresh air.

32

I WAS AT MY desk, which was just out of sight around the corner from my secretary's so-called office, also labeled the reception area, when I heard Hazel's friendly voice offer, "May I help you?"

"I'm Henry Sotello. I have an appointment with Mr. Everest."

"Please have a seat, Mr. Sotello." Hazel, always tastefully dressed, was in her late fifties. She had been with me since I began my accounting practice eight years ago. Before that she had been my secretary at the First National Bank where I had been a vice president.

The bank title had not impressed me, and the salary was even less overwhelming. So, after enduring over ten years of bureaucratic and political bull crap, I just upped and abruptly resigned one day . . . one day after I had discovered that I had, somehow, passed all four parts of the three-day National CPA Exam on my first attempt. Only five percent of those sitting for the exam ever accomplished that feat. I shrugged it off as pure luck, and the grace of God.

Anyway, Hazel's loyalty to me was without question. She had even taken a pay cut when I lost almost all of my clients ten months ago. I trusted her implicitly.

The man's face looks ruddy . . . too much sun, Hazel thought as she rose from her desk. She also decided Mr. Sotello drank too much beer as she glanced at his inflated stomach that appeared even more pronounced after he had seated himself on one of the armless metal chairs in the small waiting area.

Meanwhile, Henry Sotello was doing his own evaluation as he perused a quick mental inventory of the office while he waited. And, telling me later, concluded that *this* CPA was not doing as well as most other accountants. My office, though neat appearing, with its cheap metal furniture looked pretty sparse and tiny to Henry.

"Michael, Mr. Sotello is here for his one o'clock." Hazel stood at the door of my office.

Without looking up from my computer monitor, I said, "I don't remember him on my calendar. Who is he?"

"He called early this morning," Hazel was quick to answer, "and said he had to see you today. And, said it was extremely urgent. And by the way, don't forget to sign your memo to Catherine Steele . . . she's the Appeals Officer you met with a few months ago for Doctor Chapin. The file's there," Hazel said, and I glanced up long enough to see her point to the corner of my desk.

"Ask him to come in," I instructed as I looked away from the monitor and involuntarily glanced at Doctor Chapin's thick file. Dr. Chapin was one of only several clients who still had confidence in me since my bankruptcy hell almost a year ago.

"Mr. Everest, I'm Henry Sotello." The man extended his hand across the desk as I rose from my chair.

"Nice to meet you," I said as I shook the visitor's hand and motioned toward an aged and well-worn chair in front of my desk. "What can I do for you?"

"May I close the door?" Sotello didn't wait for an answer. As he sat down, Sotello presented a badge in his wallet, "I'm with the Drug Enforcement Administration, and we would like to talk to you about some work we need done."

I listened as my visitor spent the next ten minutes explaining how the agency had stepped up its war on illegal drugs.

The agent continued, "We're trying another approach, that, until now, we've never been able to consider. It has been impossible for us to infiltrate the top levels of the drug cartels. In fact, it's been difficult to even get into the middle levels."

At that point, I interrupted the DEA agent, "I don't have any police experience. I'm an accountant, Mr. Sotello . . . I don't even own a gun."

"We know. But we also know you speak fluent Spanish . . . and you *are* an accountant."

"I don't know what I could possibly do for you," I chided and shifted uncomfortably in my chair. For some unknown reason that I couldn't identify within any meaningful notion, I felt the adrenalin mounting and wondered why it excited me, the thought of doing something daring and dangerous. *This would definitely beat sitting at my desk all day,* flashed through my distilled mind.

Even so, I still forced myself to tell the government agent, "I'm sorry, Mr. Sotello, but I don't want to waste your time." As I said this I became aware of a terribly foreign visitor of unknown consequences overtaking my seemingly juvenile thought process as I realized I was already hooked.

"There's something I should mention," Sotello interjected while leaning forward in his chair and placing his forearms on top of my small well-used secondhand metal desk. "A person could make a lot of money doing what we're asking you to do."

Sotello paused momentarily, while contemplating his next words as he stared at me, the accountant. Then he continued, "Have you ever seen a million dollars in cash? Have you ever seen five million dollars? . . . ten million?"

My eyes locked on those of the DEA agent while my unseen right leg started twitching as if it was about to bolt out from under my desk and tell the DEA agent that *I'll brutally maim, massacre and rape anyone the government wants for those kind of bucks.* Neither of us blinked.

Sotello slowly leaned back in his chair, "The drug cartels have billions of dollars in cash stockpiled all over the place. They want to launder it into the legitimate money supply system. We want them to do that, so we'll know where all their money is. Then, we're going to take it. And, hopefully, bankrupt some of those bastards.

"They know our government is beginning to use the military and even local national guard units to try to stop the flow of drugs. We're hiring hundreds of new agents. The word is 'full force' against the cartels. And the word is coming from the top level of our government."

As I listened, my mind rocketed like a NASA space booster blasting for take-off as a completely unfamiliar thrill began playing runaway through my entire irresponsible body. It's as if I'm sitting on the bench of the big game and have always been only a spectator, and then all of a sudden the coach yells at me to get out there. I want to, but I'm scared shitless. And I come to that crossroad in my life, when it's time to poop or get off the pot. And I ask myself, *Is this what I really need? . . . danger in my life? Will this make me alive . . . Will this free me? Why can't I be happy with who I am now? Will I ever grow up? Do I really want in that fucking game?*

I didn't take my eyes off the drug agent as I leaned back in my chair and listened to more of what the man had to say. My heart was rapidly approaching Mach 1, though I believed I was masking it pretty well.

"The cartels want to get into legitimate businesses here in the states and in Europe," the DEA agent said as he leaned forward. "They know they can't use offshore banks like they used to, so they want people who can show them how to structure those enterprises and launder their cash . . . they need accountants to do that.

"One of our sources has told us they're looking for an accountant right here in Phoenix."

I took a deep breath that showed. "What brought you to me?" As well as becoming pumped, I was also becoming amused, and wondered what or who in the world had brought the United States Drug Enforcement Administration to me and my small struggling accounting firm of two.

I waited for a response as Sotello looked at me and stood and walked to the small office window. With his back to me, Henry Sotello clasped his hands behind him and stared out into the tiny parking lot that was, barely, large enough for three cars. And all three spaces were occupied, respectively, by Sotello's government-issue light-blue two-year-old Ford sedan, by Hazel's three-year-old Nissan Sentra and my nine-year-old Buick Park Avenue.

"I'll tell you why we want you." Sotello paused a few seconds as he continued looking out the window. "We know you had some financial problems during the past year. You lost everything." The big heavyset man turned away from the window and met my shell shocked face. "That fact would explain to the cartel why you would be willing to work for them."

My stomach scratched at the knot that was trying to shit can my insides. I thought about Julia. I had convinced her that the land project would make a lot of money. I had thought, maybe, *that* would have helped our marriage.

She'd hang me up by my balls to the nearest palm tree stark naked and strip my skin from my pathetic body piece by piece if I ever got into something like this, I warned myself.

I moved the foot of my crossed leg to the floor and swivelled my worn chair toward Sotello, and followed my visitor's movements as the agent returned to the seat in front of my desk. My heart was bolting even faster and I wondered if it showed now.

For a while, neither of us spoke. I just stared aimlessly across the small room, my folded hands positioned on my desk. Then I slowly blinked and set my gaze on the DEA agent. "You mentioned ten million dollars," I said pausing for a few seconds before finishing. "In cash, I believe you said." Then I waited for the drug agent's reaction, and wished I had some toilet paper and privacy to clean out my pants.

Sotello took a deep breath and sat back in the hard chair with his head slightly tilted back, and slowly exhaled. "Michael . . . is it all right if I call you Michael?"

Henry Sotello excitedly resumed, "The drug cartels will pay millions, in cash, to an accountant they can trust. One of those cartels will be your client.

"The Drug Enforcement Administration doesn't object to a CPA being paid for services rendered to his client. In fact, the DEA doesn't even care if the accountant is paid in cash. All the income you receive from us and the cartel will be reported on your tax returns and the IRS won't question from where it came."

I felt my heart popping through my shirt now. *She'll kill me . . . she "will" kill me!* I kept fighting off those warning shots as I tried to appear calm, and yet, knew that my heart would detonate any second. But I felt alive. My mind gathered up speed, now sailing a mile a minute. "I have clients who need me. What am I supposed to do with them?"

"If your assistant can't handle a couple of months without you, you'll hire an associate within the next couple of days. We'll fund his salary." Sotello had an answer for everything. "You'll have to leave by the end of the week for Williamsburg, Virginia for some schooling."

"What do I tell my wife?"

Sotello was quick to answer, "You have a new client located in Virginia. They'll want you to familiarize yourself with their operations and you'll need to be there as long as it takes. Tell your wife that you should be back here in ten to twelve weeks.

"Tell her that you'll be required to travel often for them at first. You *will* travel often for the cartel. We'll cover your overhead while you're gone."

I sadly concluded to myself, *Julia won't mind me being gone a lot.*

"Oh! . . . there's one more thing," Sotello slowly announced as he sat up straight in his chair. "If they find out . . . that you're working for us," the agent paused and looked directly at my pitted expression, and then told his new recruit, "without any hesitation they'll kill you in the most brutal manner they can contrive."

Henry Sotello's harsh statement momentarily pared my excitement . . . cropped my rapidly pumping heart.

But, even so, I couldn't remember the last time I had felt this tonic sense of being alive . . . really alive.

I stared at the DEA agent . . . and thought about Julia. *She'll kill me!* . . . "Let me think it over."

33

CATHERINE STEELE'S CASE load seemed to be heavier than ever, and she had been unable to work on the "Doctor Chapin" case for more than ten weeks from the time when she had first met with the CPA in her office back in October, over two and a half months ago.

She laid her light coat on the small couch in her office and sat down at her desk. She was in high spirits and wanted to take a few moments to relax and view the valley as she gazed out through the small window that faced south from midtown Central Avenue.

It was Friday morning and the view was breathtaking. The morning air had been crisp, and the sun shined brilliantly while the sky was a deep-blue with just a few grey clouds gathering over the Estrella Mountains.

Catherine was a little apprehensive while she tried to talk herself into thinking, *No big deal!* as she dialed and cleared her throat.

Though her heart was pounding, Catherine felt renewed. She and the twins were going to spend the weekend up in Flagstaff, just two driving hours away from Phoenix.

She listened to the buzzing sound in her ear and thought about how foolish she had been to think romantically about Michael Everest. She felt a slight tremor in her hands as she heard the pleasant voice answering at the other end, "Michael Everest's office. May I help you?"

Catherine introduced herself and asked for "Mr. Everest."

"Just a moment, please," the polite voice told her.

After Hazel buzzed me, and told me who was on the line, I purposely, and wasn't sure at all why, waited for a moment before I picked up the phone and said, "This is Michael."

I heard her overly businesslike voice in the receiver and felt a tiny chill slide up the back of my neck, "This is Catherine Steele, Mr. Everest, from the appeals office." Her voice sounded unsteady.

I sensed her uneasiness as she hesitated too long before continuing. "I've had a chance to review the information you gave me regarding Doctor Chapin, and I believe there are several items that we need to talk about."

"My client is anxious to have this settled, Ms. Steele," I advised her. "I'm leaving tonight for a couple of months, and I have a tight schedule today." As I told her this, I recalled that it had been just four days ago that Henry Sotello of the Drug Enforcement Administration had first visited my office.

There was momentary silence, awkward silence, as if both of us were lost for words . . . I know I was!

Finally I broke the lull, "I know it's really short notice, but, would you have any time to meet this evening?"

"YES!" A loud answer . . . *very* loud. Then I heard her again, sounding calmer, "Yes, I believe I could if it isn't too late. I'm also leaving the valley." She paused, then added, "for the weekend."

After that, I heard nothing coming from her end and thought, maybe, she had felt uncomfortable because of her late comment.

Before panic could pick me up, cycle and spit me out, I tried to gather myself and quickly remedy my thinking as to what I needed to do next. Then, the words just spilled out as if from a superior force, "Well, let's see"—I was still trying to think, out loud—"I have meetings until five thirty. My plane leaves at eight twenty." And then, the words just tweaked their way out past my lips without any premature reflection or guarded scrutiny on my part as I spoke into the telephone that I held quivering at my ear, "Would you be able to meet me at the Arizona Club Norte?—"

I knew she could tell I hesitated without finishing. But then, changing gears, I said, more confidently now, "Or better yet, could you meet me at *Azteca* on Central at six?"

As I hung up, sharp-edged guilt, and thoughts of The Inquisition, decided to question my integrity as well as my fidelity as I asked myself, *Would I have been this determined to finish a client case with a government agent if that person were not Catherine Steele?*

I didn't wait around long enough to answer that question as I promptly got up from my desk and headed to my car. As I rushed past Hazel, I told her I was out for the day, in fact for the next three months. I told her the new accountant—I had just hired him two days ago—could handle everything until I got back from the east coast.

I desperately needed to climb North Mountain, and I refused to even think about that despoiled question about Catherine Steele . . . I was afraid of what the answer would be.

As she hung up the phone, Catherine thought about why Michael Everest had changed his mind about the private Arizona Club. She, a government agent, wasn't permitted to accept a meal from an adversary. She thought to herself that he had been thoughtful not to compromise her.

She looked at her wall clock . . . ten-thirty. She was glad she had a lot to do that day, until six o'clock.

34

AZTECA WAS A POPULAR Mexican Food Restaurant in the midtown business strip on Central Avenue, six blocks north of Catherine's office. She had gone there a few times before for lunch with some of her coworkers.

The waiting area was packed with the overflow of young men and women executives, secretaries and clerks who had filtered out from the bar section. Everyone seemed to be laughing and talking all at the same time.

She looked to me as if her eyes had not yet adjusted to the dim light when I approached her.

"Hi!" I smiled, "It's busier than I expected. I forgot about 'happy hour.' C'mon, she has a table for us," I told Catherine as I stepped behind her.

I knew she felt the pressure of my hand lightly touching just above the small of her back as I guided her through the maze of the celebrating ritual. It was an electrifying feeling for me because I had never touched a woman like that, in that flirtatious way, in all the years since I had been married. It was frightening, but, at the same time, enchanting.

"Just follow her," I said.

The waitress handed each of us a menu after we had been seated opposite one another in a booth toward the rear of one of the dining rooms.

"I'll bring your water with lemon, Mr. Everest. What would you like to drink, Ms. Steele?" the waitress offered.

I could tell, Catherine could barely hold back a slight smile as she looked at me watching her reaction. "I'll have iced tea, please." She smiled up at the waitress.

"One of my best friends owns this place. They take very good care of me . . . and my guests," I told her with a sheepish grin after the waitress had gone. "I thought it would temper the mood a little for two adversaries."

Catherine laughed, "I'm impressed." She felt her hands stop trembling as much.

"I appreciate you meeting with me on such short notice, and I'll try not to keep you too long," I said as I picked up my napkin and placed it on my lap. "Are you leaving for business or pleasure?"

He remembered that I was leaving the valley, Catherine thought. *Was he interested or was he just making conversation? No matter, he "did" remember.* "I'm going up to Flag for the weekend."

"It's been snowing up there a lot. Are you a skier?" I asked as the waitress placed our drinks on the table.

"I grew up in Montana, Mr. Everest," Catherine laughed.

As we ate, we discussed and settled the differences of Doctor Chapin's case. Catherine agreed to send me the proposal for signature. There would be no need to take the case to Tax Court. I was sure we both felt the settlement was fair.

Less than an hour and Michael Everest is gone, Catherine thought as she sat motionless in her white one-year-old Buick Regal.

After sitting there a few insular moments, she started the engine. As she shifted into drive, she noticed the misty rain brushing across her windshield.

I'll never see him again . . .

35

Washington, D.C. . . .

THE ACID-COLD March wind seemed to ignore, almost laughingly rebuke, my heavy overcoat, penetrating every vulnerable crack in my armor, and sending chilling shivers down my neck while I gingerly maneuvered through the foot of snow that had begun blanketing Georgetown University's campus earlier in the afternoon.

I was in awe at how quiet the air seemed, even with snowflakes streaming down like a runaway stampede. The crunching of snow beneath my feet was the only sound I heard. I had not been in snow, when it was falling, for over twenty-five years.

It was seven P.M., Friday.

I had just completed my eighth week at Camp Peary, located on nine thousand acres of barbed-wire-encircled woods at Williamsburg, Virginia. It looked like a community college, with brick buildings, dorms, a cafeteria and a gym, laid out on a rustic campus.

As I trudged along, I recalled the training I had undergone so far and how it had transformed my body, and more importantly my soul, into someone new . . . someone I never would have imagined I could be . . . someone I liked much better.

* * *

I had been subjected to intense training in classrooms, learning about criminal justice procedures and civil rights law, studying various software systems and related computer hardware. I had also participated in a class titled "Flaps and Seals," where I studied the finer points of stealthily opening and resealing letters.

I also found a course titled "Tradecraft" to my liking. It included covert photography of enemy documents, the art of picking up messages from dead drops, and the use of disguises. I also participated in staged cocktail parties, learning how to strike up conversations with targeted individuals.

One of the courses that I did not take part in, included serving in solitary confinement in the camp's mock prison. I figured that the powers-that-be had already come to the conclusion that, if I was discovered by the enemy, I wouldn't live long enough to be put into a cell, so why bother.

Outside the classroom I was introduced to weapons training on the firing range, and hand-to-hand combat in the gym.

I had never had firearms training before, so this new undertaking was something I found suitable to my liking, especially stripping down the weapons and reassembling them under the required time. After just four weeks at Camp Peary, I could tear down any weapon, and clean and reassemble it as fast as any of the instructors, except for the one called Joshua Stone.

Years ago, when I was ten or eleven years old, I'd had a Daisy BB gun that I had shot out in the desert north of Phoenix once or twice a month. At Camp Peary, it was the first time I had ever shot a "real gun." It took me only five weeks to be classified as expert with several assault rifles and small firearms.

I preferred the 9mm Glock 226 semiautomatic over any of the others, and had decided by the end of the third week that the Glock was made for me.

When it came to the hand-to-hand fighting, I acted like a novice. Several times though, I was tempted to show the instructors what I knew. But I recalled what Henry Sotello had told me before I had left for Virginia, about not drawing attention to myself. Besides, I realized, These instructors were quite good. No! . . . They were VERY, VERY good . . . even the pretty, young lady with the short brown hair. *I had no way of knowing for sure at the time, but I suspected that the instructors already knew everything about me.*

As part of my training, for the past three weeks, the gorgeous young female instructor had been working out with me, using one of the newer martial arts known as Aikido . . . the "gentle martial art." Lora Parks—that was the name she had given me—told me that she had begun studying this martial art form eleven years ago in Chicago.

I, myself, had only been studying this form, in Scottsdale, for six years. I thought she was quite good, and appreciated her teaching me several new techniques.

I had grown a beard—Sotello's idea—and had not been allowed to mingle with the other trainees, except during the staged cocktail parties. Otherwise, I saw them only from a distance and was always isolated from their quarters. I was not sure why, especially, I thought, since they were supposed to be the good guys.

For the past eight weeks, at the end of each day, I had always been accompanied by at least one of my instructors to my quarters, which consisted of a study room, a small kitchen, three small bedrooms and a lounge area for eating and watching television. Though there was little time for T.V.

Another odd thing, it seemed to me, was that I had been the only student in each of my so-called crash courses. Until now, I'd had only the same three private tutors for everything.

I had also spent about two to three hours studying each evening after a seven o'clock dinner that had always been served in my quarters by two of my instructors whom I knew as David Palmer and Joshua Stone.

I had no idea which branches of the military they belonged to. They wore only Camp Peary attire, not military uniforms, the same as I, no rank or insignias were visible. I guessed that they were, or had been, in the military's "Special Forces."

I judged David Palmer to be in his early thirties, and Joshua Stone, probably middle twenties. And Lora Parks appeared to be fresh out of college within the past two or three years. So, I reckoned her age at the middle twenties also. My two male mentors were always in my quarters when I was there.

I quickly learned that all three were well trained in hand-to-hand combat fighting, and that all three were exceptionally good with weapons and extremely knowledgeable in demolition procedures.

I also discovered that all three of them spoke fluent Spanish, and, most of the time, they chose to use that language instead of English when communicating with me, their student spy.

* * *

After attentively inching my way up the icy steps, I entered the warmth of the university's auditorium. The three hundred or so, I estimated, who had braved the Icelandic weather conditions had already seated themselves.

As the guest speaker was being introduced I had to settle for an end seat in the twelfth row.

"Ladies and gentlemen . . . Mr. Warren Turner."

There was polite applause.

"Thank you, Ms. Murphy. After that quite generous introduction I should pinch myself to see if I'm God." Professor Turner smiled as he said it, and there was light laughter in the auditorium.

"I am very pleased to see so many faces tonight. The weather has not been kind." His gentle smile seemed to glow, I thought, as the elderly man looked out over the audience, his hands grasping the top of each side of the podium. He paused for a moment, as if weighing his words. Then he began to speak.

"I've always been intrigued with the treatments that people of different orientations afford one another. We are all human beings, yet, each of our different experiences . . . our families, our friends . . . our associates, our religions, and our countries . . . all of these make us human, but yet so different.

"It seems to me that we, in this country, need to realize and accept these simple, but very major differences, especially when our government makes foreign policy decisions, and we, as citizens, especially our media, constantly monitor, evaluate and judge the positions taken by our government."

I listened as Warren Turner continued for the next forty-five minutes, talking excitedly about how the country, and the world, should address the issues that divide them.

" . . . and unlimited opportunities are being literally thrown at our country's feet to help the rest of the world build a peaceful society that is welcomed by almost all countries . . . ensuring in the process that every nation is to be respected for its own individuality while maintaining, at the same time, its rightful identity and place, not position, but place in the world. . . . "

The speaker paused momentarily, allowing his listeners to digest his last few words. Finally he concluded, "I thank each and every one of you very much for taking the time to come this evening."

Everyone stood and loud applause followed.

That man has great ideas, I thought, impressed, as I stood applauding with everyone else, and watching Warren Turner leave the stage. *He should be president.*

As I watched the elderly statesman disappear out a side door, I realized how glad I was that one of the instructors, David Palmer, had suggested that I look at a flier posted on a bulletin board near one of the classrooms at Camp Peary. The flier had announced that a talk was to be given at the Georgetown University auditorium by Professor Turner, the well-known and popular foreign affairs adviser to the last four presidents.

Palmer had told me that Professor Warren Turner was being considered for National Security Advisor, I recalled as I shivered and pulled my overcoat collar up around my neck and entered hell froze over.

It had stopped snowing, and as I carefully maneuvered down the slick steps outside the auditorium, I heard a familiar voice. "Mr. Everest, I'm glad to see you here tonight."

David Palmer was planted about twenty feet away from where I stood shivering in the snow, and he appeared to be entering a black limousine stationed at the curb. "Could I drop you somewhere?"

I saw that there was someone else in the limo. "No, thanks, my ride will be here in fifteen or twenty minutes." I then pulled my overcoat up higher around my neck as the arctic air stung my face.

"You'll freeze to death in ten minutes! C'mon, we'll call your ride and cancel." Palmer had walked over to me and lightly, yet firmly, grabbed my arm.

As I climbed into the warmth of the limo I found myself face to face with the white-haired speaker.

"Hello there. I'm Warren Turner." He extended his hand as he said it.

"It's an honor to meet you, sir. I'm Michael Everest," I said while shaking Turner's gloved hand with my own gloved hand and positioning myself in the seat facing opposite the elderly statesman.

My instructor climbed in alongside Turner. After he closed the door of the limo, Palmer addressed the professor, "Mr. Everest is training at *Camp Peary*, sir. He has four more weeks to go."

36

Camp Peary, Virginia . . .

IT WAS MIDMORNING in early April when Lora Parks closed the rear door of her Qx4 after storing her last piece of luggage, and headed for the driver's side. That's when she spotted him coming out the dormitory entrance.

Lora knew Joshua Stone couldn't possibly avoid seeing her. She was only about forty yards away. She watched him as he walked to the waiting nondescript grey sedan with his suitcase in hand.

She could tell he noticed her right after he had deposited his piece of luggage into the trunk of the vehicle. She watched him stand straight up and slowly walk around to the passenger's door . . . he was looking in her direction the whole time.

Then she saw him politely smile at her and offer a shallow wave "goodbye" before disappearing into the front seat of the government car that would take him to the camp's airport. Lora did not know where Joshua Stone was off to. And she wondered why she had this uninvited forlorn vacuum stirring within her.

* * *

Lora had had absolutely no opportunities at all to talk privately with Joshua Stone during the past twelve weeks that the two of them had been at "The Farm."

It had appeared to her that Joshua Stone, himself, had demonstrated a concerted effort to avoid being alone with her. She had begun telling herself that he was beginning to "bug" the hell out of her as she found herself thinking constantly about him, and the fact that he was so incredibly gorgeous surely didn't help matters.

Of course, Lora admittedly acknowledged to herself that she had acted cold and aloof when they had first arrived at Camp Peary in January. But, she'd had reason to.

She had been deeply disappointed and passionately furious after she had been told by David Palmer that it had been decided she would not participate in the Middle East assignment with Stone that past December. She had been told, in fact, that Joshua Stone would go alone.

Lora had wanted to know why the change, and, accordingly, had badgered Palmer, including, reminding him that she reported directly to Warren Turner. She had told him that she would go directly to Turner for an explanation if it came to that.

Palmer, not wanting to pull rank on her, had relented to her pressure, and had told her that Joshua Stone had indicated to his superior that he would not be comfortable traveling with a female in Lebanon.

Palmer had also told her that Joshua Stone had felt it would be too dangerous for her.

And furthermore, Palmer reluctantly advised Lora, Joshua Stone's contact had told Warren Turner that Joshua would not go anywhere with Lora in particular. Palmer had cringed and swallowed hard at that last bit of news to her.

Later that same day, in her apartment, Lora had fumed, sworn, screamed, kicked in her bedroom closet door, and yelled at her dusty-brown and white cat, Harold . . . who, by the way, was a female.

After that, Lora Parks never wanted to be in the same state as Joshua Stone, ever . . . except, maybe, to tell him to his face what a lowdown male chauvinist prick he was, and that she never wanted to lay eyes on him ever again. Yeah, and a pig's ass isn't pork!

Several days later, during early January, She had been asked by Turner to report to Camp Peary at the beginning of the following week to assist in training a new, highly sensitive, highly secretive recruit of the agency.

She sat in Turner's office while he also told Lora that her security clearance had just been upgraded to the top bar. She now had "White House Status" clearance. Only the President of the United States possessed a higher rating.

By the time she had arrived at "The Farm," Lora had been calmed down somewhat by several tactful conversations with David Palmer, who had fast become a good, loyal and supportive friend. Palmer had been impressed by what she had accomplished at the agency in the short time that she had been at Langley.

* * *

Now as she watched Joshua Stone's car disembark, Lora felt an agonizing, empty feeling in her chest. She thought about how the two of them had kept their distance from one another and had acted admirably as professional associates toward one another over the past twelve weeks.

She was proud of herself because she had not given Joshua Stone one smidgen of any indication that he had thoroughly pissed her off before they had come to Camp Peary.

She was puzzled, however, as to why he had acted so polite to her and why he had been such a perfect gentleman to her, both professionally and socially, and always in the presence of others, for the entire time they were there, training Michael Everest.

Lora's eyes continued following Joshua's car as it began winding through the dense array of leafless trees not yet freed from winter's grasp. It dawned on her how one becomes accustomed to the barren, drab trees in the surrounding woods that time of year. They become quite unnoticeable, taken for granted. And then, just like that, one day, like an overnight miracle, they become thick with foliage, and one can never quite recall an awareness of when that occurred. And now, it was still a long time coming.

When she saw his car finally disappear, she turned and opened her car door, glanced in his direction one more time, and climbed in . . . *Probably never see the sonofabitch again, anyway.*

37

AS JOSHUA STONE surveyed the scenery drifting by, he thought about how he had been so trenchantly aware of Lora

Parks watching him as soon as he had come through the doors leading out from the dormitory. He had pretended not to notice her until after he had placed his suitcase into the trunk of the waiting car, even though out of the corner of his eye he had gazed continuously in her direction. He had purposely played out this pretense because he wasn't sure what he was going to do . . . *Just walk right up to her and say "goodbye"? . . . Yell "goodbye"? . . .*

When the time came, he still couldn't think of anything to do or say, so he simply looked up at her, gave her one of his best smiles and forced himself to wave goodbye, and climbed into the car.

The overwhelming thought was, again, burdening him as he shuffled in the front seat of the sedan. *I'm a priest, and I haven't told her. I have no business thinking about her the way I do. I can't "ever" see her again.*

He petitioned himself, *How do I forget this woman? She's everywhere. I think about her all the time. Stop it, "Father" Stone . . . STOP it!*

* * *

Joshua recalled the night in early December when "Cardinal" had told him that his new assignment was to find out what he could about a plan that Middle East terrorists had purportedly devised. Plans that, in the words of extremely reliable Western informers, would topple European governments as well as several governments of the Americas. Word from the highly paid informants was that a biological virus of some kind would be used, and was being tested now. "Cardinal" had told Joshua that time was of the essence, and that Joshua had to go to Lebanon immediately.

"Washington is of the opinion that it will be safer for you to travel with a woman. So they've arranged for you to travel with a wife," "Cardinal" had told Joshua. Bishop Adolfo Carbajal momentarily paused as he observed Joshua's reaction to what he had just been told.

The pause caused Joshua to look up at Carbajal with a questioning look. But Joshua said nothing as he waited for his mentor to continue. Joshua didn't have a problem with the idea.

Carbajal then added as he looked at Joshua, "She's the woman you met on the island in the Mediterranean."

Since Bishop Carbajal was Joshua's confessor, Joshua had already told him about Lora Parks. Joshua had confessed the whole story about how he had felt moved by Lora, and what had happened between Lora and himself . . . which was nothing really the bishop had determined and he had told Joshua so.

But, Joshua couldn't escape the feelings, the constant thoughts of her . . . whether he was awake or not.

He recalled, over and over again in his mind, what he had related to "Cardinal." "I don't want to face her. What happened on that island was just a job to her, Father. But, like a naive fool, I thought more of it. I had no right to presume anything like that. I'm a priest, and I've sinned." Joshua paused for a few seconds and looked at his dear friend. "I never want to see her again."

Within days, Joshua then went to Lebanon for almost a week that included several meetings with paid informers, and confirmed the worst fears that some kind of poison gas was being developed that would be capable of assassinating a large group of people all at one time.

After he returned from the Middle East, Joshua was advised by Bishop Carbajal that he was needed at the training facility in Virginia. The bishop had decided that it was time for Joshua to face his affliction . . . face Lora Parks.

* * *

The sedan pulled alongside the Gulfstream jet already warming up its powerful engines on the tarmac, interrupting Joshua's thoughts. He stepped from the car, snatched up his suitcase from the car's trunk and took a long look up into the blue sky. The breeze was brisk and still quite cool, and the sun teemed brightly while the sky opted a cloudless stance.

Father Joshua Stone took a deep breath of the Virginia air, climbed up into the luxury jet and settled into his seat. He politely refused refreshments from the Air Force steward, and decided he'd try to get some shuteye.

He closed his eyes and recalled seeing her early that first morning after he had arrived at Peary the previous night, twelve weeks ago.

Joshua had almost lost it after he had entered David Palmer's office and stared down at Lora Parks who sat on a small chair just left of the doorway while Palmer stood behind his desk.

Joshua recalled how he had just stood there, gawking at her. He couldn't think of anything to say . . . *I just stood there like a buffoon with his finger engaged up his nose.*

David Palmer finally had broken the constrained silence and introduced them, "Lora Parks, this is Joshua Stone. I believe the two of you have already met." And with that, Major David Palmer pursed his lips, rolled his eyes upward and sat down behind his desk.

Joshua remembered how cold Lora's reaction had been to him in that office. He had felt like a hot-stove poker had just been asswiped down his throat and stirred to the boiling point. He could still see her eyes, so indifferent, like he was just someone with whom she had gone through the motions. That look from Lora had established the ambience between the two of them, there in Virginia, for the next three months. Joshua was all business from that moment on.

He had decided, like an actor, Lora Parks had just played her role during the whole Greek affair, just doing her job, nothing more. *She was very convincing,* Joshua reluctantly admitted, and inhaled a deep breath as he felt the Gulfstream lift from the ground that was a part of the Virginia countryside.

38

Scottsdale, Arizona . . .

THE WARM DESERT winds in late April had momentarily subsided, and I felt eternally grateful for that as I tried to forget the shitload of butterflies swarming in my belly, and to forget that I felt like I was about to have an unsolicited bowel movement. It was difficult for anyone to play tennis in the blustering southwest winds that usually kicked up late evenings during that time of year. And, it was not unusual for the dust storms to play havoc with the valley during the last part of March and on into the latter part of April. I felt that I'd already been violated enough by adversities that seemed to cherish leveling themselves in unwanted apparitions totally conflicting with my sentiment, without having to worry about the elements too. And, I was wondering what the hell my mind and body were about to partake in.

It was Thursday evening, about ten minutes to seven, and I was sitting at a patio table at the Oasis Tennis Club, waiting to be called for a match. I had put in my match request just after I had spotted, in the parking lot, the person I had been waiting for. The description of the drug man's car had been given to me by Henry Sotello.

As I sat there, wondering if I should vomit now or wait until I got on the tennis court, I recalled my meeting with Sotello just a few days after I had returned from the east and Camp Peary, six days ago.

Sotello had briefed me, *"He plays at his club every Thursday night. Afterwards, he usually has a few drinks on the terrace patio overlooking the courts. He always comes to the club looking for a match."*

As I waited to be assigned a court and someone to play, hopefully the drug lord, I tried to focus what attention I could on a mixed doubles match going on at court three. The court was situated about six feet lower than where I sat, and lush green landscaping tapered down from the concrete patio toward the court, about thirty feet away.

I mulled over in my mind the code name that Sotello had given me before I had gone to Virginia... *Gaman. Must be a coincidence... coincidence, hell!* I told myself. *They probably know everything about me, probably know how often I take a leak.*

The outside loudspeaker interrupted my thoughts. "MR. EVEREST, PLEASE REPORT TO COURT SEVENTEEN." I felt as if the butterflies were now waging a major battle for control of my intestines and were about to embark en masse in the direction of my asshole as I opened the chain-link gate to court seventeen.

My opponent had already stashed his tennis bag and walked onto the court near the gate, and was taking a few practice swings at an invisible ball when I entered the court.

"Hi, I'm Hector Baldarrama." The man extended his hand.

I reached out with mine as I introduced myself, "I'm Michael Everest, nice to meet you."

While I studied the man, I guessed that he was in his late thirties, about five ten . . . slender, but with strong muscular legs. *A good-looking guy,* I thought as I stashed my tennis bag on the round white metal table sitting between the two adjacent courts numbered sixteen and seventeen. *He looks like a movie star, perfect features.* I couldn't help thinking that my opponent almost didn't look real.

While I, wild raging butterflies and all, walked out onto my side of the court, I thought of something that, until now, I had taken for granted. I nervously chuckled facetiously to myself and thought, *It'll really be funny if I can't beat this guy.*

After warming up with the drug man, and then completing the first set, I quickly discovered that my concern was for naught, as I had no difficulty at all with this opponent.

Later, as the match progressed, I noticed that Baldarrama's thick black hair had been perfectly manicured and there was not a hair on the man's head that was out of place, even after two hard-fought sets. My hair, on the other hand, and even though it wasn't that long, was already plastered down with sweat to my forehead. I, jokingly to myself, loathed nonsweaters.

After playing for almost two hours, I finally won the second of three sets in a tiebreaker. I had purposely allowed the match to be close enough so that the outcome could go either way . . . until the end. A sharp volley past the man's backhand side and into the corner of the court finished the match.

He'll want a rematch . . . no one wants to lose a close one, I reasoned as the two of us met at the net to shake hands and extend the customary, congratulatory words of thanks, while under one's breath, you call him a wart loser if you beat him.

And, if he *beats* you . . . he's a worthless cheating slime ball with a lot of luck.

After I had packed up my gear at the patio table near the net, I thanked the drug man again and hurried away while telling myself . . . *Don't seem too eager.*

To my amazement, it dawned on me as I walked towards my car . . . the butterflies had vanished.

39

I PURPOSELY STAYED away from the tennis club on Thursdays for the next three weeks, but *did* manage to play every Monday and Friday evening so the club's staff could become familiar with me . . . and I always came looking for a match.

On the fourth Monday after I had played that first time with Hector Baldarrama, I noticed the drug lord playing a singles match a few courts away from where I was playing a doubles match with three members who had asked me to fill in for a missing part of their regular foursome.

The sad thing about this situation had nothing really to do with me per se, but I couldn't help thinking about the missing "fourth" for whom I was subbing.

The poor man, bless his unwanted soul, had called at the last minute, unable to play, and would now be treated as an unreliable outcast for the rest of his miserable days, and banished to the role of an alternate.

Tennis was grave business, I couldn't help joking to myself, and then self admonished, *I've really got to be more serious about all this.* So far, I was actually enjoying my newfound role . . . even though my heart tickled a troublesome misfired beat now and then dating back to my first encounter with Hector Baldarrama.

During the doubles match, I caught him glancing in my direction several times. When my match was over, I purposely avoided an encounter with the drug lord and hurried from the club . . . *the deadly game was on.*

*   *   *

On the fourth Thursday, I found myself matched again with the drug dealer. And, as before, I made sure we played three hard-fought sets, making sure that I beat Baldarrama again, in a tiebreaker.

I knew that it was my nature to always allow close line calls to go in favor of any opponent when I was unsure if the ball was in or out. I believed I had acquired this trait from Hue. I also believed that Hue had never experienced, even for the briefest of measured time, the question of cheating for one's own personal gain. I realized at an early age that it was a thought foreign to her existence. I knew no one else like her.

With Baldarrama, I had purposely made several quite-generous important "game-point calls" in Baldarrama's favor that the drug lord obviously *knew* should have been my points.

After the match, I prepared to leave in the same hurried fashion as before. But, I noticed that Baldarrama had hastily grabbed up his own equipment so that the drug lord could walk to the clubhouse along with me.

Until then, there had been little conversation between us other than the usual court courtesies and occasional small talk. As we walked, Baldarrama invited me to have a drink with him.

We had several . . . I opted for lemonade as I knew that alcohol wouldn't mix well with what I now knew must be killer bees that had replaced the butterflies, and had found their own battleground deep inside my belly. At that moment, I swore to myself that I would pay my doctor a visit the very next day to stop these wars perpetrating in such relentless and dissatisfying portions among the various airborne insects I imagined were buried deep inside my gut.

I wasn't surprised when I was asked by the drug man for a rematch for the following Thursday.

As I drove home, I thought about the past hour spent with Hector Baldarrama. We had talked about tennis, the club, and how long each of us had been members, just like any normal members would do. I was beginning to feel more comfortable around the man . . . even liked him.

I had told him that I had joined the tennis club several months ago because I had just recently moved to the Piestewa Peak area just west of Paradise Valley—a disgustingly wealthy township that spreads out over a few square miles between northeast Phoenix and Scottsdale.

As I turned off Scottsdale Road onto Lincoln Drive, heading west, I thought about Baldarrama telling me that he was an exporting and importing consultant.

And, I had told Baldarrama that I had a small accounting practice.

After pulling my well-aged Park Avenue into the driveway, I turned off the ignition and sat staring at the rented house that was supposed to be my home . . . no lights were on. *She still isn't there . . . I wonder what she would say if she knew,* I mused as I climbed out of the Buick. I could feel the adrenaline high. I felt alive, excited . . . and afraid.

40

THE NEXT THREE months decided to escape any grasp of time whatsoever and stole past me without any recognition of their demise while I carefully cultivated my newfound friendship.

As the ball flew by my outstretched arm, I complimented my opponent, "Great shot."

"I believe that's set and match my friend," Hector Baldarrama calmly yelled as he strolled to the net. "Come, Michael, the victor owes you a drink."

So that the drug man wouldn't give up in frustration over not being able to beat me and look for someone else to play, I had let him win every few matches during the past three months that we had been playing one another.

We sat at one of the patio tables overlooking the tennis courts and talked about our match for a few minutes while idly watching other matches going on around us.

Even though the August sun had settled itself below the horizon several hours ago, I told myself that the temperature was still in the high nineties. I considerately thought several times that night to thank my creator for the monsoons delaying their ingress into the valley, bringing with them the high humidity that would make the weather even more unbearable.

The tennis courts with their green surfaces had the appearance of grass to the unknowing eye due to the special lighting which had been developed for athletic events after dark. All twenty-four courts were busy, some with highly rated players, some with beginners, and most in between. One thing, however, was certain, every court had nothing but serious participants.

Though I had not socialized with anyone else but Hector Baldarrama, I presumed that this club was no different than all other tennis clubs where the caste system was quite prevalent. In this tennis world, a person's constant goal, constant aim, was to move up in that caste order. And that order, that social level that one occupied, was determined solely upon the tennis skills one possessed. I enjoyed watching the system operate. I also reminded myself, chuckling while that thought occurred, that I must take life more seriously.

As the waiter deposited the drinks on the table, he spoke to Baldarrama in Spanish, but before Hector could respond, I answered in Spanish... for the first time in Baldarrama's presence.

The drug kingpin looked at me like a long lost brother, and the man's expression told me he was pleasantly surprised.

"Cheers," Hector said with a smile, and raised his glass of Coors beer.

"Cheers," I lifted my Sun Cooler drink.

After we had tipped our glasses, Hector began speaking in Spanish, "You told me you have a small accounting practice, Michael... and no partners. How do you get new clients?"

"Usually by referrals," I answered in Spanish as I felt my pumping heart drop to my belly button. *Is this the opening I've been waiting for?* I shifted in my chair and crossed my legs . . . and wished I hadn't done that. *Stay calm,* I reminded myself.

"Would you be interested in an importing and exporting client?"

"I'm always interested in new clients, Hector. What type of products are you talking about?" My pulse was pumping five hundred miles a minute as I tried, with some difficulty, to remain calm and concentrate on trying to relax my gaze at Hector Baldarrama.

"Could we get together at my office sometime on Monday?" the drug dealer asked.

41

TWENTY-FIVE MINUTES AFTER leaving the tennis club, I called Henry Sotello from a pay phone at the corner of Nineteenth Avenue and Osborn. Sotello had previously instructed me to never use my cell phone or my business or home phones when contacting Henry at his home or office . . . and never address one another by name.

I felt the adrenaline pumping like an Alaskan pipeline and slighting no routes within my entire body as I said into the phone, "It's happening." I paused for a second or so and then told my government contact, "And I'm scared shitless!"

"Good!" Sotello said. "If you weren't, I'd be worried."

"He asked me to meet with him Monday. It seems almost too easy." I told Sotello.

Henry warned me, his new associate, "This is just the beginning. You must never underestimate him. Always be on your guard. Hector Baldarrama is a cunning and ruthless animal.

He'll kill you without even thinking twice about it if he finds you're deceiving him."

Then, after a momentary silence, Henry's voice turned soft as he said, "I'm excited about this too, Michael."

Another brief pause, then I heard him say, "Just be careful, my friend."

42

A TALL, HEAVYSET Hispanic man, dressed in a cream-colored business suit with matching tie, shirt and shoes, greeted me at the front door of the Scottsdale mansion.

I introduced myself in English, and told the man that I had an appointment with Hector Baldarrama.

I had seen the man before with another even larger man a few times at the tennis club with Baldarrama. I had never seen either wear tennis attire, so I presumed that neither played tennis.

I later learned the man's name was Jaime and the other was Jesse . . . *Hector's bodyguards.*

This initial contact there at Baldarrama's estate marked a dramatic change in me. I was to become a liar . . . a deceiver, not at all me. Or was it?

And, for the first time, I began lamenting sharp pains at the base of my neck and between my shoulders as if I were being pierced with electric rods that had just been magnetized by lightning bolts. Up until then, during the past year or so, I had, occasionally, only felt a slight discomfort at the base of my neck, which had begun incarnating itself about the time my bankruptcy proceedings began.

From then on, the constant aura of fear fashioned its serpent presence everywhere I went, and there was no reprieve from its harshness, not even when I slept, if I slept. I became acutely aware of the danger in which I was placing myself. The fun, the excitement . . . was over. Henceforth, this business was serious . . . *deadly serious,* I strongly forewarned myself.

At that moment, I had second thoughts about going through with the whole thing. I searched my soul, more than once, and asked myself, *What the hell am I doing here? What am I getting into. Do I really want to do this?* I knew I was committing myself to a world totally foreign to me . . . Hector Baldarrama's world. There would be no turning back.

But I knew I had already tasted the nectar, sensed the danger, the high that I could trace at will, in this new life. I couldn't help myself. I was already trapped like the fly in the spider's deadly web. There was no escape.

"Please come in, Mr. Baldarrama is expecting you." Jaime was polite and spoke in English with an Hispanic accent. He led me to the outside pool patio where Hector Baldarrama was eating breakfast.

"Michael!" Baldarrama rose from his chair and shook my hand. "How about some juice? I know you don't drink coffee." The drug lord motioned to a chair.

"Juice will be fine, thanks," I said as I crossed around the shaded patio table and sat facing opposite the impressive man.

"You have a beautiful home, Hector. This view is magnificent," I told the drug lord as I gazed out at the McDowell Mountains in the distance. I judged them to be some ten or fifteen miles away.

"You should have a home such as this, Michael." I could tell that Hector Baldarrama was proud of his domain as he seemed to beam with obvious pride, and I could tell that he enjoyed the compliments while he and I viewed the splendidly manicured landscaping that covered the ten-acre estate.

The drug kingpin politely waited until I had been served, then sipped his coffee. As he set his cup down, he asked, "How do you feel about the IRS?"

The blunt question caught me off guard, and I paused momentarily as I looked into the eyes of the man across the table awaiting a response.

After a brief reflection of the question, I replied, "Well, I wouldn't have their job. At times, they have to enforce some pretty stupid laws that unfairly penalize some, more than others. They take a lot of ridicule . . . in some cases it's deserved, I suppose. I believe they're all frustrated with the system, the same as we are."

The knots in my stomach tightened and unsought shock waves of burning pain sparked in their full glory at the base of my neck, and then established a beachhead all along my shoulders, with no intent of withdrawing any time soon.

Just treat him like any other new client, I tried to convince myself as I waited for what I knew, sure as hell, was not just another new client interview . . . *this potential new client may kill me.*

"You said the tax laws were unfair. In what way?" The drug lord was persistent as he studied me, the CPA.

I consciously refrained from recrossing my legs . . . though my body considered it. *Remain calm, Everest,* I warned myself. I recalled Hue telling me once, *"When a person speaks, words are heard, but the speaker's movements may say something else to the listener . . . the speaker's movements must agree with the words if the listener is to accept what is heard as truth."*

Another pause and a measured sip from my glass of orange juice before I responded to Baldarrama's question, "I believe the tax laws are written for economic and political reasons . . . more so than to raise income to support the government. Some of my clients may not always tell me everything. I tell them that the tax laws are not moral issues, and I don't judge my clients on how they treat those laws.

"I tell them, however, as their CPA I am bound to abide by the tax laws with the information my clients give me."

I continued, purposely telling the drug leader that most people were unfairly taxed more than they should be by the government, and, that, "I'm fed up with the whole system, Hector."

Baldarrama stood. "I ate too much," he said as he motioned. "Let's walk and I'll show you the grounds."

As we strolled along winding pathways fashioned of tile, I listened as he told me about the gardens that he had built there. "I did it for my new wife five years ago. She wanted to impress her friends from Los Angeles. It lasted only a year. She was unhappy with me."

A pause, then he laughed and seemed to shrug, and said, "So she left . . . deserted me."

I said nothing as I watched the man and listened. I couldn't help liking Hector Baldarrama, and I began to feel uneasy . . . some guilt . . . betrayal. *Maybe the DEA was wrong about him,* I thought for a brief second or two . . . but, I *knew* the truth.

"I'll tell you what, my friend." Hector said, his hand on my shoulder. "Why don't you and your wife have dinner with me tonight?"

That's where I knew more than anything that I had to put a stop to this madness into which I was about to dive like a free fall with no control whatsoever. The thought of my own wife being involved in this deadly venture was further than I was willing to go . . . for Sotello, for my government, for myself.

My first reaction was to give this drug man a definitive "No! My wife is not part of this." But, without any acceptable persuasion that would allow me to withdraw from this extraneous world of death and destruction, I found little comfort in the thought of telling this man that I will not do as he asked, at least for now. And even so, I couldn't induce myself to believe that Julia would be in any danger because of one diminutive dinner engagement.

It became quite clear in my order of thinking that the deadly fruit dangling in front of me in the form of this unknown danger had completely seduced my taste buds and rendered my senses helpless to even deliberate on their own in a mature and reasonable conviction of any kind.

43

"I KNOW IT'S SHORT notice, Julia. But can't you have someone take your class tonight? This could be a big client," I told her, feeling the frustration in my voice as I gazed out through the small window of my depressing office overlooking the tiny parking lot.

I hated asking a favor of her. Whenever I did, she always reminded me, in some way, that I owed her. She kept a tab. I felt, sensed, that my wife wanted to be needed . . . by her husband. *I can't give that . . . Why won't I give her that?* But I had no answer . . . it just seemed to deliberately shield itself from my realm of thinking for unknown reasons I couldn't identify and wasn't supposed to understand in this human matrix.

Julia finally said with a sigh, loud enough for me to hear, "All right, I'll ask one of my graduate assistants to take my class. I'll be home by six. Bye!"

I hung up and tried to shift my attention to some client tax briefs before leaving. I absentmindedly massaged the back of my neck now and then while my mind kept drifting to Hector Baldarrama and the drug man's penetrating eyes.

44

AFTER DINNER AT Mountain Shadows Resort in Paradise Valley, we returned to Baldarrama's estate in northeast Scottsdale. Accompanying him was a tall statuesque woman. *In her middle to late twenties,* I judged when I was introduced to this blonde beauty. I couldn't help noticing that she was several inches taller than Hector. Admiring her expensive, tight form-fitting black dress that stopped an inch above her knees, I easily gave her a nine point nine on a scale of one to ten. Her name was Nancina Por Tero.

While the four of us chatted together with small talk in the spacious living room, Julia and I learned that Nancina had grown up in Mexico City, and had earned a Bachelor of Science degree in economics from San Diego State University and a law degree from UCLA, specializing in International Trade Law.

Later, while Nancina and Julia were freshening up, Hector told me that Nancina had been living with him for about eight months.

After the ladies had returned, Hector excused himself and me, leaving the two ladies to themselves to continue their friendly discussion about world trade and politics.

I knew that Julia was in the process of writing an article for one of the scholastic magazines concerning the economy and trade practices of Japan. She had done extensive research on the subject and was eager to get some feedback from someone who might be familiar with international trade, someone exactly like Nancina.

Julia and Nancina hit it off right away, I uncomfortably mused to myself, in a counterfeit attempt at justifying Julia's presence there. As I did so, Baldarrama sequestered us by closing double doors to his study. I almost convinced myself that this encounter for my wife was a good thing. But, I still couldn't remove the guilt that quartered itself deep inside me, for I had placed her in danger. I told myself it would not happen again.

I put the thought to rest and gazed out through the very large and quite impressive floor-to-ceiling window that presented a spectacular panoramic view of Camelback Mountain three miles away. Then, I relaxed myself in one of the two deep-cushioned sofa chairs that were placed in a tastefully arranged seating area next to a large stone fireplace that lay void for the summer.

Hector walked over to where I sat and handed me a glass of brandy that he had poured at the bar in the corner of the large study. My host had concocted himself a vodka gimlet on the rocks.

After he sat down in the other sofa chair near mine, the drug lord posed a question in Spanish, "How would someone get millions and millions of dollars into this country without having to tell from where it came?"

I sat there, holding my glass, and found myself gaping directly at him, his question still somewhere out there in the wind. It startled me, and yet taught me from that time on that I've got to be ready for the unexpected with this man. *This killer.*

I waited a few seconds to let him think that I was pondering the question. Then, I told him in Spanish, "Recognize it as income and pay taxes on it."

"And how would one explain from where it came if one did not wish to disclose its true source?"

I felt the man searching my eyes as he took a sip from his drink. It caused me to feel the hair stand on the back of my neck.

I set my glass on the coffee table and hoped Baldarrama hadn't noticed my trembling hand. After pausing momentarily, I told the drug man, "Then one would, first, invest a small amount that was already in the U.S. money system."

Neither of us spoke . . . for a while. I watched my dangerous host peer out through the huge window overlooking the impressive front yard landscaping that was enhanced now, and appeared even more magnificent, because of the elaborate and professionally well designed night-lighting that automatically came to life after the sun had nestled itself below the nearby peaks, wishing that I was on one of those mountains instead of where I found myself at that moment. As I sat there, awaiting Baldarrama's response, I suspected the drug lord was contemplating what he had just been told.

Finally, the man rose from his chair and strolled to the bar in silence.

While he poured another brandy for me and fixed another gimlet for himself, he spoke, "Nine years ago I had none of this. The only people who did were the ones who belonged to the *Chain*."

A pause, then he turned and looked across the room at me, as if searching the reaction on my face. Then he continued speaking, "This is a good country, Michael . . . except for the never-ending infamous chain of ass kissers who run this country and tell us the rules by which we must live and survive. And then, they play another game among themselves with completely different rules."

I sat forward with my forearms resting just above my knees, fixing my gaze downward toward the thick white carpet, slowly nodding in agreement . . . as I knew I should.

"Mi amigo," Hector continued in Spanish, "the so-called American dream for honest people is no longer a reality . . . unless you screw everyone and kiss asses."

"Yo se!" ("I know"), I volunteered in a quiet air nodding in agreement, still studying the carpet. *Don't overact,* I instructed myself, heart bolting like a rabbit being stalked by a starving bloodhound, as I slowly looked up at the dangerous man facing me twenty feet away.

"As you can probably tell, I have very few friends," Hector said while I stared into his sterile eyes. "Even though I have known you for only a short time, Michael, I feel that you are my friend . . . and I respect you."

I kept my eyes focused on the drug dealer as he strolled back to his chair, and said, "I would like to see you have a beautiful home like this . . . and drive a fine car."

I just continued staring at the man . . . without blinking, and, all the while, shitting truckloads of bricks in my shorts.

Baldarrama continued, his eyes pointed right at me, "I want you to work for me."

I hesitated while trying to will away World War III in my chest somewhere in the vicinity of my heart, then rose from my chair. I was only four or five feet away from Hector when I said to him, "Nothing would please me more, than to be able to give my wife a home like this." As I said it, I motioned around the luxurious room. This whole conversation was spoken only in Spanish.

After I told him this, I noticed, immediately, the somber expression on his face just before I heard him, "Please do not be offended about what I am about to say, Michael."

I couldn't help staring with an inner sense of bewilderment as my wealthy host momentarily paused, as if not sure how to proceed.

Finally, his words came, "I am aware of your unfortunate real estate failure. I also know about your business almost failing. I know that you lost almost everything. It is time for your luck to change, my friend."

At that instant, I felt the hair behind my neck stand again as I froze and stared at Hector Baldarrama. I felt the blood rushing to my head, and instinctively thought to myself, *How dare this prick spy on me!*

I had forgotten, momentarily, the reason why I was sitting in that room with that dangerous man. I felt anger . . . as well as embarrassment. Without thought at all, I lowered my eyes toward the floor. I wasn't acting.

Then, just as quickly, thank God, I gathered my composure . . . and continued staring down at the floor, purposely avoiding eye contact with the drug lord. *Show him nothing,* I told myself. *Let him think what he wants, he already believes in you, Everest,* I assured myself.

I lingered silent and didn't move for what seemed an eternity. *Did I blow it?* Finally, I told the drug lord, "I had a lot of bitterness a year ago." I was barely able to utter my words—mouth as dry as a desert gulch in July—as I looked up at the powerful drug lord. "I lost most of my accounting practice, I lost my home . . . I lost my reputation. Someday I'll repay what my clients lost. I will do anything . . . I don't care what it takes or how long, I will repay them." I meant every word of it.

Hector leaned forward toward me, and like a soothing parent, said very slowly, almost in a whisper, "I want to help you change all that. I can make you a wealthy man, Michael." The man's eyes seemed to scrutinize mine, and then the drug man added, "You can help me as well, my friend."

Baldarrama rose from his chair and casually walked over to the huge window and asked as he stared out, "How would you like to repay those people within the next year and also have a home like this?"

On hearing those words, I knew my bowel movement in the next ten seconds was a foregone conclusion. I rose from the chair, walked over to the window and stood next to him, and gazed out at the mountains in the distance. "Who would I have to kill?" I jokingly said.

Hector turned to me and leaned against the wall next to the window before saying, "I'm serious, Michael. You could repay them and buy a home like this and have it paid for. I need someone like you to tell me how to set up businesses and tell me how these businesses can operate so that I will know how to manage them. I want to learn how cash can flow through these companies legitimately."

I walked over to the chair I had sat in earlier and turned toward the dangerous schemer, and asked, "Could I make a million dollars during the next year?"

Baldarrama hesitated and looked at me as if weighing my question, and studying me, then answered, "It will require some traveling. It will require dealing with some very powerful people. Those people have certain businesses that may not be the most desirable, but those businesses have provided them with enormous sums of money."

He paused as he drank from his glass. Then he set the glass on a small marble table, and told me, "They now want to invest this money in the United States and Europe. They want to invest this cash into desirable businesses."

Baldarrama sat down on the sofa as he continued, "An accountant with clients such as these will make much, much more than a million dollars in a year. You can be that accountant."

45

I COULDN'T SLEEP that night, and found myself tossing endlessly, imagining having ten million dollars. I also imagined all kinds of secret agent situations . . . including being killed . . . my wife murdered.

This was what I had been waiting for. I felt excited . . . and, scared shitless! I kept seeing Hector Baldarrama's dark eyes steeling into mine like an ignited spear.

As I lay there, I pensively examined myself, *Was Hector Baldarrama seeing right through me . . . and reading my mind?*

46

DURING THE NEXT month, I spent most of my waking hours reviewing industry accounting practices and tax laws relating to the types of businesses that I had recommended to the drug kingpin. The CPA that I had hired just two days before going to Camp Peary, was handling all my other accounting clients so that I could manage my new client . . . my *scary* new client.

Based on my recommendations, Baldarrama decided on franchising small fast food restaurants that would be set up all over the United States and Europe.

A ton of their filthy money could run through these, I told myself. *So easy . . . So damn easy!*

Each restaurant would be called *Lunas Primaveras,* and each one would have the same decor and would be a joint venture consisting of Hector Baldarrama's foreign trust and some foreign investors. I had learned that the foreign investors were made up of twenty-two foreign trusts that had been set up in Switzerland many years ago.

I recommended to Baldarrama that each restaurant should have one local owner who would pay a franchise fee equaling ninety-two percent of gross monthly sales, yet, still be guaranteed at least twelve thousand dollars of income per month, not to exceed eight percent of sales.

The twelve thousand dollars per month was the amount that Baldarrama felt was enough to keep the local owner happy, and quiet. If the local owner would get greedy, later on . . . well, I didn't even want to think about that.

The formula for determining the maximum amount of cash to launder through any single location was simple. I just had to keep the monthly sales at any single location under one hundred fifty thousand dollars. Eight percent of that amount equals twelve thousand dollars. And so, I easily calculated, one location could launder up to one million eight hundred thousand dollars per year.

Eventually, with five hundred locations throughout the United States and Europe, close to nine hundred million dollars could be laundered each year, and converted to honest-to-goodness squeaky clean cash.

My plan was to buy the first restaurant with cash that Hector Baldarrama had already put into the legitimate money system and use the large profits from cash laundered through that initial restaurant to invest in another. And then the profits from those two franchises would be invested in another, and another, and another, and so forth.

My instructions called for the daily records from each franchise restaurant to be forwarded to *Lunas Primaveras's* headquarters in Phoenix, where I would oversee the accounting records for each location.

A local bank checking account was to be set up in each restaurant's area with the only authorized signatories to be Hector Baldarrama and me. The local restaurant owner, the franchisee, would have absolutely no access to that checking account.

Once a week someone from the Phoenix office headquarters—one of Baldarrama's men—would pick up the receipts and deposit them into the local bank. Of course, the deposits would include additional cash, a lot of additional cash. All checks, including payroll checks, would be drawn on the local bank of each location, but would be prepared at the Phoenix headquarters by a staff of bookkeepers that I would hire in Phoenix.

I also suggested to Baldarrama that it would be cost effective to purchase small existing restaurants that were barely surviving, refurbish them, and enlist their existing owners to be franchisees. It didn't matter if these restaurants made a profit. What *did* matter, was that the restaurants stayed in business.

Eventually—I had planned—the drug lord's partnership, *Lunas Primaveras,* would be its own food and supplies provider . . . more cash profits to launder into the country's money supply. *Might as well make sure they're all profitable.* I knew, with this kind of money to promote them, and with good management, they could be quite profitable even without the phantom income.

I also knew that I had to make sure food and beverage costs ratios to sales were similar to industry trends, a simple task. I had each restaurant purchase the appropriate amount of food and beverages in relation to reported sales, and the excess was routed to the local food banks . . . under the strict condition that the donor remain anonymous.

During the next seventy days, I set up three restaurants: one in Phoenix, one in Manhattan Beach, California and one in Carlsbad, California.

As part of my strategy, I recommended to Baldarrama that the franchise partnership set up restaurants in other areas such as the Midwest, with three or four in each metropolitan area.

Hector Baldarrama, to say the least, was impressed with his new accountant.

47

WE SAT TOGETHER in Baldarrama's office—Hector at his desk, me opposite, two days before Thanksgiving.

"Here's another three hundred thousand for you." Baldarrama handed me the Lunas Primaveras check, payable to my now-thriving accounting firm.

"I appreciate this, Hector," I expressed as I sat back in the luxurious leather chair, seemingly a little embarrassed. "I don't know what to say." *Never in my wildest dreams,* I thought to myself. At that moment, I felt giddy, and a little guilty.

"Hell! Don't say anything. You've earned it. And there's more coming. We're just beginning," Hector said with a big smile. "This makes seven hundred twenty-five thousand dollars you've been paid so far. That's not bad after just three months, my friend." We always spoke in Spanish when we were alone.

Hector rose from his desk and stepped over to the small bar built into the paneled wall of teak wood about six feet from his desk, and said as he poured himself a vodka gimlet and a lemonade for me, his visitor, "You are going to be a very wealthy accountant. My foreign partners are quite pleased with our progress."

"In fact," he continued as he handed me the cold glass, "it's time to look at Europe. You and I have been invited to visit my most important partner during the first week in December. We are going to Spain . . . and, Michael . . . bring Julia."

48

THANKSGIVING HAD just been noted the previous week, and it had been only a month or so since the Valley of the Sun had finally begun to command relief from the summer's torrid blast. The sun frolicked in its game of hide-and-seek among the popcorn-shaped white clouds drifting lazily along like icebergs through the bright ocean of blue sky.

The gentle breeze danced teasingly with her hair as Catherine Steele stepped out of her office building on Central Avenue.

It was eleven-thirty in the morning and the temperature, in the high seventies, was unusually warm for the first week in December. Catherine began to have second thoughts about walking to Saint Francis. *Maybe, I should drive today.*

She couldn't make up her mind. *It's so beautiful, though . . . No! I'm walking,* she finally decided and set out, up Central Avenue. The church was located a little over a mile north of her office.

Catherine had been attending noon mass once a week for the past five weeks. There was no particular reason. It just seemed to fill a void. *Besides,* she informed herself with a jesting smile, *not only am I making points, but the walking is helping my figure.*

She knew her figure really didn't need much improvement. She exercised with aerobic videos every night after putting the twins to bed, and she thought about how lucky she was to have good genes and coveted bone structure. She knew she looked quite good.

As she walked up Central Avenue, and crossed Indian School Road, every male, who saw her, smiled and thanked God . . . and every female, who saw her, wished to God something or other. It took about fifteen minutes for her to reach St. Francis.

Catherine, momentarily startled, almost lost her balance as she moved into the church pew. *The man, a dozen rows in front* . . . she couldn't be sure. She knelt and crossed herself.

Mass began, and she couldn't avoid glancing at the back of him now and then.

After about twenty minutes, everyone rose to receive the Eucharist. Catherine stared at him as he turned toward the center aisle. Her heart raced as she straightened. It *was* him.

She had tried not to think about him for the past eleven months. *Why am I shaking?* She felt weak as she took deep breaths. She asked herself, *Why this man?*

Catherine Steele knew why.

She wanted to know him. Be his friend, talk to him . . . look at him, touch him . . . have him touch her . . . hold her.

After the Eucharist, Catherine refused to look in his direction.

Five minutes later, Mass ended.

She walked toward the rear of the church. Once outside, she stood under the covered porch, and hopelessly stared in complete defeat. It was a downpour.

She glanced back to see if he was coming. There was no one. Everyone had gone. *He must have gone out the side entrance,* she thought dejectedly.

She looked at the rain as she pondered her dilemma. *How in God's name am I going to get back to my office without getting drenched?* Then she told herself she didn't care.

Catherine stood staring at the rain for a moment, and then began walking down the church steps toward Central Avenue. The rain, coming down in buckets, quickly soaked her before she had walked a block.

It felt good at first. The huge raindrops were like a cleansing. They were exhilarating. Then they became colder, turning to sleet, and beating down on her. There was nowhere for her to go, nowhere to escape the deluge.

She kept telling herself that it didn't matter. She felt lonely . . . she felt empty inside. Catherine Steele began to cry.

The horn startled her. She had walked almost three blocks from Saint Francis. The Porsche sitting alongside her wasn't familiar.

Then the passenger door opened.

"HI, MS. STEELE," the voice rang out from the compact car trying to defeat the sound of the downpour. Catherine could tell, he hesitated, then yelled out again, even louder, "I'M MICHAEL EVEREST. I SAW YOU IN CHURCH." A pause for a second, then he added, "I'M THE ACCOUNTANT . . . FOR DOCTOR CHAPIN."

As if I didn't remember. If only you knew, Mr. Everest, Catherine brooded to herself as she stood in the pouring rain, staring down into the sports car in disbelief. Her heart had just magnified its pumping beat by infinitesimals as she envisioned herself, *I must look like a female creature from the black lagoon.*

"C'MON! YOU DON'T WANT TO DROWN, DO YOU?" she heard his loud voice still trying to compete with the torrent hammering down on them.

At the time, from that luxury vehicle, the dark sky appeared menacing to Catherine as it continued to hurl its barrage at the valley. She couldn't see out of through the windshield or side window as huge gusts of showers pounded the Porsche. She felt like they were all alone, a million miles from anywhere . . . from anyone. Fright beckoned her reasoning in small allotments as she sensed her driver was having difficulty seeing, too.

She also felt a little apprehensive, and began to lament mixed emotions about her predicament. On one hand here she was, alone with him. Yet, on the other, she thought, *are we going to have an accident because of all of this rain, and both be killed?*

As they slowly motored along Fifteenth Avenue with the waterline seeming to Catherine as if it were almost up to the doors of the little car, he joked about hoping that his Porsche could float. She forced a chuckle along with him at that remark.

"You know," he said, seemingly to Catherine, trying to sound somewhat more serious, "these raindrops are pretty. I just wish to heck I could see where I'm going." He laughed again as he said it, and Catherine hoped that he was exaggerating.

While they drove on, they talked some more, about how fast the rain had come, unexpectedly. They talked about how good the rain was for the valley. They mentioned to one another something about each other's work, how was it going? Uneasy silence froze the air for a moment before she heard him ask her about her ski trip to Flagstaff, last January.

That question brought a smile to Catherine's lips as she humorously thought to herself, *Now that's really scratching, Mr. Everest, trying to keep the conversation going.* She thought her driver was adorable. *He remembered,* she noted with another smile . . . *he remembered, after almost eleven months, that I went to Flagstaff.*

Somewhere along the way, as they drove, she asked him to call her "Catherine," and he told her to call him "Michael." They continued with more small talk as they drove through the rain-filled streets.

The rain was still pouring down with no sign of consigning itself toward other needy locales when they finally pulled into Catherine's apartment complex parking lot.

He had insisted on taking her home to change clothes, and she directed him to a covered parking spot. It had taken almost thirty minutes because of the half-flooded streets. During the trip she had told him it normally took less than fifteen minutes to get to her apartment from her office. She was grateful, but she wished this trip had gone on forever. Catherine's feelings reminded her of how Guinevere must have felt when she had first encountered Lancelot . . . excitement with hopelessness as a rider.

After he pulled into the parking space, he turned off the engine and told her, "I'll wait here for you to change," and then crawled out of the sports car and maneuvered around to the passenger side. And, after he opened her door, she heard him say, "Then, I'll run you back to your office."

The rain had stopped by the time the two-seater reached the front of Catherine's office building. The sun was shining its best behavior even though occasionally drifting in and out of a few dissipating clouds.

She climbed out, closed the passenger's door and leaned down, looking through the open window at the driver's sky-blue eyes. "I really don't know how to thank you. I don't know what I would have done. Thanks again!"

She felt warmth where her heart fluttered, and was so light-headed that she imagined she was going to faint. *This isn't real,* she thought as she stared inside the car at her rescuer.

"I'm glad I was there," he smiled. "Well, good seeing you." Catherine waved at him as he roared away. She could tell he was watching her through his rearview mirror.

The cool breeze caressed her face, and she smiled for the first time ever . . . the first time ever, after Michael Everest had just left her.

I'm in love with him.

49

Southern Coast of Spain . . .

AFTER HAVING GONE from the city of Granada earlier that day, I could tell that Julia and Nancina Por Tero were fascinated with the Spanish countryside as the limousine swung westward at La Rabita, an ancient fishing village in the comfortable shelter of a small fortress surrounded by cultivated land at the eastern end of the rugged coast of southern Spain, known as the *Costa Tropical.*

The paved road ran parallel to the Mediterranean Sea coastline, skirting beaches and mountain spurs along the way in the southern province of Granada.

We passed the seaside village of La Mamola with its large beaches. And we passed Castell de Ferro, a small place at the foot of a hill, and saw the first of many ancient watchtowers along the coast.

These, Hector Baldarrama pointed out, were lookout observation points for warning the villagers of impending danger from pirates who roamed the Mediterranean searching for weak prey among the small fishing villages lining the coastline.

From there we entered the tourist-oriented sector on the Granada part of the Costa Del Sol.

The mild, fresh sea air swept through the open windows of the limo. *And to think I almost didn't come,* Julia thought as she continued devouring the passing sights in the first foreign country she had ever been to except for several border towns of Mexico. Julia could see that Nancina was also enjoying the spectacular views as well.

As the limo raced along, Julia pointed out workers in the fields to Nancina, who, along with Hector, faced the rear opposite Julia and her husband in the passenger section of the limo.

"There *have* to be many more shops ahead for us to explore," Julia jokingly said to Nancina as the cool breeze continued playing with their hair through the open windows. Julia had begun to get a chill but didn't want the windows closed, and so she wrapped her sweater around her shoulders and slumped down a little to avoid the draft.

I noticed this, and purposely made no comment or overtures that a gentleman might have extended, such as an offer to close the windows, or even more . . . place my arm around her. I hated the thought that I wanted, so badly, to touch her . . . to hold her.

We had been traveling for the past three hours, stopping along the way now and then to take in the scenery and tourist shops.

While the ladies eagerly visited another cluster of shops, Hector and I strolled along the roadway, but didn't discuss business at all . . . just small talk about the place where we were.

I was thankful for that. But, I was always aware of which shop Julia was in and wondered why in hell I even cared at all where she was. I wanted to hate her.

As we walked, I made an observation to Hector, "It seems that the men of this village cater to their women like puppy dogs. Almost like the men are in heat and the women know it, and feel the power."

Hector replied with a smile on his face, "These men obviously have not learned that it is far less hazardous to a man's sanity when the man chooses a wife that 'he turns on' rather than when he selects a wife who 'turns him on.' "

I looked at Hector and chuckled as we reached the limo. The ladies were already inside.

During the next half hour or so, we passed five or six more fishing villages until we reached Maro, a small village in the Province of Malaga. After another ten minutes, Hector's bodyguard, Jaime, swung the limo a hard left.

Jesse, Baldarrama's other bodyguard, rode in the front passenger seat.

The black luxury automobile began climbing a steep winding dirt road that was barely wide enough for one car. Two minutes later we pulled to an abrupt stop.

"My God! How glorious!" Julia excitedly shouted as we stepped from the limo.

The adobe mansion sat on the pinnacle of the highest hill within miles. The hill jutted out over the Mediterranean, gradually sloping down on all sides, then dropping abruptly to the sea on three sides. The northeastern side of the hill contained a circular dirt road that appeared to be the only access to the villa from the valley below.

Seven or eight gardeners were seen taking care of the landscaping. *They don't seem to be working too hard at it,* I thought. *They're all probably just a reach away from an automatic.*

With her eyes closed briefly Julia took a deep breath, slowly exhaled and then looked at the sea below and proclaimed, "I have never seen anything more beautiful." She spun back around to let me know she was speaking to me.

"It *is* beautiful," I replied. I too, could not help being impressed by the scenery.

The gusty December wind easily filled the sails of five small boats visible on the deep-blue choppy water below. The only clouds to be seen hung above the distant horizon toward the northwest.

Not foreign to me anymore, I felt the ever-present butterflies waging their war again for dominance over my stomach. *Another time,* I couldn't help thinking as we began ascending the steps toward the now-opened double doors. *I would give anything to be here at another time.*

After we had entered through the doors into the entry way, I found himself staring into dark piercing eyes as Hector Baldarrama introduced me to, possibly, the most powerful drug lord in the world. I felt the hairs at the back of my neck cower and huddle together in preparation for the no good that was surely to come someday from this man. *He probably knows more about me than I do,* I thought as I stared into the dark eyes of my host. *Probably already figured out how he's going to kill me, when the time comes.*

Rodrigo Lara Orasco took my outstretched hand with a firm grip, "Welcome to my home, Michael."

As the man slowly released my hand, I introduced my wife.

Orasco gently took her hand. "I am very happy to meet you, Julia."

The soft-spoken Orasco demonstrated perfect English as Julia detected no apparent Spanish accent. She felt almost hypnotized as she looked into his eyes. Then a strange feeling came over her.

While Orasco briefly held her hand she felt as though he could see into her eyes and into her soul itself . . . as if a window had opened exposing her inner being. Her face felt flushed. She felt like Rodrigo Lara Orasco could see right through her. She knew he was not an ordinary man.

Orasco was almost six feet tall and appeared to Julia to be in his late forties. *Very confident man,* she thought as she gathered her composure and quickly sized up Mr. Orasco . . . *Charming and exceptionally good looking . . . with sad eyes.* She wondered where his wife was.

"I am sure you wish to relax and freshen up before dinner," Orasco said with a smile, and gestured toward the stairs. "Avilla will show you your rooms." It was four-thirty in the afternoon.

50

JULIA, AFTER HAVING spent twenty minutes or so unpacking, sat alone on the veranda overlooking the sea.

She kept looking inside toward the bed. *There's only one.* She couldn't recall the last time she had slept in the same bed as her husband. She felt warmth in her breasts and her thighs slightly squeezed together. It was a subconscious reaction before she realized what she had done. *We're like strangers. Why did Michael bring me here?* she asked herself as she absentmindedly brushed her fingers across her nipples, which she could feel hardened inside her blouse, and her eyes momentarily closed.

She savored that sensation only briefly, and then rose and strolled along the edge of the veranda, looking out at the rugged coastline snaking itself in and out until it disappeared in the distance.

Maybe this romantic place can save us, she thought as the wind suddenly picked up, startling her.

51

JULIA AND NANCINA were seated to the left and right, respectively, of Rodrigo Lara Orasco, I noted. *Charming man ... this killer. Letting me know my wife sits to his left, the side of the heart.*

I had also noticed that, when I had met earlier with Orasco and Baldarrama in the study, there appeared to be a common trust and respect between the two drug kingpins. It was subtle, but clearly obvious to me, however, that Orasco made the final decisions.

"Since this is your first venture to my country," Orasco said as he stood at the head of the twelve-foot-long exquisitely fashioned dark-wood dining table, "my renowned chef has prepared for your dining pleasure, a variety of dishes originating from several major gastronomic zones in mainland Spain.

"May I present to you, Master Chef Carlos Galdiano."

Orasco began lightly applauding and everyone else followed suit as a very slender, medium height, gentleman, who was obviously of Spanish origin, entered the dining room.

The chef's slightly high-pitched voice began in broken English as he tentatively forced a nervous smile, "Ladies and gentlemen, I prepare for your pleasure, from Andalasia... Gazpacho, an exquisite cold vegetable soup, and Jabugo ham from the province of Huelva, a true delicacy.

"From the North, I prepare Vizcayan style codfish and a side dish of 'fabada,' which you will find is a magnificent bean stew, as you refer to it in America.

"From the Pyrenees, I prepare 'chilindrones' which are some of the marinade sauces served along with ham from Teruel."

Carlos' voice rose to an even higher pitch as he excitedly continued in his broken English, "I prepare for your tastes, several casseroles that are," he took a breath, "quite popular in Catalonia along with 'ali-oli', a world famous sauce made with garlic and olive oil."

Orasco's smile expressed his obvious approval as the chef continued. The two ladies, absent condescending tones of any hue, thought the chef was "darling."

"And to finish, I prepare from the Balearic Isles, the light pastries we call 'ensaimadas.'"

After the dinner, which was magnificent everyone agreed, Orasco escorted his guests into the huge living room, revealing a forty-foot-long wall of floor-to-ceiling windows and veranda doors overlooking the Mediterranean.

Julia was impressed by the articulate Spaniard as the evening passed. Mr. Orasco seemed, to her, to be highly educated and obviously well acquainted with high-ranking dignitaries not only in his country, but throughout Europe and even the United States.

She wondered curiously, *Where is his family? He hasn't mentioned them. Where is his wife?*

52

DARKNESS PROVOKED a chilling wind that danced through the soft white transparent draperies of the opened veranda doorway.

As her head lay on the soft pillows, Julia was still able to see, through the sheer curtains, the winding coastline... upon which, she watched a clement amber moon cast a quiet glow.

Now and then her view would turn to darkness as the moon would be withdrawn at short intervals by small clouds with halos around them when concealing the moonlight.

She sensed her husband wasn't asleep, and she felt warmth rising from him as he lay with his back to her. The wind made it difficult for her to listen to his breathing.

She had forgotten what it was like for him to hold her—a memory... and taste... misplaced for more than three years.

Will he ever hold me again? she wondered. She felt warm inside. *I want him now... I need his touch... I need him to stop the fire inside me,* she shamelessly fantasized.

She lay there awake for a very long time, watching the coastline appear and then turn dark... and then reappear again as the full moon continued to slowly sail in and out of the gathering storm clouds.

After a while longer, she felt cold and pulled the blankets up around her and began recalling the sights of the day in that prepossessing foreign land. Finally, her eyes became heavy and she drifted off.

He sat in a cushioned patio chair on the veranda outside his bedroom, staring into the darkness. He could not bare to look at the somber moon when it slid past a cloud now and then. He may not have even known, at the moment, that it was there. The moonlight that bore down on him was *far* too melancholy for his thoughts.

The blackness out over the sea seemed to calm him... he had already allowed himself two extra glasses of the exquisite

Bordeaux from a prized first growth chateau in France. Now he was almost finished with what he knew was the final glass, for him, that night.

And he'd had his fill of the Cohiba Siglo II Cuban cigar, from the Vuelta Abajo highlands of Pinar del Rio province, that was still more than half of its original length as he laid it in the ashtray on the small wrought-iron table next to him.

The wind grew more forceful as it blew in from across the sea causing a chill he did not recognize.

Rodrigo Lara Orasco let out a sigh. He thought about his family. The first time he had done so in many years. He had difficulty recalling their faces. A mist formed in his eyes. It seemed now that they had never existed.

53

Evansville, Indiana . . .

LIGHT SNOWFLAKES SWIRLED around us, and settled on our godforsaken unprotected heads and half frozen faces as we expeditiously walked along Riverside Drive with our frostbitten hands buried deep inside our pockets.

Our shoulders were hunched as we tried to submerse our faces down inside the pulled-up collars of our light overcoats. We had just passed Sunset Park, which was on the opposite side of the broad thoroughfare that ran parallel to the half-mile-wide Ohio River.

My chattering teeth barely conceded me the ability to enunciate my words to Hector Baldarrama, "There's the restaurant, about a block and a half away." The sight of air escaping from my own mouth with each word chilled me even more.

I swore under my breath at myself for not having the hindsight to pack gloves and a sock cap, and especially ear muffs. At that moment, I felt as if my exposed ears were being pricked with thousands of burning needles from the stinging-cold air from hell, and thought they would shatter like crushed ice from the slightest touch.

God, how I yearned for southern Spain from where we had just returned less than two weeks ago . . . *warm* southern Spain.

Jaime and Jesse trailed not far behind Baldarrama and me. The two bodyguards swore, under their breaths, about having to come to this frozen hell on earth when they had been totally unprepared, and, especially now, because they and their employer had gotten lost and we had parked twelve blocks away from the restaurant.

We four travelers had been walking for more than fifteen minutes, and we had sadly discovered that our light jackets, more than adequate in the Valley of the Sun, were useless pieces of squirrel shit against the December Midwestern winds.

The two trailing henchmen swore to one another that they'd never come to this Godforsaken place again . . . *Hector Baldarrama could cut off our balls first.*

Speaking of which, we continued our "double time" strides that we *hoped* would keep our little balls from turning into Popsicles.

In the last five minutes the unanimous concurrence was that the temperature had dropped another twenty degrees. All of us, thinking the same thing at this point, felt that, if even a soft feather touched down on the front of our shoes, the agonizing pain from that occurring on our frozen toes would drive us into a state of shock.

As we traipsed up Riverside Drive, I glanced across the street toward the grey river, and observed two long barges passing each other from opposite directions. One was headed east, upriver. *Probably going to Cincinnati,* I imagined, *and the other was heading west toward the Mississippi River. It would go by New Orleans, eventually, and then out to the Gulf of Mexico,* I further speculated. But, right then, I could have cared less if those two boats sank right there in front of my eyes.

I was more than anxious to retreat back to the warm sunshine of the Valley of the Sun. My teeth continued to chatter uncontrollably. I was amazed at how dismal the colorless landscape appeared, with its leafless trees under the dispirited steel-grey sky.

I recalled how green and beautiful it had been the day that Hue had brought me there, many years ago. We had been on vacation. It had been early June and I was twelve years old.

That was the first day that Hue had ever mentioned, to me, anything about my father.

* * *

The two of us reclined in the shade on the tree-filled green lawn of Sunset Park for most of the afternoon. Hue had brought a picnic basket.

Later, after the sun had set, we watched the hundreds of bright lights silhouetting white river boats that slowly paddled up and down the river, "Maybe headed toward Owensboro," Hue had speculated, "or, maybe, to Louisville."

Lightning bugs could be seen randomly throughout the park, silently twinkling on and off in the darkness, like distant lighthouses along coastlines. I had never seen anything like it.

I could see the shadows of the rustling limbs with their thick forested leaves gently swaying as if the sounds of a slow waltz prompted their patterned performance while they were heartened by a gentle breeze that fluttered just enough to cool the humid summer night.

I had always admired Hue's gentle voice. She had never shouted at me, even whenever she had criticized me. She appeared, to me, to be always under flawless control of her nature . . . she seldom showed emotion, and rarely did she speak of the past. I frequently wondered what she was really thinking.

Even so, Hue and I were close, I thought. But, sometimes I found myself feeling lonely . . . even when I was with her. I had never felt so close to her as I did that summer night, there in Sunset Park . . . and I never felt that closeness with her again.

"Can you imagine, Michael, if our eyes could see energy," she said with a smile as she gazed out across the river toward the opposite bank, where Kentucky was. "It would be like looking at fire, engulfing us, everything around us burning."

I listened to her evangelizing to me with her Asian accent, "We are all linked together by energy, the same as if we are all . . . one. Because of this, it's natural that we treat all people, and all things, as if we are that person or that thing. Because, in reality, Michael, we truly are that person, we are that thing. We are everyone, and we are everything.

"Remember that all of us impart enormous amounts of energy to whomever is around us . . . to everything around us. We transmit positive energy." *She hesitated, and with a very slight motion of her small hand, waved away a mosquito that hovered in front of her face. Then, she finished saying,* "And, sadly and far too often, we father negative energy.

"Conflict breeds negative energy, and negative energy depletes the positive that we possess, and it dispels positive energy that others possess. Always remember, Michael, that positive energy, flowing back and forth between people, and things, makes both stronger . . . and this creates joy while negative energy encourages the absence of joy."

Slowly, Hue withdrew her gaze from the river, turned, and looked into my eyes that were illuminated by a park lamp some fifty feet away and said, "Someday, you will understand."

We sat there relaxing on the soft cool grass in quiet reflection. I could hear the waves lashing up against the riverbank some one hundred yards away.

It's like clockwork, *I thought.* Every time a river boat or barge passes, the waves grow larger and flow faster, and then, after a few minutes, they quiet themselves . . . and wait for the next barge or boat. *I felt as if I were part of the waves . . . part of the river. It was a new feeling for me. It was a comfortable feeling. I did not feel strange to this place.*

Later that night, Hue told me she had never been there before. But that confused me; I could tell that she knew a lot about this small city that lay near the southwestern tip of Indiana on the north side of the Ohio River. I wondered why she had brought me there.

We continued reclining on the grass with neither of us saying a word. Finally, I said, "It's beautiful here, Sinsai! How did you know about this place?"

She looked at me with a hint of a smile, and then quietly replied, "Your father was born here ... he grew up here, near Pigeon Creek."

* * *

It was twenty minutes before ten in the morning when we entered the warm diner through the glass door that was veiled with frost from the freezing cold outside.

We were already ten minutes late.

I quickly realized that the sit-down counter, with it's twenty or so chairs, was filled, as was the row of double-seated table booths adjacent to the outside wall with its windows that, along the wall's entire length, ran halfway down from the ceiling and ended at the height of the booths' tables. The windows were so heavily coated with ice, no one could see outside from within the diner.

Two men and two women were standing just inside the entrance door waiting for somewhere to sit, and there was barely enough elbow room. Baldarrama and I had to turn sideways to squeeze past them.

Hector was the first to spot the man with whom we had briefly met the previous evening. My boss nudged my arm and headed down the aisle while motioning as he said, "He's in the last booth."

As we started toward the rear, I glanced back at Jaime and Jesse who had entered the cramped waiting area and stood looking at the filled diner. Jesse mumbled something into Jaime's ear and they both looked disgusted with the whole situation. They weren't about to go back outside into that frozen wasteland.

"Well, Hector, Michael, I hope ya got a good night's sleep." Jerry Merkel was the speaker. He stood up as he greeted us two visitors from Arizona. The heavyset man shook our hands and introduced his wife, Audrey, who had remained seated in the booth.

"My wife, here, and me are really excited about this," Jerry said as the three of us sat down.

"It sounds like we can wrap this up then," Hector remarked, and nodded his head to coffee from a gesture by the efficient waitress.

"Let me get this straight," Jerry couldn't believe it. "You guys are puttin' up all the money and all we gotta do, is run the restaurant and we're guaranteed a hunert n' forty-four thousand dollars a year?" Jerry didn't give Baldarrama or me time to answer. "Hell, that's all ma' wife and I've done for the past twenty-eight years, just run a small restaurant. We just never had the money ta' have a place of our own."

"Well, you do now, Jerry," Hector Baldarrama said. I could tell Hector was amused, and was probably telling himself that Jerry Merkel had done his arithmetic.

"Just sign these franchise agreements and we'll get everything going," Hector declared as he slid some papers across the table to Jerry. "You should be able to open in four weeks. Michael will handle the bookkeeping and you and your wife will make some bucks."

I knew Hector wanted to get the hell out of there. He had accompanied me on this *one* single trip so that he would have some idea of what kind of people were going to run his franchises, and now he had seen enough . . . this was his last trip. I was sure of that.

As we climbed into the rented Le Sabre, I reminded Hector that we were late for our next meeting with a Mr. Hamilton.

* * *

Bob Hamilton felt a little guilty while he waited inside the local café in Newburgh which overlooked the Ohio River, just east of Evansville.

The offer's too good . . . these lambs are payin too much for my rundown place, he chuckled to himself. *Maybe, they'll wanna open a few more, so I can compete with the big boys. I'll hafta' drop a little hint. Hell, I could manage ten of these damn things.*

Bob raised his cup to get the waitress's attention. "Honey, could ya' warm this for me?"

He saw the investors enter the restaurant.

54

Southern Coast of Spain . . .

"THAT WAS EXTRAORDINARY, Mr. Orasco," Alan Keith Graves told his host. Graves was a third-term member of the United States Senate, and chairperson of the powerful Senate Armed Services Committee. He had just finished a full course meal as a guest of Rodrigo Lara Orasco.

"The finer things in life, Senator Graves, that and of course family is what is important," the patronizing Orasco was speaking. "Come, let us resume our discussion where we will be more comfortable."

Orasco led the way from the dining room into the elegant library.

The senator appreciated his surroundings. He had never been to Spain before, and he could clearly see that money was no object as he glanced around at the luxuriously decorated mansion. Even his expensive home in Delaware did not compare to these surroundings.

Alan Graves was a highly decorated Vietnam War fighter pilot. He had been one of the lucky ones who didn't see the prisoner of war camps, even though he had been forced to ditch his F-4 Phantom jets on three separate occasions. Each time he had been plucked from the deep waters of the South China Sea by the heroic air rescue units, twice from the carrier, USS *Ranger*, and once from the carrier, USS *Enterprise*.

Graves, an Air Force Captain at the time, had always been thankful that he had never been assigned a mission which would have required him to bomb civilians.

Every day, he had feared his luck would run out, and he would be ordered to face that terrible ordeal. It would have been an order that he knew he would have, though reluctantly, followed. And, in any case, it would have been an assignment which he surely would have completed to the best of his ability.

Graves had never expressed his feelings to his fellow fighter pilots or to his commanders, and he'd always had sympathy for those comrades who'd had to carry that heavy burden. To this day, Alan Graves continued to thank his God for being spared that horrifying tribulation.

Unlike his very close friend, Jim Franklin, who was now President of the United States, Senator Graves harbored no further political aspirations other than to continue representing his constituents from Delaware. There were plenty of perks available to him in his present job.

His wife, Mary, loved being an insider in Washington because of the Senator's power in the upper chamber. The well known fact that her husband was the best friend of the President of the United States didn't hurt either. Obviously, Senator Graves was privy to high-level decision making.

With their twenty-five-year-old son in his third year of medical school at Harvard, the highly respected and popular family was envied by all of Washington.

"I'm pleased that you were able to accept my invitation, Senator. I know that the Christmas season is rather hectic for everyone." Orasco motioned to a chair for his guest, "Please, sit here."

"It's not every day that I have the opportunity to meet a philanthropist such as yourself, Mr. Orasco." The Senator continued speaking as he settled into the comfortable easy chair. "I'm pleased that you have an interest in helping less-advantaged children improve their lives."

He paused long enough to acknowledge a silent "thank you" as he accepted a drink from Orasco's butler. "I'm well aware of your contributions here in Spain that enable so many underprivileged children to attend college, Señor Orasco."

Senator Graves tasted a sip of the smooth and, obviously, quite expensive brandy before continuing, "And I appreciate your noble gesture to assist my humble endeavor in setting up similar programs in the United States."

"It is an extraordinary cause, indeed, Senator Graves. Now, if you will permit me, I will show you why it is important that you be here tonight."

Orasco turned toward his servant and calmly instructed, "Avilla, please turn down the lights." Orasco smiled to himself as the video was snapped on by the loyal Avilla.

Senator Alan Graves froze as he watched in horror as the scenes, clearly displayed on the large screen, changed his life. The hidden camera did not lie. It had, quite profoundly, captured everything . . . everything that had happened, that night, just a month ago.

55

"MICHAEL EVEREST IS calling. Are you available?" Kellie giggled over the intercom.

Catherine Steele smiled as she punched the blinking button to one of the outside lines. "This is Catherine."

"Hi!" Every time she heard that voice over the phone, she felt like her heart was singing.

"Hello, Mr. Everest," she said as she leaned back in her chair. "And what important business do you have with your government today?" She laughed mischievously, loud enough to be heard through the phone line.

"Since we're only two days away from Christmas, I was wondering if you'll have lunch with me today," she heard him say. "You know, the holiday spirit and all."

"I believe my busy schedule will permit that, Mr. Everest." Catherine laughed again aloud.

She heard him tell her he would pick her up at eleven-thirty in front of her office. Then, just before the disconnection told her he was gone, the phone added, "See you then. Bye!"

She hung up and smiled as she thought about how the two of them had been calling one another two or three times a week since he had rescued her from the rain, more than five weeks ago. She hadn't seen him since.

The phone dialogues started with a call that he had initiated. He had needed, or, so he had told her, a suggestion on how to handle a tax matter for a client.

Then, a week later, Catherine had suspicious ideas about a suspected less-than-scrupulous taxpayer involved in a tax case she was working on. She had wanted an outsider's viewpoint on several matters related to the case, so she had called Michael Everest for his advice.

Then, a few days later, she had heard a joke in her office, and so she had called him again, and told him the joke, over which they had a good laugh.

More frequent calls just seemed to *happen* after that.

Catherine had heard that *Thomassino's* was a ridiculously expensive restaurant out on East Camelback Road, near Scottsdale. Its Northern Italian cuisine had always been highly praised by local food editors. The popular establishment had been around for over thirty years, and it catered to the wealthy, or so she had heard. On any given day, visiting Hollywood celebrities could usually be spotted there, enjoying the European ambience along with the local elite.

While he held the restaurant's door open, Catherine melted to his smile as he remarked, "I don't know anyone here. But, we have reservations."

As she glanced at her lunch date, she felt somewhat intimidated. *He looks even more handsome now than when I last saw him.* She felt him take her breath away.

As I entered the flashy restaurant behind her, I obviously was still denying any wrongdoing on my part by simply not addressing myself to the subject of fidelity. I told myself that an innocent luncheon with a friend, even though that friend was a female, an extremely attractive female, constituted no crime or ill-mannered behavior on my part. I wasn't totally—or even remotely—convinced of that, but decided I could deal with it later, and pacified my own guilt by strategically dispatching my conscience to the bench, while, matter of fact, announcing to myself, *There's a first time for everything. If it's wrong, so what! My wife doesn't give a diddly shit, anyway.*

The subtle lighting at Thomassino's seemed almost magical as we sat across from each other at the small table with the burgundy-red tablecloth.

We were sitting next to a lime-green textured wall with its subtle water colors depicting various outdoor scenes that were, Catherine guessed, late nineteenth century European.

I joked about the menu marked only in Italian as we tried to decide what to order. I asked about her plans for the holidays. Was she going home to see her parents?

Catherine told me her parents had come in from Montana to see her and the twins for the holidays.

I told her how lucky she was to have children, and that I had none.

She told me the story about Ronnie, her high school sweetheart; how she had gotten pregnant just before Ronnie had gone away to college the summer before her senior year . . . and that she never saw him again.

Catherine seemed oblivious to everyone around them. She hardly took her eyes off him as she listened to him telling her that he had wanted children when he had first been married. "But, my wife had wanted to wait," he told her. "Then, after about seven or eight years, Julia finished her doctorate and was ready to begin a family."

That was the first time Catherine heard his wife's name. A wife who was no longer just a person whom Catherine did not know. His wife had a name, and she was real. And the realization that he was married to her hit Catherine like a hammer pounding Catherine's heart into crumpled pieces.

A pause and a sip from his water glass before she heard him say, "Julia had wanted children too late, and I felt there was something missing between us. I wasn't sure where we were headed . . . and I couldn't see us having children then . . . and so, they just didn't happen."

As Catherine listened she felt as if she could float away, and wondered how the man across the table felt about her at that moment . . . she refused to think about him married.

She was helpless.

56

JANUARY IMPARTED ITSELF with an exceptional gesture as much needed rain accounted for half its days. February manifested itself with a cold wave for the first twelve days, and then shifted into a warm posture that invited everyone in the valley out to taste its blessings. March brought, of course, the aroma of the orange blossoms that penetrated even the most adverse mind and made it sing. April brought the so-called "March Winds" that reallocated the sand in the desert. And I, Michael Everest, didn't have occasion to recall any of this as I was preoccupied with becoming rich and trying to keep my ass on straight hoping to avoid experiencing a premature death.

May began as bright and gently warm and I pursued it into the afternoon as I spoke from a public phone booth at Thirty-third Avenue just north of Buckeye Road, "There are twenty-three *Lunas Primaveras* restaurants now."

While speaking I carefully observed the inhabitants of where I found myself, as this south Phoenix spot I had chosen was a rough neighborhood that bore old industrial buildings and old rundown and mostly abandoned small houses, and fifty or so homeless individuals seemed to find my presence annoying. Several of them were voicing their opposition to me using their phone.

I loathed the putrid smell and sticky feel of the telephone's receiver, which I purposely held slightly, and contemptuously, away from my ear.

As I scanned both north and south up and down Thirty-third Avenue I also resented the pecking feeling that I was constantly being watched. I tried to be careful never choosing a phone booth at two major intersections anymore and always made phone calls to Henry Sotello from the middle of a block. Then, I only had two directions, instead of four, to worry about if I was being followed . . . one of the tricks that Sotello had taught me.

For fear of our conversations being traced, I also never used the same public phone twice when speaking with Henry, nor did I dare use my cellular phone.

"Right now, they can probably run forty million dollars a year through the existing restaurants without drawing attention," I reported to my mentor. "Baldarrama wants to get the total figure up to a billion a year. So he wants two hundred more restaurants set up in Europe and another two hundred fifty in the states within the next eighteen months.

"Right now, I'm working with sales reps who'll go out and open up these restaurants. And, next week I'm meeting with Rodrigo Orasco at his villa in Spain," I told Sotello, and then waited for some input from the opposite end of the line.

"Things are moving now," I heard Henry's gruff voice say through the receiver. "We want them to put every dime they have into the legitimate money system. And we'll know exactly where it is."

"How long before we can take it?" I asked my government contact. I, myself, had already been paid more than one and a half million dollars in cash by Baldarrama plus another million that had been paid to my accounting firm. That was just over a seven month period—August through April.

But I was finding it difficult to sleep, and the relentless number of hours required of me seemed endless . . . not to mention the pain between my shoulders at the base of my neck that seemed to be occurring more frequently and with more intensity.

I had been putting in more than a hundred hours a week ever since I had begun setting up the franchise restaurants. And now, I was well aware that even more would be expected of me because of the European restaurants that Baldarrama wanted opened as soon as possible.

I also felt constant pressure from the fear of being discovered by the cartel. This ever-present trepidation caused me to undergo frequent nightmares, including one recurring dream that depicted me as being tied up in a chair and having my arms sawed off just above the elbows with a chainsaw.

"We're hoping your second visit with Rodrigo Lara Orasco will give us some leads about his associates," I heard Sotello say from the private phone line that had been wired into Sotello's home by federal people from Washington—that's all I had been told by Sotello. *That's probably all that Henry was told,* I conjectured as I involuntarily breathed out a sigh of frustration into the receiver, and knew my partner at the other end of the line heard it.

Sotello began speaking again, "Orasco has some kind of connection with people in the Middle East, and we're not sure which countries are involved. The wheels in D.C. have received information that something big is going down within the next year. And Orasco is a major part of it.

"It's no longer just a drug war, my friend," Sotella continued after a fleeting pause. "Now, it's gotten more complicated. It could possibly be that we are on the verge of a World War."

The DEA agent's words caused me to shudder as I pondered the thought of the responsibility that had been stamped upon me. It was an obligation I had never expected, nor asked for.

But I knew the excitement of what I was doing shot the shit out of the shortcomings . . . the long hours . . . the constant fear that I will slip up somewhere and be discovered. This new life had awakened something inside me that I could not totally explain. I was someone else now, and *that,* I would not, could not . . . change.

If I had to make the choice again, I *knew* I would do it over, and I always knew in the beginning that the money had *never* been a factor in my decision to work with Henry Sotello.

57

THE BOEING 747 LIFTED off from Phoenix Sky Harbor International Airport and veered left toward the south, while I idly peered out the window at the brilliantly lit bright-orange sky, and took a last glimpse of the setting sun, before the jumbo jet skewed eastward.

I bore an uninvited wonderment as to why Rodrigo Orasco had invited Julia, and was surprised when she hadn't hesitated to say yes when I had asked her to come.

Nothing had changed after Julia and I had returned from that first visit to Rodrigo Lara Orasco's villa back in December, five months ago. We still hardly spoke to one another and, when we did, I felt like we were strangers. And I was convinced that I was hopelessly stamped by fate to nurse loneliness even in my own home for the rest of my days, even though my soul seemed to be racing to somewhere forbidden with Catherine Steele.

As the Boeing slightly quaked from turbulence, I laid my head back in the seat and tried to doze off while flirting with images pervading my senses about when I had first met Julia twenty years earlier.

* * *

I had just recently turned nineteen, and Julia was eighteen. While attending Phoenix Junior College I had been working nights as a bookkeeper at The Arizona Bank.

I first saw her when I came around a room divider separating my small work station from the other work areas. She was sitting at my desk with her back to me as she filed papers into a divider folder that contained pending documents that I had to review and process into the bank's computer system that night.

My eyes grew transfixed on her beautiful long neck just below her short hairline. Months later, I told her that I had fallen in love with her even before she had turned around.

In less than three weeks we began dating. Before that, I had not had the confidence nor the courage to ask her out. I had done so only after one of my coworkers had told me that Julia wanted to go out with me.

During the first few weeks we dated, I felt like I'd discovered a dreamlike and unreachable course whose likes could never be captured in this ordinary world . . . yet, I, one of the chosen, had done so. It was ecstasy and, at the same time, torment. After just a few weeks of dating, I began to sense that Julia was not in love with me. She no longer seemed as excited to see me as she had in the beginning.

I hopelessly grasped for comfort of any sort that must have existed somewhere, but not in my universe. For I had allowed myself to commit the unthinkable, I had fallen in love.

From that moment on I reminded myself countless times what Hue had always told me, "Never let your emotions control you. Love nothing . . . no one, and you will never feel the worst kind of pain."

I abhorred the defenseless feeling. Hue had been right. I had no control over it, and I hated Julia's indifference toward me. She had become flighty . . . seemed too confident about my feelings for her.

I tried to pull away from her. For months at a time during our stormy two-year courtship I tried to stop seeing her.

But, I needed someone then . . . I missed Hue. Hue had died seven months before I had met Julia, giving me an excuse at the time to drop out of school.

The kata and dojos had been my only escape from the loneliness. But those workouts wouldn't take away the pain. Julia saved me. We had known each other for almost two years before we married.

Soon after that, I began working days at a grocery store and went to school in the evenings while Julia worked the three thirty afternoon-to-midnight shift at the bank.

We seldom saw one another during the first year of marriage, and when we did, we just seemed to ignore each other or constantly argue over meaningless things. From the very beginning I detected that Julia always, for whatever reasons, tried to find something to quarrel about, even when the two of us would be having an amiable conversation.

The night it happened, we had been married for about fourteen months. I had come down with bronchial pneumonia and valley fever, and had to sit upright in bed so I could breathe more easily.

On that particular night my breathing difficulties worsened, and kept me awake for most of the first few hours I was in bed.

I recalled checking the clock the first time, and discovered it was one-thirty in the morning, and Julia wasn't home yet . . . already an hour late.

We could afford only the bare necessities when it came to furniture, so the room bore just a small double-bed and two three-drawer cardboard dressers sitting against the wall at the foot of the bed.

Time seemed to have wanted to take side roads in its inept attempts to go forward in a reasonable fashion, and I could not find the secret to unlock my sleeplessness, and began to worry. I reached down and snatched up the alarm clock from the floor next to the bed . . . three thirty A.M.

Time continued its hateful remedy of progression as every minute seemed to be an hour.

When I heard the front door finally open, I glanced down at the clock on the floor again. It was twenty minutes past four.

As I lay there, I sensed her trying to quietly close the door. I felt like vomiting.

* * *

My dreaming was suddenly interrupted as I was startled awake by something and saw the steward standing over us.

"Sir, here's your bottled water," the steward politely offered. Then, he reached across Julia who was sitting in the first-class aisle seat next to me and handed me the plastic container.

"Could you tell us how soon we'll be landing?" Julia asked.

The steward glanced at his watch and said as he handed her a glass containing ice and Seven-Up, "It looks like another forty minutes, ma'am."

"Thank you," she said as she rose from her seat. Then she turned her head addressing me without really looking at me, "I'm going to freshen up."

I took three huge gulps of the cold water and let my head lay back against the headrest again, and haunting thoughts returned me again to that night seventeen years ago.

* * *

After Julia had quietly slipped into bed, I remained motionless for several minutes, pretending to be asleep, my whole body quaking and my stomach churning while my raspy breathing filled the night.

After lying there for what seemed like an hour, I finally asked, "Why are you so late? I was worried and called the bank," I lied.

My eyes saw nothing but darkness . . . deadening silence and total blackness. I was convinced that my heartbeat was rocketing into the next dimension and not entirely healthy as I waited for an answer. I felt no movement from her, and the stillness pierced the air and overshadowed the dismal room for what seemed like a lifetime that mattered little anymore. Finally, I heard her quietly answer, "I was talking to someone."

My wispy breaths continued, but I didn't dare move. Beads of sweat had masterminded an overthrow of my senses and began trickling down my forehead. I was half sitting, half lying, with my back against the wall. The bed had no headboard.

More silence . . . lasting forever, it seemed. My face felt flushed as I tried to suppress the wheezing sound coming from my throat each time I drew a breath. At the same time, my head felt like it was on fire and felt as if it were being crushed in a vise.

* * *

Julia returned to her seat and finished her drink while I, silently staring out into the darkness, drank the rest of mine.

Then she turned off the overhead light, which had been the only one on in the darkened aircraft, and reclined her seat back as far as it would go. She lay back and closed her eyes . . . the eyes that, I noted, had not even once looked in my direction.

As I relaxed my head against the headrest, I thought about the time—several years ago—when I had asked Julia why she had married me. I could still recall the sheepish half smile on her face as she looked at me, shrugged, and said, matter of fact, "I don't know."

I had then asked her why she had stayed with me. She had simply answered, "I have nowhere else to go."

After reflecting on that, my thoughts again took me back to that night. I didn't really know how long we had lain there together in that canyon of black vacuity and gnawing silence before she said anything else.

* * *

"I was talking to someone I work with," she finally managed to say.

"Was it a man?" I was thankful that there was no light to see her . . . for her to see me. *"Yes,"* she said, and paused a few seconds before finishing, *"I needed someone to talk to. That's all we did."*

"Where were you?"

"In his car."

* * *

A jolt from the aircraft, as it began its descent, startled me, and I sat up and saw through the cabin window a sea of lights below . . . Miami, Florida. We would change planes there and then have a nonstop to Madrid.

I looked over at Julia reclining on the seat next to me, and she appeared to be asleep. As I watched her, I felt myself becoming aroused. I wanted to make love to her. I wanted to take her and screw her brains out.

Yet, at that moment, as my soul had been so often stirred over the years with the same frustrating and helpless feeling, I despised her . . . for not loving me.

58

Southern Coast of Spain . . .

I CLIMBED INTO the limo after shaking hands with Rodrigo Lara Orasco who stood outside the black luxury automobile in front of his villa.

I had left Julia a few minutes earlier, and she had already showered and dressed in causal slacks and a sweatshirt along with tennis shoes and was last seen sitting in a recliner on the veranda outside our bedroom, drinking hot tea.

I knew I had been somewhat a little formal and distant when I had told her goodbye. After so many years sleeping alone, it had actually made me feel some discomfort, awkwardness this past night, sleeping in the same bed as my wife.

I sensed that she wasn't pleased that I was leaving for Paris without her, and that puzzled me.

As I observed the passing countryside, well defined by the bright sunshine, I thought about dinner with Orasco the night before.

Orasco had been, not surprisingly, charming and respectful to Julia and me. But occasionally, I thought I had detected some obvious flirting between my wife and our host. It had made me feel like "three's a crowd," and it wasn't hard for me to figure out who was on the outside looking in.

After dinner, the drug lord and I had retired to the library to discuss my itinerary for the next eleven days. In accordance with Orasco's instructions, I was to meet in Paris a guide by the name of Jacques (pronounced *Zshock*) Guzman.

Orasco had explained to me, "Jacques speaks English, French, German, and Dutch as well as Spanish, and will accompany you to Berlin, Amsterdam, Brussels and Geneva. All of your appointments in each city have been prearranged."

As I pondered that, I tried to relax and settle myself back in the leather-cushioned seat as the limo muscled closer to Malaga where Orasco's private jet would take me to my first stop, Paris . . . and Jacques Guzman.

59

I TUGGED OPEN the heavy door from inside my suite at the Plaza Athenee in the Chaillot Quarter, near the Champs-Elysees Quarter in Paris. My eyes grew wide as I stood speechless gawking at the stunning young woman standing in my doorway.

She spoke perfect English. "How do you do, Mr. Everest? I am Jacques Guzman. You were expecting me, I believe." She extended her hand . . . and I, flustered with my mouth dangling open and lost for words, slowly reached out to a gentle handshake.

I could not take my eyes away from those soft, incredibly beauteous turquoise blue eyes. I had always believed, until that moment, that no one was better at maintaining more control over oneself than I, Michael Everest, the master. And standing there at that moment, I felt myself fully blushing as I tried to salvage my composure.

"It's very nice to meet you, Ms. Guzman. Please call me Michael," I said with a futile attempt at concealing my inept clumsiness, while knowing full well that this lovely creature had won the first round.

"And please call me Jacques, Michael," she appended as she entered the suite past where I stood still startled and regrettably aware that I looked nothing at all like a well-disciplined and professional accountant.

My eyes followed her tall, slender form as she slowly strolled across the thick vanilla custard-shaded carpet to the opened balcony doorway that unfolded into quite a spectacular view of the top of the prominent Eiffel Tower a short distance on the opposite side of the Seine.

Her long black hair trailed down to the middle of her back, and her skirt stopped just above her slender knees, revealing long, tanned legs. She wore a navy-blue suit that clung to her curves, but not overdone. She appeared to be, I decided, purely a sophisticated woman of utmost class . . . *and she knows it.*

"What a lovely view you have," she said as she slowly pivoted to face me.

"Yes, I do." As I said it, I became suddenly embarrassed as I thought she might think I was referring to her, which I rapidly realized, I was. I cleared my inept throat and tried to cover up immediately, "A very competent someone knew what they were doing when they arranged this room for me."

"I know," she said without pausing, "I am that guilty party." It was the first glint of a foreign accent that I detected in her English.

As I looked at her smile, I thought I would melt. *God! I'm going to hate the next two weeks,* I facetiously thought to myself. "I appreciate it," I politely said. I began to feel more at ease and my self confidence began to recapture its normal course.

"Well, then. If you are ready, Michael, I will show you the finest brunch in Paris so that we may prepare for our first meeting this afternoon at one o'clock."

I seldom ate breakfast or lunch. Every morning, I always took two tablespoons of apple vinegar chased with a glass of orange juice before I shaved and performed my *kata*.

I had made sure, that morning in my suite, I had awoken in plenty of time to complete my workout routine and shower before meeting Jacques Guzman.

And now, the pastries were too tempting as I sat across from the olive-skin beauty outside a Paris café where glass-topped tables, supported by brown wrought-iron supports, were placed along a sidewalk accompanied by amply padded matching chairs that were surprisingly quite comfortable.

I had just devoured a Napoleon pastry and had even drank, for the first time in almost twenty years, a cup of coffee, the smoothest that I had ever recalled tasting. Contrary to what I had heard about the thick black coffees of Europe, mine glazed just a shade darker brown than most American beers.

This 'Delila' has obviously lured and trapped me, and now, I'm hopelessly beguiled under her magical spell, I jokingly thought as I savored the warm sun and cozy breeze washing over us.

At that moment, with the unfamiliar caffeine taking control, rock solid, or so I thought, I began to taste the rich morsel of my second Napoleon pastry along with a second cup of . . . *that delicious honey-brown brew.*

What other forbidden fruits will this maiden prevail on me, I could but wonder as I joked to myself—trying humorously to think European—while, eagerly, looking forward to the next week and a half traveling across Europe with this goddess.

The two of us spent the next hour, leisurely sitting at the street-side table, laughing and talking about anything and everything . . . but not about business.

60

Madrid . . .

"THAT IS BREATHTAKING, Rodrigo," Julia Everest proclaimed—louder than she had intended—as she viewed the *Les Vessenols en Auvers* original by Vincent van Gogh.

"Yes, it is." Rodrigo Lara Orasco was quite delighted that his guest enjoyed beautiful works of art. He found as much pleasure in viewing her as she found in viewing the classical works by Fra Angellico, Van Eyck, Durer, Rembrandt, Hais, Titian, Van Dyck and Rubens.

They also studied works by the impressionists such as Manet, Monet, Renoir, Gaugain, Toulouse-Lautrec and Cezanne as well as van Gogh.

Orasco admiringly observed this beautiful American woman as he fancied her smile while she perused the extraordinary collection of paintings by the masters that consisted of more than seven hundred paintings preserved at the Thyssen-Bornemisza Museum in Madrid.

"On another occasion, I will bring you to the Prado Museum nearby," he promised her. "And you will see works by El Greco, Velazquez, Ribera, Murillo and Goya, some of the greatest paintings in the history of the world. You will be helpless to restrain your admiration."

Julia glanced at him and wandered toward the next masterpiece . . . her smile lit up her eyes. Orasco was pleased. They had been there for over an hour, and didn't leave until another pleasurable hour had passed.

The soft cool breeze seemed to Julia to bless with its presence all souls within its boundaries while she observed the sun beginning to mask itself behind tall buildings. She sat outside with him in wicker basket chairs at a small wicker table covered by a bright-orange tablecloth on Paseo del Pinro Rosales.

Julia listened attentively to Rodrigo Lara Orasco as he provided her with a brief history of Madrid.

"The principal traces of the origins of Madrid date back to the ninth century," Orasco began. "Mohammed was responsible for the construction of a fortress for defense of the Kingdom of Toledo, and he built a wall around the town, then known by the name of Magerit.

"The Moors withstood many attacks from Christian kings and ruled up until King Alfonso VI finally conquered this place in 1083."

Julia was fascinated by this articulate and extremely handsome man. *He must be in his late forties or early fifties.* Her curiosity was becoming more intense, and more emboldened for answers as she continued to ask herself, *Why isn't Rodrigo married? Is he gay?*

The scurrying, and quite attentive, waiter brought them delicious Madrid stew with its chickpeas. Rodrigo would reward him, handsomely. Orasco wanted this night and every night with this fascinating woman to be perfect.

Julia tasted piquant *chorizo* sausage, black pudding and *callos a la madrilena* which was tripe prepared with white wine, brandy, red pepper, onion, ham and spicy seasoning.

An hour later, the white and lime fusion of colored lighting radiating from the beautiful archways of the Puerta de Alcala, one of the beloved symbols of Madrid, could be seen several blocks away as Julia strolled along the sidewalk with Orasco.

"Oh, Rodrigo, this is the most beautiful place I have ever seen. Everything here seems so magical, like a fairy tale."

"Yes, I was captivated by this extraordinary place, the moment I saw it. I promised myself that I would return and live my life here as soon as possible."

They walked a block or so in silence, enjoying the serenity of their surroundings, even though the bustling traffic seemed much heavier than it had been earlier.

Finally, it was Julia who broke the silence as she quietly remarked, "I know little about you, Rodrigo. Tell me."

Rodrigo stopped walking and looked at her. He took the light jacket he had been carrying and placed it around her shoulders and they continued their transient walk.

"I come from Bogota, Columbia. I was married to a charming and beautiful woman. She was a good wife, better than I thought I deserved. She gave me three beautiful babies . . . three daughters."

Julia sensed Orasco hesitate before he continued, "All of them perished in a fire many years ago. I cannot forget. So, I never meet another woman and fall in love."

Orasco was silent for a while and they continued slowly walking. Then, after they had gone almost another block, Julia heard him quietly say, "I have never spoken to anyone about them . . . until now."

As they walked, Julia slowly reached for his hand and held it. She didn't say anything as moisture fashioned its presence in the corners of her joyless eyes.

61

Geneva . . .

"ALL RIGHT, MICHAEL, this is our last night in this glorious place. I am in charge now," Jacques Guzman declared with authority and in Spanish as she giggled and dragged me along by my arm as we just seemed to shuffle out through the doorway of the historic and quite discreet Hotel Les Armures. "Hurry, here is our ride," she excitedly proclaimed as we dashed into the chauffeured Mercedes. I almost lost one of my shoes.

As I forged into one of the luxury sedan's well-cushioned seats, I thought the past week and a half had gone by much too quickly.

"No more work. It is time to celebrate," Jacques continued speaking in Spanish as she sank back into her plush seat.

In the very beginning, she had decided that we would speak in Spanish, her native language—the one with which she was most comfortable.

After we had both settled ourselves into the luxury sedan, she asked me, "How does it feel to be going home tomorrow? Aren't you going to miss me?" She had already had several cocktails at the hotel, so she was feeling quite blissful.

I wasn't sure how to answer.

"It will be nice to get home. I guess I'm not much of a traveler," I said in a more serious tone than I had intended. And, yes, I was going to miss this incredibly beautiful, fun-loving, and extremely intelligent woman.

I looked at her and laughed before saying, "If I were fifteen years younger I would never allow you out of my sight."

"I'm not really twenty-four," she countered with an enticing laugh. "I'm thirty."

"Yeah, and I'm nineteen," I told her as I mockingly grabbed her hand and kissed it like a gentleman. *Is this what my daughter, the daughter I never had, would have been like?*

"Seriously, Michael . . . I was supposed to seduce you, you know." Her half-pouting lips feigned sadness.

I looked at her and remarked, "At first, you could have easily done that, lady. But, not after that first day in Paris . . . when I realized how much I liked you." I was definitely going to miss her. We had bonded an instant friendship.

I thought about the occasional flirting between us in the beginning as we had settled the business affairs that had brought us together traveling from Paris to Berlin, then to Amsterdam, and Brussels and finally to Geneva. It had taken eleven days.

* * *

The next evening, as I squared myself into the opulent chair on the private jet returning me from Paris to Malaga, I opened a bottle of spring water and gulped down two huge swallows. The luxury aircraft found its cruising speed once it reached nine thousand feet and, by then, I had finished off my drink.

As I relaxed in the extravagance of my dimly lighted surroundings, I reflected on what Jacques had told me about herself while I gazed out through the small windows down at the unfamiliar clusters of pale lights coming to life and barely evident due to the afterglow of dusk that seemingly refused to relinquish its grip and allow the night to once again breathe its shade of indigo over sky and earth.

* * *

She had spent most of her life in boarding schools in Switzerland and France. Her parents had died when she was five years old . . . she couldn't remember anything about them. Just over a year ago, she had graduated with honors from one of the prestigious universities in Madrid, with three majors . . . English, German and French, with a minor in Business Administration with emphasis in Finance and Economics.

She was now attending a graduate school of international trade in Paris. She also spoke fluent Portuguese and Spanish.

She had a trust fund that had been set up by her parents, and wasn't sure how much, but she thought it was many millions of American dollars. She had been told by a lawyer in Madrid that she will be able to access the trust when she reaches the age of twenty-five.

* * *

I found it refreshing that Jacques could swear with the best of them, drink with the best of them and, yet, not have the slightest doubt of who she was while displaying as much class as any woman I had ever known, refined and confident . . . and I felt I certainly qualified as an expert, for I knew I had most definitely been privileged to have encountered some very first rate ladies in my lifetime, including my very own wife. *I'm sure, also, it's not a handicap for Jacques, that she's so damn gorgeous,* I reflected and couldn't help smiling.

It had amused me when I had observed men, of all ages, watching and flirting with her wherever she and I had gone. And she had been quite aware of the attention, and, in fact, had flirted back with most of them.

I found himself warming to a smile again about that while I lazily listened to the soft music calming itself in quiet tones through the luxury jet's cabin. *What a sheltered life I've led,* I opined to myself.

It was not until I had begun to relax in my seat that it struck me . . . *"I was supposed to seduce you."*

62

Southern Coast of Spain . . .

"MICHAEL WILL BE returning late tonight, and since I must leave early in the morning, I will be unable to see you and Michael off," Rodrigo Orasco told Julia in English, the language he had chosen to use during the past eleven days that he had served as her host even though he knew she spoke fluent Spanish as well as her husband.

Orasco was sitting in an upright reclining chair on the veranda outside the living room. It was eight-thirty in the evening.

The Mediterranean below appeared to be a black canyon as far as the eye could see. Only the sounds of the waves crashing on the rocks below confirmed that the sea was there.

The black-stone thunder clouds had stolen the moonlight and seemed to be forewarning that the storm, breeding far out at sea, was surely on its way.

Julia sat in a chair next to her host. "I've had an enchanting time, Rodrigo. I have never laughed so much in a long time."

"I've even had the pleasure of seeing your tears," Rodrigo said, smiling as Julia was reminded of their stroll past the Puerta de Alcala in Madrid.

"That is something you will not see again," she retorted, accompanied by a slight giggle. "I am not allowed that luxury." She thought the cognac, of which she decided she had already consumed far too much, had forced her to choose those words.

"What do you mean, 'that luxury'?" he asked as he eyed his guest—she could tell he did not expect a response.

Then she heard him softly say to her, "A tear is a manifestation of a person's life . . . it is a breathing out of past experiences, a release of those experiences of that person's life, and all those experiences drawn together, as one, are added to the present experience.

"The next teardrop will carry the present experience as well as all of those that the past tears had held . . . with each becoming more valuable than the one before."

Julia eyed Rodrigo Orasco while he paused momentarily, staring out at the darkness, and, then, she watched him turn towards her and address her in a somber tone, "Someone once said, that a tear . . . so precious . . . so divine . . . should be a sacrament."

Neither spoke.

She watched his face as he turned and appeared to gaze in the direction of the sea again.

Finally, Rodrigo broke the silence as he turned toward her once again before saying, "To shed a tear is a right we have." He hesitated, momentarily . . . and she saw a smile form on his handsome face. Then she heard him say with a laugh, seemingly she thought, trying to hide his seriousness, "As long as we do not embarrass ourselves, of course." They both laughed.

But, Julia *knew* he was serious.

For a few moments Julia reflected on what Rodrigo had just said. *Apparently, the cognac carries more kick than I imagine,* she mischievously thought as she responded, "From childhood, Japanese are told, 'Gaman Shinasai' . . . bear up, be stoic in the face of hardship, display no tears.

"Their children are taught in school about the samurai who, not wanting to bother other people, showed no emotion when his beloved father died."

She lingered as she looked at Rodrigo, and then remarked, "Michael was taught that, at an early age from someone he admired and respected."

"Gaman Shinasai," Orasco slowly repeated it aloud. Then he rose and stood facing her, and asked, "Do you believe that, lovely lady?"

"I believe it because Michael believes it," she answered with an affirming smile.

She followed Orasco with her eyes as he took the glass from her and walked over to the bar and poured them both more cognac. Then he returned with her glass, and posed another question, "Are we only to share our joy with one another? Do we not also have the right to share pain?" Then, he asked her, "From which do we grow more? . . . joy or pain?"

She studied this mysterious man as he paused briefly and looked into her eyes, causing her to shudder as he softly said, "I believe it is pain."

63

Bogota, Columbia . . .

"DON'T FORGET Papa! My party begins at four." It was her thirteenth birthday. Rosa Orantes threw him a kiss as she darted back inside.

He felt her excitement as he watched his beautiful daughter disappear behind the closed door with her dog, Blanca, trailing at her heels.

Roberto Luis Orantes whistled as he started his motor car's engine. He prayed silently, Thank you, El Señor, for this wonderful day. And thank you for my precious daughters.

He pushed down on the clutch pedal and manually shifted gears, and questioned himself aloud, "Did I kiss Ernestina goodbye?" He couldn't recall. "If not, I'll make it up to her, tonight." He thought about her full lips and, oh, how he loved to kiss them . . . how he loved his wife's sensuous lips to make love to him.

But, now, Roberto Orantes could hardly wait to get to his office . . . his new office as the Metropolitan Police Commander. At the age of thirty-two, he knew he would be the youngest ever.

Servani, the mayor, was going to announce the name of the new commander today to succeed Tomas Aguillar who had died of a heart attack in a brothel over a week ago.

Orantes had thought Aguillar would be the police commander for many, many years since Aguillar had been only forty-one years old. The deceased man's premature death had shocked not only the people of Bogata, but the whole country.

Almost every citizen in Columbia knew about the young commander who was fearlessly trying to rid their country of the vicious drug lords who had enslaved every living soul of Columbia in some manner or other.

Roberto Orantes was no less shocked. He thought that his commander, and friend, was as healthy as anyone Roberto knew.

There had been no previous knowledge from anyone that indicated Aquillar had a heart problem.

Orantes had always been loyal to his commander. Both of them hated the drug dealers and both worked tirelessly trying to rid their city of those scum who peddled the addictive powder and took advantage of the poor in the outlying villages.

Orantes had been almost assured to be the new commander, he thought. Mayor Servani, himself, had told me that I was the strongest candidate. *Roberto could barely keep from smiling as he pulled his automobile into his private parking place at the municipal building.*

"Roberto! Come in here," Santo Ybarra nervously motioned toward a small office off the corridor. "Hurry, my friend!"

Orantes had just entered the front door of the police headquarters, and it was quite apparent that Ybarra had obviously been waiting for him.

"What is it?" Orantes asked as Ybarra, his hand on Orantes' shoulder, pulled Roberto into the tiny room and quickly closed the door.

Captain Ybarra was directly under Major Roberto Orantes in the police chain of command, and was considered by Orantes to be a loyal associate and friend.

With a white handkerchief Ybarra wiped the sweat from his forehead as he took a deep breath and hesitated for a brief moment. He did not know how, nor did he wish to tell Orantes the news.

Finally, he summoned the courage and said, "The mayor is in the commander's office now with General Hidalgo from our military and two federales from the United States. He is preparing to announce the new police commander in a matter of minutes."

Ybarra hesitated, as he looked at Orantes. Then he slowly said, to his superior and friend, "It will not be you."

Orantes stared at Ybarra. The expression on Orantes' face told Ybarra that his friend did not believe what he had just been told.

Orantes slowly sat down on the worn wooden chair; his right forearm rested on the small wooden table that had not been painted, or even cleaned, in years. Roberto's other hand rested in his lap. He still stared up at Ybarra with the look of disbelief. Roberto could not speak. His glazed eyes turned toward the wall.

Finally, after a moment of frozen silence, Orantes slowly looked up at his assistant, his friend, and quietly asked, "Quien?" . . . ("Who?")

"Colonel Calderon."

Orantes slowly shook his head in disbelief. He knew the colonel. The colonel was always seen with General Hidalgo.

Orantes pleaded, "Why do they want someone from the armed forces again? Calderon knows nothing about running a police department."

Ybarra sat down on the opposite side of the table and remarked to his friend, "I was told by the general that the government of the United States wanted someone from the army."

Roberto could not believe it. He had worked hard. He had been loyal to his job. He knew he would do a very good job as police commander. He could not imagine someone from the military—the corrupt military—being selected for the position.

There was no proof, but Orantes and the deceased police commander had suspected for months that high levels of the military were assisting the Columbian drug cartels.

"Who are these men from the United States?" Orantes asked. He now stood with his hands on his hips.

"They carry authority directly from their President," Santo answered disgustedly. "This is what I was told by Mayor Servani."

Roberto paced back and forth in the nine-foot-by-seven-foot room with its unpainted, plastered and crudely patched walls. What am I to do now?

Orantes accelerated so his motor car would make it up the hill of the dirt road. It was already six o'clock in the evening. He had promised his daughter that he would be home by four. How was he to know that his motor car would require a new water pump that day?

He felt the lump in his throat, and the hopeless, empty feeling in his heart. He did not wish to face Ernestina.

Roberto had teased his wife that, from now on, beginning with the next time she saw him, she would always have to salute him because he would be the Metropolitan Police Commander.

He had jokingly promised her that they would move into the city and live in a palace . . . well, at least a place with running water.

As he saw his modest stucco home a quarter mile away, he could still hear, over and over again, the mayor's haunting voice.

* * *

"Believe me, Roberto, there will be other opportunities. This time we are required to let politics dictate to us. The United States President insisted that we install Colonel Calderon. They wish to work more closely with our military and they believe it would be wise to have someone running our police department who has an understanding of the military . . ."

* * *

WHERE is Blanca? *Orantes asked himself as he pulled into the small yard, his eyes searching the grounds for the tiny dog. His heart skipped a few beats.* Blanca always barks when I arrive home, *he told himself with an alarmed look.*

"BLANCA! COME HERE," *he anxiously called out as he gingerly stepped from the automobile. It seemed too quiet.*

He began to feel panic as he rushed into the house, calling, "Ernestina! Atencia! Rosa! Ramona! Where are you?"

When he entered the front room, he froze. His mouth fell open, but there was no sound as he stared. Then his mind told him what he saw.

Near the doorway lay his brother-in-law, Franz, spread eagled on his back with a dark crimson splotch over his heart. His forehead had a small dark red hole, and dried blood had trickled down across his eye and onto the coarsely laid wood planked floor.

Then Roberto saw them.

"NO! NO! . . . NO! NO! NO! OH, GOD! NOOOO!" *he screamed, and dropped to his knees, his buttocks resting on his heels and his hands helplessly at his side, his eyes only a blank stare.*

He remained that way for what seemed like an eternity, crying . . . loudly at first, then quiet sobs.

After a while, he managed to raise his head, and look at his family. He rose and slowly moved toward them.

His wife Ernestina and his daughters lay on their backs. Their clothing had been stripped away in the front. His wife and Ramona, the youngest at nine years of age, lay in the middle of the small room.

Atencia, the second daughter who was eleven, lay in the doorway leading to the kitchen. Rosa was in one of the corners of the living room. Her dog lay near her . . . its head had been decapitated.

Against a wall lay Orantes' sister, Sarrita . . . Franz's wife.

Roberto saw the puddles of blood on the floor below their necks. He stared at the blood that had distilled to the floor from between their legs. He saw the smeared blood that had dried on their arms and legs.

Orantes knew they had been raped and their throats ripped open by bayonets . . . military bayonets.

And Roberto Luis Orantes knew, that he, too, was supposed to have been there.

The smoke from the hills in the countryside could be seen from Bogota.

The old, dirty motorcar left a trail of dust as it rambled away from the city. Orantes knew he must hide . . . for now. "We are going away for a while, Jacquelina. I will take care of you now," he said as he gently patted her knee.

The little girl sitting in the passenger seat did not acknowledge him. She stared out the window and said nothing. The tears had dried. The five-year-old knew she would never see her mother or father again. Roberto had found her hiding in the brush.

Orantes glanced back through the rear window one last time at his home, now engulfed in flames. The metal container of petrol that he had spread throughout the house would guarantee that no one would see his precious babies or his beautiful wife.

Roberto Luis Orantes is dead today, he raged to himself. They will pay . . . they will all pay.

There were no more tears from Roberto Luis Orantes.

*   *   *

Bogota . . . two years later

"SEÑOR, this is for you," the young boy said as he handed an envelope to the police officer.

The startled Major Santo Ybarra ceased his brisk walk outside police headquarters. For some reason, instinct maybe, Ybarra stuck the unexpected mail into his uniform's coat pocket and entered the building.

When he had closed the door to his office, Ybarra opened the envelope and sat down in his chair and began to read it.

It was written in Spanish.

SANTO:
BE AT THE TELEPHONE BOOTH AT
THE CORNER OF CALLE VIA LOMA LINDA
AND AVENIDA CENTRAL AT ELEVEN
THIS MORNING. I WILL CALL.
        RLO

The streets were busy as motorcars of all shapes raced by. Ybarra watched the pedestrian traffic as he waited by the telephone booth. Once, he had to stop an elderly lady from using the phone. And just a minute ago he had to refuse the phone to two young girls. None of them questioned him because of his uniform.

He jerked awkwardly as the phone rang . . . it seemed very loud to him.

"Diga!" he said into the receiver.

The voice shocked him. Santo Ybarra could not believe what he heard.

"Ola! Mi amigo. It is Roberto."

"But you are dead! You have been dead for more than two years," Ybarra cried into the phone.

"It is I, Santo. And I am not dead."

"Madre de Dios! I cannot believe it. They found your bones in the house."

"No, Santo, they found the bones of my brother-in-law. I am very much alive. I want you to work for me."

"What am I to do?" Ybarra took a deep breath. "I know only being a police officer. I cannot believe it is you. When they found your bones . . . your body—"

"I need your assistance now, my friend. Who, in the police department that we can trust, are still there?"

"I would have to think, Roberto. After your death, or what we thought was your death, nineteen police officers resigned within three months, including Avillo Juarez. They were the smartest and strongest of any of us."

"I know, they work for me now," Orantes told him.

Santo Ybarra was in shock as he listened.

Orantes continued, "Tomorrow I will call you at your office. And I would like for you to read me tomorrow's headline of the Independencia Periodical. I also would like for you to have the police report related to this headline on your desk when I call."

"I still cannot believe it is you." Ybarra mumbled under his breath.

"No one else is to know, Santo. Goodbye for now, my friend."

* * *

"This is Major Ybarra speaking," Santo stared, in disbelief, at the newspaper headline lying on his desk.

"This is Roberto. Please read the headline to me."

Santo shifted in his chair, "MAYOR'S FAMILY EXECUTED."

Orantes wanted Ybarra to read him the details. "What does the newspaper say happened?"

Ybarra briefly read the column. "It just says that the mayor and his wife had been executed and found in the mayor's home along with his seven grandchildren, his four daughters and their husbands.

"They were having a birthday party for one of the grandchildren. The police are questioning suspects now. That's all it says."

"How does the police report describe it?" Orantes asked.

That was what astounded Santo Ybarra. He had already read the police report. He stammered as he told Orantes the details. "The mayor's wife and daughters, and grandchildren, had been raped and their bodies had been mutilated. The mayor's four sons-in-law had been shot in the back of their heads as they lay in a row on their bellies."

Ybarra continued reading the report to Orantes. "The mayor was still alive when they found him. He died later from loss of blood. His penis and testicles had been cut from his body with a chainsaw found beside him.

"It appears that he witnessed everything before this was done to him." Ybarra wanted to puke.

"I will call you again tomorrow, Santo. You will need to read tomorrow's headline to me. Goodbye."

* * *

"Ola! This is captain Ybarra." Santo could not believe the newspaper headline and the police report lying on his desk.

"It is I, Santo," Orantes's voice was calm.

"What are you doing, Roberto? This is madness." Ybarra was frightened.

"Please read the headline to me."

Ybarrra read, "GENERAL HIDALGO ASSASSINATED."

"Read me the police report."

Santo picked up the report with his trembling hands. "The bodies of General Hidalgo, Colonel Calderon, the Metropolitan Police Commander, and twelve of their closest aids were found at the general's villa."

He swallowed hard and continued reading the report to Orantes. "Also, the bodies of Juan Elpido Duarte and Enrique Javier Ochoa were found there. They were the most powerful drug lords of the Medellin and Cali cartels, Roberto.

"All of them, every one of them, were found with their throats slashed. Bayonets were still embedded in each of their throats." Ybarra dropped the report on his desk and put his hand to his forehead.

"What else did the report say, Santo?"

Ybarra did not have to reread the police report to answer. "It said that each one of them had had their testicles ripped from their bodies with some kind of pliers.

"This is madness, Roberto," Ybarra cried.

"Now, you will be the new Metropolitan Police Commander, Santo. And you will work for me."

Then, without waiting for a response, Rodrigo Lara Orasco calmly hung up the receiver and walked away from the telephone booth.

64

"HI!" TESS SAID in a seemingly tired way as Julia opened the front door and a July blast of heat rushed across her.

"Hi, Tess, I didn't expect you. Come in." Julia led her best friend into the kitchen and offered, "Want some sun tea?"

"That sounds good," Tess replied. Julia picked up on Tess's tone as being somewhat tense.

Sensing a serious conversation coming on with her university associate and feeling a bit awkward, Julia didn't say anything as she dropped ice cubes into two glasses sitting on the counter. She poured tea into each, then added a teaspoon of sugar and set both glasses down on the kitchen table where Tess had already camped herself in one of the chairs that she normally did not sit in.

"Is something wrong?" Julia curiously asked as she sat down in the closest chair next to her friend. Julia became disconcerted as Tess looked at her for a few seconds without saying anything.

Then, an inner cry of alarm crept over Julia as she noted without any doubt the serious look on Tess's face, and anxiously rearranged herself in the chair as she waited for her friend to explain.

Finally, Tess began, "I need to tell you something." A pause before finishing, "But, I'm not quite sure . . . how to go about it."

Julia placed her glass on the table. She had become exasperated by now, and instructed her friend, "Just say it, Tess." Julia knew, now, that this was not going to be pleasant.

Tess hesitated again, then forced it out, "I climbed Piestewa Peak a few evenings ago, and . . . I saw Michael." Tess briefly wavered again, then, muttered barely audible, "He was with someone."

Tess turned her eyes away from Julia and studied the table for a few seconds. Then she looked up at her best friend, and said with finality, "He was holding her hand, and they were walking to the parking area together. Then Michael hugged her for a few minutes before she got into her car and left."

Julia stared at Tess, who, all at once, seemed to be half a football field away, as if Tess was at the opposite end of a black tunnel encircled with borders that appeared to be out of focus. And Julia felt like someone had just hammered the top of her head with a blunt instrument . . . not at all unlike what she had felt when she had been in an automobile rollover accident during her junior year of high school. The thought of Michael ever being with another woman was something that had never entered Julia's mind. At first, she felt more anger than misery.

65

IT WAS EIGHT-THIRTY that evening when I shut the front door and strolled into the master bedroom where Julia was sitting on the bed leaning back on a pile of pillows that she had positioned against the headboard. She appeared to be reading part of *The Arizona Republic,* and had several sections spread across the bed.

She looked up at me after I had given her the customary "Hi!" but didn't answer, and avoided me by glancing back down at the newspaper without saying anything.

I felt the wind deflate my lungs, and guilt choked my senses as if I knew she could read my mind.

I didn't say anything else and walked into my closet that was adjacent to the bathroom, and emptied my pockets, dropping keys and coins on my caddy, which was on a shelf just inside the closet. It had never occurred to me, until that moment, but I questioned myself then as to why I had continued using the second closet in her bedroom. For the past three years I had always slept in another room.

When I came out from the closet, Julia, eyes glaring, confronted me with a volley of words in an indisputable fiery tone, "Tess saw you with someone at the mountain. Are you having an affair?" Julia was never known as someone who minced words. Beating around the bush was a blatant waste of valuable time and energy as far as she was concerned.

I could see her watching my reaction as I stopped in my tracks and stood staring at her. I most certainly felt the air vacate the room leaving nothing for normal breathing. The expression on my face, I was certain, told her what she did not wish to believe.

I stood there for a few tacit moments with my eyes apprehensively darting around the room, at nothing in particular, but I definitely did not let them rest on her again. Finally, I gazed sharply at my wife and said with a very shaky voice not at all my own, "I've spent some time with someone."

Well, *that* just plain didn't sound right, and I knew it. My recognition of all thought at that instant pretty much reminded me that my whole body had just been sucked naked into a glass cookie jar for Julia and everyone in the whole world to see.

She was fuming now, and she wanted details. She rose from the bed and hurled the newspaper onto the floor, and fired off another barrage of words. "Who is she? Where did you meet her? How long?" She didn't expect nor want any explanations.

I could see the rage and contempt erupting from her. *She probably feels satisfaction,* I couldn't help thinking. *She's caught 'me'! Now, we're even.*

"YOU BASTARD!" she cried as she stomped from the room.

Ten stunned minutes beat through my life before I saw her lying on the sofa in the living room when I first stepped into the foyer with a small suitcase. I promptly opened the front door and left.

For more than an hour Julia lay on the sofa. Over and over again she could still recall the sound of the front door open and close. When she had heard it sealed shut, fear had swept over her, and she could not remember such a time that hopelessness had ever vented itself in such bold dispositions, even more so than on that horrible day when she was just five years old.

Though they had not slept together, except at Rodrigo Lara Orasco's villa, nor made love in more than three years, she had never considered or imagined not being with Michael.

She slumped face down into the cushion sobbing. For hours she lay there, confused, feeling lost . . . desolate . . . and more alone than she had ever felt.

Finally, feeling totally diminished of energy . . . and hope, she drifted off into a slumber that tendered mercy.

66

AUGUST WAS TURNING its final days, and it had been six weeks since I had walked out the door from Julia . . . seemed to me like six months. Even the slightest morsel of guilt wouldn't bring its sort forward in any persuading dimension within my deliberations that would condemn me for having deceived her. *What the hell did she expect?* I missed my wife, terribly.

Julia never loved me, I concluded. But, somewhere deep inside, beyond my grasp, I still could not be convinced . . . hoping I was wrong. Yet, unknowingly, I continued searching for reasons to dismiss Julia from my life, so I could, once and for all, be free of her spell over me. *Is that what I really want?* I kept asking myself.

She's probably been seeing someone else for years, I tried to convince myself. At that moment, I despised her . . . detested the *hold* she had on me.

My thoughts rambled as I rationalized, *Besides, Catherine and I haven't done anything wrong. We've embraced a few times, and adopted a few innocent body holds . . . that's all! Hell, we've only kissed a few times, and only as greetings or goodbyes on the cheek.* But, I knew I was just kidding myself. I knew damn well it was wrong, and I had deceived my wife . . . and I was wrong.

And, I admitted to myself, I knew Catherine Steele was in love with me. *I'm not that damn naive. I can read between the lines.*

I had recognized the subtle words that Catherine would so carefully articulate when she would express her feelings toward me, but, at the same time, careful not to actually tell me that she was in love with me.

I wasn't sure what it was that I felt for Catherine. I knew I enjoyed being with her. And often, I had realized, I would be anxiously anticipating, longing for the next occasion when I would see her again. And many days I'd daydream, and discover how much I missed her when I wasn't with her.

But, Jesus, I miss Julia. Why can't she love me . . . why doesn't she desire me? Why is she so flighty with her feelings . . . it's as if she purposely tries to hide them, I incessantly reminded myself over and over in such defeated furor that it probed into every chamber where speculations manifested themselves everywhere my consciousness bared itself.

As I sat there in my office I tried to weigh everything. I admitted to myself that I wasn't being fair to Catherine, leading her on. And to make things even worse, and more confusing, I was actually beginning to enjoy living alone.

Why don't I feel lonely without Julia? Is it because I have Catherine available at my beck and call. Is she my security blanket? Is that all she is? All of these questions demanding answers kept firing at will in my meditations. And I had no decent rejoinder for any of them.

My hopeless pondering continued digressing me from the tax-planning material I had been working on at my *fancy* desk. I laid my *fancy* pencil down and leaned way back in my *fancy* chair, and gazed out through the huge windows of my *fancy* office, the Scottsdale office that Hector Baldarrama's dollars had bought me. At that moment all that *fancy* extravagance didn't mean shit to me.

From where I sat, there in my office, I could see the large man-made lake less than a hundred feet away. I felt a wave of depression as I lazily observed the small white caps on the water's surface being rustled by wind gusts that were now becoming more intense, much stronger than earlier in the afternoon when I had practiced hitting ground strokes with the pro at the tennis club just a half-mile from my office. I had hoped *that* workout on a hot humid day would send my frustrations packing . . . but, it didn't seem to do much good.

My melancholy thoughts finally scattered and went searching for the storage provinces of my mind for later contemplations as I allowed my attention to be drawn to the dark monsoon clouds rising above the horizon over the southeastern part of the valley where Tempe, Mesa, Chandler and Gilbert were. It looked like there was going to be a late monsoon-season lightning display later in the evening over South Mountain, and maybe even over the Estrellas.

That spectacle was a summer distraction that most valley dwellers looked forward to after enduring dry months upon end of cloudless sky everywhere in sight. The flashing streaks across the black night heavens, one right after the other, reminded one of fireworks. And, sometimes, this ornamental array would go on for hours. It was most common in late July and most of the month of August.

The antique clock on the wall chimed seven thirty, and I couldn't tell from my office at that moment, but imagined the sun low in the western sky, and most likely it was about to evanesce behind the mountains.

I wished now I hadn't told Catherine I'd climb Piestewa Peak with her later. I'd much rather go home and crash, watch a ball game, observe the lightning show . . . *be by myself.*

All my life, I had been afraid of being alone. I had this desperate yearning that seemed to consume me and plant itself in my being that demanded that I always needed to be with someone. I had always had Hue.

After she had been gone for several months I had felt as if loneliness had installed itself into every module my reasoning could possibly strike and had refused to surrender its tortured presence in any decent form. At that time I thought I was destined to live the rest of my life with that depressing sense, *that despoiled feeling of isolation.*

But then, a few months later, I met Julia and everything was all right.

With that thought ending, my daydreaming was interrupted by the telephone on my desk. I briefly regarded it, but then rejected picking it up. Instead, I rose from my chair, grabbed my keys and cellular phone from the top drawer of one of the lateral filing cabinets near the doorway of my office, turned out the lights and headed down the hall.

I climbed into my Porsche, and as I pulled out of the parking lot—a very large parking lot—I recalled how Hector Baldarrama had surprised me with the sports car eight months ago . . . we had just begun working together a few months earlier.

* * *

I had tried to convince Hector that the convertible Porsche was much too pretentious for me. I told my "boss" that I would rather have something less flashy, like an Oldsmobile or even a Buick Park Avenue with all the goodies. "I could deal with that image."

"Everest," I had even told myself, "why are you so damned conservative? You're just a tight-ass right winger . . . live a little!"

But Hector wouldn't listen to me anyway. The drug kingpin wanted to reward his talented accountant, and so, as he handed the keys of the Porsche to me, he told me, "This little beauty was made just for you, amigo,"

And that was that!

* * *

I swung north off Lincoln Drive and headed up toward the parking area at Piestewa Peak. As I drove through the upper-middle-class neighborhood, I began appraising the past two years.

I thought about how my life had become so dramatically recast. It almost seemed to me now like the past year and a half had been nothing more than a dream, and I would wake up any second.

I had been in charge of opening seventy-two Lunas Primaveras restaurants in Europe and twenty-four in the United States, and I was tired, genuinely worn out. All of a sudden, over the past few weeks, I felt old . . . *really* old.

"Quit feeling sorry for yourself, you're getting rich," I muttered to himself. I massaged the back of my neck—this act now becoming a frequent ritual—as I climbed out of the sports car at the foot of the Peak.

67

AFTER HIKING THE mountain with Catherine, and the sun having already wrestled itself from the valley, I quartered a somewhat more acceptable attitude in my thinking relative to my whole situation at that time in my life, even though the August heat was still unbearable as all hell, and even though I *did* mention *that* ungratifying fact to myself more than once and in less than appropriate language that was definitely better suited to a locale of sailors.

Bidding Catherine goodbye and leaving the Peak parking lot I drove south on Central Avenue until I reached Thomas Road where I swung a right and stopped at a pay phone near a parking area at Phoenix College. This took me out of the way by five or six miles, but it enabled me to most likely lose anyone who might be tracking me. It was almost nine o'clock at night and it was still hotter than hell.

I dialed Sotello's number.

"Diga!" Henry answered the phone the same way every time I called him. Eventually, after I had become accustomed to this, I found himself silently mimicking the 'Diga!' at the same time that I heard Henry uttering the abrupt greeting.

I meant no disrespect to Henry. It was all in fun and just an innocent pantomime that I found humorous ... it helped me unwind.

"It's me! We have to meet." I told my contact.

"Okay! I'll be there in forty minutes," I heard over the phone before it went dead in my ear.

68

I GUIDED THE sports car through the entrance of North Mountain Park at Seventh Street and Peoria Avenue. That was the designated place where Sotello and I met when we didn't want to discuss something over the telephone, or whenever we needed to discuss a matter at length. Unless it was absolutely necessary, the two of us had agreed, we would avoid meeting in person.

I maneuvered up and around the winding road, which was the only one leading into the park, and stopped the Porsche near one of the covered picnic areas. I had always selected a different parking spot each time I had to meet with Henry.

I was eminently mindful that my Porsche was not the most discreet automobile in the world, and I often mused to myself that it was the reason Hector Baldarrama had given me the luxury vehicle. I knew I had to be careful where I parked it ... preferably hidden from the view of a slow-moving car that might be roaming the paved road searching for a certain accountant's sports car.

After parking, I walked for a quarter of a mile, and climbed up the same bluff as always that overlooked the winding road. The bluff wasn't as high as North Mountain, but was tucked next to the mother mountain on the east side facing Seventh Street.

From the bluff, it was impossible not to observe anyone approaching from the road, or, for that matter, on foot anywhere from the surrounding desert, even at night.

This bluff provided another advantage that I found suitable. It could be reached from a multitude of directions, and, on the flip side of that, it could be evacuated quite discreetly in those same different directions.

I knew North Mountain Park like the back of my hand, and probably, I had decided long ago, as well as any Native American of the past who had ever roamed the mountains hunting game.

For more than sixteen years, just about every day, I had run up and down North Mountain, and occasionally Piestewa Peak, with Hue. I felt especially comfortable at North Mountain, and felt like I could probably climb to the top with my eyes closed if need be. And I knew it would be virtually impossible for anyone to follow me without me knowing it. That mountain trail was my river of safety, just like the Mississippi protected Mark Twain's *Huck Finn*.

I sat there admiring the night sky when the sultry breeze suddenly cloaked my face, and its discordant whisper, for some unknown reason, took me back thirty-three years, there at North Mountain, to younger but not more innocent days . . . just before my nightmares began to cast their unsought notions on my nights.

* * *

I panted hard as I stood struggling to catch my breath. I bent over with my hands resting on my thighs just above my slightly bent knees, allowing my lungs to relax and adjust themselves to the change in the air entering more easily, more effortlessly.

I had done it. I had run up all the way, all the way up North Mountain . . . and, I had finally beaten Hue to the top.

I was barely seven years old.

After finally inducing my breathing to its normal cadence, I straightened up, and my eyes followed Hue reaching the top as she gasped for air. She had not let me beat her.

But we couldn't stop yet. I set out down the slopes, Hue just a few steps behind. There was to be no rest until we reached the base of the mountain.

* * *

Once at the top of the butte, I sat on a small boulder and waited for Henry Sotello to climb up. Even though it was dark and the moon was well hidden behind some lazy slow-drifting clouds, I could still follow Sotello's moves from the time Henry left his car until he reached the top of the bluff. It took him almost ten minutes. And I was absolutely certain that no one had followed my friend.

"Como esta, amigo," Henry, breathing heavily, vocalized with some difficulty as he half waved one hand and wiped the sweat from his brow with the other.

"Bien, gracias!" I casually returned the huffing and puffing man's greeting.

We continued speaking in Spanish as I made a statement to the winded DEA agent that caught his attention, "Well, Henry, you've wanted to know where all of the cartel's cash is going—"

I purposely hesitated for a few seconds to make sure my government contact was grasping what he was being told, and then continued, while smiling with an obvious twinkle in my eye, "I think I know."

"Ah! It's about time we had some good news. Tell me all about it, my friend," Henry said as he carefully, and with some effort, seated himself on a boulder about ten feet away from me, and gazed out at the blanket of lights that were spread out across the black valley floor far below.

The first time Henry Sotello and I had met up there I learned that Henry had lived in Phoenix all of his life, and, until he and I had begun meeting on the butte, Henry had never examined the valley from North Mountain Park, even during the day, and he still had not climbed to the top of the mountain.

"What a view!" Henry sighed and gingerly leaned back, adjusting himself against a boulder that supported his back.

* * *

Hue and I sat on one of the concrete picnic tables at the base of the trail. I was overjoyed and busting my buttons, proud that I had finally beaten her.

But as I studied her sitting on the opposite side of the table, I tasted a sadness that tempered my thoughts of achievement. I wondered how she felt . . . what she was thinking. She had lost to me for the first time.

How was I to know, because I sure didn't know at that moment, that my life, on that day, would change forever. Hue began to teach me . . . teach me to live with pain . . . to survive.

She had always loved me, even though I sometimes wondered if she did. But, from that day on, she would no longer let me feel it.

The late-evening warm April wind blew gently across the desert as she and I sat there together at the base of the mountain.

North Mountain was my favorite place and time on earth, there in the semidarkness of the surrounding desert and mountains, populated by tall cacti and mesquite and palo verde trees and even Carolina Jasmin with their yellow flowers blooming and sheathing a golden glow across the desert landscape. And there was always, every March and April, a multitude of wildflowers such as brittle bush, desert globe swallow and penstemon blushing their enticing colors.

And when the desert had its fair share of winter rain, there would be Mexican gold and California poppies and desert bluebells staging their glorious productions. And from the top of North Mountain, I could see every star in the northern hemisphere.

And now, at the age of seven, I had won the race to the top. But, on the following day, I lost my childhood forever.

"Get up, Michael," Hue yelled as she rushed through my bedroom door. She knew it was time. Time to prepare me.

It was four forty-five in the morning.

As Hue instructed me, I stood facing her. I felt like I was still half asleep.

"From this day forward, Michael, I am your Sinsai. I will teach you 'Kata.' You will learn them all. We begin with 'Naihanchi Shodan.' I am your mirror, do as I do. Place your feet and toes together. Find your Ki. Lightly flex your calves and forearms, nothing else, shoulders down. Breathe in deeply . . . hold . . . for one . . . two . . . exhale slowly. And so it began.

For the next twelve years, it was the same every morning at four forty-five . . . until just before Hue died.

She taught me all of the 'Shorin Ryu Kata.' She taught me the deadly 'Ju-Jutsu' and 'Mai Thai' fighting methods. For twelve years Hue taught me those deadly techniques. Just as her master had taught her.

And she continued to run up North Mountain and, occasionally, Piestewa Peak with me every day, until she became ill, just before her death.

She never told me how devoted she was to me, nor how much she loved me. But, she thought I knew. She just knew I felt her . . . her energy . . . her love.

She was wrong.

Shortly after the martial arts pedagogy began each morning, I began to have the same dream every few weeks, up until I was almost fifteen years old.

I would wake up in the middle of the night, crying. It was the only time I ever cried, the only time I was permitted to cry . . . secretly.

Elephants floated all around me in the dream. But they weren't elephants . . . they were huge like elephants. But they didn't have elephant trunks or tails. They were round and each one was as large as my room.

The dream would begin when I would see the evil eyes of one of those gross creatures staring at me from a far distance up in a black sky. And then, in a flash, the creature's wide opened sneering eyes would be inches away from mine as I lay in my bed. And then, the creature would post its face up against mine, and its huge menacing eyes would glare right through me.

I would wake, screaming. But no one would come, and I'd be afraid to go back to sleep. No one ever came . . . no one came to save me.

*   *   *

I had Sotello's undivided attention as I began my report about what I had discovered, "Hector Baldarrama told me Rodrigo Orasco was a big wheel in the National Police of Columbia, fifteen or twenty years ago. Then, one day Orasco got pissed off and resigned. Baldarrama wasn't sure about all the details.

"Anyway," I continued, "Orasco set up a cartel consisting of twenty-two member shares. One share was owned by each of the initial members, and all profits were to be distributed equally to each of them. Orasco had the same sharing percentage as the other members.

"A few years later—Orasco's recommendation—the members voted to add Hector Baldarrama. And *that* increased their happy group to twenty-three members.

"According to Baldarrama, he first met Orasco ten or twelve years ago when he just happened to be taking a stroll along a street one night in Vallarta, Mexico and ran into four thugs hassling Orasco who was there alone on vacation.

"Hector told me that he and Orasco kicked some ass, and Hector was a hero in Orasco's eyes. According to Baldarrama, Orasco thought the thugs probably would have killed him if Hector hadn't come along.

"So . . . then they became drinking buddies, and ultimately Orasco brought Baldarrama into their group. During the fight that night, Hector had his face busted up pretty good, so Orasco had Hector get a make-over from a top cosmetic plastic surgeon in San Diego. Hector told me that his face looked better after the fight than it had before and, because it was so dark, Orasco would never know that. Hector thought *that* was funnier than shit."

I paused long enough to take a swig from a plastic bottle of water, then proceeded telling the DEA agent, "The cartel's rules stated that, if any member was killed, his ownership reverted to a trust which had been set up by that member. All accumulated profits of the deceased member were to go to the trust, as would all future profits allocated to that member for a period of fifteen years from the date the cartel had been formed."

I took another swig before resuming my dissertation, "At the end of fifteen years, the cartel would cease to exist and each member could go his own way with his own profits.

"By setting up the trusts that way, Orasco was ingenious because of the way he structured everything. He prevented any of the members from getting greedy and knocking off one another, and, thus, avoided any internal power struggles."

All the talking I was doing caused me to finally finish off the last drops of my bottled water before pushing on, "It would do no good, for the other members, if one of them died, because the deceased's trust would have all the rights to that deceased member's earnings until the fifteen years were up. The bottom line was that no one benefitted from internal fighting or killing."

Sotello grunted and raised himself from the boulder, and massaged his buttocks, which, from his reaction, seemed to me to have cramped a little from the hard rock, although he still appeared to be intently grasping every word of my byline. I knew Henry was fast becoming a fan of Rodrigo Orasco, at least as far as respecting Orasco's ingenuity.

"Also, Henry," I stood and stretched as I continued, "any member could leave at any time during the fifteen years and take with him his accumulated profits, and there would be no hard feelings. The departing member would simply forfeit his rights to any future profits, and the remaining members and their trusts would get a bigger piece of the pie."

Sotello apparently wondered, and asked me, "Where did they keep their cash all that time?"

"As far as I could tell," I answered, "they all agreed to hide their cash in different places, mainly in bank safe deposit boxes. Some of the cash, small amounts, was put into foreign banks under the names of each of the individual trusts."

I diverted my message momentarily, "By the way, some of the trusts had designated portions of their profits to such beneficiaries as orphanages, churches, nonprofit organizations, and even the arts, as well as to the families of the members."

Henry Sotello was impressed with the information that I had provided, and he took in everything I told him. And, I wasn't quite finished.

"Each member took his allocated profits in cash every year and hid them. Only the member and beneficiaries knew the location. Now, these trusts want the billions of dollars, in cash, made legitimate," I said as I concluded my report.

"Oh, one other thing, Henry!" I added as an afterthought. "It had been agreed by all members from the very beginning that Orasco had total control over the organization, and his word was final in all decisions. Rodrigo Lara Orasco was leader supreme."

My story completed, I stepped over to the edge of the butte and gazed out at the black valley sprinkled with the thousands of sparkling diamonds and shiny multicolored gems and precious stones, and remarked, "Baldarrama told me that Orasco had been extremely brutal at times when it came to his enemies . . . even to their families."

After pausing for that to sink in, I turned toward Sotello and quietly observed to my associate, "I think Baldarrama may suspect I'm not who I say I am. Several times I've caught one of his henchmen following me. Maybe this should be our last contact, Henry, until I come out."

Henry walked over to the edge of the butte, and planted his feet next to mine. The DEA agent stood there, staring out across the valley. He told me how the view reminded him of a spilled pirate's treasure chest with jewels, diamonds and rubies . . . orange and yellow, white and red, and green. He also told me how much he loved the quiet up there. We could hear no other sound but the wind playing its song of refuge and gliding free across the rolling hills . . . *so peaceful*.

As the two of us stood there gazing out, Henry quietly told me, "Okay, Michael, no more contact. But, we've got to find out how Orasco fits in with the Arab terrorists. And, we need to find out where those bank accounts and safe deposit boxes are."

"This might help," I said with a sly grin as I waved in my hand a computer disc that I had pulled from my shirt pocket, and then handed to Sotello.

The DEA agent gladly took the disc from his spy, a rather good one at that—I just knew Henry was thinking. He then carefully placed it in his own shirt pocket, and looked out across the valley again . . . and smiled.

69

"I SAW HIM AT a pay phone again, Hector. I think he tried to lose me," Jaime reported to his boss. "This time he didn't."

"How long did he talk?" Baldarrama quizzed.

"Less than a minute, Jefe. It looked like he made two calls," Jaime answered. "He looked nervous, and kept looking around as if he was checking to see if he was being followed. I don't trust him, Jefe."

"Where did he go after that?"

"I'm sorry, Hector, I lost him after that." Jaime felt like an idiot. Jaime didn't think it would be wise to tell Baldarrama about the beautiful young girl with short brown hair, who had interrupted Jaime, and caused him to lose sight of Everest.

The woman, in her twenties, Jaime guessed, had promised him that she would have some drinks with him if he would take her to a bar in Glendale to meet a friend. She had told him that her car had broken down.

Jaime remembered that she spoke beautiful Spanish, and she even spoke French. Jaime didn't speak French, but it sounded like French to him. It was too bad he couldn't find her in the bar after he had dropped her off and parked his car.

Baldarrama didn't say anything. He just stared with disgust at Jaime.

Hector Baldarrama wanted to believe that Michael was his friend, his loyal associate, but the drug lord was beginning to wonder. He sat back in the sofa in his living room with one leg crossed over the other, wondering if and why Michael Everest had tried to make sure that he was not being followed.

I have paid Michael more than six million dollars, the drug lord mused. *Why would he do this? Why would he use a pay telephone when he has a cellular phone?*

"From now on, watch him closely," he ordered Jaime, "Watch him very closely."

The young woman pushed open the door, and smiled as she welcomed the cool blast of air sweeping over her as she entered her condo on east Bethany Home Road. Even after having just faced, for the first time, almost the entire summer of hell in the Valley, she still had not become accustomed to the blistering heat that made her feel like she was being baked inside an oven that had been preheated to four hundred fifty degrees, even at ten thirty at night.

But, she concluded, *this sure beats . . . all to hell . . . the five months of training I went through with those "Delta Boys" at Fort Bragg just before "this" assignment.* She was passionately determined, *I'm damn well going to be better than Jericho . . . I "have" to be.*

Anyway, there was good news. Her neighbors had promised that the welcomed cool weather was just around the corner, just six or seven weeks away. She supposed she would still be around then as she snapped the bolt lock on the door.

After she kicked off her high heel shoes and gave no attention as to which direction they flew, she headed straight for the small refrigerator for an ice-cold Perrier.

As she popped the cap and inhaled a couple of huge gulps, she thought about the "slime ball" who, earlier that night, had given her a ride to Glendale. The putrid pot stench inside his car still lingered in her clothing, which she promptly discarded into a plastic bag.

As she removed her government standard-issue high-powered Browning 9–millimeter semiautomatic from her purse and placed it on the floor between the bed and the nightstand on the farside of the bed away from the doorway, Lora Parks wondered if, someday, she would have to kill the man.

70

Washington, D.C. . . .

"YES, MR. PRESIDENT, we know exactly where those foreign accounts are, and we know how much is in each one," Warren

Turner confidently told James Franklin, who sat on a sofa listening attentively to Turner, his newly appointed National Security Advisor.

The two men paid little attention, if any, to the scene outside the bulletproof windows behind the president's desk in the Oval Office where the snow-covered White House lawn had been blanketed from the overnight early-November snowstorm that still continued to rage itself with a fury that suggested the gods wanted recourse for some unknown injustice that mankind had committed against nature that was finally unforgivable.

So far, Turner could tell that the president was quite pleased with the information that Turner had given him. "If there are any withdrawals from any of those accounts, we'll be able to follow the funds wherever they go," Turner added.

The new National Security Advisor hesitated momentarily . . . he wanted to be sure that his briefing was clear and well understood by his president.

Then he continued, "We don't know yet, but we're diligently trying to find out where the bulk of the cash is. Meanwhile, we're prepared to freeze the account funds at a moment's notice."

"How much is in the accounts?" the president asked.

"The last figure we had about a week ago," Turner replied, "was approximately two billion American dollars." Warren could see, from the unchanged expression on James Franklin's face, that the president was not surprised at the amount.

"The accounts are spread out, pretty much equally, over twenty-three trust accounts in banks of eight foreign countries, Mr. President. We expect *that* amount to grow dramatically over the next six months, and eventually increase by an average of about seventy-five million a month."

Turner paused briefly, and waited for that last bit of information to sink in. "We don't know how much cash is hidden away in safe deposit boxes, either, Mr. President."

"Probably billions more," Jim Franklin offered, as he stood up from the sofa.

Turner, as a courtesy to the most powerful man in the world, also stood up from the blue, white and gold sofa chair to which he earlier had been assigned by the president when Turner had first entered the—inordinately formal and, thus, not so comfortable—Oval Office.

Though he thought the president was satisfied that he had received as much information as Warren had, Warren could not help noticing that the president's solemn face looked concerned.

He heard Jim Franklin ask as they slowly strolled toward one of the Oval Office doors, "Have we had any new information about 'Gardenstone'? I'm beginning to feel a little antsy . . . I don't think it's just the weather causing it, Warren."

"No new information, Mr. President," Turner hesitated for a few seconds before finishing, "but, we've got several agents snooping around in Europe and the Middle East. We still believe Rodrigo Lara Orasco is behind it or, at least, he's closely connected to it in some way."

Warren paused again, then told the somber Franklin, "I, too, fear we are running out of time."

Franklin extended his hand, "I have another appointment now, Warren. I appreciate what you're doing. *Gaman* has provided us with extremely vital information, and we appreciate it. I hope everything works out."

"Thank you, Mr. President . . . so do I."

71

"JULIA'S HERE, MICHAEL," I heard Hazel tell me as I glanced up at Hazel and decided immediately that she sounded and looked a little apprehensive as she stood in the doorway of my private office.

I had not seen my wife since I had moved out back in August . . . that was four months ago.

Totally caught off guard, I shuffled some papers on my desk, sighed and reluctantly said, "Okay!" and nodded my head. "Tell her to come on back."

When Julia entered my office, she brandished what I would describe as a nervous smile, and said in a clear tone, "Hi!" and seated herself in one of the well-padded leather visitors' chairs in front of my desk. It was obvious she was uncomfortable being there, and I wasn't exactly the rock of Gibraltar.

I couldn't help noticing how beautiful my wife was... I hated that she looked so good. Julia was Hispanic, and, as I watched her sitting there, I was reminded about the time that, a few years ago in Dana Point, California, an elderly lady had commented on how pretty Julia was. The lady had asked her if she was Hawaiian.

On other occasions, friends and coworkers had wondered if she was Italian. She also had been mistaken for a Greek woman once. *Hispanic! Hawaiian! Whatever!* I thought as I looked at her now. *She is so damn gorgeous... and sensuous!*

I sat there admiring the dark-green suit she wore. It made her light-olive skin look radiant. Her dark brown eyes were soft, and had always been, to me, the most beautiful I had ever seen, especially when she smiled. She smiled nervously now.

While I sat with my hands clasped together and resting on my desk I sensed she was unsure of herself as she sat across from me. I continued looking in her direction while not actually looking at her. That was my familiar way of letting her know I was ready to listen to whatever she had to say, and, at the same time, letting her know I wasn't particularly happy that she was there. At least that's what I wanted her to think... of course I was full of crap. My heart was fluttering a little... *a lot.*

She had now crossed one leg over the other, allowing her skirt to rise just above her slender knees, revealing her perfect calves. Her hands were placed on her purse, in her lap. What made her so desirable and appealing to men, *and* women, other than her obvious natural beauty, was her total unawareness of the sensuality she cast.

At this point, I was still lost for words, and began to feel more tense than I had already been when she had first walked into my office. And I couldn't think of anything to say that would break the wall of silence.

Finally, and definitely with awkwardness, I managed to say, "You surprised me. I didn't expect you to come here."

"I've missed you," she said softly. She was looking directly into my eyes. I thought I would melt... *dammit!*

I thought to myself, *She has never said that to me before. Why now? Is it because she thinks I have someone else?* I felt the fire and bitterness germinating inside as I asked, "Why?" I stared right at her.

I could barely hear her shaky voice, cracking at times, almost mumbling, "Because . . . I love you. I miss you. I've missed you for years . . . and didn't know it.

"I . . . ," her voice cracked, and I knew she could barely speak, "I was afraid . . . afraid to commit myself . . . to allow myself to be in love with you . . . it was safe."

My tone hardened even more, and uncontrolled bitterness manifested itself with such force it even frightened me. But I had gone too far and couldn't stop the words from spilling from my mouth, "What's changed your mind? Is it because you're lonely? . . . Or, because you think I have another woman?"

I knew . . . and I was helpless to control it . . . the furor stirring inside me for so many years—for what I felt was mental abuse from my wife in the form of neglect and indifference—was ready to erupt . . . to free me. To finally free me from her power over me.

And so I roared on, "Did you think that, since another woman wanted me, then maybe, I'm worth having now, that I'm worth more than someone for whom you've just settled?" The words just kept coming, and I couldn't stop. The subconscious cut of me demanded I tell her what I felt.

Glaring at her, I could see her mouth open slightly as she tried to maintain control . . . determined not to cry, and she turned her face away and spent her eyes toward the window.

I sat there, not uttering another word, almost in shock at what I had just done. As I watched her, I thought she would break down into a valley of tears any second. I had *never* seen her crawl before . . . for me.

As quickly as it had come, my rage stamped itself out like a harsh winter wind would extinguish a flame in a batting of an eye. Then, only sadness found itself charging every thought and feeling I could summon at that moment.

I wanted to hold her. But, something, deep inside, still would not let me move.

Her voice quivered even more as she strained to hold back the tears. "I just know . . . I just know that I don't want anyone but you," she said in a crying whisper as she turned to look at me. The desk still separated us.

"I want you to come home," she pleaded. "Please . . . please give us another chance. I'll go to counseling like you've always wanted. I'll do anything . . . just come home."

I felt air and energy drain from my body . . . from my soul. And I surrendered no discernible emotion as I sat looking at my wife. For what seemed like an eternity, I just sat there without saying anything, looking away from her, searching the room . . . aimlessly. Then I finally allowed my eyes to strike her, this dispirited incredibly gorgeous woman, and I thought about how I had always believed that I had possessed enough passion for her that would more than compensate for the lack of it she had for me.

Finally, I stood and slowly walked around the desk. I took her hands in mine and lightly coaxed her to her feet. And held her. We held each other.

I stroked her hair, and smelled her fragrance, and felt the wetness of her tears on my shirt as her face was buried in my chest. We remained still, standing . . . holding one another, and time seemed to estrange itself from our closeness.

I gazed out the window as I continued holding her, still standing, still softly stroking her hair. I was not sure what this meant for us. But, I was certain of one thing. At that moment . . . she felt wonderful to hold.

We went home . . . together.

And made love . . . tender, sensuous love at first, our bodies gently pressed together, trembling, both burning with fire, lightly caressing . . . new unfamiliar touching as if we were being joined together for the first time. Then, later, more passionately, more frantically, more desperately, we two lovers demanded more from one another, urging one another on with our hands, our mouths, discovering the openness of love . . . the physical love that neither of us was ever capable of experiencing before.

I knew then that I was free from her power over me . . . I no longer obsessed her, needed her. Now I could love her because I *chose*, I *willed* it so.

And that night, we finally gave ourselves... all of ourselves... to one another... mind, body and the depths of our being.

72

The Middle East...

SHAMAN ZODARU WATCHED through the thick protective glass window as the ever-cautious technician nervously finished tightening the coarse steel-black cap of the cylinder, which had an exterior surface similar in color and texture as the cap. The cylinder was approximately three centimeters in diameter and seven centimeters in length.

From his position outside the steel-enclosed laboratory, Zodaru could easily detect the heavy perspiration on Oman Shahnir's forehead just before the technician swept his brow with his own shirtsleeve.

Shahnir turned to look at his superior, who was a displaced Palestinian forced to live in Lebanon, and silently worded through the thick glass window with his lips, "It is done!" Shahnir's tired face displayed the look of pride... and relief. Though he welcomed that glorious day when he would see Allah, Oman was not ready to die a horrible death... not that day... not that night!

Oman Shahnir knew that if he had made even a slight miscalculation, he would have breathed in the deadly gas, and his body would have died a horrifying death in two or three minutes, with each minute seeming like an eternity of agonizing convulsions and excruciating pain from blood vessels expanding and finally exploding inside his body.

After observing the technician's completion, Zodaru made no gesture and said nothing as he began to reflect to himself, as if in prayer, about why all of this had come to be... *For you, my grandfather, for you my dear father, for all of your brothers and sisters, and for my family. Now, the thieves will pay once more. Allah has always guided me. He will guide me again.*

The Jew swine, and their European pagans and American Pimps will all pay for taking your lands from you... for taking your homes from you... for spitting on you... for taking your lives.

For over fifty years, the infidels have treated all of us as if we are less than dirt... as if we are nothing.

No more! I swear it... Allah wills it!

Zodaru turned towards the two men waiting just outside the door to the laboratory. He nodded for them to proceed.

Zodaru watched as the two men promptly opened the steel door without hesitation, and carried a wooden crate of olives into the isolated steel chamber and over to the table where the cylinder had been assembled. The two men, now appearing quite jittery, set the crate on the floor and removed half of the olives and placed them on the floor next to the crate.

By now, Zodaru had entered the chamber. He stood within a few feet of the crate and continued observing everything as Shahnir carefully placed the sealed cylinder on top of the remaining olives in the center of the crate and meticulously packed foam around the deadly chemical container. Then Shahnir covered it with most of the olives that lay on the floor.

Once the insulated cylinder had been completely hidden by the olives, the two men fastened the lid to the top of the crate and carefully carried it to the waiting truck outside... to join the other five crates.

"Oman," Zodaru said as he bowed slightly to the smaller man, "Allah will always bless you."

Oman returned the courtesy as he bowed, acknowledging Shaman Zodaru's gratitude. Nothing needed to be said.

Three minutes later, Oman Shahnir watched the truck, with Shaman Zodaru, his two soldiers and the shipment of olives, until it disappeared in the trailing dust and cold darkness of the Libyan desert.

73

CATHERINE STEELE WALKED slowly along the side of the canal that wound through Encanto Park, which was located in central Phoenix just a mile east of her office. The weather had turned unusually cold in the Valley of the Sun, even for late December.

The freezing wind blew relentlessly, and storm clouds covered the sky. Catherine thought it was going to snow any minute as she tugged at her coat collar, trying to pull it up around her face.

She strolled transiently and surveyed the small ripples on top of the ashen grey water. She wondered why he had sounded so strange on the phone. *Never before had he seemed so serious when calling me.* Knots tightened inside. She knew something was different, something was wrong. She looked at her watch . . . *four-forty-five. He's late!*

She continued her slow pace, and spotted a small flock of pigeons that had gathered together looking for bread crumbs near one of the concrete picnic tables on the canal bank. She watched another gathering of them, huddled together under the table, trying to shield themselves from the wind. It seemed to her to be blowing harder now.

She glanced at her watch again when she finally recognized him walking in her direction. It was almost five-fifteen. He was still some distance away on the other side of the canal, coming from the parking lot.

She watched him head toward the walk bridge that provided access to her side of the thirty-foot-wide canal. Her eyes followed him as he began crossing. He was still at least forty yards away. The wind blew even harder, and the sky became darker.

As she watched him reach her side of the canal, Catherine felt a lump in her throat. *Oh, God! I love him so much. Why do I love him so? It hurts . . . it hurts so much!*

By the time he finally reached her, Catherine felt numb, yet she could feel her heart racing to sadness, like it was ready to vault from her being and flee so abruptly she couldn't catch up with it. The freezing wind continued its attack as it blew itself heavy into her face without any toleration for kindness whatsoever, but she didn't feel it.

She studied his expression, searching for a sign of hope, a spark in any ration, that would give her comfort, even if only briefly.

"Hi!" she barely heard him say. She watched him flash a slight apprehensive polite kind of smile. His eyes told her what was to come as she blinked and swallowed hard.

"Hi, Michael!" It was a quiet sound forced out by her as she attempted a smile. She didn't reach out to him, and she felt him hold back the same. For *some* time, as her encounters with him, their friendship, or whatever, had evolved, they had begun to embrace one another when they would first meet on each occasion. But, Catherine knew . . . not now.

She could tell he kept a distance between them, an extra foot or so. *Just enough to let me know,* she thought, *let me know things had changed. Everything had changed . . . everything was different now.*

She swallowed hard, and her heart was no longer a part of her as it bolted even faster. She wanted to run, telling herself, *I won't have to listen to him. Just turn and run, Catherine!*

Somewhere deep inside, she managed to hear him say, "Can we sit down?"

She was crying, inside, as she sat, sideways, onto the park bench. She was facing him, waiting for him to tell her what she already knew. She shivered as the cruel wind snarled its disposition all the way down inside her coat collar.

He sat down next to her, facing straight ahead. He seemed to Catherine to be looking out at distant things. He was leaning forward with his forearms resting just above his knees. She watched him rub his palms against one another, then touch his fingers all together, straight, forming a steeple.

She knew he didn't know how to begin. "What's wrong Michael?" She couldn't wait any longer. "What do you want to tell me?"

"I can't see you anymore!" she heard him say, and watched him lower his eyes toward the ground.

His words sounded *So Final!* Her body trembled, and her chest tightened as she tried to hold back the tears, the tears she did not want him to see.

She looked past him at trees waving frantically, at people walking in the wind, at the grey sky suspended at the horizons, at holiday lights adorning skyscrapers a mile away on Central Avenue. She didn't say anything.

He placed his arm around her, and she laid her head against his chest. She no longer felt the wind heaving itself at them. Soft sobs escaped her lips as she began to cry aloud, even though she didn't want to.

It became dark. After a while she raised her head and looked away. Her eyes scanned across the canal at trees and bushes bending aggressively in the howling wind as if they were fighting for their lives to stay rooted as park lamps sprayed their orange glows on them.

She felt the cold now. The wind continued to blow fiercely, and its relentless fit stifled everything else, and she barely heard him say, "I'm sorry! I never wanted to hurt you."

She looked at his face, and he was looking at her. *His beautiful eyes,* she thought. *His soft eyes looking at me. The dim lights from the park lamps, glistening down on the side of his face . . . make him look like a young school boy. And the way he's looking at me tells me that misery is tearing his insides. Oh, God, how I love him!*

She placed her hand on his shoulder as she sat facing him. *His face, so somber, so serious.* She looked away and sighed involuntarily, as if trying to catch her breath after a good cry.

They sat there for a long time, neither saying anything. The wind continued blowing hard. Catherine stared out across the water, where the canal expanded into a small lake where several dozen ducks, highlighted by the lamps, were bobbing on the choppy water. Every now and then one of them would flick its beak into the icy pond.

She finally broke the silence. Her voice barely audible, "I always had that little bit of hope . . . that we would be together some day."

She hesitated for a few seconds, searching for the right words. "But, down deep... I always knew... I always knew..." her voice trailed off as she slowly shook her head, and continued looking out across the park while tears swelled in her eyes again. And then, she felt the cold again as a discordant gust of wind slapped across her face.

I said to her, "I love you, Steele." I was looking at her when she turned toward me.

It was the first time she had ever heard me say it. She looked into my eyes and then slowly looked away. "Yes!" I heard her finally say, and then she hesitated briefly before she told me, matter of fact, as she stared out across the lake, "Yes ... you love me—" Another hesitation, and then she turned towards me again and I felt her eyes searching mine, and she asked, "But ... are you in *love* with me?"

She watched my reaction as I just stared at her. I had been caught off guard by the question. She continued eyeing me, as if demanding an answer, until I looked down, away from her.

After a tormenting march of time that seemed to have abandoned all movement forward while thrusting itself off the edge of the world never to be acknowledged again, I finally mustered the balls to answer her, "I don't know what I feel anymore. It's like my feelings have shut down." I wanted to get the hell out of there.

Her eyes followed me as I rose from the park bench and turned around, facing across the park in the direction behind the bench. I started to say something again, but, then hesitated while I searched for the right damn words.

I could feel her stare frozen to my face. I finally said, "I love Julia ... and I love you, Catherine." I turned and looked at her. "I've had no right to see you the way I have. I knew, I felt it ... that you were in love with me. It made me feel wanted, for the first time in my life."

And then I added, "Except for that first week I met Julia."

I looked away from her and still felt her eyes locked on me, and, without forethought, in a subtle barely noticeable motion, I sadly moved my head from side to side. Then, while still gazing out across the lake, I told her, "Every man longs to be wanted . . . same as a woman. I'm no different."

I paused, searching for words that wouldn't hurt her as much before I continued torturing her . . . and myself, "I don't know if I'm capable of being in love, with you, or with Julia . . . or with anyone! It's like I'm afraid to feel, afraid to let myself be hurt . . . be controlled by someone else." At that moment, as I said this, I believed it was the truth.

Catherine stood and faced him, "I'm in love with you, Michael," she said solemnly. "I didn't plan it. But, I did allow it to happen. The feeling, the happiness, is not like anything I've ever felt before." The tears—*damn tears*—came again.

At that moment, Catherine couldn't free herself from feeling the wickedness of hopelessness, abandonment and betrayal that, without a doubt, had stamped themselves into her person with a vengeance, and she, for an instant, pondered that only time was capable of fading these godless goods, but then again, only maybe.

After a few agonizing moments of silence, Catherine turned toward the park bench, picked up her purse and looked at him. He wouldn't look at her . . . she knew he couldn't bear to.

She reached her hand to him and lightly brushed his cheek with the tips of her fingers, and softly said, "I have to go. Goodbye, Michael."

She slowly turned and walked away. Her tears could come now . . . and, they flooded her eyes like an ocean tidal wave sweeping unsuspectingly over innocent things.

As she crossed the bridge over the canal, Catherine felt the ice-cold misty spray of the rain against her face. She didn't look back.

74

Somewhere in the Italian Alps...

MARCUS GIULLIANO WAS in his first year as a medical student at the University in Milan. He had no memory of his father, a bricklayer, who had died when he had fallen from a four-story structure because the scaffolding had collapsed. Marcus was just two years old at the time.

Marcus's mother was a baker's assistant. Maria Giulliano had worked hard at raising her son alone. She had always encouraged Marcus and closely watched his progress at the schools he had attended in Milan.

She knew her son had a gift of learning, and she had beamed with pride at his secondary school graduation when the headmaster of his school announced that Marcus had been awarded a scholastic scholarship to the University in Milan.

Even with the scholarship, Marcus barely had enough to get by during his premed training. He had never, in his entire life, seen a thousand American dollars in cash.

He tried not to mind the freezing February wind that propelled the surging snowflakes across the windshield of the worn truck as it strained, struggling to finish its last climb up through the frozen mountain passes and begin its descent down into the less cold valleys.

It was two-thirty in the morning. The road was passable... just barely. The swirling snowflakes continued to fall across the vehicle's path as its tires grabbed at the slick frozen snow that was now up to two- or three-inches high on the pavement... the pavement that Marcus could barely make out through the windshield.

His hands, packed with tension, tightly gripped the steering wheel as if they were welded to it. He felt sweat trickling down his forehead... even on such a freezing night.

The twenty-year-old Marcus would soon have his pockets full, full of the American cash, just for driving this truck through the mountains.

Only fifteen more hours, he thought, smiling to himself. *Just as soon as I mail these crates of olives in Milan, I will be a rich man . . . at least for a day or two,* he smiled to himself.

First, I will buy Mama the shawl that she has always wanted. Then, I will take Pauletta to that grand restaurant in Milan, which neither she nor I have ever even seen the inside.

Sixteen hours passed. Marcus still felt the cold, but he was glad to be in Milan. It was not as cold there. As soon as he had taken care of his duties with the shipment, he had telephoned his mama to let her know he had arrived safely.

She had made him promise to tell her when he had gotten there because she would worry about him driving through the winter mountains. He would be home in an hour or so, he had told her.

Marcus waited, as he had been instructed, in the truck along the dirt road just several miles outside the city. He thought about the shipment of crates, and their destinations.

Someday, I will go to Bonn . . . to London, England . . . to Paris. I will take Mama and Pauletta. And children . . . Pauletta and I will have children, and we will take them. And we will also go to Baltimore in Maryland, in the United States.

Yes, we will go to those places, just like the olives.

He saw the dust trailing the motorcar a half mile away. He smiled as he watched the black automobile come closer.

He thought, *How lucky I was to be near the villa that day. I had just gone for a walk. The foreigner had touched my shoulder, and had asked me if I could drive a truck. Of course! I had said. He had asked if I could drive the truck through the Alps. Of course I could do that! How lucky I was!*

Marcus climbed from the filthy truck as the motorcar pulled to the side of the road in front of him.

"Do you have the receipts that verify the crates have been shipped?" the middle-aged Arab asked as he and another Arab, about the same age, approached Marcus. The man spoke in Italian with a Middle Eastern accent.

"Yes! Of course! Here they are, sir." Marcus handed the shipping receipts to the man. "I was told, sir, that you would pay me the money."

"Yes, of course. It is there in my motorcar. But, first I need to get something from the truck . . . Come!" Shaman Zodaru said to Marcus.

As Marcus followed Zodaru toward the rear of the truck, the second man followed closely behind.

But, before they reached the rear of the truck, the nine-millimeter piece of lead entered cleanly through the back of the young student's head.

75

March . . . Tuesday, 8:22 P.M.

"HE IS OF no further use to us," Hector Baldarrama told Jesse, who sat in the plush captain's seat across the table from Baldarrama in the leased private jet as the pilot prepared to land at L.A. International.

"But, Jefe—"

Baldarrama cut in sharply, not letting his bodyguard finish, "I want him taken care of before we get back to Scottsdale on Thursday."

"But, Hector! He's a cop . . . a Phoenix cop!" Jesse did not agree with his boss. "Maybe, you should discuss it with Orasco before we—"

Again, Baldarrama cut the man off as the drug chieftain slammed his fist down on the table in front of them. "I don't give a shit if he's the *fucking* king of England! He's getting greedy. I want his ass done, NOW! UNDERSTAND?"

Baldarrama's bodyguard let out a sigh and said, "Okay, Jefe. I'll have Doogan take care of it."

As Hector glared at his henchman, his deliberations instantly vaporized as he was startled by the lights appearing all of a sudden outside the window next to him as the luxury jet suddenly swooped down from the thick clouds that hung low over LAX and grasped hard the tarmac within a split second afterward. It frightened him for a moment as he realized how low to the ground the cloud cover was. And then, as an afterthought, he told his *peone,* "There is no need to mention any of this to Orasco. Understand?"

"Si, Jefe! I understand," Jessie reluctantly answered his *full of shit* boss.

As the jet taxied toward the private hangars, Hector thought about Nancina Por Tero . . . *she's somewhere in this Goddamned fucking city. Who the fuck does she think, she is? Just leave me whenever she wants? . . . Fuck her! I've been through this before. Nobody tells me to fuck off! . . . Nobody!*

* * *

"Por favor!" she pleaded in Spanish, "Don't hit me again." Gloria Baldarrama lay on the bed trying to hide her face behind her folded-up legs as she held her arms up in front of herself, trying to block her husband's vicious blows.

"You goddamn whore!" Hector yelled as he slammed his opened hand against the side of her head. "Every fucking time we go out, you are making eyes at someone . . . you fucking bitch!"

Then he began punching his fists at her as she tried to shield herself. Her face had already taken two hard blows. She knew he had broken her nose again.

"Don't you ever embarrass me like that again? Do you fucking hear me? . . . Do you?" he yelled as he stood over her.

"I wasn't doing anything, Hector!" Gloria half screamed, "I just thanked the waiter for picking up my coat and—"

"You were fucking coming on to the bastard!" Hector yelled as he raised his hand as if he were going to strike her again. "If you ever do that again, I'll fucking kill you . . . Do you hear me? . . . Do you fucking hear me?"

"Yes!" Gloria cried, "Yes! I hear you."

After he had stormed from the room, Gloria strained to sit up, still sobbing. The pain from her battered face and head had finally registered in her brain. She brought her hand slowly to *her mouth, and, with her finger tips, gently touched the swelling which she knew was there. She moaned.*

"This is the last time that bastard will ever do this to me," she told herself as she climbed to her feet. "I must get away from this madman! He'll come to me tomorrow and tell me, again, how sorry he was, and that he'll never do it again."

Gloria thought about the past year, married to Hector Baldarrama. *He had beaten her badly, before. At least a dozen times, she thought.* Twice, Jaime and Jesse had to take me to the hospital. This is the last time . . . I'm leaving that sonofabitch.

She groaned as she raised herself from the bed and hobbled into the bathroom, feeling the sharp pains, even in her legs, from Baldarrama's blows. She looked in the mirror and delicately touched the cuts on her face with the cool wet wash towel. She sobbed to herself as she thought, I can't call the police . . . he'll kill me for sure. I have to sneak away when he's gone.

The heart surgeon finally appeared from behind the emergency operating-room double doors, each with a small window about eye level in height. He walked hurriedly toward Hector Baldarrama who stood in the hallway by the door that lead into the waiting room.

The doctor had a grave look on his face as he approached Baldarrama. When the doctor finally reached the anxiously awaiting husband, he said, in a quiet and sympathetic tone, "I'm sorry, Mr. Baldarrama! There was nothing we could do. There was extreme trauma in the heart area. We tried everything we could. Whenever someone has had a massive heart attack such as your wife, there's really not much that can be done. I'm very sorry!"

Hector Baldarrama quickly passed through the hospital doors with a somber look. He climbed into the limousine and the door closed behind him.

After Jesse and Jaime had climbed into the driver's and passenger's seats, respectively, and closed their doors, Hector laughed loudly and said to his bodyguards, "Let's go get some pussy!" *He laughed out loud again as the hospital disappeared from view.*

76

Wednesday, 8:15 A.M.

VINCENT EDGARS GLANCED over at Henry Sotello, who sat at his desk filling out some kind of report. Edgars thought to himself that Sotello had seemed edgy lately . . . like something big was going down. Edgars tried not to be too obvious as he kept watching his acting boss.

He thought to himself, *With Stan Dodd out of town for a few weeks, and Sotello the acting Agent in Charge, why hasn't Sotello told me anything?*

"Hey, Sotello!" one of the other DEA agents yelled across four rolls of desks, "line three."

"Okay! Just a second!" Sotello answered back. He continued writing.

Edgars saw his chance. He picked up the phone and tried to sound like the muffled voice of Sotello, "Hello!"

He immediately heard a startled voice on the other line. "Uh, this is *Gaman!*"

Edgars quickly responded as if surprised, "Oh, hold it, pal! I got the wrong line. Who'd you want?"

"Henry Sotello!" the voice from the phone stammered, obviously unnerved.

"Hey, Sotello! It's for you!" Edgars yelled at Sotello.

"Okay I've got it!" Sotello picked up the phone, "Hello, Sotello!"

Edgars listened, but didn't dare look at Sotello, and pretended to be filling out some paperwork.

Henry didn't speak momentarily, and Edgars felt his stare. Edgars kept writing and didn't look up. He knew this was not an ordinary contact on the other end of the phone.

"Its okay, he's one of our agents," Sotello finally said into the receiver as he anxiously blinked his eyes.

* * *

8:40 A.M.

"This is Vince Edgars! I need to talk to Señor Orasco right now!" He stood at a phone booth outside a Circle K convenience market on West McDowell Road.

"This is Orasco. What is happening?" They spoke in English.

"It may be nothing, Señor Orasco," Edgars' voice was urgent. "Then, again, it may be important. I tried to get a hold of Baldarrama, but he's outta town. So, I thought I should talk to you."

"Well, what is it you wish to tell me?" Orasco did not like Edgars. He thought the man had no integrity, no sense of honor. And, he did not trust the informant. But, he would use the DEA agent a while longer.

Orasco continued listening as Edgars spoke, "I overheard one of our agents on the telephone. The person identified himself as Gaman. I don't know if that means anything to you, Señor Orasco. But I—"

The drug lord continued to hear Edgars' voice over the phone, but Rodrigo Lara Orasco was no longer listening. He felt the hair on his neck rise as everything around him prompted itself to an abrupt halt and he felt like he could only move in slow motion. Even the sound of the waves from the Mediterranean seemed to have closed their roar.

He remembered Julia telling him . . . "Gaman Shinasai."

"GAMAN!" Orasco shrieked as he lost all composure.

Edgars wasn't sure what was happening on the other end of the line. Frightened, he continued to hold the receiver to his ear. He just listened.

Avilla came running into the living room with his semi-automatic drawn and ready to fire. He had heard Orasco's agonizing scream.

Once Avilla saw that Orasco was all right, Avilla stopped in his tracks, lowered his weapon and stood staring at his boss.

Orasco remained speechless as he stood there slowly shaking his head in disbelief, his mouth tight as he rubbed his lips together. He looked at Avilla, but stared right through him, and continued to clutch the cell phone in his hand which now hung down at his side. Rodrigo Lara Orasco was ready to explode.

After time had delivered itself unrecognizable for an unknown and disturbing spell for the three men, Orasco finally sat down in the nearest chair and put the telephone to his ear. He spoke quietly, and calmly, into the receiver, "I will send someone to meet you within a few hours. They will take care of Gaman."

He closed the cellular and turned toward Avilla and said to him, in Spanish, "I want Antonio and Zalo to be in Phoenix, Arizona . . . TODAY!"

6:40 P.M.

Ralph Doogan didn't want to have to waste the cop's wife too. But, as Doogan sat in the stolen Chevy Camaro in the upper-middle-class neighborhood, he thought to himself that he'd have to wait until it got dark and go in and take them both out. *Whatever! It doesn't matter one way or the other to me.*

He thought about the two and a half hours he had already been waiting. *Since the guy had been in the damn police station all day, there was no way I could take his ass out.* "Fuck it!" He said out loud. "Whatever's meant to be, is meant to be!" He was getting anxious.

The cool wind began to chill him as he rolled up the window of the Camaro and reached down to touch the bundle inside his pants. Doogan was not going to let the two thousand dollars in hundreds burn a hole in his pocket.

He had plans. *Friday, I'm gonna take Cheryl to see the horses run at Turf Paradise and show her the time of her life.* He thought about how he had just met her at *Mr. Lucky's*—a night club out on Grand Avenue—two weeks ago. Good piece of ass, and not bad lookin', he congratulated himself.

As he watched the house on the corner and thought about the money, he mumbled to himself, "Now, I just hafta earn it."

It wasn't five minutes later when Doogan sat up straight, staring at the person getting into the car. He said to himself in a low whisper, "Holy Shit! My man is movin'!"

He started his engine and moved forward slowly and dared not let the white late-model Pontiac out of his sight as he followed it along Thunderbird Road remaining comfortably back with a few cars between them.

After a mile or so, the Pontiac turned into Moon Valley Country Club Estates with Doogan following half a block behind. The setting sun had already vanished behind Moon Mountain, which formed the west boundary of the luxurious neighborhood.

As the two cars, Doogan's a block behind, turned onto a narrow lane, Doogan excitedly proclaimed, "Now's my chance!" And, he quickly tried to close the distance between them.

But, all of a sudden, the Pontiac slowed and then pulled to the side of the lane by a single tennis court and stopped. There was another car already parked there and two men in tennis clothes stood next to it.

Doogan slowed down and drove by without looking at the men. He thought to himself, *Shit! I'll wait until it gets dark.*

* * *

An hour and a half had passed while Doogan sat in the shadows of his car, watching, about thirty yards away from the tennis court.

Shit, man, he thought, *it's time to go to work.* He reached across to the passenger side and grabbed the Springfield M1A rifle and opened the car door. He smelled orange blossoms as he climbed out.

His legs felt stiff after being confined to his car for so long, so he looked down at the ground and bent his knees to stretch. That's when he heard them.

He barely had time to look up before their automatic assault rifles unleashed across his chest slamming him back against the Camaro.

His rifle clattered to the pavement, and Ralph Doogan didn't even have time to comprehend what was happening as his lifeless form slumped to the lane.

He never saw the two men quickly turn and begin spraying their automatics at the tennis players as the two men raced toward the tennis court.

Present Day

77

Thursday, 1:40 A.M.

AS I HEAD EAST on Interstate 10, I keep seeing the haunting image in my office mirror staring back at me, and I'm unable to wrestle myself from the thought of Walter Barron and Ted Mills, lying on the tennis court, not moving... and Jack Hopkins ... all of them, lying there in their own blood.

I killed them... I'm the reason they're dead. This tormenting force rages across my deliberations with unrelenting absurdness that refuses to curtail in any manner of compassion its judgment of me, only to condemn me in the most damning conviction. *Only five hours ago I caused the death of five men.*

I keep smelling the death of the two men I killed. *Jesus! They tried to kill me!* The frightening thought sinks in, *They tried to kill "me"! I had no choice... I "had" to do it. God!... What have I done?*

At first, I think about staying on the I-10 and heading down to Tucson, but, for some unknown reason, decide right when I get to the Superstition Freeway Junction in Tempe to swerve the Porsche onto the off-ramp and head east toward Mesa. *I've got to get away for a while, need time to think.* I frantically massage the back of my neck.

The sports car roars east on the Superstition, doing barely sixty-five... the speed limit.

I head towards Apache Junction, which will then take me to Miami and Globe, two small copper mining towns up in the mountains. The two towns are nestled side by side about ninety-five miles east of Phoenix.

I'm not a stranger to the Globe-Miami area. Julia's from Miami.

It takes an hour and twenty minutes to reach Live Oak Street, a *so-called* highway, and the only main drag in Miami. The windows and top of the Porsche are closed now because the night wind has turned cold, especially up here where it can be ten to twenty degrees cooler than down in the valley.

I enter Miami city limits and glance to my left, a block away, and see the roof and steeple of Our Lady of the Blessed Sacrament Catholic Church where Julia and I once professed to one another our undying love, loyalty and devotion.

Seeing the church now, stirs up recalls of our wedding reception in the hall across the street from the church. *It was the most miserable day of my life.*

It seemed like the whole town of Miami had come . . . out of respect for Julia's father, Agapito Contreras, a staunch Democrat and union leader.

Even though he had not finished elementary school, Agapito was as smart as anyone I ever met. My father-in-law knew the cut of people, inside and out.

He felt deeply about equality. He believed that some men had obvious social and financial, even physical, advantages over others. That was each man's lot in life. But that was okay with Agapito Contreras. That was the way things were . . . as long as a man was fair with the next man, and treated that man as an equal.

I miss him now as I recall that he was never intimidated by anyone, no matter what that person's social status. Agapito could converse with the same confidence and ease with someone such as the president of the United states, as well as with a man or woman who could be labeled at the lowest wring of the social ladder. Agapito never felt that he was better than the next man, nor less.

If my father-in-law had any shortcomings, in my view, it was the fact that he always claimed to vote the straight Democratic ticket. He always joked, with a twinkle in his eye, to anyone who would listen, that a dumb crooked Democrat was still better than a capable honest Republican. There were many humorous discussions between me, myself a Democrat, and my father-in-law about that fable.

I miss the Spanish lessons from Agapito and miss our conversations about life that often continued late into early mornings. I was fortunate to have learned fluent Spanish from the elderly man as a result of those vigorous training sessions.

He was a constant tease . . . to both Julia and me. He reinforced my already cultivated ability to laugh at myself. Now, I wish with all my might that Agapito Contreras was still here. *He would know what to do.*

I hardly knew anyone, and wondered if Julia knew even half the people attending our wedding. I can still visualize her now, in the wedding dress that she insisted I buy her. *Took every dime I had . . . that, and her wedding rings.*

I never, not once, noticed Julia looking at me at all during that whole afternoon. I did recall her acknowledging me when we cut the wedding cake. *Other than that,* I reminisce as my sports car moves slowly through the east end of Miami, *it was like we were in two different places that day.*

I pull into a Whiting Gas Station between Globe and Miami where I refuel the Porsche. I'm trying to avoid thinking in detail about what happened the night before in the valley, but its trepidations won't consent to allow comfort to bare itself in any welcomed fashion and the scenes keep hammering my thoughts. *Jesus! All those dead bodies . . . my friends' bodies!*

Ten or twelve minutes later, I begin heading back through Miami toward the valley and glance at the car's digital clock . . . three ten in the morning.

As I near the western city limits of Miami, now traveling the speed limit of twenty-five miles per hour, I notice a local police car sitting quietly in an empty parking area where a Dairy Queen once stood along Live Oak. Otherwise, the dying town and vacant highway are quiet and deserted. And, as I suffer a stream of fear crawling up the back of my neck, I wonder if anyone is following me.

After having been gone from Miami for about five or six minutes, the Porsche climbs up the dark mountain road toward the summit known as "Top of The World" that accommodates in a hit-and-miss fashion an assortment of cabins and mobile homes scattered on both sides of the highway along a half mile or so of a straight stretch of the winding highway near the top of the mountain range about halfway between Miami and Superior, another small mining town that I had to pass through to get to Miami from the valley.

As I roar up the highway I can't help but attach my gaze momentarily on the WORMS FOR SALE sign with the slovenly written black lettering on a white background that is boldly posted at the curve entering the tiny community.

It reminds me of my wedding night and the drive to Phoenix. Both Julia and I should have been overwhelmed with joyous excitement and anticipation . . . eager to get to our apartment in Phoenix.

Before our wedding day, other than making out and a little feel once in a while, I never made love to Julia, *all the way*. And neither of us had ever ventured that far with anyone else before.

I remember how broke we were . . . no money for a honeymoon. I recall that I had my right arm around her as I drove through the mountains with one hand . . . and that she had felt like a stranger. The energy I felt in the car that night told me she felt the same.

Forty-five minutes pass, and the lights of the oncoming car bring me back to the present as I merge onto the Superstition Freeway at Apache junction. I begin to feel more tension; I know it's because I'm returning to the valley . . . and I don't want to. I can feel the knots in my stomach tighten even more.

I begin laboring over and over in my mind how I might have slipped up. I recall that one of the assassins called me *Gaman*. I imagine to myself, *Someone at the DEA betrayed me . . . or someone in Washington. Who can I trust?*

I know, though I don't want to admit it . . . she's *the only one*.

78

4:35 A.M.

AFTER LISTENING TO endless ringing in the phone's receiver, I finally hear the connection, and Catherine Steele's sheepish voice answers, "Hello."

It startles me at first. It's been more than two months since I last saw her walking away from me at Encanto Park... someone whom I had been accustomed to talking to almost every day for the past year.

Finally, after searching for words that have without discerned logic sequestered themselves from my mind as if on a rebellious vacation away from my brain, and maybe intending to criticize my selfish action and warning me to hang up the phone, I finally manage to speak into the receiver, "This is Michael."

I listen for her reaction, but there's nothing. And then I tell her, "I'm in trouble... I need your help."

I try to imagine what she's thinking at that moment and visualize her lying there, her eyes narrowing and she's probably thinking about the bullshit I told her the last time we were together, there in the park. While I listen to the silence, I question myself, *Why in hell would she want to help me?*

Her voice sounds foreign to me now as I hear her ask, "What's wrong?" I sense that her sentiment approaches a detachment that suggests only a subconscious reaction to politeness.

I feel anxious, defeated, and finally tell her, pleading, "I don't know where else to go!"

"What do you want me to do?" she asks coldly.

All at once I feel damned with no where to turn. And I know now that I should never have called her.

My eyes search out from the telephone booth on Van Buren Avenue near downtown Phoenix, and I can think of absolutely nothing that I, at that moment, have any right to ask her to do.

After affirming that thought to myself, I finally say in a defeated tone, and honestly mean it, "I think I made a mistake calling you, I'm sorry . . . I have to go!" My voice becomes quiet, calmer, as I tell her, "Look, I'm sorry! I'm truly sorry—."

"No! Wait, Michael!" she interrupts, her voice loud. Then, softer, "Please, Michael . . . let me help you!"

I take a deep breath and slowly exhale. I recall what the marriage counselor told me when I described to her the depression that had consumed me after I had stopped seeing Catherine. *"You are in a stage of mourning, Michael. Someone who was a very important part of your life is no longer a part of it. When you feel that you will never see that person again, it's like that person has died. The feeling of loss will eventually pass. It will take time."*

Now, I need Catherine. But, I don't want to hurt her again. I listen to her voice over the phone, quietly pleading, "Please, Michael, don't be afraid of me. I love you . . . I know I can't be with you, I know that! Please, let me help you, nothing more . . . just let me be the friend who wants to help you."

I manage to say, guilt creeping in, "I can't come there, it's too dangerous. Can you meet me at the park?"

"I'll be there in half an hour."

Except for North Mountain, Encanto Park, with its lush green landscaping, has always been my favorite place in the valley for quiet purpose. It lies a mile or so west of Central Avenue where the midtown commercial high rises tower in the distance. One of the older parks in Phoenix, it begins along the east side of Fifteenth Avenue about three blocks south of Thomas Road where it borders a public golf course of the same name. The park continues south along Fifteenth until ending a few blocks north of McDowell Road. It is actually located only about four miles from downtown Phoenix.

The park is about two or three blocks wide, and is bordered on the south and east by the Palmaire District that embodies older homes built sixty to seventy years ago. Yuppies began taking over the district about twenty-five years ago, rebuilding and remodeling the area with upper-class homes.

The early morning air chills me as I sit on top of a concrete picnic table watching Catherine about fifty yards away, walking impetuously along one of the cement paths that wind throughout the deserted park.

As she approaches I notice she's wearing a dark sweatshirt and faded jeans, and looks like she just stepped out of Vogue Magazine, even at five o'clock in the morning. As I study her coming toward me, I wonder what she'll think when I tell her everything. I don't want to put her in any danger, and tell myself not to get her mixed up in this mess . . . but, I can't be persuaded. I feel my heart pounding faster and faster the closer she comes, and my mind is too weak and constrains me like a prisoner to remain . . . waiting for someone to take away my pain.

Her reaction tells me my appearance shocks her when she's just a few feet away as she yells out, "My God! What happened to you?"

And then, all at once, I feel like my whole body is collapsing as all my strength seems to renounce me, and I'm unable to control myself as I slide off the table and reach out to her.

I cling to her and can't help wishing she was Julia, and feel like an asshole even thinking that. And then, I feel Catherine's warmth, her softness close to me, clutching me, and that takes away any thoughts of Julia.

Then, something, foreign and from a distance I cannot touch, overpowers me, and I can no longer hold back. I attempt, and fail, to suppress a sobbing breath that escapes my lips. Like a dam bursting I feel the torrent gushing through me, and for the first time in almost a lifetime I am able to allow the long forgotten feeling to overwhelm me . . . not just from fear or thoughts of my friends lying in death, but from all the year's of emptiness that I have borne without the warmth of tenderness, without the true intimacy I somehow knew existed but had never experienced . . . until the past few months with Julia.

And now I stand there with Catherine Steele and savor her strength as she holds onto me while my head lies on her shoulder. I feel her arms encircle me, trying to shield me from the pain, from every pain I have ever felt . . . every pain that has desecrated my soul, buried deep inside, unable to release itself in any sort . . . until now.

And, for the first time in my life, I weep uncontrollably... without shame. And cry out in my sorrow, "Hue! Hue!... Hue ..."

79

8:05 A.M.

"LIEUTENANT MANUCCI, I'm Guy Hernandez," the CPA says as he enters the reception area and extends his hand. "I'm Mr. Everest's associate. Please, come back to my office." Manucci admires the CPA's long-sleeve light-blue Polo shirt and cranberry-red tie along with the dark-blue dress slacks, no coat, and Detective Joseph Manucci feels like a homeless person in comparison.

Joseph settles into an expensive leather visitor's chair in Hernandez's exceptionally large and luxurious office with its walls beautifully paneled in cherry wood.

There are three visitors' chairs in all. Joseph continues his admiration mode as he studies a large brown leather sofa positioned against the wall to the right and a glass enclosed bookcase running all the way to the ceiling against the wall behind him.

Completing the arrangement is a credenza that matches Guy Hernandez's large desk also made of cherry wood, and positioned about four feet behind the CPA's leather executive chair.

Manucci notices, to his left, through four French doors centered along the wall, a landscaped area of luscious winter-green grass that slopes down to a generous-size manmade lake. He admires several paintings, diplomas, memberships and professional licenses, all expensively framed and tastefully adorning the walls.

Manucci hears Hernandez ask as he watches the CPA settle into the luxurious chair, "What can I do for you, Lieutenant?"

The CPA clasps his hands together in his lap and leans back in his chair and Manucci feels the CPA's dark brown eyes scrutinizing him.

"Some police officers were gunned down last night while they were playing tennis," Manucci tells him. "We believe Michael Everest was with them at the time, and we're trying to locate him."

Joseph stares at Hernandez and watches the CPA shift in his chair and then lean forward placing his forearms on the desk before answering, "Michael left a message that he's been called out of town for a few days. He travels a lot. Are you sure he was there?"

Manucci sits back and crosses his right leg over his left, his arms resting on the chair's heavily padded sidearms. "We're quite certain he was there. I need to know where he is now."

"The truth is, Lieutenant, we don't know. Michael was supposed to be here this morning to review a client's tax projection with me. It's quite important. Normally, if he has to leave town unexpectedly, he'll call me at home. He's very conscientious about his clients."

"Are you involved with all of Mr. Everest's clients?"

"Yes," Hernandez answers then hesitates for a second . . . "except for one. Michael spends most of his time on that client's work. He's required to travel for them now and then."

"Can you give me the name of the client?"

As he sits across from Detective Manucci, Guy Hernandez recalls when, just over two years ago, he was hired by Michael, paying Guy five times as much as he earned before at a large national firm. He now feels that he and Michael have become very good friends. And equally important, he feels they trust each other. "I'm sorry, Lieutenant, I also want to know where Michael is. But, that's information I'm not permitted to give you."

Guy cringes to himself like any other certified public accountants worth their salt would do if they were to hear that disjointed and stabbing diction just pronounced by the detective, "I can get a subpoena."

"If you'll do that, I'll show you whatever you wish." Guy then rises from his chair and tells the detective, "If Michael's in trouble I want to help. But, professional ethics won't allow me to discuss clients without a court order."

80

JULIA EVEREST SLEPT only a few hours. She spent the night on the living room sofa, and the sun, coursing through the half-open wooden shutters on the picture window overlooking the front lawn, woke her an hour ago. Then she took a hot shower and slipped on some Philadelphia Eagles warmups that brought back memories of her father watching football on T.V. and following his adopted team.

Once, she reminisces, he actually saw a live professional football game in Philadelphia where he had attended a national convention for his union. He fell in love with the victorious Eagles that day and remained faithful until the day he passed away.

Now Julia sits at the breakfast table in the kitchen's eating area overlooking the pool and meticulously manicured landscaping in the rear yard. Piestewa Peak, a half mile away, towers upward into the Carolina-blue sky.

She glances at the blue-and-white porcelain clock on the wall as she steeps the *Brown & Ashley Tea Co.* "Morning Mist" gourmet tea in her cup. It's half past eight.

Still no word from Michael. She wonders if she should call the detective to see if he's heard from her husband.

At that instant, the phone rings.

"Julia, anything new?" It's Tess.

"No, nothing yet! I'll call you as soon as I know more," Julia assures her best friend.

"Do you want me to come over?"

"No, Tess. I'll call you as soon as I know something."

As Julia hangs up the phone, she hears chimes from the front doorbell.

"Mrs. Everest?" one of the two men asks.

"Yes." Julia doesn't recognize either man. Both are tall and heavyset, both wearing short-sleeve sports shirts that hang out over their khaki pants.

The morning air, somewhat cool, is breezy, and sweeps across her face, causing a few strands of hair to trickle down along her high cheek bones.

"Your husband's been hurt and we're supposed to take you to him right away." The man speaking has thick hair, Julia notices. *Coal-black . . . it doesn't look natural*, she critiques to herself.

She glances at the gold jewelry necklace hanging loosely around his neck that disappears inside his loose-fitting shirt. She judges that he's in his late forties or early fifties, trying to look younger. The other man appears to be in his late twenties.

"Where is he? Is he all right?" she anxiously questions, and swallows hard as she tries to take no notice of the lump in her throat that tells her Michael is not all right.

"We were just told to take you to him, Mrs. Everest," the same man replies.

"All right, I'll follow you in my car. Let me get my purse."

"We're supposed to take you in *our* car," the younger man finally speaks, sounding impatient.

The older man interrupts, and touches the arm of the younger one as if telling him to back off. Then, the older man says, "Mrs. Everest, we have to hurry. Your husband is hurt bad. We don't have time to waste. Please come with us now."

Julia feels the hairs on her neck rise. It crosses her mind now. *They haven't identified themselves as police officers.* She tells them, "I'll come with you, but I need to drive my own car."

"FUCK!" The young man has run out of patience. "Just grab her ass and let's get the fuck outta here," he orders.

Julia tries to close the front door, but the older man slams his arms against it and the door flies open, knocking her off balance. Before she can recover, both men grab her, and she feels a sting in her upper arm while she wrestles with the two intruders. After a few seconds, she feels woozy, stops resisting and collapses unconscious.

She doesn't hear the older man speak as they carry her limp body to their car.

"The plane's at the Scottsdale Airport."

81

"IT'S TIME TO go . . . it's almost nine o'clock," I whisper into Catherine's ear as I brush hair from her face. We fell asleep about two and a half hours ago inside her Buick Regal, which is now parked outside her apartment complex.

She stirs, and raises her head from my shoulder. I can see that the brilliant sunlight presses her to squint, and, after a moment adjusting her eyes and pressing a slight smile, she looks at me sitting in the passenger side front seat next to her.

She says nothing and reaches her hand up and touches the back of my neck, then gently squeezes with her hand, and climbs out of the car.

As we agreed, Catherine will rent a car for the day and I will use hers. After leaving the park earlier that morning I stashed the Porsche in St. Joseph Hospital and Medical Center's five-story parking garage. The hospital's only a half mile or so from Encanto Park, and I thought that, because people come and go all night long, my car along with doctors' luxury cars won't draw attention and no one will think to search there.

When Catherine walks into her office reception area in the Central Trust Towers, the entire staff is mingling and, with a definite aura of excitement charging the air, is discussing the shootings and massacre from the night before. The clock on the wall reads nine fifty-five.

On one of the desks nearby, Catherine notices *The Arizona Republic* headline: "POSSIBLE CONSPIRACY." She goes directly to her office and dials Henry Sotello's number.

A courteous female voice answers, "Drug Enforcement Administration, may I help you?"

Catherine follows Michael's instructions, "May I speak with Henry Sotello?" Catherine's afraid her voice sounds shaky, and she can't stop trembling.

The polite lady on the other end of the line replies, "Agent Sotello is out of the office at the moment. Would you like to speak to another agent?"

"Can you tell me when you expect him back?" Catherine sounds defeated as she asks.

"He'll be back today, ma'am, but I'm not sure when. Would you like to leave a message?"

"No! . . . No, I'm . . . I'm not at a number where I can be reached. I'll call later. Thank you." She remembers that Michael warned her not to speak with anyone but Henry Sotello.

After hanging up the phone, Catherine realizes how frightened she is . . . for Michael. *I have to help him.* She thinks about everything he told her earlier that morning . . . Baldarrama, Orasco, Moon Valley. *Nothing can happen to him.*

82

AS SOON AS I left Catherine I called the administration offices at Arizona State University West, and was told that Julia had not shown up for her two morning classes.

It's now ten fifteen when I enter the back door of my house, and I'm scared shitless to the nth degree. I expected that they'd be watching the front, so I parked Catherine's car up on a mountain road several streets away with a clear view of the front and back of the house.

While I was slipping across the stretch of desert leading down to my enclosed backyard, two jackrabbits skipped across my path ten or twelve yards in front of me, and I was reminded, *The world goes on!*

Where's Julia? I wonder in a furor that has deepened its penetration into my thoughts as I search the house, carefully avoiding the windows. There's no sign of her, so I look in the garage and discover her car there . . . and panic.

"Where are you, Julia? Where the hell are you?" I complain aloud.

As hopelessness intensifies itself with no apology or repentance, I grab a pair of binoculars from a shelf in the garage and dash out the back door, and then hustle across the desert up to the waiting car as fast as my legs will propel me while thinking every second that I'm going to be riddled with bullets.

The sun is blazing hot now as I climb into the car. But, even so, I decide I have to wait for a while. I *have* to find out where Julia is.

83

IT TAKES JOSEPH Manucci more than three hours to get the subpoena for Everest's office. It's already ten after eleven when he pulls into a Jack-in-the-Box on Central Avenue just south of Osborn Road.

"Coffee, please," he tells the microphone. "Not the same as talking to *Jack*," Manucci complains aloud to himself. "Why'd they ever get rid of the *Jack in the Box?" Everybody runs out of time, even Jack . . . even Joseph Manucci.*

As he waits . . . suddenly, without warning, he sees the image of the dead student's face from the dry Salt River bed the previous night. He wishes he was working only *that* case. *I'm going to catch those fuckers. You can bet money on it,* he vows to himself and smacks his lips together.

Well, Jack's made a comeback, he reasons to himself as he accepts the Styrofoam cup of steaming hot coffee handed to him through the drive-thru window and dismisses, for the time being, the image of the dead girl. *So can Joseph Manucci.*

He maneuvers the grey sedan into traffic on Central, carefully takes a sip of the coffee and heads north towards Camelback Road. As he approaches Indian School Road, he speculates to himself, *Wonder what I'd be doing now if I had taught school.*

Always wanted to teach high school... clean life, summers off... long vacations. I'm running out of time. He thinks about Assistant Chief Walter Barron. *Six months from now, no one will remember.*

Manucci turns right on Camelback and heads east towards Scottsdale. The traffic seems heavier than usual at this time of day.

A few minutes later his portable phone buzzes. "This is Manucci," he responds.

"Joseph, this is Robb. Just got word that Jack Hopkins came out of his coma. He can't have visitors, but he'll pull through."

Manucci lets out a sigh of relief and quietly says, "Thanks, Robb. I'll stop and see him later. Any word on Ted Mills?"

"Naw! He hasn't come out of it yet. I guess it's still touch and go. Everybody's pretty much shook up over all this."

"Okay, I'll keep in touch," Manucci says as he works his way into the traffic flow on the Piestewa Freeway. It takes him another ten or twelve minutes to get to Everest's office up near Shea Boulevard and Scottsdale Road in north Scottsdale.

As he walks in past the heavy doors, Joseph is greeted cordially by Hazel. "Hi!" she says as she stands up from her desk. "I'll tell Guy you're here."

Manucci likes Hazel. She reminds him of his mother when his mother was in her fifties... *nice looking, neat dresser, good taste, doesn't dress old fashion.*

He has to wait until Hernandez finishes with a phone call. When Manucci was there earlier that morning, other than appreciating Guy Hernandez's office, Joseph didn't have time to really notice the rest of the suite. But now, as he peruses the reception area and regards the expensive-looking wood paneling, he concludes, *These two accountants are doing very well. They must have some very wealthy clients.*

84

12:08 P.M.

I'VE WAITED IN the hot sun for more than two and a half hours, alternating between the inside and outside of Catherine's car. *Still no sign of Julia . . . or anyone else,* I remind myself. At the moment I wish I'd brought some bottled water from the house. My mouth is dry and I can feel the sunburn symptoms on my face. I curse myself because I didn't have enough sense to at least bring a ball cap with me.

Another ten minutes pass, and I decide to try to get hold of Catherine. *I've "got" to talk to Sotello,* I can't help thinking and agonizing to myself.

Still afraid to use my cellular, I call Catherine's office from a pay phone in front of a grocery store on Glendale Avenue.

"I've tried his office three times, Michael," she tells me. "He hasn't been in. What are you going to do?"

"Keep trying!" I instruct her in as calm a voice as I can summon. "I'll call you in a couple of hours." I pause before telling her goodbye, "Thanks, Steele. I'm sorry I've gotten you involved. As soon as you contact Sotello, I don't want you to do anything else. I'll let you know when everything's okay."

"Be careful, Michael."

After Joseph Manucci leaves Michael Everest's associate, he drives directly to northeast Scottsdale. He found the address from the client's files in Everest's office. His watch reads almost one thiry as he slowly drives by the front of Hector Baldarrama's estate.

This place has "got" to be worth a few megabucks, Joseph speculates. *And I'll bet it's drug money.*

He turns his car around at the next intersection and heads back by to take another look. A half block before he gets there he sees someone come out the front door of the mansion that sets back forty or fifty yards from the street.

Manucci pulls over to the side of the road in front of the neighboring house, grabs his binoculars from the back seat and focuses them out through the windshield of his sedan. He gets a good look at the man's face before the man climbs into the car parked in the circular drive.

Manucci knows he's seen the man before, and not too long ago, but he can't remember where.

He watches the car pull onto the street, and quickly slips the binoculars out of sight down below the window, and then, nabs the license plate number through the binoculars after the car passes a half block away. Joseph waits a few minutes after the car has gone, and then heads for John C. Lincoln Hospital.

When Manucci arrives, he sees two uniformed Phoenix police officers outside the individually partitioned section of the intensive care unit where Jack Hopkins' bed is located. The officers tell Manucci that Hopkins still can't have visitors other than his wife who left ten or fifteen minutes ago. So, Joseph decides to head to his downtown office.

85

CATHERINE STEELE HAS tried to reach Henry Sotello two more times. It's now two fifty in the afternoon. Sotello still isn't in. It's been more than an hour since she last called.

A male voice answers this time, "Drug Enforcement!"

Catherine is momentarily thrown off guard because it's not the same lady who has answered the phone for Catherine's previous calls. "I was wondering if Mr. Sotello has come in, yet?"

"Yes, ma'am, but he had to leave," the voice answers. "Would you like to leave a message?"

Catherine doesn't know what to do. *I should have left a message before, and he would have called me by now.* She's becoming more frantic. Michael told her that she had to reach Sotello.

She hesitates, then remembers again Michael telling her not to talk to anyone but Sotello. *But, Michael needs help, NOW!* She agonizes.

She *has* to do something, she reasons, and speaks into the phone, "Will you tell Mr. Sotello that I'm calling for Gaman." She spelled it for him . . . "G-A-M-A-N. I need to speak with Mr. Sotello as soon as possible. I'll call back in an hour."

"Yes, ma'am, I'll see that he gets the message," Agent Vince Edgars politely assures her.

An hour later, Catherine calls again, and the female voice tells her that Henry Sotello is still out. Catherine wonders where Michael is as she hangs up the phone. *What should I do?*

She frantically pulls open one of the bottom drawers of her desk and snatches up the business telephone directory for the metro Phoenix area.

She flips through the listings, searching for an address. Once she finds it, she recognizes where it is, downtown.

"I'm leaving, Kellie! I'll check in on my voice mail for messages," Catherine says as she skirts past the receptionist.

Once in her car, it only takes her ten minutes to reach the Drug Enforcement Administration's downtown office. It's now ten minutes past four.

A man enters the hallway from a private office about forty feet away from the reception area, and walks toward Catherine. No one is at the receptionist desk. "Can I help you?" he asks.

"Yes," she says softly, her voice unsteady. "I'd like to see Henry Sotello, please." Catherine's knees are shaking so hard now she consciously feels that her legs are going to waterloo.

"He's not in now. I'm Agent Edgars. I work with him. Can I help you?" The agent is courteous.

"No . . . thank you. I'll wait for him."

"I don't believe he'll be back today," the agent tells her. "If you'll leave your name and phone number, I'll see that he gets the message to call you."

Catherine hesitates, then tells the polite agent, "All right . . . My name is Catherine Steele, and my number is 602-555-9000, extension 346. If Agent Sotello can't reach me there, he can leave a message and I'll call him back."

86

JOSEPH MANUCCI SIPS stale coffee as he sits at his desk and reviews the notes he took during his meeting with Everest's associate, Guy Hernandez. He checks his watch, it's four fifteen.

When Joseph was at Everest's office, he looked through the CPA's personal calendars for the past three years, and wrote down dates and listed trips that Everest had taken.

It looks to Manucci like Everest made five trips to Europe during the past year and a half, and two of those times he went to Spain. All the trips also included visits to Switzerland, Germany, France and Belgium.

As he scans his notes, it occurs to him how odd it seems that Guy Hernandez works with Everest on all of the CPA firm's clients except for this *one* client with the huge home in Scottsdale.

Manucci wonders, *Mr. Everest, are you helping this guy launder drug money? Are you the one they were after last night? If so,* he questions, *Why? Why do they want you dead?*

Joseph picks up his phone as he convinces himself, *It's time to pick you up, Mr. Everest, wherever you are.*

After a few minutes of getting out an "All Points Bulletin" on Michael Everest, Manucci hangs up the phone and leans back in his hard steno chair. Gazing up at the ceiling, he concludes to himself, *I need to know more about you, too, Mr. Baldarrama.*

87

VINCENT EDGARS JOTS down the information that Catherine Steele gives him, and tells her he'll leave it on Agent Sotello's desk.

After she leaves the DEA office, Edgars shoves the piece of paper in his pocket, and trails her out the door. He watches her climb into a red Toyota Corolla, and then races to his Maxima, around the corner.

He's too late. By the time Edgars swings his car onto First Avenue, there's no sign of her. He decides to circle around Monroe and Adams Streets, but has no luck spotting her. He tries Van Buren and Central Avenue, all the way up to Roosevelt . . . *still no sign of her.*

Fifteen minutes later, Agent Edgars is speaking on a pay phone at First Avenue and Polk. "Yes, Mr. Baldarrama, it's the local IRS office, it's just a recording. Her name's Catherine Steele. She's a looker, too." Edgars thinks to himself, *There'll be a big bonus for this.*

"Gaman is dead," Hector Baldarrama reminds Edgars. "But, he may have told her something. Find out exactly who she is. Find out from *this* Sotello what she knows. I need to know by noon tomorrow. I'm leaving for Spain now, so I will call *you.*

Hector Baldarrama disconnects his cellular phone and pulls his Mercedes into Scottsdale Municipal Airport. Even though he has medicated himself on vodka gimlets, he's still in a shaded state of shock because of the phone call he received earlier that morning from Rodrigo Lara Orasco.

Baldarrama still recalls, vividly, the conversation, and what he felt when he heard Orasco tell him that Michael Everest was a rat for the DEA . . . code name *Gaman.*

That fucking Everest. I trusted that bastard . . . the prick was my friend, Baldarrama reflects as he staggers aboard Orasco's private jet.

Hector has already had eight vodka gimlets within the past hour and a half, and it took all of the concentration he could rally just to get his Mercedes to the airport without being arrested.

After his eyes adjust to the dim lighting in the aircraft's cabin, Hector smiles as he gazes down at his sleeping guest. Julia Everest has been on board since early morning.

Baldarrama chuckles as he recalls Orasco's voice from their phone conversation earlier that day, *"We need to find out how much Julia Everest knows. See that she's not harmed. I'll deal with her."*

Hector relaxes in the plush seat and sips another vodka gimlet as the aircraft prepares to leave. "Fuck you, Everest, I hope you're in hell," he chants to himself and awards himself another taste of the gimlet. He wickedly smiles as he thinks about Jaime and Jesse finishing up the job he started an hour earlier. *Just a little fringe benefit for their service and loyalty.*

88

Sonoran Desert, Arizona . . .

THE RAGING JULY heat from the scorching sun bore down on the small band of travelers. They were young men and young women, fourteen in all.

One by one, they slumped to the ground, finding little relief from the thin layer of shade patterned by the sparse numbers of palo verde trees and mesquite brush. It was early afternoon.

Their leader was referred to as "Coyote." The travelers, or their families, had each already paid him seven hundred American dollars to lead them to the land of plenty.

Until now, they had only dreamed about it . . . never believing it would be possible to go to the rich United States of America. A place where everyone had jobs. A place where everyone had good food to eat . . . enough food to eat. Friends and relatives, who had already realized the dream, had written them about it, or by word of mouth, had praised this land with the promise of a new life, a better life.

Now, the travelers wondered if it had been nothing more than a worthless dream. Would they live to see it?

Coyote was more fortunate than they. He had hidden extra water in his belongings, but could not show it to the others or else he too might die.

He observed them as he reclined against a palo verde that barely shaded him. His group would have been picked up the night before if the clouds had not hidden the moon and he had not drank so much tequila.

While the unbearable heat persisted in slowing the passage of time, Coyote watched as two men pulled up the dress of one of the young girls who lay next to a large mesquite bush. She was barely alive because of exposure and dehydration. Coyote, his eyes squinting from the desert sands reflecting the sun's rays, watched the two men, in their early twenties.

They knew they would soon die. They would not do so without pleasure one last time.

He watched as they raped the young girl. She barely made a sound . . . she was dead before the second one had finished with her.

Coyote watched . . . and became aroused.

He looked around, scanning the twenty to thirty yard square area where the travelers had dispiritedly tried to shelter themselves. His eyes searched for the one he had been watching. "She is beautiful . . . aristocratic," he hopelessly told himself.

He knew she had not looked at him twice. If she had, he knew it was only to gaze at his pockmarked face and crooked nose that was far too large for his small face, the same face his mother had despised.

He remembered . . . it was nine years ago . . . he was ten years old.

* * *

"You ugly little bastard," she said as she smashed the back of her hand across his face. "I told you not to come back here until you had enough.

"Twenty-three dineros are not enough," she screamed at him. She was already drunk. It was four thirty in the afternoon.

The blow sent the boy flying backwards, crushing the flimsy-built wooden chair woven together from mesquite.

"Now, look what you've done, you little worm!" she screamed even louder, and rushed toward him.

The boy rolled away for protection. But, there was no where to go. He felt her kicks battering his back and legs as he cradled himself into a ball, his hands and arms covering his face and head, trying to shield himself from the blows.

This was just one of the hundreds of beatings his whore mother had given him. But this was the last of them. He had had enough. He ran away that night. And he never saw the slut bitch again.

* * *

Now, as he ran his tongue across his lips, he saw the young girl. She had collapsed with her back leaning against a palo verde tree with barely enough shade to partially veil her from the sun.

Coyote slowly moved to her ... he felt light-headed. He whispered to her as he fell to his knees beside her. "Señorita, be brave. Soon, you will be in Tucson."

The listless, half-closed eyes of the teenaged girl rotated slowly toward Coyote. She did not raise her head from the tree supporting her. She was unable to speak ... her tongue had swelled and she could barely breathe.

Half delirious, her pleading eyes gazed at him. Coyote looked around ... he began to tremble all over and his mouth became even dryer. He and the dying girl were alone.

"Mi señorita bonita, I will help you. Do not be afraid," he whispered. "I have moistness for you ... It will make you feel better."

His whole body shook as he eagerly lowered his trousers, exposing himself. Then the Coyote pushed himself to her as she sat motionless.

Her mouth barely opened, and Hector Baldarrama shuddered uncontrollably as he found release ... and smashed the huge rock he held into the side of her head. "Bitch"!

89

Washington, D.C. . . . Thursday, 11:35 P.M.

EVEN THOUGH THE double doors remain open, she knocks before entering her husband's study.

She can see him easily from the doorway, sitting in his favorite chair staring out through the frost-covered huge bay window into the cold darkness, catching a glimpse of a distant flashing of light now and then from an occasional automobile passing on the treacherous icy road that courses below at the bottom of the hill.

The flames in the fireplace have long expired. His hands lay in his lap and his shoulders slump. He still wears his dark-grey business suit trousers and his snow-white dress shirt after having removed his coat and tie earlier in the evening along with his black wingtips. He doesn't respond to his wife, and remains motionless, making no attempt to acknowledge her as she enters.

Mary Graves is wearing a yellow robe and bedroom slippers. For the past hour she has been patiently waiting for him to come to bed. She knows this room is his refuge from the daily pressures of being one of the most powerful senators in Washington. This is where he escapes for contemplating difficult decisions. This is his Camp David.

Mary quietly walks over to him, sits down at his feet on the thick carpet and lays her head in his lap. He doesn't acknowledge her. She doesn't speak. She knows he will eventually talk to her.

After a few minutes, the senator lays his left hand on his wife's head and lightly brushes her hair and quietly tells her, "I've had a lot of calls to make over the years." He pauses briefly, and then continues. "I believe this one is the toughest."

Alan Graves knows his study is free from any electronic bugs. He personally checks the room almost daily. The last time was shortly after he arrived home earlier in the evening.

He's glad he spent three years in "SPECIAL OPS" before retiring from the Air Force. He was just an aid and gopher to one of the section commanders during his tour there. But he was able to learn quite a bit about electronic surveillance.

The senator doesn't speak again for several minutes. He continues, lovingly, caressing Mary's head while he stares out at the black night that has imposed for now its dominant self on the landscape.

Finally he sits up straight, and, with a huge sigh, says to his wife of twenty-eight years, "I've never asked you . . . never thought I would ever have to ask you, to be involved with my work or run any errands for me. But, I need your help now, Hon."

Mary Graves doesn't move. She waits for her husband to continue.

After a brief pause, as he reflects on what he is about to tell her, he says, "I'm being blackmailed. I'm being forced to help these madmen do something terrible."

Mary sits up, turns her head and looks up at him as shivers run down her neck with no intention of freeing themselves from her discord until they have satisfied themselves that their acknowledgment has forged its mark.

90

Scottsdale . . . 11:10 P.M.

AFTER A LONG and grueling conference with a Superior Court Judge, Joseph Manucci and a deputy county attorney are still not able to get a search warrant for Hector Baldarrama's house.

So, Manucci has no choice but to explore Baldarrama's domain in a more discreet manner. After much soul searching, taking all of almost half a micro-second, he decides that he has no choice but to go in alone.

The beautifully manicured lawn and shrubs of the estate are a welcome sight, he decides, when compared to the more common Arizona desert landscaping used for most homes with that much acreage.

In Manucci's humble assessment, the outside night lights definitely enhance the entire setting even more. He is quite impressed. When he drove by earlier that afternoon it wasn't possible to see the artistic effect in the sunlight.

As he struggles up and over the rear block fence he concludes, facetiously, to himself, I can be happy here, just living outside the main house, under a palm tree.

Immediately, he discovers there's a guesthouse that sits isolated at the back side of the large swimming pool which is some thirty yards away from the main house. As he studies it, he mumbles, dejectedly, to himself, "The guest house is *bigger* than *my* house." He also notices there's a light on inside.

Being careful to avoid stepping into any lighted areas, Manucci cautiously remains in the shadows and alertly maneuvers his way toward one of the lighted windows.

When he takes his first glance through the window, he freezes . . .

On the edge of one of two king-size beds, positioned on opposite walls, sits an Hispanic man, stark naked with his huge belly sagging down and his elbows resting on his knees. He holds a half-empty whiskey bottle in one hand, from which he takes a hurried swig, causing most of the bottle's contents to dribble down his chin onto the reddish-brown Mexican tile floor.

The man is huffing and puffing, as if he has just finished doing fifty pushups. Manucci easily concludes that the man is quite drunk.

Then, Manucci sees, sprawled across the other bed, a nude woman, glistening with sweat, arms tied to the bedposts with some kind of leather straps.

Another large and nude Hispanic man is mounted on top of her, panting hard. The woman—very young, Manucci judges—seems to be unconscious.

Through the closed window, he can hear the grunting and panting coming from the man. He senses that the man is having, or about to have, an orgasm.

And then, Joseph Manucci is stunned at what he sees. He can't order his body to move quickly enough as he watches the grunting man, lying on top of the woman, raise a pistol and point it to the side of her forehead and fire it, splattering blood and brain across the bed and splashing all across the wall.

"NOOOO!" Manucci screams. Desperately, he smashes the window with his .38 revolver and reels off a barrage of bullets at the killer. All three rounds rip into the man. One enters between the nose and mouth, one through the front of the lower neck and one rips through Jesse's cheek bone, just below his left eye.

The first man on the other bed has little time to do anything, other than to glance at the dead man on the woman, and then at the broken window. By the time the drunken man is able to steady himself enough to pull himself up on his feet, three more discharges from Manucci's .38 tear into his chest. Jaime staggers back and collapses backwards onto the bed.

Manucci slumps to the ground with his back against the building. He's oblivious to the blood oozing from the back of his hand that was cut when he smashed the window with his revolver. The cool night air prickles the sweat on his face as he breathes heavily with his head resting against the wall of the guest house.

Joseph just sits there, not moving. He waits for his eyes to clear from sweat, and tears that have swelled unnoticed . . . not only for what he has just witnessed, but also for years of frustration from sights his job has demanded that he see and become a part of.

But, even with all the gruesome crime scenes he's witnessed during his thirty-one years in the department, he finds what just happened unbelievable.

After a while, seething with anger, he opens his eyes. All he can think about are Baldarrama and Everest. *Where are those bastards? I'm going to find them, and I'm going to hang them by their balls until they rot.*

He slouches there for another four or five minutes before calling for backup on his portable phone. Then he struggles to his feet and slowly heads over to the main house.

It's empty. There's no sign of Baldarrama or Everest, or anyone else. Manucci hears sirens.

91

Phoenix . . . 11:55 P.M.

THE COOL BREEZE washes over me, and I find myself saliently welcoming its refreshing carriage as I peer out from the butte. There's no sign of Henry Sotello.

I wonder to myself where Julia is. *They must have her.* I shake my head as numerous thoughts bound through my brain like powerful freight trains racing side by side toward unforeseen perils, and the thoughts hurdle themselves like perpetual motion, not able to stop or even slow down while accomplishing nothing more than only confounding me. *Where would they take her?*

And my sanity distresses over Catherine. I have no desire to have her part of this nightmare any longer, and dejectedly admit to myself that I can't call her again.

For a brief moment, I allow myself one final critique of the valley lights and begin climbing down the mountain. Feeling a total sense of defeat, I decide to put off trying to reach Henry until morning.

The ashen full moon seems exceptionally bright in the cloudless sky as it lights up the whole mountain for my stride down one of the familiar trails.

When I reach Catherine's car, I recognize for the first time that I ache all over. I feel like I've been strung up and whipped by a lynch mob and left for the flies, and remind myself that I haven't slept since I woke up early yesterday morning . . . Wednesday, except when I cat-napped a few hours in Catherine's car earlier this morning. A hot shower also seems real appetizing to me right now.

Once in the car, I head south on Seventh Street toward the freeway to search for any small motel out on I-10, west of Phoenix.

92

Washington, D.C. . . . Friday 9:05 A.M.

THE BARBARIC LATE-WINTER wind lashes its bitter attitude across her exposed face as she closes the front door and walks briskly to the car. The threatening clouds pack the dark sky as winter refuses to abdicate its waning power over the land. "It looks like more snow," she predicts as she pulls her coat collar up higher around her neck.

It's freezing cold and there's no sun to offer relief as mother nature strikes her fury all along the east coast from northern Florida all the way to Maine. Right now, Mary Graves doesn't care about Florida or Maine. Her concern is to get to Dulles International Airport as quickly as possible.

She curses under her breath. The ice on the vehicle's windshield reminds her that she forgot to put her Suburban in the garage the night before. She knows she'll have to wait awhile as she turns on the heater and defroster.

While she shivers inside the car, she can't purge herself from the hurt and despondent sense of failure and hopelessness, thinking about what her husband told her the night before. She recalls the tears streaming down her face. Her chest felt like someone crushed it with a sledgehammer, and she remembers crying over and over, "NO! NO! NO!"

Her husband purposely spared her most of the details. She'll be forever grateful to him for that. She can still see him sitting in the chair refusing to look at her as he tried carefully to choose his words, to soften the blows of the horrible acts about which he was forced to tell her.

The poor man, his heart broken, she thinks to herself, having to keep this to himself all these months . . . to protect me.

She recalls her husband's words, *"When I visited Rodrigo Lara Orasco in Spain a year ago this past December, I was shown a video of our son having sex with a very young boy . . . couldn't have been more than eleven or twelve years old."*

Mary can still see the pain in Alan's eyes as he told her, "*Orasco said he will reveal this to the press if I don't do what he wants.*"

The frost finally melts away enough for her windshield wipers to clear her view, and so she backs out of the driveway and heads for Dulles. She asks herself as she glances into the rear view mirror, "How many of you bastards are following me?"

As she drives slowly on the snow-packed street, the memories return.

* * *

She saw the horrors of war. She was a surgical nurse in Vietnam. She still remembers the agonizing screams, the pleading for help, the amputations, the endless cries of pain . . . and worse yet, the silence of death.

She remembers finding refuge in storage closets, crouching down in a corner, in the darkness, with brooms, mops and rancid buckets of decaying mop water . . . and crying.

She truly wanted to help the soldiers, but their helpless eyes were too much for her. Everything overwhelmed her. She felt like a weakling, not strong like the others.

The explosions began all around them, until one hit directly in the operating room, obliterating the medical barracks.

Mary's friends, eight very young nurses—six women and two men—were blown apart along with five young and extraordinary surgeons—two men and three women.

Mary was hiding in her space. It saved her life, and she escaped with only a few scrapes. But, mentally, she was devastated. She was alive, and her friends were gone . . . forever. They were gone because they were trying to help, and Mary was alive because she was hiding.

She helped prepare her friends, what was left of them, for their last trip home. Mary went home too, to a hospital that tried to repair her mind. That's where she met Alan Keith Graves.

He was recuperating from injuries suffered while jumping from his third downed jet fighter over the South China Sea. The last jump cost Alan the loss of his right leg from the middle of his thigh down.

Alan's incredibly optimistic demeanor overwhelmed Mary, and helped her begin to face her demons. His love rescued her.

It took many years for her to no longer need the pills that helped her sleep to escape the images of the helpless and hopeless eyes of her dying comrades. But, nurtured and deeply loved by an extraordinary man, Mary persevered.

* * *

She hasn't forgotten. She has hardened to it . . . but she will never forget.

And now, this! *How can my son, my baby . . . do these hideous things. Evil men made him do it!* She reasons . . . she prays.

Forty minutes later at Dulles International, just west of Washington, she boards Northern Airways Flight 242 to Boston. Mary whispers to the young lady as Mary discreetly places the envelope into the hands of the stewardess who is greeting passengers as they board. "Give this to the captain right away. It's an emergency."

The startled young woman looks dubiously at Mary and quickly turns and moves toward the cockpit, thinking to herself, *Oh, God, we're being hijacked!*

The captain immediately tears open the envelope. It was written by Senator Alan Graves.

93

Phoenix . . . 8:06 A.M.

AGENT VINCENT EDGARS approaches the desk of Henry Sotello where Sotello stands removing his coat . . . Sotello just came in.

Edgars tells Sotello, "A woman was here to see you yesterday afternoon. She called quite a few times . . . said something about calling for someone named Gaman, something or other. The message is on your desk. Anything I can do?"

Sotello absentmindedly picks up the message, then remembers that Edgars asked him a question. "Uh . . . no . . . uh," Sotello reads the message as he addresses Edgars. "I'll call her and see what the hell she's talking about."

Sotello waits a few minutes at his desk and shuffles a few papers, trying to give the impression that the message isn't that big a deal. After three or four minutes, he goes into Stan Cobb's empty office and sits down at the desk.

Busying himself at his own desk, Agent Edgars's eyes discreetly observe Sotello.

Henry dials the number and listens as the receptionist politely answers at the other end. "Internal Revenue Service, Appeals, may I help you?"

"May I speak to Catherine Steele, please?"

Five seconds later Sotello hears Catherine's voice, "This is Catherine Steele!"

"Ms. Steele, this is Agent Sotello from the Drug Enforcement Administration."

"Thank God! I've been trying to reach you since yesterday. Gaman—"

Sotello cuts her off, "I can't talk, now. Can we meet somewhere? Where's your office? . . . Okay! I'll be there in thirty minutes. Don't talk to anyone else."

* * *

Langley Air Force Base, Virginia 10:20 A.M.

"Yes sir! Captain. Please hold while I try to locate Mr. Turner."

Before the Marine Sergeant first-class can put the caller on hold, the Northern Airways Flight 242 Captain's voice is heard in the receiver. "Again, Sergeant, I must remind you . . . I am unable to speak with anyone other than the National Security Advisor. And, again, I must remind you that . . . he must be on a secure line."

* * *

Phoenix ... 8:55 A.M.

He waits out of sight, and has a clear view of the lobby. *Sooner or later she'll come out of one of the elevators, alone or with Sotello,* Edgars tells himself.

After waiting about twenty minutes, he watches the gorgeous lady exit the elevator, with Sotello. Edgars knows he has to act fast.

Sotello's car is on the second level of the garage. They rush off the elevator near his car, and Henry opens the passenger-side door for Catherine and hurries around to the driver's side.

As Henry opens the car door, Edgars rushes up from behind him. "AGENT SOTELLO!" Edgars yells.

Startled, Sotello spins around, and three silent bursts from Edgars' 9mm semiautomatic explode into Sotello's unbuttoned suit coat.

Henry Sotello makes no sound . . . his legs collapse and he drops like dead weight to the pavement as if the executioner opened the trapdoor.

Catherine isn't sure what is happening as Edgars slides into the driver's seat and starts the engine. He excitedly tells her, "Ms. Steele, that man was about to betray Gaman. We've got to get out of here!" Edgars still grips his pistol in his right hand.

As the car speeds down the garage ramp, the excited Edgars loudly tells Catherine, "You may not believe me now, but you'll soon know I'm telling the truth."

Catherine is too frightened to say anything, it all happened so fast. The only thing she can think of is, *Where are we going?*

94

Aboard Northern Airlines Flight 242 . . . somewhere over the coast of New Jersey 10:40 A.M.

MARY GRAVES opens the small folded piece of paper that the stewardess discreetly slipped to her while serving Mary a beverage.

Mary gingerly glances around as she quietly unfolds the note. She reads the following handwritten message . . .

WARREN TURNER SAYS A TAXI WILL BE
WAITING IN THE DEPARTURE AREA IN
BOSTON. YOU WILL BE TOLD WHICH ONE.
YOU WILL BE TAKEN TO TURNER. NO ONE
WILL FOLLOW.

The note is signed: CAPTAIN DICK BLOEMER. Below the captain's name, the note finishes with: GOOD LUCK!

Arnold Drury doesn't like chasing some old bag around, especially early in the morning. But, for now, he has become accustomed to Mary Graves making him rise early.

Drury has been following the senator's wife for the past three weeks. He can tell what day it is, whether it's morning, afternoon or night, just by where he is, watching her. He's getting bored. But he was told just yesterday that it will be for only a few more days.

Now, she's changed her schedule, and she almost gave him the slip. Drury didn't think he was going to make the plane in time. It was overbooked.

He thinks about the young woman whom he approached, to see if she would sell him her boarding pass. An extra two hundred bucks did the trick, that and his fake police badge. *I'm definitely gonna' get reimbursed for this,* he tells himself. *That bitch wasn't even gonna' let me have her ticket until I showed her my shield. What a cunt!*

He glances towards Mary Graves, four rows in front of him, and feels the jolt of the aircraft preparing for its descent.

* * *

Boston . . . 12:35 P.M.

Mary Graves follows the porter through the doors leading out from the terminal at Logan International. As soon as she steps outside, Mary instinctively bears up against the freezing wind and huge gusting snowflakes kissing her eyelids intent on demanding her fortitude and resignation.

The porter walks directly to a taxi sitting at the curb and quickly places her bags into the open trunk. After Mary hurriedly climbs into the warm back seat, the taxi quickly dashes away from the curb.

They proceed several blocks when she hears a loud noise behind them. Her reflexes take over and she jerks her head around, and views through the snowstorm, about a block behind on the snow-packed street, the rest of the collisions as three or four cars collide with a bus that now blocks all traffic from getting through.

No one will follow.

"It's good to see you, Mary," Warren Turner remarks as he embraces the senator's wife.

"You too, Warren," Mary warmly greets him. Mary thinks highly of the National Security Advisor to the president. She often envisions *him* as president someday.

"Come, we can talk inside where it's warm," Turner says, and lightly takes her arm as she cautiously advances up the recently shoveled concrete walkway that is still slippery from snowflakes now rapidly packing the ground.

Mary presumes this well-hidden farmhouse is more than it appears. Bone bare trees spaced tightly together are still capable of concealing the huge private residence from the road more than two hundred yards away. Everything is overlaid with ten to fifteen inches of snow that continues to stream down.

After glancing at her watch, she knows it took twenty-five minutes for her to get to this place from Logan.

She relaxes some, knowing she's safe for now and that no unknown persons are watching her every move. One of the National Security Advisor's aides politely takes her overcoat in which she placed her gloves and earmuffs.

"Please bring some hot tea for Mrs. Graves," Warren Turner instructs the aid. "Here, Mary, please!" Warren gestures toward the end of a sofa.

He pulls a small chair up close and, once seated, leans toward her and rests his forearms on his thighs. The relaxed gesture makes Mary feel much more comfortable with where she is, and she is grateful to Warren Turner for that kindly act. She feels warmth from a fire blazing in a large red brick fireplace just seven or eight feet away.

Mary recalls what her husband told her and how to present it to Warren Turner. *I'm safe now. Everything's going to be all right.* She looks into the man's gentle eyes and begins.

95

Peoria, Arizona 10:50 A.M.

HE UNLOCKS THE door and steps aside for Catherine Steele to enter the tiny apartment in this fast-growing city that borders on a part of Glendale and northwest Phoenix.

Catherine is still frightened, but she's regained some of her composure. She flinches when the man abruptly grabs her arm and handcuffs her to a white wooden railing that separates the kitchen from the tiny eating area. All she can think about is that he's going to murder her. But, after a few minutes, she isn't so tense, and decides that he wouldn't have handcuffed her if he intends to kill her, at least for now.

She wonders where Michael is, and thinks about Henry Sotello, lying there as they drove away. *Is he dead?*

* * *

I don't want to call Henry Sotello's office at all. But, I can't reach Catherine. I called her at twenty minutes to ten and she wasn't in. I tried again at eleven o'clock. Still, no sign of her.

It's now noon, and uninvited anxieties pervade my world while I interrogate myself with no mercy as to why I ever got into this mess. I dial her office again. This time I decide to ask more than just to speak with her. "Can you tell me if she left with anyone?"

"Yes," Kellie replies, "she left with a gentleman a little before nine thirty this morning." The receptionist gives me a description of the man.

It's Sotello . . . I dial Henry's office.

The female voice answers, "Drug Enforcement Administration. May I help you?"

"May I speak with Henry Sotello, please?"

A pause . . . "Who is calling, please?"

Alarms go off. Heated flashes begin reeling through my head as I sense something wrong. They've never asked that before! After unplanned silence and hesitation I finally answer the lady, "I'm working on a case with Agent Sotello."

Her voice cracks, "Agent Sotello was killed this morning."

It had to have been a semitruck that smashed into me, because I cannot even comprehend where I am at this moment of time in my life. Then I realize I'm holding a pay phone . . . away from my ear, and I know for sure that at any moment my brain is going to explode. Numbness takes possession of my senses everywhere else, and everything around me looms like it's now nothing more than frozen matter. I finally hear the receptionist's voice calling to me in the receiver, "Sir . . . Sir! Did you hear me . . . Sir?"

Softly, I answer . . . "Yes . . ."

Calm, resolved, I ask about Catherine. "Can you tell me . . . was anyone else with him?"

"No, sir! No one was with him."

"Thank you . . . I'm very sorry," I say quietly into the receiver, then hang up.

"They've got Catherine!" I vent out loud, almost shouting.

96

IN THE APARTMENT with Catherine Steele, Vince Edgars picks up the phone on the first ring, "Hello!"

He hears a voice in Spanish, "This is Baldarrama, what news do you have?" Hector Baldarrama is gazing out at the Mediterranean Sea from Rodrigo Orasco's villa in Spain, and sipping coffee in the hope of removing the hangover from hell that he foolishly engendered the previous day.

Edgars answers in Spanish, "I have some bad news, Jefe." He nervously, and promptly, continues speaking into the phone so his boss won't have time to yell, "It's Jaime and Jesse. They're dead, Hector! The cops killed 'em last night at your place. I heard about it in my office this afternoon. It happened too late for the newspapers to pick it up."

Vince listens and waits, but there's no response from the other end. After a few unwelcome moments of cold-steel silence, he tells Baldarrama more bad news, "The cop is still alive. He's at John C. Lincoln."

"FUCK!" He hears Baldarrama's howling voice.

There's more silence for a moment. Vince listens to breathing at the other end, and finally hears Baldarrama's pissed-off voice again, yelling, "YOU GO TO THAT MOTHERFUCKIN' HOSPITAL AND WASTE HIS ASS, NOW!"

"Okay! Hector. I'll take care of it."

"YOU FUCKIN' TAKE CARE OF IT NOW!" Baldarrama screams. Then he says more calmly, "What about the other problem?"

Edgars tells Baldarrama that Henry Sotello's dead and the woman is there with Edgars. He concludes by saying, "She is very beautiful, Jefe!"

"Orasco's jet has returned to Scottsdale," Vince hears Baldarrama say. "It was supposed to pick up Jaime and Jesse. Take the woman there first . . . and, Vince, make sure no one gives her anything to eat or drink until she gets here at the villa. . . . We need to ripen her."

97

Aboard Air Force Boeing 737 . . . somewhere over Maryland 4:10 P.M.

IT'S BEEN MORE than two hours since Warren Turner met with Mary Graves. After their meeting, Turner arranged for the senator's wife to be discreetly dispatched to her son's college dorm by taxi . . . a harmless visit by a mother with her son.

Turner takes the time, now, to dwell on and digest the conversation he had with Mary and what she told him.

* * *

"Someone will contact my husband on Sunday, and will tell Alan where to pick up three packages. The packages will be small enough to fit into his suit pockets without being noticed by anyone.

"Alan has an appointment with the president on Monday morning, and he is to hide one of the packages under the President's sofa in the Oval Office. Alan was told that someone will be watching to make sure he does what they want."

Mary also told Warren, "Later, that morning, Alan is to hide each of the other two packages somewhere in the Senate and House chambers.

"My husband was told that these packages will be detonated simultaneously by someone in Washington. Alan believes that Rodrigo Lara Orasco will authorize the detonation with a signal of some kind. He heard Orasco mention something about 'A New World Order.'

"Alan also believes that this same act of terrorism may be happening simultaneously in some European cities."

Warren advised Mary Graves to tell her husband to do whatever he is instructed. Turner told Mary, *"If Senator Graves refuses to do what they say, they'll find a way to kill him. We don't know who is involved, so there will be no guarantee that we can protect him.*

"They may have a Plan B about which we have no information. At least we know about Plan A. For now, Mary, we have to do what they want."

Turner also told Mary, *"Our best chance is to get the packages and switch them, and put them in a safe place, away . . . far away from our country's leaders."*

* * *

Turner's thoughts are interrupted by the steward, an Air Force Sergeant. "We're approaching Andrews, sir. We'll be landing in ten minutes,"

Turner acknowledges with a nod, and continues his thoughts. It appears to him that the explosions will not be the primary killers. *It must be some kind of poison gas. We have to make the switch before Alan Graves delivers the packages.*

The aircraft touches down at Andrews Air Force Base in a snowstorm, and Turner deliberates about the other countries. *How do we alert them without alarming Orasco? We have to cut off the head. We "have" to find Orasco.*

The worried look on Warren Turner's face betrays his confidence. *Where are you, Michael?*

98

Phoenix . . . 2:25 P.M.

EVEN WITH A STOUT March wind picking up and though I'm wearing dark sunglasses, the glaring sun still bears down with sultry, piercing stings that ploy an unwelcome concert across my unprotected face. No clouds are visible anywhere in the turquoise-blue sky.

I settle in as best I can in Catherine's car, parked several blocks away from Hector Baldarrama's estate. When I first cruised by fifteen minutes earlier, I saw three marked police cars . . . two from Phoenix and one from Scottsdale.

Two other cars were also parked in the circular drive. Probably unmarked cop cars, I'm almost sure. Crazy thoughts clash in my brain like a dozen Rottweilers snarling and tearing each other apart as they sniff death, and I'm not overly impressed with any of these idiotic views. *Have the police found Julia, or Catherine, or both? Are they alive? Where's Baldarrama . . . and his henchmen? What's happened there at Hector's estate?*

I've convinced myself that I need to wait until the police go, before trying to get inside Hector's house. If they hang around too long, then I'll have to come up with some way of getting in, or at least some way of finding out what's happened.

Minutes pass and a wild idea springs into my contriving little mind without any reason that explains with any understanding why it has lodged itself into existence. But, it may work. So I turn the ignition, make a U-turn and head to Biltmore Estates, another disgustingly sinful assemblage of expensive homes in northeast Phoenix that rival the largest and most expensive in the famous Beverly Hills in California.

After a few minutes of cruising through the wealthy area with its polished appearing black paved road that bears no sidewalks on either side, but instead is bordered on both sides by manicured lawns and occasional flower boxes that obviously invite no pedestrians or strangers of any sort, I spot what I'm searching for.

The pickup truck pulls into Hector Baldarrama's circular driveway. The driver glances at his watch, fifteen minutes until four. The sun still hammers its heat in undesired tones with no thought of easing its spirit in any welcoming fashion. The sky, still void of clouds, is now a deep blue that fades to baby blue around the horizons. Only one Phoenix police car remains parked in the driveway.

The pool-cleaner, wearing denim slacks and a white T-shirt displaying black logo on the back, DESERT POOL MAINTENANCE, climbs from the truck and retrieves his personally customized wooden carrying case that holds his pool chemicals and gauges, and enters the side gate carrying his equipment.

He strides toward the pool, which, he estimates, sits back about sixty feet from the main house. There's a guesthouse located about forty feet in back of the pool decking that itself is about fifteen feet wide encircling the entire perimeter of the pool.

The pool has a rectangular shape and has a waterfall splashing down about ten feet off of huge boulders, about midway of the length of the pool on the side opposite the mansion. The pool is twenty-five feet wide and sixty feet long. The pool cleaner knows this for a fact because Hector Baldarrama told him so.

A uniformed police officer stands on a patio in front of the guest house that, the pool cleaner ventures to guess with little effort, is completely encircled by the familiar yellow crime scene tape.

"HOLD IT!" the police officer loudly orders. "WHAT ARE YOU DOING HERE?"

"I'm here to service the pool," I answer in somewhat of a loud tone. "Is anything wrong?" As I ask this, I scan the grounds with my eyes while my head remains facing directly at the man, and I continue moving toward him, walking casually while taking extra long strides that I hope the law enforcement officer doesn't notice.

Looks like there's only one cop, I assure myself, with somewhat convincing spirits and barely a noticeable weight of doubt that the law enforcement man and I are alone on the estate.

"You'll have to leave," the officer tells me. "You'll have to come back another time."

"Yes, sir!" I reply in my most courteous tone. I now stand about six feet from the police officer. "But I need Mr. Baldarrama to sign my service sheet, so I can prove I was here." As I say this, strangely, I don't feel nervous or anxious in the least bit. And the pain at the back of my neck and shoulders has apparently taken leave and perpetrated itself on some other poor soul to harass and declare miserable. *And don't come back, you devilish fool of pain!*

Then, I notice the broken window of the guest house. "Holy shit!" I purposely cry out. "What the hell happened there?"

The officer turns his attention away from me—the pool cleaner—and glances at the broken window, giving me the split second I need. After all that's happened the past two days, my confidence level has peaked as high as the mountains surrounding the valley.

Like a flash, it seems to the officer, but to me, my movements are like slow motion because they've been so fine-tuned with the unwavering tightly bound inner concentration of energy that now consumes me. And I find myself amazed at how my mind feels so well disciplined that it is centered only on what is taking place now . . . being nowhere else.

My left hand, primarily my two middle fingers and thumb, clamps down on top of the wrist and right hand of the officer.

In Aikido this technique is referred to as *Kotegaeshi Undo*, and requires twisting, with little effort on my part, until the police officer instantly drops to the ground, on his knees at first, and then rapidly ends up on his rear end in a sitting position with his back to me. This entire movement takes less than a second.

I, while subconsciously maintaining my Ki—my center of gravity—now stand behind the sitting man while continuing to apply pressure to his wrist.

The police officer, obviously in some discomfort, is unable to move or break the hold without causing more pain to himself, or causing his wrist to break.

Thank God, most of these cops don't continue practicing their self-defense training once they leave the academy, I assure myself with no lack of confidence.

When I was younger, in fact, up until about fifteen years ago, I worked out at several dojos four or five times a week, training in the martial arts that Hue had taught me.

I recall that many local police officers also worked out at the karate dojos. Some were better than others, but most of them were, more or less, beginners, achieving a rank of "Blue Belt" at best, which is at the fourth level of belt rank, and is seven levels below "Black Belt." At that "Blue Belt" level, most of them felt adequate since *that* karate and Ju-Jutsu level exceeded what they learned at the police academy.

However, I discovered that, from taking Aikido classes three times a week over the past six years, many Arizona Highway Patrol officers were quite good at that martial art, many of them rising to a "Black Belt" rank.

Now, after having achieved an Aikido Black Belt rank myself, I am convinced that every police officer in the country should become proficient in Aikido.

"I want to know what happened here!" I demand while applying more pressure on the lawman's wrist.

The officer, on his buttocks, groans as he shifts his weight, trying to ease the pressure. He's barely able to speak as he winces and replies with small grunts in between his words, "Uh . . . last night . . . one of our detectives . . . shot and killed . . . uh . . . two men . . . who uh . . . who raped and killed a woman."

A pause, then he grimaces from the pain and says, "It happened there, in the guesthouse."

I panic and almost lose my grip, "Who was the woman?"

The officer clenches his teeth because of the Aikido hold, and responds while loudly exhaling, "They haven't identified her yet."

"Where did they take her?" I feel like everything in my belly is about to spew all over the manicured walkway.

"The county morgue in Phoenix," the officer answers.

My grip remains firm, and I apply more pressure to remind my captive that I'm still in control as I pepper more questions at him, "Who were the two men who were killed? Where were they killed?"

The officer grunts, "They were employees, here . . . I guess. They were there, in the guesthouse."

Images of Jaime and Jesse are conjured up in my mind, and I calmly quiz my captive again, "Where's Hector Baldarrama?"

I finally release my grip because I now have the police officer's handgun pointed at him. I repeat again in a tone absent any doubt whatsoever of seriousness on my part, "Where's Baldarrama?"

"We don't know. No one else was here."

I scan the grounds and decide on a safe place for the police officer. I handcuff his left hand to the pool's diving board and place one of the patio tables with an umbrella next to him for shade. Then I place the key to the handcuffs, along with the pistol and portable phone, far enough away so that he can't reach them.

Then, with no small measure of caution whatsoever, I search through Baldarrama's house.

I find nothing there that awards me any speculation as to where Julia and Catherine are, and the turmoil fully incarnating itself inside my stomach renders me no solace whatsoever in my wonderment. *Is one of them at the morgue?* I reluctantly ponder, and feel the knots tightening like a vise in my gut. *God, what have I caused?*

After making sure my prisoner's still handcuffed to the diving board, I head directly to Biltmore Estates to return the pickup truck and untie the pool cleaner whom I left, unharmed, in the rear yard of one of the mansions.

I tell the young man Baldarrama's address and instruct him to call 911 and send someone there right away, and check out the back yard.

Then I apologize to him and throw myself into Catherine's Buick Regal and head to the morgue . . . along with a dry mouth and a nauseous stomach that is now firmly camped where my chest lies, reminding me of what I might find there.

99

Scottsdale . . . 5:35 P.M.

JUST A LITTLE while ago, Joseph Manucci spoke with an embarrassed patrol officer who spent almost an hour and a half handcuffed to the springs of a diving board . . . with the officer's own handcuffs.

Now, as Manucci places the portable phone on his car seat and heads down Scottsdale Road, it chimes alive. He grabs it up and recites into the receiver, "This is Manucci!"

"Lieutenant, this is Robb." His voice is quiet, "I have some bad news . . . Mills didn't make it."

Manucci's mouth opens slightly . . . he doesn't say anything. Then his lips tighten and stone cold defeated eyes gaze out through the passenger side window of the Chevy, and moor on the *Praying Monk* near the camel's head on Camelback Mountain about two miles away. It appears like a shadow because the sun, nearing the western horizon, has positioned itself behind the kneeling friar made of rock.

After a while or so, he hears Robb's still quiet voice again over the receiver, "I'm sorry, Joseph . . . I'm really sorry."

"Fuck!" Manucci reacts loudly into the receiver.

Regaining his composure, he calmly says, "I'm going to the hospital . . . I'll call you later . . . Robb."

Manucci disconnects.

"Where the fuck *are* you, Everest, you sonofabitch!" he bellows.

* * *

Vince Edgars watches as Lara Orasco's private jet lifts off from Scottsdale Municipal Airport. He smiles and thinks to himself, *I've given Baldarrama the girl . . . she's the only living link between Baldarrama and Gaman. She is one helluva' good lookin' piece of ass . . . I should've tasted some of that while I had the chance.*

But, on second thought, Vince thinks better of that idea. *Oh, what the shit! It's not worth gettin' my balls cut off. Shit, next week I'm gonna' have so much fuckin' pussy anyway! Now, there's just one more little item to clear up.*

100

6:10 P.M.

THE COUNTY MORGUE attendant strives to be helpful . . . and sympathetic. "Please, Mr. Forsyth, this way." Her voice always seems to her to conciliate those who have come to perform a most difficult task that is but one of the ensuing steps of mourning the death of a loved one. She sincerely respects the remains of all of the deceased who have been placed there.

She was taught that her domain is a sanctuary that guarantees repute seldom granted in dying, for the remains of these luckless mortals.

Her teachers are the medical examiners whose pledge and duty are to respect, uphold and protect the dignity of those given to their care. Though seemingly cold to it all, it may appear to any observer, she knows that most of these teachers and fact finders are quite protective of their charges under this code.

And now, she, the attendant, was just told by Mr. Forsyth that he was notified by the police department that his sister may have been brought here last night or early this morning.

I—Forsyth—explain to the kind lady that my sister was killed in Scottsdale the night before and that a police officer had shot and killed two men who murdered her.

My heart pounds at a rate I cannot imagine being healthful as I trail behind the attendant through metal double doors and onto a sparkling white-tiled floor in a hallway with clean beige walls made of, what appears to be, Sheetrock.

The brightly lit hallway seems to be about about forty feet long, and ends with another set of swinging double doors through which I'm led.

The attendant tells me she knows the one I'm looking for. I imagine her feeling badly because of the pain she knows I must be going through.

As she pulls the sheet away from the face, a shiver bolts through me, transforming into a hot flash and then projecting downward through my entire body as I stare at the young woman with the flaxen face, void of life . . . a stranger to my existence. Shock turns to relief, then a brief sense of guilt and melancholy. I don't consciously comprehend the conflicting feelings at first . . . no one ever does.

It's like a stirring of both joy and sorrow, I've been told. First, for a split second, repairing the heart because the body lying there is not who one expects, and then, secondly, in the same split second, injuring the heart because grief is naturally felt for the person who lies there. It is still a person. And we are still human beings.

Dejected at what I see, but at the same time relieved, I pace out of the morgue and search my muddled mind to consider what I have to do now.

Where would they take Julia and Catherine? Jaime and Jesse spring into my contemplations, and the dead girl lying there in the morgue. *What a terrible waste! How the hell did I let myself get into this unreal, bizarre mess of shit?*

At the moment, I know well that I have to watch my own back and expect at any moment that someone is going to end my life. And, I decide, the police have my description by now and have most likely placed me on a short list of very wanted persons.

I've got to get to Orasco . . . I can't go to the airport. My mind's firing with untold scenarios. *I'll go to California . . . they won't be looking for me there. But, who's going to help me? I have no one.*

Hopelessness and helplessness are neck and neck in stamping themselves into my recognition of the sorry state of my affairs spawning themselves visible as I unlock Catherine's car.

As I drag the door open, I don't notice company walking up the sidewalk toward me until we're about ten feet apart. Then, my face burrows itself into shock after my head turns and I glare at the man's face . . . "You!"

101

Cambridge, Massachusetts . . . 8:30 P.M.

THE WARMTH INSIDE the campus library gives her new resolve as she finally convinces herself that she must see him . . . she cannot leave until she settles this torment.

After leaving the library, Mary Graves toils for several blocks in order to gather her thoughts and decide what she will say.

There's no letup as the unusually late-season snowstorm still pummels the New England landscape.

She can't help but notice that only a few students brave the harshness of winter's final stand and stubborn grasp at prolonging its term as she watches them trudge through the snow that is now three or four inches high on the shadowy walkways and still drifting down in a steady flow amply emboldened by the jarring wind.

She finally reaches the small apartment complex with its rustic New England exterior. It has no second floor.

She feels the trembling in her freezing hands as she knocks. After a few seconds, the door to the apartment opens, and Mary Graves shivers, but not just because of the cold. With different eyes, she intuitively studies him. *He is so handsome,* she can't help thinking.

"Mom! What are you doing here?" Tom Graves stammers with a startled look on his face as he flings open the door.

Mary notices that he's wearing cutoffs and a T-shirt. *Good! . . . It looks to her like he's not on his way out . . . At least, I'm not interrupting anything.* She hasn't been at her son's apartment since the first day he moved in, three years ago.

"I had an errand to run in Boston for your father," she tells him, sounding much too serious, and not looking at her son as she enters the one-bedroom apartment near the university's campus.

"I need to talk to you about something. It's very serious, Tom," she firmly declares as she glances at him, but only for a second, and removes her coat.

"Sure! Let's sit on the couch," she hears him say, with what seems to her a disconcerted voice. She senses that he's uncomfortable because of her presence.

It reminds her of how he was when he came home the Christmas before last. *He only stayed for three days instead of the normal week . . . giving me the excuse of having to finish a term paper that one of his professors had allowed him to resubmit in order to raise his grade one more level.*

Mary felt like something was wrong then. Tom acted strange . . . distant. But she thought at the time that it was because her husband was unable to come home for Christmas, and she thought that Tom was disappointed.

Now, of course, Mary understands why her husband didn't spend Christmas with her and her son. *After what Alan had seen, he couldn't face our son.*

She reminds herself, *Tom didn't come home at all this past Christmas.*

Mary feels the first sprinkling of tears forming in her eyes as her shaky voice begins telling her son the terrible thing she was told by his father.

As she relates to her son what she knows, she maintains her composure quite well, she judges, commending herself. But, then, after she finishes, she begins weeping uncontrollably.

After a moment, or so, Mary gathers her composure again, and sits silently, staring at the bare and cold fireplace that seems to parallel the ache in her heart at that moment. Her hands are in her lap, clinging tightly to the wadded-up pieces of tissues that she has used to wipe her eyes. She can't bear to look at her son. Mary Graves knows now what a broken heart feels like.

And Tom Graves realizes he has caused enormous pain to his mother, and father. How can he forget that night.

* * *

Cambridge, Massachusetts . . . fifteen months ago

Her long dark hair fell across the smooth white skin on her face. She casually stroked strands out of her eyes as she smiled at him. She knew he was the one.

Twice a week, Fridays and Saturdays, for the past three weeks, she had sat at the bar on the same stool. Before that, she had made sure that their eyes had met . . . and she had conveniently passed close to him often enough so that they had spoken "hello's" to one another more than once or twice.

She knew he felt her presence. He's shy, but he will come to me, *she had confidently assured herself.*

And, he had . . .

A week ago he had finally summoned the courage to talk to her. It wasn't as if Tom Graves hadn't dated gorgeous women before. But, this one . . . he had thought to himself . . . was different. He had never seen such dark eyes, and such a small and slender body. Her face, with its small features, had captivated him.

The noise was at a high crescendo, everyone seemed to be shouting at once . . . the spirits quenching their thirsts and giving them their high. The packed room of students, elbow to elbow, celebrating the Thanksgiving weekend, demanded loud voices if one was to be heard.

Tom Graves swallowed down the last drops of his beer and set the glass on the bar. He felt a lightheaded sensation, which seemed a little strange . . . and very frisky, *he heartily thought to himself as he smiled and slid his legs around on the barstool to face her.*

She was the most erotic and mysterious woman Tom Graves had ever met. She had told him she was a secretary for a federal government agency in Boston. He felt lucky that she had chosen him. He knew every male student in the place envied him. Tough shit, assholes!

Now, as she flirted with the tall, blond, and quite shy, medical student, she thought to herself, It's time to enjoy him!

"It's getting late, Tom, let's go!" he heard her say, after she slid off the barstool and placed her purse strap over her shoulder. Then she pushed the hair back from her face and looked at him with such a provocative, sensuous and inviting air that he thought he actually could feel the blood warm within his body.

Tom knew, that he, and for that matter, every other male who could see her, marveled at this petite woman's incredibly-shaped long legs that looked like they belonged to a professional dancer. She wore a short black dress, well above her knees, and black high-heel shoes that glorified her legs even more.

Tom didn't argue. I'd go to hell with you, honey! *he thought to himself as he slid off the bar stool. He tried to steady himself as he headed for the door with her hand pulling his. Her place was only three blocks from the night club.*

"Here, let me make you more comfortable," she purred softly as she unbuttoned his shirt and, with some difficulty, slid his arms out of the long sleeves.

The room was almost pitch black, except for a few dim rays from street lights culling their way through the battered Venetian blinds on the small window.

Tom Graves stood next to the bed. "No! Yes! It's there," he drunkenly decided with a lazy smile about the bed's whereabouts. He was floating in the sky. But, he was sure that the bed was there . . . he just couldn't see it. He couldn't see anything . . . he didn't care.

He felt her unzipping his Calvin Klein jeans and pulling them down to his ankles. He had difficulty keeping himself from falling flat on his face, but . . . he still continued smiling.

He felt her hands on his as she moved them around to his back . . . instructing him that she wanted his hands out of the way. Whatever you say, lady, *he said to himself as he began breathing harder.*

He was helpless as her soft, full lips took his manliness and made love to it . . . until he could hold back no longer. He moaned and shuttered as he finished.

He staggered, smiling to himself. Then he heard her soft voice, seemingly distant, say, "Lie down on the bed."

Tom couldn't see it, but he knew it was just in front of him. He felt like everything was spinning all around him, even though he couldn't see a damn thing. He reached down with his hands, trying to steady himself at the same time, and felt for the bed. He smiled a shit-eating grin and lay down reaching for her.

Too much beer! *he thought.* Man, this whole fuckin' room is spinning!

Then, he felt her small firm buttocks slide next to him as she lay on her side with her back to him.

He reached his hand around her hip and caressed her stomach, and then lowered his hand toward the patch of hair between her legs . . .

* * *

"Mom, listen to me," her son excitedly tells her. Tom Graves laughs, as if he has just discovered a toy under a Christmas tree.

He slides closer to her on the couch and places his hands on hers, and exclaims, "It was a set-up! Don't you see? . . . it was a set-up!"

Then he puts his arm around her shoulders and continues explaining what he, himself, has just discovered, "At the time I didn't understand why? Now, I know! It was to get to Dad!"

Confused, Mary looks up at him as he relates to her his recollection of that night. "The room was dark . . . I couldn't see anything. Besides, I had drank quite a bit of beer.

"They . . . she . . . probably spiked my drinks. I remember feeling a little strange . . . quite good, in fact . . . fantastic. Beer had never made me feel like that before.

"She was this incredible-looking woman. Every man in the tavern was looking at her. I had met her several weeks before. We went to her apartment. I remember the room being pitch black. I thought I was floating in space, and could barely stand up.

"Then she undressed me."

Mary Graves measures her son as he hesitates and rises from the couch. She can tell that he has become quite aware that he is talking to his mother. *He's embarrassed.*

She says to her son as she dabs at her wet eyes with the tissue, "Please tell me the rest, Tom. You don't have to give all the details. I just want to understand what happened."

"She performed oral sex," Mary's only child begins as he carefully chooses his words out of respect for his mother. "But, it wasn't her. In the dark, she switched places with a boy that she, or someone else, had snuck into the room. I didn't realize what was going on until I was in bed with him.

"Even though I was plowed at the time, I never moved so fast out of a bed. The video obviously didn't show that, or the sounds of my screaming."

Tom rises from the couch, standing over his mother, and tells her, "Mom, I have friends who are gay, but I'm not gay . . . and I'm definitely not a pervert."

Mary, still resting on the couch, can't prevent tears slipping from the corner of her eyes again, and her son sits down next to her and tenderly places his arms around his mother.

102

Phoenix . . . 6:25 P.M.

IT'S DINNER HOUR at John C. Lincoln Hospital. There are few visitors. The lobby is deserted except for the receptionist sitting behind the counter. Even the overhead lighting seems subdued.

Vince Edgars enters the elevator and punches the touch button for the fourth floor—Medical Intensive Care Unit.

As he approaches the ICU nurse station, he looks for signs of uniformed cops . . . there aren't any.

"I'm a police officer," he announces as he displays his DEA badge to the nurse. "I want to see Assistant Chief Hopkins."

Joseph Manucci walks to the elevators from the receptionist's desk in the hospital's main lobby. He's just been told that Assistant Chief Hopkins is out of the Intensive Care Unit... he's on the sixth floor.

As Manucci enters Jack Hopkins' room, he can see that Hopkins is lying on his back, asleep, with an I-V tube in his left forearm. A white sheet covers Hopkins as far up as his chest. His arms lie on the bed at his side.

There are no uniformed officers outside his door. *The Department's conclusion was unanimous,* Manucci reflects. *The shooting was a hit on Everest, drug related, nothing more. The assistant chiefs were innocent bystanders, unluckily part of a blundered massacre.*

He stands over Hopkins a few moments. *Hopkins is lucky,* Manucci supposes. *Only two bullets entered his body, one cleanly all the way through the right shoulder. The second one lodged in the side of his thigh, a ricochet from the pavement. Damn lucky!*

Manucci was told by doctors that Hopkins' greatest danger was the amount of blood he had lost before the paramedics arrived... there will be no permanent damage.

Joseph decides not to wake the sleeping assistant police chief, and leaves the room and heads for the elevators... the hospital's cafeteria is on the first floor.

Ten minutes later, Manucci strolls out of the elevator carrying a cup of coffee, and starts down the hallway towards Hopkins' room just as he sees a man entering the room.

The man glances back just before disappearing out of sight.

At first, Manucci doesn't give it a second thought. His first reaction is to not enter the room until the visitor has gone. He feels like he's seen the man before... several times.

Suddenly, he remembers... *Coming out of Baldarrama's house... the guy that got into the car.*

He dispatches his coffee that splashes all over the floor behind him, races down the hallway, slams open the closed door and barrels into the room with his revolver in both hands, aimed directly at the visitor, who's holding his own pistol, aiming at Hopkins.

As soon as he hears the banging noise from the door, Vince Edgars instinctively begins turning his weapon away from Jack Hopkins and towards Manucci.

Manucci drops to the floor and, at the same instant, rolls to the left and fires his .38 . . . three times!

Vince Edgars' face explodes and his handgun fires harmlessly into the ceiling as he whirls backward, slamming into the wall and crumpling to the floor face down.

103

THE HOSPITAL ROOM is now charged with a message of discerned isolation for Joseph Manucci and Jack Hopkins, the last of at least two dozen people who have been in and out of the room since the shooting occurred two hours earlier.

They are two cops who, as casual friends, have a mutual respect for each other, and, who, deep inside, proudly perceive the comradeship they share as members of one of the finest law enforcement departments in the world.

For police officers, there's a time to wind down after a stressful situation, especially one that has been jointly experienced and has a satisfactory ending.

There's relief whenever no civilian or police officer has been injured or killed. There is sadness because of a bad situation that has resulted in a civilian or police officer being injured, or even killed. And, there is the realization of how vulnerable each member of the department is. All these thoughts are common to all law enforcement officers.

Joseph Manucci and Jack Hopkins, now, in silence, share these same unspoken thoughts . . . while the odor of cordite still pitches its breed in the air.

Soon, they will relocate Hopkins to another room. But, he will still smell death . . . for a long time.

Two uniforms stand guard outside the door.

Manucci spent the past hour or so downtown, meeting with the chief of police and a few of the chief's staff. Now, Joseph sits in a hard folding-type chair, that doesn't fold, next to the bed staring without any acknowledged purpose at the opposite wall. His mind is relaxed, his body totally exhausted, and he feels it now for the first time.

As he relives in his mind the events of the past forty-eight hours, Manucci is keenly aware of Jack Hopkins' presence in the room.

He watches Jack lying on his back, staring up at the ceiling. Joseph, without really knowing, detects that the two of them have some unfinished business to attend to. Neither speak.

Manucci reminisces to himself about how long he's known Jack Hopkins. *Ever since Jack enrolled in the police academy. We were patrol officers together . . . there's a mutual respect.*

Joseph recalls, *The times I was fifth man out, for their foursome on Wednesdays. Most of the time it was to sub for Michael Everest . . . Jack and I go back a long way.* Manucci feels tired as that last thought sinks in.

Ten more minutes of silence.

Finally, Manucci sees Jack Hopkins turn his head toward him and say, "You saved my life, Joseph. How did you know?"

Manucci blinks his eyes a couple of times before he looks at Hopkins and replies in a quiet tone, "I saw him come out of Hector Baldarrama's house yesterday. I had seen him before, but I couldn't recall where. Now, since I know who he is, I remember him at some briefings we had with DEA."

Manucci's eyes tighten and his brow slightly furrows as he looks at Hopkins and asks, "Why was he trying to kill you, Jack?"

Joseph watches the man lying in the bed look away, toward the ceiling for a few seconds, before he hears the answer to his question, "I'm on their payroll . . . I'm on Hector Baldarrama's payroll."

Manucci abruptly stops him, "Jack, do you want an attorney?"

"No! I'm a dead man if I don't tell you everything. I'll be a witness, but . . . " Hopkins pauses, "I want a deal . . . I won't last twenty-four hours in prison."

They stop there.

Manucci rises from his chair and asks the assistant police chief one final question, "Is Michael Everest mixed up in the drug dealing?"

Hopkins looks at Manucci and tells him, "I'm not aware of him being involved with Baldarrama. The hit was meant only for me, as far as I know."

He steps out of the elevator and answers the ringing portable phone in his left hand, "This is Manucci!"

He hears Robb's voice through the receiver, "Joseph, can you come back downtown? There's a Stan Cobb here who wants to talk to you about Michael Everest. Cobb's the local agent in charge of the DEA."

As he walks to his car, Manucci reflects on the murdered young women he has seen *far* too many times at the Salt River. He doesn't *ever* want to forget them.

As he unlocks the chevy's door, he looks in the distance at the silhouette of Piestewa Peak stabbing upward toward the black sky. *It's gotta be at least four or five miles away, he surmises. Hardly, noticeable this far away. Funny, at night, up close it's like a gigantic ebony pyramid!*

As those thoughts melt away he becomes aware that the night air carries a chill. But, even so, it tastes refreshing . . . to Detective Joseph Manucci.

104

Luke Air Force Base, Arizona . . . Saturday 7:00 A.M.

I SIT LEISURELY at one of the mess hall tables eating a warm breakfast of bacon and eggs with Army "Special Forces" Major

David Palmer. I had just finished a fair nights sleep of six hours and enjoyed a hot shower followed by fresh clean clothes.

Now my attention is on Palmer while he tells me how he flew cross-country from Washington, D.C., per instructions from Warren Turner, and then, after scouring Phoenix most of Friday, along with help from Lora Parks, was finally able to track me down outside the Maricopa County morgue the previous night.

Under orders from Warren Turner, Palmer and I came directly to this air force base, located a few miles west of Glendale.

Major Palmer, the professional soldier, and I now wear identical clothing, except for the color of our military-style long-sleeved shirts. My shirt is light blue and David Palmer's is tan. I can't help wondering why, but don't bother to ask. *Probably has something to do with Palmer actually being in the military,* I conjecture.

Other than that, we both wear black combat pants with black sweatshirts along with black windbreakers and lightweight black combat boots. I'm surprised at how comfortable the boots feel.

Both of us easily conceal shoulder holsters that hold our choices of semiautomatic pistols under our respective wind breakers. Palmer prefers the Sig Sauer P220 .45, while I continue using my nine-millimeter Glock 226.

Just as I finish detailing to Palmer what's taken place over the past three days, we're interrupted by a young air force officer whose closely cropped hair is, to my thinking, as remarkable as a stunning cardinal-red Arizona sunset.

"Sirs, your ride is ready," First Lieutenant Preach advises as he approaches us, trying to be quite the professional.

The young officer appears to be boyishly excited about us two visitors who are placed in his care. The whole base is *probably aware,* or they've *heard* from a buddy, that two very *Top Secret* officials were brought onto the base late last night.

The lieutenant feels like it's an honor to work with these two V.I.P. guys *who*—the word spreading throughout Luke Air Force Base says—are *Special Forces* commandos.

Everyone on the base is quite aware that the entire Air Force jet-fighter training facility is closed up tighter than a pig's ass at pruning time. The consensus is that something big is going down, and Lieutenant Preach probably *knows,* but can't talk about it. I'm sure, the word also spread around now, is that the lieutenant is "The Man."

David Palmer calmly reassures me, his comrade, "Let's go, Michael, we'll find both of the ladies."

While I taste something pretty wretched in my saliva wondering where *the ladies* are, the two of us rise from the table, and Major Palmer turns and acknowledges the eager air force officer, "Much obliged, Lieutenant, for your hospitality."

After we climb aboard the jet transport and settle in, my attention's directed toward Palmer as the major proceeds to tell me about Senator Graves and the poison gas plot to wipe out the legislative and executive branches of the government of the United States, as well as governing branches of major European countries.

We two shadow warriors are airborne by 0815 hours, and I'm told by my partner where we're headed . . . destination, a U.S. military base in southern Europe, and then a brief helocopter ride to an aircraft carrier battle group in the Mediterranean Sea.

105

Washington, D.C. . . . 1:00 P.M.

WARREN TURNER LISTENS as he scans the members of the Joint Chiefs of Staff sitting around the huge conference table.

"We'll bring them in close to the shoreline tomorrow night here at Nerja at 2350 hours," Admiral Joe Hennessey announces as he flashes his red pointer light to the location on the overhead screen displaying the map of Spain and the Mediterranean Sea. "It will leave them about ten kilometers from their destination.

"Mr. Turner's agent, code name *Gaman*, is familiar with the target. Accompanying *Gaman* will be Major David Palmer and

Captains Lora Parks and Joshua Stone. All except *Gaman* are "Special Forces." Also, a SEAL team is on standby ready for backup if needed."

The admiral turns away from the screen and faces the group at the table, then continues, "They'll begin the assault on Monday at 0600 hours, local time . . . just after sunrise."

At first, Turner didn't want Michael to go with them. But Warren decided he had no choice. *Michael's familiar with Rodrigo Lara Orasco's villa. This operation has to be discreet because Orasco probably has Julia Everest and Catherine Steele. An all out assault would probably kill the two women.*

During an earlier telephone call with Major Palmer, Turner was briefed about the information that Michael provided the major, including the unknown whereabouts of the two ladies.

"That's about it, gentlemen," Admiral Hennessey concludes his briefing.

Ten minutes later, Turner sits alone in the Undersecretary of Defense's dimly lit office. He's waiting for a call from MI-6, now more commonly referred to as the SIS, in London.

This clandestine British equivalent to our Central Intelligence Agency now known as the Secret Intelligence Service is coordinating the search for Lara Orasco's terrorists in England, Germany and France.

While he waits, Warren reflects on how Michael's life has finally come to this . . . *it was inevitable.*

* * *

It was two days before Christmas, forty years ago . . . two-thirty in the morning.

The clouds, packed with snow, had been threatening the Washington, D.C. area for the past three days. Everyone was still hopeful for a white Christmas.

The three of them . . . Beth and Jonathon Becker, and Warren Turner were together in Beth's hospital room. She had just borne Jonathon's baby.

Beaming and overwhelmed with pride, Jonathon sat in the chair holding his three-hour-old son.

Warren stood next to Beth's bed, softly caressing her hand that rested on the bed along side of her. She was barely awake... it had been less than an easy delivery. She was exhausted. But she was deliriously happy as she watched the man of her dreams holding her son.

Discreetly—so as not to be noticed by Warren—Jonathon looked at Beth and nodded his head toward Warren, as if seeking, asking Beth for approval. She nodded affirmatively.

Jonathon looked at Warren and said, "At this moment, no one could be luckier than I. Here I sit, holding my son, in this room with my two best friends... one of whom I'm in love with and undeserving of her. And the other... God! If only, I were a woman."

All three bellowed out in laughter. Beth tried to restrain herself because of the pain, but didn't succeed.

"Seriously, Warren, you know how we feel about you," Jonathon spoke softly now, his voice beginning to crack just a little. "We want you to name him."

Warren who had been looking at Jonathon, quickly glanced at Beth, and then back at Jonathon. Beth clung tightly to Warren's hand. He didn't know what to say!

* * *

The phone on the desk rings loudly, scattering the National Security Advisor's images. "This is Warren Turner."

"This is Tommy, Warren," the SIS Director's deep voice is easily recognized by Turner as he holds the phone to his ear.

"How are you, Thomas?"

Warren Turner and Thomas Andrews have worked together on numerous occasions over the years for their respective countries. Warren knows there's strong mutual admiration and respect between them.

"We've been busy buggers here, Warren. We located our man. He's a member of Parliament. We tracked him down from your suggestion of reviewing the Prime Minister's calendar for this coming Monday."

Turner listens as the head of MI-6 continues, "It was a rather simple task, actually. The Prime Minister only had four meetings set up on Monday with members of our Parliament.

"Again, at your suggestion, we went about reviewing itineraries of those four, three men and one woman, for the past two years, and took a look see at any brief excursions that one of them may have had to Spain. Naturally, it was done quite discreetly.

"And, just before we attempted to contact him, our man called our office and asked to meet . . . it seems he wished to tell us all about what was going on."

The Briton pauses briefly to make sure Warren is catching it all, then continues, "We'll solve the problem the same as your people are doing. Obviously, Warren, we're still looking for the delivery people. But since all of the packages will be dropped off at predesignated spots, we don't have much to go on.

"Other than that, everything should work out quite satisfactorily . . . don't you think?"

Warren breathes a sigh of relief and inquires of his friend, "Have you heard any news from the others, Tom?"

"As a matter of fact, we have, Warren. Our good friend, Lawrence Bliquez, in Paris and the people in Bonn report to us that they have, each, isolated their man, or in the case of Paris, their woman, using, of course, the same methods as we. And, glad to say, both of their targets came immediately to their own government's security offices and notified them about the goings on.

"By the way, my dear friend, we also contacted Moscow in the event they might be involved. Their people advise me that they have no plans for any joint government meetings during the next few weeks, and they assure me that none of their parliamentary people have been to Spain for quite some time. So, the Russians surely are not part of this game."

"Thanks, Thomas, for your help. We'll keep in touch until this is over."

Warren replaces the phone and renders a reflective glance at the framed photograph of the attractive young woman sitting on the undersecretary's desk, staring back at Warren. It dawns on him that he is in a strange office. Until now, he has been, to put it mildly, somewhat preoccupied with the situation at hand. And now, he suddenly becomes cognizant of the unfamiliar surroundings for the first time.

Warren takes his eyes from the woman's gaze and allows his mind to travel back . . .

* * *

"That's so perfect," Beth said as she repeated Warren's choice... "Michael Jonathon Becker."

Beth and Jonathon both knew that "Michael the Archangel" was Warren's self-chosen patron saint. Warren beamed as the new parents smiled at him.

* * *

With that thought, Warren decides it's time, and raises himself from the comfortable executive chair in the undersecretary's office and heads out the door... for Virginia.

Heavy snowflakes plunge earthbound with fierce purpose as the limo pulls out of the private parking garage located underneath the Defense Department's huge octagon-shaped complex. Upon discovering the snowstorm with such force, Warren asks his driver to stop.

The glossy black limousine comes to a slow halt, and then Warren opens the rear passenger's door and carefully steps out onto the foot of snow already based on the ground.

He almost loses his balance as he stumbles a little while sinking down into the slippery ivory crust that has not yet compressed. He pauses for a moment and takes in the scene.

As the Washington monument oversees Warren from a distance, he, with a smile, oddly notices, for the first time in his life, the contrast between the loud echoing of rain cascading downward and the quiet that now surrounds him... the silence of snowflake flurries plummeting to the ground. *Silent turmoil* ... he reflects to himself.

106

Southern Spain . . . 5:50 P.M.

THE WEATHER REMINDS a beclouded and somewhat giddy Julia Everest of Carlsbad, California. She recalls that she and Michael spent their first vacation together in that small coastal southern California tourist village that lies just twenty-five minutes north of San Diego. That was the first time she had ever seen the ocean.

The sun has now sequestered itself below the western horizon of the Mediterranean and grants only a remaining glow as a reminder that it had been there, and the breeze, bearing the damp smell of the sea, carries a chill.

She lies on one of the reclining lounge chairs and feels as if she's in a dream . . . floating . . . high in the clouds.

At her waist, she clumsily tugs the light blanket up higher, up to her shoulders while still letting a portion of it remain hanging down over her feet while a battle wages between her trance-like bearing and her determination to open her eyes at will.

From the second-story veranda, high above the Mediterranean, with barely open eyes she dreamily gazes at the serpentine coastline that seems to go on for miles.

She's not at all sure why, but she can't stop smiling to herself as images drift through her mind. *Michael brought me here before . . . several times . . . Yes! Michael . . . where is my Michael? Why isn't Michael here? . . . This is Rodrigo's home . . . where is Michael? . . .*

Julia wrestles with unknown contrariety to open her eyes, barely victorious at this simple task as her mind continues to ramble . . . *I feel so relaxed . . . Why am I here? Where is Michael? . . . it is so beautiful here . . .*

His soft voice suddenly interrupts her thoughts, "What are you thinking, lovely lady?"

Rodrigo Lara Orasco sits down on the edge of the lounge chair where she lies. He softly strokes her hair above her forehead.

The scent of Rodrigo's Armani cologne is familiar to her . . . never evident unless she is very near him, she recalls. *Like the times Michael brought me here, and left me with Rodrigo . . . Rodrigo always sits close to me . . . and we flirt with one another. Does Rodrigo find me attractive? Yes . . . Rodrigo finds me attractive. Rodrigo is in love with me . . . I sense it.* Julia still feels skittish and continues experiencing a floating sensation.

Michael would disappear . . . Where would he go? He would leave me alone with Rodrigo . . . My head, I feel so . . . why can't I get up? . . . It is so beautiful here, her thoughts continue to mystify her.

She looks at Rodrigo and smiles as he lightly brushes her hair with the tips of his fingers. She is pressed with weightlessness so much so that she finds it difficult to speak.

She sighs between her words and vocalizes softly, "I believe . . . this is . . . the most . . . beautiful . . . place anywhere . . . in the world." Her heavy eyelids permit with reluctance her desire to scan the view below.

The sedatives are taking longer to wear off . . . longer than Rodrigo had thought.

"I envy you, terribly, . . . for having all of this," she sighs.

"It is yours now. I give it all to you," Rodrigo whispers. He leans over and gently kisses her cheek. Her scent captivates him and molds his helpless senses into welcomed slavery.

Rodrigo wanted Julia the first time he saw her. He has made love to scores of beautiful women during the past fifteen years, but he has never been able to love any of them. Long ago he accepted that he will never be able to love another woman besides Ernestina.

The first time he saw Julia, Rodrigo knew he was mistaken. Now, he must make love to her.

His mind fills with memories of the times Julia was his guest while her husband was sent off to Paris or Geneva, or Brussels, or wherever.

Rodrigo recalls the things that he and Julia did together during Michael's absence. They sailed, rode horses . . . visited the shops in the small villages nearby. And, in Madrid, they went to the finest restaurants, and to the great museums.

Rodrigo remembers the many hours they spent together on this very balcony, discussing almost every subject while they watched, together, the spectacular sunsets where the world seemed to end, across the Mediterranean.

She is extremely intelligent . . . witty and charming . . . and very beautiful, he declares to himself. Rodrigo Lara Orasco is mesmerized as he gazes upon her lying there.

Sadly for him, he realizes, he no longer can be satisfied with only making love to her. He has gone beyond that now, far beyond what he intended. Now, he wishes . . . he longs . . . for Julia Everest to love him the same way he loves her.

The final hint of the sun's passing merges itself into an indigo blue before settling into blackness at the sea's horizon, and the wind, now turned cold, begins blowing with even more purpose.

Julia, aware of Rodrigo's presence next to her, clutches her blanket even higher, but not because of him.

Orasco stands and removes his jacket and places it over her, on top of her blanket.

He possesses an overwhelming desire to kiss her beautiful lips. He imagines her touch, *If only she would allow me to hold her.*

But, it is no good, he cries to himself in frustration, because he does not wish for her to respond to him only because she has been drugged.

"Come, I will escort you inside . . . you will catch a chill." Rodrigo aches so badly to hold her. It is maddening. It is unfair.

Julia looks into his eyes. She smiles and her eyes are barely open. Slowly, she draws a deep breath, and softly petitions, "Will you always be my friend, dear Rodrigo?"

"Si, mi bonita," his voice trembles.

Julia wishes for him to hold her. With all of her strength she raises herself and extends her arms out to him.

Rodrigo sits and leans toward her and engages his arms around her, drawing her to him, and his lips softly brush the side of her neck . . . he has never felt such warmth from a woman like this. It is maddening indeed . . . it is ecstacy. She holds him tighter. Her fragrance engulfs him. They cling to one another . . . both oblivious to the cold breeze as they wrap themselves together . . . both seeking shelter from unknown images that do not identify themselves.

107

Washington, D.C. . . . 3:40 P.M.

THE DRIVER, HEADING for Virginia, is cautious as he negotiates the snow-packed streets of the nation's capital.

Warren Turner can barely see the falling snow through the car's frosted windows. His thoughts refuse to give way to anything else, other than recalling events so many years ago that converge on Michael's parents. Those memories that have been tucked away tenderly in the core of his mind are now so vivid to Warren.

He keeps thinking about how the three of them had worked together ever since they had joined the CIA . . . four years before Michael was born.

Warren remembers that he was madly in love with Elizabeth Archer . . . *she always knew it. She loved me, but Beth was "in love" only with Jonathon.*

Warren recalls when Beth and Jonathon told him they were going to marry. *Naturally, my heart was broken . . . but, of course, I was best man.*

The soothing flames crackle in the fireplace while he spawns his pipe to life and reclines in his favorite easy chair. Just before entering his study, he noted the time on the foyer wall . . . twenty minutes until nine o'clock, Saturday night.

Warren Turner wishes things could have been different. He remembers Hue as she finds her place among the images he conjures up now.

She did a remarkable job of raising Michael. Warren is keenly aware of how deeply Hue loved Jonathon and Beth, *and of course, Michael.*

Hue gave Michael his new last name . . . she knew he would be tall . . . tall, like Mount Everest.

Hue hid Michael . . . and she protected him, Warren rousingly acknowledges to himself with a smile.

As he slowly draws in on his pipe and surveys flames in the fireplace that render themselves into a gentle dance of leisurely inflections, Warren wishes he could have been part of Michael's life instead of just observing from a distance all those years. But he's convinced, *It would have been far too dangerous for Michael.*

Warren reminisces about all of the monthly phone calls from Hue while Michael was growing up, keeping Warren updated on Michael's life. Warren could tell, from her voice, her excitement, a mother's voice, a mother's excitement, how much Hue loved the boy . . . how proud she was of him.

With that thought, Warren rises from his chair and walks to the breakfront with its dark-wood grain, where his humidor occupies its place of honor just inside the glass doors. He submerges his pipe into the special blend created just for him, and with his thumb, lightly compresses the tobacco down into the bowl. Then, with deliberate and calculated effort, he strikes a match across the stones that form the fireplace and lights the tobacco, drawing deep, rapid breaths through the pipe stem. The aromatic smoke fills the air.

He stands still, gazing out the window, at nothing in particular, because there is nothing interesting to him outside, as his mind has already begun recalling the final days in Indonesia . . . thirty-eight years ago.

* * *

It was supposed to be a vacation. Jonathon, Beth and Michael had been in Singapore a week before Warren and Hue flew in from Hong Kong, the homebase of Jonathon, Beth and Warren.

In Hong Kong, the three of them had been tracking some heroin dealers and trying to infiltrate the dealers' cartels.

Hue was a Vietnamese woman in her late fifties. She had worked with the three of them for almost two years. She often took care of Michael when Beth couldn't. She loved Michael as she would have loved her own son.

It was seven-thirty in the evening, and Singapore was extremely hot and humid ... there was a light drizzle, nothing more than a mist, actually.

Shortly after Warren and Hue arrived, Beth decided to leave the hotel room and jog in the rain to cool off.

Warren catnapped on one of the two small beds. Jonathon and Hue sat in wicker chairs at a small wicker table, drinking herbal tea, and Hue was listening to Jonathon as he told her more stories about his childhood in Indiana. Hue could not get enough. She was the attentive, eager audience, always wanting to hear anything that would make her feel closer to the great United States.

Two-year-old Michael was at the window watching the rain and watching his mother begin her jog down the street.

She was about ninety feet away.

At that instant, he saw her ripped apart as four men stitched across her body with automatic weapons. Warren and Hue had been followed.

Michael's voice shrieked as he cried, "MAMMA! MAMMA!"

At the sound of the automatic gunfire, all three inside the room moved swiftly, absent thought of any measured heartbeat.

Instantly, Jonathon ducked to the floor, his chair flying backwards at the same time, and rolled to Michael, snatching him away from the window. Hue grabbed her pistol as she slid to the floor.

Within a split second, Warren had awoken and lay on the floor ... he held his semiautomatic pistol with both hands, aiming toward the room's entrance door.

"WE'VE GOT TO GET OUT OF HERE! WE'VE GOT TO FIND BETH," Jonathon yelled.

Michael looked at his father and cried, "Mamma hurt!"

* * *

Warren continues to stand there in his office gazing out

across the snow-covered Virginia hills for awhile as time does not allow itself to address him in any recognizable fashion. Finally, he empties the ashes from his pipe into the fireplace . . . and wonders to himself how much Michael remembers.

After briefly reflecting on that last thought, he places the pipe in the rack on his desk and slowly paces to his bedroom.

As he undresses, he thinks about his wife who died of breast cancer eight years ago. Warren and Frances were never able to have children. *I loved Frances even more than I had loved Beth. They would have liked each other . . . very much,* he imagines.

108

Southern Spain . . . Sunday 8:10 A.M.

HER EYES SLOWLY open. At first she isn't sure where she is. Then, lying there in the bed on her side, Julia serenely captures in her view the choppy waters of the Mediterranean through the opened veranda doors.

Orasco's villa! *How did I get here? How long have I been here?* She feels like vomiting, and her head samples unmanaged vertigo as she strains to sit up.

Her mind begins to clear as she tries recalling what happened. *The two men! They brought me here. Why? What day is this? Where's Michael?*

After sitting there for a moment, dizziness still pervades her senses as she climbs out of bed and, with some effort, struggles toward the bathroom.

She can't recall ever feeling this lightheaded before, and wonders if this is what it's like to have a hangover. She knows she's never been one to drink more than one or two servings of an alcoholic beverage whenever she and Michael went anywhere because the alcohol always made her drowsy.

Once in the bathroom, she quickly, almost frantically, peels off her Eagles warmup shirt and sweat pants along with her underwear . . . the same clothes she was wearing when the two strange men came to her house. She has no idea how many days have gone by.

With eager anticipation, she turns on the faucets in the shower, and allows the mist to warm itself for a minute or so before stepping into heaven and medicating herself with the surging water as it cascades down, blessing her with long forgotten pleasures that often are so common that they occasionally hide themselves from recognition.

She lets the fine spray pelt her face and body, medicating painful spots. She discovers several bruises on her arms and legs that she presumes are the result of her skirmish with the two men at her home.

She blissfully moans in ecstacy as the gently warm water continues splashing on her. For a few moments she feels frivolous, almost giddy, from the safety of the embracing flow.

She allows herself this luxury for about a half hour, after which, her mind begins to clear and the lightheadedness pretty much wastes itself into only a memory. Then she begins to experience a sense of anxiety as she keeps seeing in her mind the encounter with the two men at her home.

Is Michael here? She wonders . . . she hopes.

After drying herself with soft oversized Egyptian towels smelling of a subtle lemon fragrance, Julia discovers a multitude of colognes and assorted toiletries inside a large mirrored medicine cabinet above the white granite sink.

Then, as she searches through the clothes hanging in the huge walk-in closet, she discovers a casual, white Ralph Lauren dress to her liking.

From the beige chest of drawers opposite her bed she selects, from quite an assortment of various types and sizes, a pair of white panties and matching bra. *Direct from Victoria's Secret,* she amusingly guesses.

And lastly, she chooses, from about forty or fifty pairs of shoes in the closet, a pair of white Cole Haan sandals that fit perfectly.

After that, Julia tries to get her bearing. The freshest thing in her mind is when she was on the veranda the night before . . . with Rodrigo.

She remembers him sitting alongside her and holding her. *Why did I let him do that?* she wonders. *He carried me to my bed.* She remembers being chilled from the night air. *Rodrigo covered me with blankets.*

Then, she recalls, *he said, something like, "Maybe, some day, mujer hermosa (beautiful woman)!" And then he left. What did he mean by that?* she ponders as she decides to explore the villa.

She steps gingerly down the stairs leading to the foyer, and freezes on the last step. She's unprepared for the surprise when she peers to the right of the foyer and fixes her gaze on Hector Baldarrama sitting at a desk near the opposite corner of the monumental living room.

Looking past the desk, she can see, through the wall of windows, the twisting coastline and the strikingly blue cloudless sky. The waving motions of the leaves on the palm, cork and jacaranda trees and surrounding bushes suggest a robust breeze is blowing in off the Mediterranean.

She observes Baldarrama glancing up from the desk and remarking to her, in a condescending manner, "Good morning, Julia. Did you sleep well?"

She remains standing at the foot of the stairs, clinging to the railing with one hand, and still holds herself a little unsteady as she stares past Baldarrama without answering, as if he isn't there.

The fire and spirit of this daughter of an extremely strong-willed and independent-minded copper miner have been amply ignited and are now surging through her blood . . . and that blood is now boiling mad.

She continues to ignore the man and steps with determination over to the front door and opens it.

Two men stand facing her just outside the front door. She can clearly see that both of them have a rifle of some kind slung over their shoulders. *Probably machine guns,* she ventures a guess. It's obvious to her that they aren't going to let her leave.

"Rodrigo had to run some errands," she hears Baldarrama say from across the room after she closes the front door in the foyer. "He'll be gone until tonight.

"Would you like some breakfast?" he asks, but doesn't bother looking up from the desk.

Julia doesn't acknowledge that she hears him, or even that he's in the next room. She treads as quickly as she can back to the staircase and promptly climbs up the stairway and hastens to her bedroom.

After closing the door, Julia opens the veranda doors and steps outside. The wind is cool, yet, comfortable, and seems to be blowing with purposeful intentions across the deck.

The sky has erased all clouds and reflects its brilliant blue shade on the water. She watches sailboats of assorted sizes in the distance. There are twenty or thirty of them spread out a half mile or so, she judges, from the coastline, with their full sails, jutting across the choppy sea.

Julia stands and leans her hands on the four-foot-high wrought-iron railing that guards the edges of the veranda. She reflects on what has happened during the past week, and asks herself, *what is happening "right" now? Why did they bring me here?*

She knows—the feeling has taken no prisoners in its inclination to overwhelm her—she's being held against her will. And she's sure she has no way of escaping without help from someone as she has already searched the entire veranda that completely encircles the second level of the villa.

Michael and I are finally learning how to give our feelings to one another, she wistfully tells herself. *Now, this is happening . . . whatever "this" is.*

She agonizes over and over in her mind, the questions, *What have you done, Michael? What have you gotten us into? Who are Rodrigo Lara Orasco and Hector Baldarrama?*

She feels tears shaping their texture as she grips the railing and squeezes with all her might. *After all these years of shutting myself out . . . I'm finally able to throw away my fears . . . be vulnerable . . . be free to love Michael. And now, this!*

She lets out a sigh and brushes away wetness that has positioned itself in small measures in the corners of her eyes as she slowly slides a few feet over and sits down on one of the padded chairs next to a round white-metal table that sits next to the edge of the veranda. Even though she's sitting, Julia still has a clear view of the sea.

A few minutes pass and she doesn't move. She doesn't know why, at this particular time, but she finds herself thinking of her mother. *Why did you leave Papa and me so suddenly? Why did you leave me so alone?*

She rises from the chair while her conscious thoughts shout hopelessness, and stands by the railing again. She leans on one foot for a while, then the other, as she continues holding on to the railing.

Most of the sailboats have faded down the coast now, and so she strains to see as many as she can. But only three remain visible. They, too, will soon vanish.

As she watches the last one disappear, Julia reflects on the sessions that she and Michael have been having with a family counselor.

Julia recalls when the adviser recently asked her to think back to her childhood . . . thirty-three years ago.

109

SHE WAS JUST five years old, standing, with her hands behind her back on the small porch near the front door. She felt lost among the crowd of grownup people standing all around her.

She could see her father sitting just a few feet away on the porch swing. He was the only one sitting . . . men and women stood around him. Lots of other people stood all around the tiny porch. There was little talking . . . a hushed murmur now and then.

Because she was the only small child there, she felt out of place. No one noticed her, she thought. Everyone's attention, it seemed to Julia, was focused on her father. Her eyes too were glued to her Papa. She had never seen him cry before . . . never. Never . . . before now.

Something terrible had happened to her Mamma! But Julia Contreras didn't know what. "I should ask my Papa!" she told herself. "But will the people let me see him? Will they let me see my Papa, now?"

She decided to wait . . .

* * *

Julia slowly moves away from the balcony railing and sits on one of the patio chairs again, and stares out at the restless sea as she continues recalling that dreadful day.

* * *

Mrs. Echeveste, a close neighbor, took Julia from the porch as the sun was setting behind the mountain of tailings from the mine, and took her over to the house next door to spend the night with Mrs. Echeveste's daughter, Elina. Elina was six . . . just a year older than Julia.

Julia had no way of knowing that she wouldn't see her father again until the day of her mother's funeral. Her father was devastated at the loss of his wife.

Theresa Contreras had been struck by a car as she carried two bags of groceries across the highway . . . the main street running through Miami, Arizona.

She had died instantly. No time to say goodbye to her husband . . . no time to say goodbye to her daughter. No time for them to hold their wife and mother. There was no time for them to say goodbye.

* * *

Julia's reflections fade as she squints while gazing out to watch seagulls gracefully drifting, absent any thought of effort, above the coastline. She wonders how her life would have been different if her mother had raised her.

She recalls how lonely she was for so many years after her mother's death. Her father became distant. But, Julia knows that he loved her . . . she just knew.

* * *

Her Papa would do little things to let her know he cared. Like the time, when she was eight-years-old, when he came home in his old pickup truck, and, as he climbed from the truck, he saw her standing with her hands behind her, leaning on one foot, then the other as she watched the neighboring children ice skating on the frozen driveways . . . Julia had no ice skates.

Agapito Contreras worked in the copper mines of Miami, Arizona. He had no money to spend on luxuries . . . only necessities. And even then, he struggled to survive.

He had learned to repair washing machines, and that had helped. The back porch of their small home was always littered with at least two or three old washing machines that were in different stages of repair.

Scattered parts covered most of the rest of the porch and even had found their way into different sections of the rear yard, covered with black tarp to protect them from the weather, even though it only occasionally rained or snowed in Miami, Arizona.

It was not easy being the only parent, and raising a daughter . . . paying for baby sitters while he worked at the mine . . . paying the tuition so his only child could attend the parochial grade school . . . paying for her clothes so she wouldn't be embarrassed. Thank God for school uniforms. Agapito meticulously washed her one uniform by hand every night.

* * *

Julia meditatively imagines how her father felt, as she turns her attention away from the direction of the Mediterranean and surveys the veranda and surrounding hills of Orasco's estate.

Seeing his daughter, watching the ice skaters and not being able to skate with them, must have torn at his heart.
Again, her thoughts drift back.

* * *

After watching Julia standing there by herself, Agapito hurried into the house for just a few minutes. Then he came out and, without saying a word to Julia, climbed into his truck and left for a while.

When he returned, he pulled the pickup into the dirt driveway and called to her to get into the truck.

Her Papa took her to the mine's company store, where everyone, who worked for the mines, shopped. He told her to pick out whichever pair of skates she wanted.

*   *   *

Julia recalls, it wasn't until she was fourteen or fifteen years old when she learned that her papa had pawned his watch to get the money for her skates.

She smiles to herself, now, as she thinks about it. *Papa never hugged me or kissed me. I never saw him show any emotion, except that day on the porch when Mamma died. Still, I know he loved me. I just wish . . . I just wish . . . sometimes he had told me so.*

She squints as the sun begins sliding around the corner of the villa. Soon, the spot where she sits will be shaded. She thinks about how much she loves Michael.

She recalls the first time she ever saw him.

*   *   *

She was instructed to file the stack of bank loan documents in alphabetical order into the Rolodex. Then the night bookkeeper would post them to the bank customers' ledger that night.

She had sat at the night bookkeeper's desk all day. She had been told that he would come in at five o'clock in the evening.

Just before five, she heard his voice behind her, "Hi! I'm Michael Everest!"

Julia turned around . . . and fell . . . instantly . . . ecstatically . . . in love.

As she looked at him, she smiled and said with a very shaky voice, "Hi! I'm Julia Contreras." God! I sounded like a meek little lamb, *she thought. She felt embarrassed.*

The tall, slender, golden-tanned, dark-haired and blue-eyed young man had taken her breath away.

Her work day was finished at five-thirty, so she only worked with Michael for a half-hour each day. But, Julia managed to freshen up just before five o'clock every day, before he came in. She wanted to look perfect for him.

She could tell that Michael was shy. So, within three weeks of their first meeting, Julia played detective and set out to find Michael's closest coworker. That done, she promptly developed a quick friendship with the young man, and asked him if Michael Everest was dating anyone.

The coworker told her yes, but that it wasn't serious. Julia then told the coworker she thought Michael was nice. That's all it took for Michael to ask Julia to go out with him.

For the first few weeks, Julia was charged by the never-imagined feelings that captured her heart and convinced her that fairy tale dreams do cast themselves into real life souls. She was madly in love with Michael, but her insecurity forged itself into a pointed dagger that pierced the core of her spirit, so she began to be afraid of losing him.

She would wake up in the middle of the night from the dreams, her body soaked with sweat. In her dreams she would see Michael and another woman walking down the aisle of a church. Each time, the church was different. Each time, the woman was different, but always beautiful. The women always wore wedding dresses.

Or, she would see, in her dreams, Michael being struck by a large truck. He would make no sound as the truck ran over him. She could see his face . . . it showed no emotion, his eyes just stared as if she were looking at a photograph.

And so, Julia, without realizing it, began to shield herself from the love she felt for Michael. She became distant . . . she knew it. But, she couldn't help it.

She was the same way on their wedding day. As they walked out of the church that morning in Miami, the dreams of the women in the wedding gowns haunted her.

The dreams came and went in her mind, all day . . . during the reception in the church hall . . . and also when she and Michael drove to Phoenix that night from Miami.

She was even afraid to look at him . . . afraid he wouldn't be there. Afraid he didn't love her the way she loved him.

As weeks turned into months, and months into years, Julia was unable to control her feelings. And so, she unknowingly built a protection wall between herself and her love for Michael. She became terrified that she would lose him. And she convinced herself she could live safely without him.

And the years sadly passed in emptiness . . . not unlike the vast, barren . . . and bitterly cold . . . desert plains in winter.

110

Washington D.C. . . . still Sunday, 4:20 P.M.

HE NERVOUSLY PICKS up the phone, and acknowledges in a hollow tone, "Hello, this is Senator Graves."

He detects that the voice at the other end of the line has a definite Middle-Eastern accent as the man tells him, "You will go now, to the gymnasium at Georgetown University. There you will find a package behind the waste container on the left side of the front entrance. Go now! You will be watched. Do not tell anyone!"

The phone line abruptly drones dead in his ear as Senator Alan Graves apprehensively glances at Mary Graves who sits by the fireplace in a chair across the room anxiously watching her husband.

It takes Graves a little more than an hour to pick up the bundle and return home. After the garage door closes, the senator nervously shuffles out of his car and turns the package over to an FBI agent who waits for him there in the garage.

"Thank you, Senator Graves. I'll have these returned to you before the sun rises," the agent assures him. "And please . . . don't worry about your surveillance. We've secured this area tight enough to spot anything larger than a boll weevil in a field of ripe cotton. I'll have no trouble getting out of here . . . and getting back."

The agent ended with, "You have a nice evening, now, Senator."

111

Mediterranean Sea . . . 9:50 P.M.

"DO YOU REMEMBER Lora Parks and Joshua Stone, Michael?" Major David Palmer asks as soon as the major and I enter the briefing room on the nuclear-powered Nimitz-class aircraft carrier USS *George Washington*.

I was told that the United States Naval Carrier Battle Group is forty-five miles off the coast somewhere northeast of Gibraltar in the Mediterranean Sea, and powering full speed ahead due east by northeast.

"Yes!" I answer and can't hide a smile, "You took care of me while I was at Camp Peary."

Palmer reintroduces me to the two commandos, "This is, for this particular mission, Captain Parks and this is Captain Stone. They work with me and they wanna tag along if it's okay with you."

I cheerfully shake their hands, and a sense of warmth, like being bundled inside a long-forgotten security blanket, soothes my pathetic bones, and I eagerly tell them, "I'm glad to see some friendly faces for a change."

We all laugh.

As we sit around the compact table, David Palmer tells me he's already briefed Stone and Parks about what I've done for the DEA during the past two years. Both were also told by Major Palmer what has happened the past week. They also know that they've been assigned to help rescue Julia Everest and Catherine Steele, and to find Rodrigo Lara Orasco.

This is the first time I've ever been on a naval vessel of any kind, and I'm incapable of unveiling soothing thoughts about my surroundings, and admit to myself, with no dash of remorse or shame, that I could never adapt in any fashion whatsoever to a mark that could project me toward an acceptable bearing to life on a naval ship.

Everything's made of iron . . . hard steel . . . too compact. Too confining . . . there's no wasted space, I tell myself. *And those damn stairs . . . they're like ladders, narrow metal ladders that go straight up, forever.* And I wonder, how many sailors have fallen from them . . . to their deaths.

For the next hour and a half, Major Palmer and the two other professional government mercenaries and I review together, over and over again, each of our individual roles after we hit the beach of southern Spain. Beforehand, from memory, I drew a sketch of the villa, and now brief my associates about the surrounding topography of the estate.

Lora Parks tries to listen attentively, but can't dismiss the uneasiness, yet excitement of a school girl with a crush, due to the presence of Joshua Stone who sits next to her across the small table from Palmer and Everest. She dares not allow herself to make any eye contact of any sort at all with the man known as *Jericho*.

Until Lora walked into the briefing room, and found Joshua sitting at the table alone, she had not seen him since she had watched him leave Camp Peary after the training session for Michael Everest *that* April . . . almost two years ago. She only had time to say "Hello" before Palmer and Everest entered the room. She isn't even sure if Joshua Stone returned her greeting.

While she listens to Everest describe the villa, Lora's thoughts about the man sitting next to her elicit their own avenues into her concentration as she is unable to dismiss his overwhelming presence.

If only I could have five minutes alone with him. What is he feeling? Does he wish he could be alone with me? Does he want to kiss me as badly as I want him to? Oh, God, Parks! This is not the time!

If not for the extraordinary ability to mentally assimilate a multitude of assorted, even unrelated, information at the same time, Lora would have remembered nary a word Everest was saying while describing the villa. But, even so, assembling all of the self-discipline she can muster, Lora forces herself to erase any more thoughts of Joshua Stone . . . for now.

112

Virginia...

IT'S FIVE O'CLOCK in the evening as Warren Turner listens to the chimes from the antique clock that stands guard in the entryway. *Michael has arrived in Spain!*

Turner reclines on the oversized sofa in the living room about five feet from the fireplace so he can feel the warmth of the newly born fire that is leisurely gaining momentum for itself. Already having changed into his nightrobe and slippers, he concludes that he won't sleep much during the next twenty-four hours. He purposely avoided going to his study, trying to escape from reminders of his enormous responsibilities, if only for a few hours.

He lights his pipe and settles back, hoping Michael feels positive energy from him. Warren reflects on the final hours in Singapore . . . he will tell Michael everything.

* * *

As soon as Hue had slipped away with Michael an hour earlier, Jonathon and Warren made themselves somewhat visible, yet, cautious in the process. They wanted the killers to follow them and not Hue and Michael.

"Wait here, Warren!" Jonathon told him.

Warren remained in a darkened doorway as Jonathon began slipping up the dimly lit road. Warren could see him move warily in and out of the shadows of each doorway.

After Jonathon worked his way up about fifty to sixty yards, he disappeared into another doorway. Then, a few seconds later, he stepped out and motioned for Warren to follow.

Warren alertly began slipping in and out of the same doorways as Jonathon, working his way toward his partner.

When Warren stepped out into the open roadway about thirty yards from Jonathon, they opened fire.

Jonathon knew that Warren had no cover, so Jonathon leaped out of the shadows, rolled to the pavement and began firing his semiautomatic pistol, hoping Warren would have time to gain cover.

The killers turned their machine guns on Jonathon.

Warren began running toward Jonathon while firing his pistol at the four dark figures silhouetted against the street light a block away.

Warren saw three of them fall before he had time to reload. He continued running toward Jonathon. The fourth killer quickly disappeared in the darkness.

When Warren reached Jonathon, he stopped suddenly.... - Jonathon didn't move.

Warren quickly knelt down and desperately rolled his best friend over on his back. Warren gaped in horror at the missing part of the right side of Jonathon's forehead. Blood oozed from Jonathon's eyes and mouth with each struggled breath.

Warren also saw the blood that oozed all over the lower front of the khaki shirt that cloaked his best friend's stomach.

He slipped his arm under Jonathon's neck and supported his dying friend's head.

Jonathon's last words were... "Don't forget your promise... I love you, Warr—" he didn't finish.

* * *

Warren Turner's face perspires as he grimaces at the images in his mind, and closes his eyes. He knows that Jonathon Becker saved his life. And Warren knows that he has broken the promise he made to Jonathon just two weeks before Jonathon's death.

* * *

"You know, partner!" Jonathon declared with slurred words to Warren as they sat in Wonto's Bar in Hong Kong. "This business is making us old, fast!"

Jonathon and Warren were drinking heavily in memory of one of their associates who had just been found floating in Kowloon Bay.

Warren listened with blurry eyes as Jonathon unloaded, "You've got to promise me that you'll take care of Michael if anything happens to me and Beth. I don't want my son to ever do what we do. You've got to promise me . . . promise me!"

"I promise, Jonathon."

113

Coast of Southern Spain . . . 11:55 P.M.

IN THE SMALL raft we are exposed to the dismal wind that makes us glad we're wearing the heavy navy-pullover sweaters and stocking caps that house the hearing devices for the almost weightless and tiny microphones that extend out around the contours of our jaws and to the side of our mouths.

After eight minutes on the choppy sea, we land on the spongy white beach at the eastern side of the small village of Nerja. Rodrigo Lara Orasco's villa is about ten kilometers west of the town.

I was advised earlier by David Palmer that the rocks and cliffs on the shoreline near Orasco's villa would have been far too difficult to deal with if we had tried to come in further west.

Lora Parks and Joshua Stone quickly begin camouflaging the raft. I didn't see them together at all after the briefing on the carrier.

Joshua, frustrated that he can't tell Lora how much he's missed her, despairingly appeals to his God. *Why do you allow me to have these feelings? Why are they so wrong? You send me, with her, into this dangerous place . . . with unspoken words and unsettled issues.*

My God, I "beg" You . . . tell me, how much have I sinned already? I love her. I can't deny it! Am I to die for that? Am I to lose my soul . . . for falling in love with someone?

Two minutes later, after finishing with the raft, Joshua and Lora, both down on one knee with their Uzi's held firmly in their hands, watch and listen as Palmer quietly tells me, "The raft won't be discovered until the sunbathers hit the beach somewhere around 0900 hours. By then, it'll all be over but the shouting."

I try, with little success, to swallow while unwanted dryness savors its own mastery inside my mouth as its purpose seems designed to live forever with no intent whatsoever of relinquishing its tonality. And, I am captive to the adrenaline rocketing through me with no assurance of any kind that it is good or bad, and I can't help thinking, wondering and worrying about Julia and Catherine. I find myself telling my companions, "I hope at least one of you is as nervous as I am."

"We're all nervous," David Palmer assures my wavering heart.

"Okay." Palmer motions with his right hand and announces, "It's one kilometer to the town and nine more to the villa. Let's go."

Lora Parks takes the point.

We scoot around the south side of the village, staying close to the beach. I accept much needed ease in noting that the beach and streets are deserted. For some unknown reason this seems to reassure me that everything will be all right, and Julia and Catherine are safe from the turmoil that has violated all of our worlds.

Near where the town ends, our hunting party suddenly hears a crescendo of male voices. It's coming from a tavern a block away on the very western edge of the village. Framed rays of light can be seen illuminating out through a doorway and a side window.

The unmistakable putrid stench of dead fish masses itself in the air forcing each of us to alter our breathing in unnatural patterns as we drop down to the safety of sagebrush growing between the road and the beach while we observe about a dozen men sitting and standing on the tavern's front porch that curves around to one side of the building. The drunken men are laughing and talking loudly. The wine has been flowing a while.

I tell myself, *Diehards, still celebrating the weekend, they're harmless. But, we have to avoid them.*

Palmer lightly touches my arm and motions toward the other side of the building. The major tells the three of us, as a whisper into his microphone, "We'll try to pass behind the building."

I'm directly behind Palmer, who now takes the lead, and the four of us, with Joshua last and circumspectly making sure no one is following, move between two buildings near the tavern.

As we do so, I realize that the full moon doesn't help conceal us. But, on the other hand, its brightness enables us to see much more easily. None of us carry night-vision glasses. We all agree that the glasses distort our perception, especially since none of us have recently had time to become accustomed to wearing the awkward things.

After leaving the village behind, we double-time along the side of a narrow highway. Three times, before reaching the dirt road leading up to the villa, we are forced to duck into the brush behind sagebrush and mesquite trees to avoid detection because of passing vehicles.

114

Virginia . . . 11:35 P.M.

HE FLIPS ON the switch at the doorway and the dim lamplight comes to life, allowing him to see well enough to enter his study. In this room Warren Turner feels he's more a part of the operation now taking place in Spain.

For the first time since he can remember, he recognizes adrenaline coursing through him and making alive nerves that have felt only passive natures for the past forty years of his life. With this renewed grasping of life he relaxes himself into his comfortable chair.

The fireplace delivers no sign of life. Even though his study is chilled he has no desire to bother with starting a fire.

Twenty-five more minutes, and it will begin, he nervously envisions. He's barely able to see out through the frosted window at the raging snowstorm, and he instinctively bundles up more snugly in his bathrobe.

I hope you'll forgive me, Michael, Warren implores, and reflects on how all of this began in Phoenix . . . just eleven months before Michael was contacted by the Drug Enforcement Administration.

* * *

The two men shook hands as they greeted each other. "Pleased to meet you, Mr. Campbell," David Palmer said as he settled into one of the two visitors' chairs in the plush and expensively paneled private office of William Campbell. "I really appreciate you coming to your office to see me. I understand you don't work on Fridays."

"Frankly, Mr. Palmer, my curiosity got the better of me," the fifty-four-year-old construction contractor said as he leaned back in his well-padded executive chair. "I was still tryin' to digest the fact that you had my unlisted home telephone number . . . while I dialed the confirmation number you'd given me to call the President of the United States.

"When the president's voice answered the phone, I didn't believe it at first. He and I spoke for a few minutes and I knew he was legit. He's a good man, you know!"

"Yes, sir!" Palmer answered. "I'll get right to the point, Mr. Campbell."

David Palmer did not waste time with his explanation, "I work for an area of the government that deals with top priority government projects. My superior reports directly to the president.

"Our area of expertise is dealing with terrorism and hostage situations, and for all practical matters, anything else the president needs to address and deems is of a discreet nature and relevant to the national security of our country.

"My group works closely with the FBI, CIA, DEA, ATF, Secret Service and all areas of the military. You might say we're roving troubleshooters."

"Well, I'm impressed Mr . . . . or should I be addressing you by your rank, Mr. Palmer?"

"You can call me David, Mr. Campbell."

"Okay . . . how do I help you guys? . . . and call me Billy! Everyone else does."

Palmer sat straight in the chair with both of his feet fixed firmly on the thickly padded butterscotch-brown carpet and got directly to the point. "The subject of our conversation is Michael Everest."

Campbell's eyes opened wide as they gazed at the stranger sent by the President. Billy loudly proclaimed, "Why, he's my CPA!"

If he didn't before, David Palmer now had the man's attention. "We know that, Mr. Campbell. That's why I'm here."

Billy Campbell said in a much calmer voice now, "I'm definitely listenin'."

Palmer continued sitting straight, showing no movement whatsoever to the wealthy construction contractor. "Mr. Campbell, we know about the real estate project that you and other clients of Mr. Everest are involved in. We know that Mr. Everest has invested heavily in it."

Campbell listened as Palmer continued speaking in a quiet and deliberate manner, "The president of the United States needs assistance from Mr. Everest on an extremely important matter of national security."

"I have to interrupt you, David," Campbell leaned forward placing his elbows on his desk, and the transplant to Arizona, in a very definitive Midwestern accent, asked, "Am I cleared, or whatever you call it, for you to be talkin' to me about top secret things concernin' national security?"

"Mr. Campbell, believe me, we've done our homework on you. Do you remember when you and some of your high school buddies *poured gasoline and urinated inside your high school bully's car?"*

"How th—? No one knew about that but me and three of my best friends!" Billy blurted out as he leaned back causing his chair to almost tip over backwards. "Man, you guys are scary!"

Palmer displayed no alteration to his facial expression. He still sat straight in the plush chair, hardly moving. "The real estate project needs to fail. We understand you have not formally committed to the investment yet."

How do these guys find out these things?' Billy thought as he listened. Big brother is watchin!

"We want you to back out of it," Palmer told the contractor. He was looking directly at Campbell when he said it.

Billy Campbell stared at the government man, and Campbell's face got real serious. He thought to himself, *Enough is enough!*

Then he said, "I can't do that, David." He hesitated for a second or two, and continued, "I can't do that to my friend."

"I understand how you feel. I promise you, you'll be compensated for any—"

Campbell cut the man off, "I don't give a rat's ass about the money." Billy's blood pressure was going sky high. "I won't do that to Michael. He's worked hard on this, and he's come up with a great plan. We're gonna make a bundle on this."

"Mr. Campbell, we will compensate everyone in Michael's project for their investments and any profits that would have been made. But, the project must fail.

"Michael Everest has already invested an enormous amount. We need him to fail . . . "

The government man paused as Billy Campbell stared at him.

Campbell finally broke the silence, "I want to talk to Michael."

"No!" Palmer shifted in the chair for the first time, and exclaimed, "You can't do that. . . . You can't tell Mr. Everest about our meeting. You will simply tell him that you have changed your mind."

Palmer rose from his chair and said, "When everything is over, then Mr. Everest will be told. He'll also be told about your loyalty to him."

Campbell stood and shrugged as he said, "Until then, though, Michael will hate me."

After David Palmer opened the door and climbed into his rented car, he pulled the sheet of paper from his inside coat pocket and looked at the name and address for his next appointment: DONALD WORTHINGTON . . . 1845 EAST HAPPY VALLEY ROAD.

* * *

Warren Turner looks at his watch, 12:01 A.M. *It's starting!*

115

Southern Spain . . . Monday, 6:00 A.M.

THE THREE SPECIAL FORCES commandos and I are approximately fifty meters from Rodrigo Lara Orasco's villa. Each of us carries a compact Uzi automatic weapon as well as a holstered semiautomatic pistol attached to the side of one of our thighs. We still wear warm navy-blue clothing.

We have separated ourselves from one another and wait behind desert boulders, yet we're joined as if we are connected to one umbilical cord as none of us is able to speak, even in a whisper, without being heard by the others through the headsets.

In the east I watch the sky undertake to brighten its darkness as angel hair mists of clouds frozen to stillness are suddenly buffed a deep red-orange from the solar brush of a sun that still hides itself before beginning its daily peregrinate to style its dominance upon everything dwelling beneath.

Minutes pass without consistent paces as I continue to sit alone, hidden the same as the others behind the rocky boulders, where each of us is able to clearly see the villa. From where I am, I gaze out at the Mediterranean. I am between the sea and the sun that has now fashioned itself full in the sky. And, with its brightness at my back, there's no glare on the water, and, in less than a minute, the solar planet changes its color from orange to lemon causing the sea to fade from blue-grey to turquoise along the shoreline. And, at the same time, the breeze stirs white ruffles that seem to dance along the surface of the water.

As my eyes solemnize this magic overture, I envision how this act of nature, this energy within itself, never ends. Even man, with all his knowledge, and arrogance, can never control, can never interrupt this magical frolic that has performed so magnificently since the beginning of time . . . when Abraham lived, when Julius Caesar lived, when Jesus Christ lived, when Christopher Columbus lived. And now . . . while we live.

My contemplations are interrupted as Lora Parks reports on where the guards are located.

Joshua Stone watches her from about thirty yards away as he listens to her voice transmitting in a whisper through the tiny microphone that brushes against the side of her mouth. She's the most beautiful commando Joshua has ever seen. He prays to himself, *Please protect her!*

Lora's voice continues, "Three are standing together about twenty meters from the front of the house, east of the circular drive. We'll have to take them first.

"There's another one outside by the cliffs, in back of the house."

I fumble my clammy hands against the cool metal of my Uzi, and hear Parks finish her observation, "I only saw one inside, in the living room."

"Besides Orasco, there are probably another three or four inside," I interject quietly into my mike.

As I wait, still hidden behind a small mound of rocks, I hear David Palmer's calm commands rise through the headset, "Stone and Parks go with me to take the three in front . . . Everest is familiar with the terrain, so he takes the one on the cliff in back.

"After we clear the outside, Everest will go in through the back of the house and take out the one in the living room.

"Once that's secure, Parks will cover the living room, and the rest of us will sweep the place. Okay, guys . . . and lady . . . we go!"

As soon as I round the rear corner of the villa I spot the guard sitting in a lounge chair that's been placed near the edge of the cliff.

The man holds his automatic rifle in his lap and faces the sea while its deafening waves smash into the rocks below, drowning out all other sound.

I maneuver up behind the foolish guard while my breathing labors and my heart thrashes in all directions as if it's taken over all matter in my body with no thought whatsoever of finding its proper place and offering me relief of any kind from its deviant presence. I recall what David Palmer told me earlier, *"It's got to be a kill, Michael . . . there are no prisoners on our missions."*

God forgive me, I pray as I grip the end of my automatic within inches of the back of the man's head.

I can't do it!

Instead, I attempt to slam the butt of my Uzi into the guard's skull . . . not a fatal blow.

But before I can bring my weapon down on its target, the guard instantly jumps up and spins around facing me. The man has already begun to swing his rifle up to fire.

Just a split second before he can squeeze the trigger, my silent automatic has already blurted out five or six quick bursts into his chest knocking him backwards toward the edge of the cliff where he drops lifeless on the manicured grassy knoll.

I brace myself motionless for a moment and close my eyes, and hear nothing but the thundering sound of the waves, and I wonder about the man whom I've just killed. I wonder about those whose lives were sealed shut by my fellow commandos within the last few minutes. *Who were these luckless beings? At no fault of their own, were they denied, in their innocence, the seasons of goodwill, love, hope and fairness? Were they such that none ever savored a mother's bosom that rendered repose, not only for comfort, but as children learning the ways of tenderness?*

I want to scream with all my might . . . I want to cry . . . I want to stop all of this.

But . . . there's no time. I take in a deep breath, tighten my lips, and let out a huge sigh as I exhale. "My man's down," my shaky voice whispers into my mike. "I'm going in."

At once I hear Palmer's confirmation through his headset, "Front Secure. Go!"

116

THE PATIO DOORS sit open, and I step into the recreation room and head toward the kitchen. I intend to enter the living room from the adjacent dining room which can be accessed from the kitchen.

But, luck doesn't take kindly to my intentions and has designs of its own as it shapes unwanted whims that interfere with my advance . . . I don't make it to the living room. A startled guard strolls into the kitchen and stands there face to face with me as I freeze and don't even fret at the feeling of having to piss my pants. But, *some* luck is with me, the guard has no weapon that I can see.

"What the fuck!" the man yells.

I don't have time to fire my Uzi as the surprised man throws himself toward me before I can swing it up. Orasco's henchman grabs hold of the front of my shirt with both hands and forces me to drop my weapon. As a reflex, I step back with my left foot, causing me to make a one-quarter-turn to the left, and spin the man off balance past where I'm stationed.

As I execute this, I bend my flexed legs and slash my right forearm down, smashing into the top nerves of the man's forearms halfway between his wrists and elbows.

The impact causes him to release his grip on my shirt, and at the same instant, forces his arms to drop instinctively away from the pain.

As if in one motion, I chop the back of my right forearm across the right side of his neck, causing him to bend backwards.

Since the man is wearing a thin T-shirt, I step my left foot toward the dazed man, and, at the same time, with full force I pound my left handed fist, with my big finger's knuckle jutting out, into the man's right rib cage. I hear the crunch of ribs snapping.

As the man's reflexes from the impact to his ribs force him to straighten and turn slightly to his right, I instantly sweep my clawed right hand across his eyes. Then, as he instinctively straightens up even more and his head bends backwards, I finish with a front kick torpedoing into his groin.

The force from the kick shoves the stunned man backwards against the island counter in the kitchen and he slides down to the floor in a dazed sitting position.

But he seems to recover and reaches for a knife tucked in a holster at his side.

Without thinking at all, and in one flashing motion, I side step to the wretched man and snap a side kick just above his left ear, crushing his skull because his head is caught between my blow and the brick wall of the kitchen island.

Within seconds, I hear Lora Parks say as she scrambles into the kitchen, "The main floor is secure. Major Palmer is going to the lower area. You and Joshua will take the upstairs."

The sickening stagnant air cleaves to the insides of her nostrils. Catherine Steele is barely coherent, yet, still recognizes the oppressive heat that feels to her like its presence far exceeds a hundred degrees in the musty room. She sees no windows.

She gasps with each breath as she frantically struggles to break free from the ropes that bind her wrists to a bed's metal headboard. She's positioned on her back on top of the bed.

She feels nauseous, and she's afraid she's about to vomit any second. Her body tingles and her head aches. Her mouth is dry, yet feels full. She coughs . . . her swollen tongue makes it difficult to breathe.

She's had nothing to eat or drink since before she left her office with Sotello on Friday morning, and she knows she's been kept in this room, which is like a sauna, ever since she was brought to this place. She has no idea what day it is or where she is. She's becoming delirious as she fights the pain and consciousness. *Michael, where are you? Help me! . . . Please!*

She hears a distant sound . . . a door opening. Catherine tries to focus her eyes as light bolts into the dark room. The glare prevents her from seeing who it is.

She hears the door slam shut.

She still can't tell who is in the dimly lighted room. The man's voice is in Spanish. Catherine doesn't recognize it, nor does she understand what he's saying.

"They understated your beauty, your body . . . " he speaks in English now.

Hector Baldarrama gazes with lust and anticipation at her form lying there in front of him, with her dress, soaked from her own perspiration, clinging tightly to her body and rising to the top of her long legs.

Hector's body trembles and his mouth hungers as he slowly removes his shirt, and then his pants until he is naked. His loins ache as he watches her slowly wrenching, trying to break free. He can tell she's barely able to move at all.

He walks slowly over to her and cuts one of her bleeding wrists free with the knife in his right hand.

She's too weak to fight him.

He pulls at her dress, ripping the front from her. He looks at her as she lies on the bed shielded only by her black bra and panties. Her smooth tanned skin shining from sweat drives Baldarrama wild.

He breathes heavier and begins to shake, almost uncontrollably. He tells himself that she is the best one yet.

He rips the bra from her, and the sight of her pale breasts drives him to a new, higher level of ecstacy that he knows no other man can possibly imagine. Catherine gasps and groans from the pain. It excites him even more.

He wants to make this last. *Yes . . . last forever.* He trembles even more, and he can barely stand. He wants to relish every minute as he grabs her panties and rips them from her.

"Aqui! mujer hermosa (Here! beautiful woman), I have something for you to drink," she hears his husky, sickening voice mumble. Then he places his knees on the bed to the side of her body and moves toward her face where he positions himself a few inches above her.

Suddenly, the door smashes open from David Palmer's kick and he tears into the room.

"YOU MOTHERFUCKING SCUM!" Palmer snarls as he charges Baldarrama, and, with an open hand straight-arms him in the chin, forcing it back into the startled man's neck just above the Adam's apple, snapping the drug lord's head back.

Baldarrama gasps for air as his hands fly to the front of his neck.

Palmer, the supposedly well-disciplined professional soldier, now filled with uncontrollable rage, doesn't even have time to consider his actions as he becomes a deadly animal whose maddening instincts engulf him, and he quickly pulls his own knife from its sheath and, in an instant, the potent, hacking steel practically severs the naked man's penis and testicles.

The rapist is choking to death as he lies on the floor in a puddle of blood composing from the flow pouring from his loins, thrashing frantically gasping to breathe through his crushed throat.

David Palmer, meanwhile, quickly snaps the rope away from the bed with the blood-smeared knife, and immediately throws a blanket over Catherine, and in the same motion picks up the helpless woman and races up the stairs to the living room where he carefully places her on a sofa before rushing to the kitchen.

Within seconds he returns with a container of ice and pops a piece in his mouth, rapidly chewing it, and then carefully placing one of the crushed pieces into the semiconscious woman's mouth. At the same time, Lora Parks has grabbed a towel from the kitchen and soaked it in cool water and begins applying it to Catherine's forehead and then to the rest of Catherine's face and neck.

After a few minutes, Catherine struggles to open her eyes and then slowly looks up at them.

David Palmer, army major, smiles as he finds himself agreeable to his evaluation that well establishes this woman as being quite attractive. She coughs and he places another small piece of ice into her mouth.

117

THEY STILL DON'T know we're here, I declare to myself as I follow Joshua Stone up the stairs. *It's so damn quiet,* I reflect to myself in an avowed state of uninvited anxiety, and this causes me to realize, after all that has happened, that I'm still human as my mind swirls and I grope with the uneasiness stirring me. *Men have just died. Sons, loving sons of mothers have died . . . Jesus, it's too quiet.*

This new world to which I have committed myself, without really considering in a judicious avenue before now, I belatedly admit to myself, appears almost imaginary. And I know it tolerates no latitude for mistakes at any level nor does it concede to thoughts of contrition for past actions that have destroyed lives.

I sense myself succumbing to uncontrolled trembling, and I'm acutely aware of the knot that's captured all matter in my belly as I continue trailing the ever-vigilant Joshua Stone up the stairway. We soon discover there's no one else at the villa.

David Palmer is sitting on the floor next to the couch watching over Catherine, still feeding her ice.

Lora Parks, wondering where Joshua Stone is, somewhere in the villa, stands watch near the front door observing Palmer while he comforts the distressed woman.

Catherine has begun breathing easier. The swelling in her tongue has subsided, but she's still incoherent at times, and won't let go of David Palmer's hand.

After completing the sweep of the premises with Joshua, I enter the living room, and seeing Catherine lying on the sofa, rush over to her.

I breathe easier when Palmer quickly assures me that she'll be okay. In fact, it appears to me that Catherine will be well taken care of.

Standing at the back of the couch, I reach down and take her other hand, and quietly tell her, "You saved my life."

She gives me a warm smile while slowly blinking her eyes and gently squeezing my hand. As I look down at her, I realize that she knows this is the last time we will ever see one another. Then I capture her lips say without sound, *I love you, Michael Everest.* . . .

David Palmer doesn't leave Catherine's side even after medics from the carrier battle group arrive on the first helicopter. He remains with her until she's placed into the evac-helo and it rises and disappears from his view, motoring for sick bay in the battle group.

118

Aboard the **USS** *George Washington . . . 9:20* A.M.

"YES SIR, CAPTAIN," the radar technician reports. "We tracked it from Malaga for about an hour and twenty minutes, and then lost it near Paris."

Captain Jerry Mattingly turns toward us four mercenaries and says, "Gentlemen, and lady . . . you heard. Any ideas?"

"That's probably Orasco's jet," Major Palmer replies as he turns to me looking for a suggestion. "What do you think?"

My mind searches for answers, and one thought keeps reappearing and overpowering all others as I focus on one person . . . *Jacques. Damn! I could never get her to talk about how she had become involved with Orasco. How much does she know? Who is she?* "I know where he is."

119

Paris . . . 8:35 P.M.

"STARS ARE castles in the sky. They sparkle like diamonds, with energy bursting out all over the universe, engulfing everything in their paths . . . paths that voyage like ocean waves scattering in song across every conceivable existence.

"And we, here on this insignificant planet, are unknowingly consumed with this energy that passionately invites us to be a part in ways that we have not yet begun to imagine.

"So far away are they . . . those castles in the sky.

"And yet, simply reaching out toward them with our minds . . . with our actions, the way we choose to live, we touch them. Our energies become one. Our energies become eternally united . . . with those castles in the sky.

"Someday when you pass from this life, Michael, your energy may well find another life on this earth, or your energy will discover its place out there among the stars . . . forever . . . and know it all.

I recall Hue's poetic words to me while we sat together on a ledge high up on North Mountain and gazed at the dark solar system that was ours that night. It was a rare time that I had heard her tell me she loved me. It was the last time I ever heard her say it. I wasn't quite six years old.

As I sit alone now on the park bench on the bank of the Seine with the cold wind tendering itself in a chilling disposition, I find myself drawn to the beauty around me . . . the dim yellow-orange glow from the street lamps reflecting on the dark water, the crisp cold breeze, smells from nearby restaurants, the sounds and movements of the traffic in the streets . . . life . . . energy . . . all of those things.

As I gaze upward, the stars that are visible appear brilliant to me in their diamond like excellence even though the bright magical lights of Paris hinder my view in a minor way . . . my view of the castles in the sky.

The soft ring from my cellular interrupts my thoughts. "Yes?" I quietly answer.

The voice on the phone is brief, "She's there now."

"All right," I reply, and snap the phone shut, and glance at my watch. It's almost nine o'clock.

After one final critique of my onyx sky I rise from the park bench and casually walk the four blocks along the quiet but fast moving waters of the Seine . . . its small waves lapping at the shore. I feel its dampness.

It takes me almost ten minutes to reach her condo and knock on the expensive hardwood door, and wait, listening for any sound. Suddenly it opens.

She stands staring at me for a brief moment, her eyes wide open. "Michael! What a wonderful surprise!" Jacques cries out in Spanish. "What are you doing here?"

I'm taken aback somewhat, surprised by her reaction. I thought she would be expecting me. She wasn't.

"Please, come in!" she excitedly invites as she opens the door all the way. "I cannot believe you are here," she happily proclaims, and rushes up and tightly hugs me.

"I have some business to take care of," I tell her in English as I awkwardly return her embrace.

At once, I can tell that Jacques detects the somberness in my voice. She closes the door behind me, and shifts to English, "Michael, you sound so serious. Is something wrong?"

I glance around the luxury condo as caution warns my senses that tell me Rodrigo Lara Orasco could be hiding here somewhere. I have been in the condo several times before, so I'm familiar with its large size. In fact, I spent several nights there in the guest bedroom during previous trips to Europe.

"I'm looking for Rodrigo Orasco," I tell her as my eyes continue scanning the apartment. "Is he here?" I sense from the inquisitive look on her face, that Jacques has no idea what's going on.

"Has he been here, Jacques?" My voice is softer now, less demanding. "Has Orasco been here?"

Perplexed, Jacques raises her arm and sweeps the back of her wrist across her forehead and answers—in Spanish—"No! I have not seen Rodrigo. Will you please tell me what is happening?"

As I prepare to sit in one of the sofa chairs in her living room, I say to her, in Spanish, "Please, Jacques, sit down."

I watch her move to the sofa and can't help but notice behind her, through the veranda doorway, the prominent Eiffel Tower several miles away, its historied loveliness displayed in silent breaths of illuminated gold animation that breathes out its soul like a seasoned warrior laying in still iron and pampered elegance, amused by us mere propitious mortals parading in awe under its sacred watchfulness.

"How did you meet Orasco?" I ask.

"How did I meet him!" Jacques says this not as a question, but more as a pondered response.

Then she shocks me with her answer. "Rodrigo is my uncle!"

120

JULIA EVEREST WATCHES from the upstairs window as the man sits by the pool with Rodrigo Orasco. The pool light echoing through the water makes it easy for her to see them. The stranger appears to be from the Middle East, and wears a jacket.

The two of them are having, it seems to her, a heated argument. When she was first brought there, she was immediately locked inside the bedroom by two men whom she presumes are Orasco's bodyguards. She had never seen either of them before.

They took her from Orasco's villa in Spain early that morning before sunrise, and locked her in one of the small compartments on Orasco's jet.

It's dark now, and her windows are locked shut so she can't tell how warm or cool it is outside, and stakes no guess at all as to where she is.

Until now, Julia has not seen nor spoken with Orasco since Saturday night when he carried her into her bedroom at his villa.

She watches the two men for about ten minutes as they continue their conversation. From their gestures Julia is certain now that they are engaged in a heated argument. Finally, they stand, and the Arab hastily stalks away in a huff.

Orasco stands there momentarily and watches the man leave. Then Julia sees Orasco slowly turn and glare up at her, and then walk from her view.

121

"I DIDN'T TELL you before, Michael, because I didn't want anyone to think that I had this position with Rodrigo's commerce because I am his niece. Since I have been in school for so many years, I have only just recently begun to see him on a regular basis.

"He has taken care of me all my life. I do not remember much about my mother, his sister. She and my father died in a fire when I was very small.

"Rodrigo brought me to Spain right after that. He made sure that I was able to be educated in the finest schools in Spain, France and Switzerland. During all those years, I only saw him four or five times before I graduated from the university. Even though I saw very little of him, he would write me letters, three or four times a year."

As I listen, I can't help being transfixed by Jacques's beautiful, troubled face as she sits so straight on the couch with her hands in her lap and her knees properly together.

She's in her bare feet and wearing a dusty-lilac cashmere sweater and plain old white American jeans. I study her as she speaks and wish this gorgeous young lady was my daughter.

At first, I'm not sure how much I should tell her about her uncle, though I'm sure the expression on my face gives me away, it's too serious.

"Michael, please tell me! Please tell me what is wrong," she pleads.

I rise from the chair, stroll over to her, and seat myself next to her on the sofa. I place my hands on hers and grip them firmly as her hands lay in her lap.

"I don't know where to begin, Jacques. It hurts to have to tell you."

"I've never had a father that I knew, Michael. I've never had a friend, a real friend. I have been alone all of my life, but I found a friend, I found you. You have made me feel special, special to you. I now know what it is like to be cared for by someone, being important to someone, someone like you. Someone like you, who wants nothing from me, but to be part of my life . . . as a dear friend.

"As long as I believe that, I will never be alone. As long as I am not alone, I can bare any pain. As long as you will be my friend and be there when I need you . . . then I know I will be safe. Please, Michael, tell me."

I place my arm around her shoulders as the two of us sit back in the sofa and she lays her head on my chest. I tell her everything I know about Rodrigo Lara Orasco, and she cries as she listens, while I hold her.

When I finish, Jacques tells me where Orasco's chateau is, in the country . . . just outside Paris.

122

AS SOON AS Julia is brought into the living room by one of the men guarding her, Orasco enters from outside. Julia sits down on an oversized sofa and glares at him.

She estimates that it's been about twenty-five minutes since the Arab man left Orasco so abruptly. And she now knows what time it is since she's able to see a clock that sits on the fireplace mantle. *It's two-thirty.* She's also aware that it's night, still dark outside the windows.

Julia watches Orasco as he approaches. She shows no emotion and displays only a serious facial look . . . an undeniable expression of contempt. She scowls at him. *Who is he? What is he?*

The powerful drug lord sits next to her, facing her while she says nothing and continues to glare at him.

"I have some terrible news, Julia." He hesitates, and then tells her, "Michael has been killed."

Her heart sinks and her mouth instinctively opens, and deep breaths overwhelm her with their reassuring presence that intends only to guard against her losing consciousness. She tries not to cry out as she continues to breath deeper, and faster.

Stunned, she stares at a large flower arrangement that sits on a glass coffee table in front of her. Consoling reflections of any degree refuse to reveal their sort to her because they're not needed as she comforts her own self, and without recognizable thought imparts her eyes to see nothing else other than the flower arrangement.

Then she hears his loud voice again, "Did you hear me, Julia? Michael is dead!"

She blinks and offhandedly turns toward Rodrigo Orasco with no whisper of an identifiable sentiment on her face. This time she doesn't look into his eyes as she always had before. Now, she looks at his entire face, as if looking right through him . . . past him.

Her stare lasts only a few seconds as the outside sound of automatic gunfire begins erupting.

Orasco leaps up, glancing around in all directions. He isn't sure where it's coming from. Only, that there's a lot of it. He frantically looks at Julia.

She's confused at first, but then a warm feeling embraces her with its promise of goodness . . . of righteousness.

Orasco suddenly grabs her by her arm, yanks her up from the sofa and drags her along with him as he bolts up the stairs. As they disappear down the hallway, Rodrigo and Julia hear the sound of the front door being smashed open.

Because of the gunfire coming from outside, neither of them hear me as I charge through the open door.

"JULIA! JULIA! WHERE ARE YOU?" I yell and drop to the floor, rolling several times to my left before coming to rest near a sofa . . . my Uzi is aimed ready to spit death as my eyes search the huge room for movement.

After waiting for ten or fifteen seconds and almost without a thought of any kind to interfere with my resolve to find my wife, I scramble to my feet and dash up the stairs taking two steps at a time, all the while my eyes scanning left and right.

Once I reach the landing at the top, I cautiously begin a room by room search . . . the adrenalin rushing through me portions no time for regarding the status of the activity in my stomach that has taken on its own renewed battle, but otherwise, I feel remarkably calm.

The intense gunfire outside ends almost as abruptly as it began. Although I still hear sporadic bursts now and then.

David Palmer, Lora Parks and Joshua Stone, along with a team of Delta Force Commandos are wreaking havoc, I half smile to myself. And, I find it odd, funny . . . amusing that I can find humor in such a place as this. A place so full of anarchy . . . and chaos. *I'd sure hate to have them pissed off at me.*

Shaman Zodaru hears automatic gunfire about five hundred meters away. It sounds to him like it is coming from Rodrigo Orasco's chateau . . . the one he just left a few minutes earlier.

He smiles to himself, *Allah watches over me. If I had left a minute or two later . . . who knows?*

Allah has a reason!

It will become even more difficult . . . we must work harder. Allah will guide us, father. For your life under these parasites . . . for your death by these dogs. For these things they will all burn in hell for what they have done to you. Allah wills it!

We will have our revenge on these pagans. They will pay for their sins . . . someday!

And we will find this murderer of our soldiers . . . we will find and destroy this "Jericho." Allah wills it!

Zodaru's motorcar turns east . . . towards home!

I scream out her name again, "JULIA! JULIA! WHERE ARE YOU?" *Where are you Julia? Where's Orasco?*

It's quiet now as I step toward the last room, with my calves comfortably flexed. I listen for any sound. Nothing! *Maybe, they're not here!*

Then, her loud voice breaks the silence, "MICHAEL, HE'S LETTING ME OUT! I'M COMING OUT!"

The door slowly opens . . . part of the way.

I see my frightened wife squeeze herself past the opening. I crouch down near the wall adjacent to the door away from the railing overlooking the living room below. I'm about a dozen feet from the doorway now.

As Julia rushes to me, she whimpers as she pleads, "Rodrigo didn't want me hurt. He wanted me out of the way so that I wouldn't be harmed. Please don't hurt him, Michael!"

As soon as she reaches me, I rise slightly, grab her arm and immediately pull her down to the floor and fall over her.

And then, without warning, Orasco comes barreling through the door with an automatic rifle ripping at anything in his way.

He aims high.

At that same instant, gunfire erupts in my ears from behind. As I look up at Orasco, I see Orasco's chest punctured like a dispatched flat stone skipping across a lake by a burst of Uzi rapid fire leashed by Joshua Stone who had quietly crawled up to five feet behind where Julia and I lie together against the wall.

I can only watch as Orasco is thrown sideways from the force of the automatic's steel pounding into him, causing his body to slam over the railing and plummet head first to the living room, thirty feet below.

I quickly slide over to the railing and stare down at the lifeless form. I'm certain Rodrigo Lara Orasco did not feel his body smack into the rustic tile floor. The dead drug lord lies face up. His eyes are open and staring at nothing. He landed on his back and on his bent right leg, so that the leg is pinned in a disgustedly gross position beneath his body.

Julia, sobbing, rushes over and drops down beside me, clinging to me with all her strength. "I love you," she whispers between sobs, and pulls me even closer. "I love you."

As I hold her and continue staring at the lifeless form below, I tell my wife, "I love you, too . . . more than anything!"

After a few moments sitting there holding my wife, I rise and guide her to her feet. Then I turn and gesture to Joshua with a nod and lips pursed in a slight smile of gratitude for saving both, Julia's and my life.

Joshua Stone returns the *thank you* in a like manner, just a nod . . . you're welcome!

Then, I instinctively ask Joshua, "Where's David and Lora. Are they all right?"

"Palmer rushed Lora to a military base hospital nearby. She has a flesh wound on her left arm just below her shoulder. David said she'll be all right," Joshua replies as he looks back at Julia and me and begins descending the stairs.

When he reaches the bottom of the stairway, Joshua once again turns back in our direction and says, "Since you don't need me anymore, I'm going to catch a quick flight back to the states. Hope to see you soon, Michael." And then he disappears out the front door.

As I lead her down the stairs, I turn to Julia, flash a light smile, and tell her, "C'mon! We're going to Paris. I want you to meet someone."

Epilogue

Washington, D.C. . . . April

SPRING FINALLY REWARDS the nation's capital with a glowing promise of gentle days, and the bright sun sprays its soothing warmth on us while a comfortable breeze whispers contentment through our hair. We casually stroll up the steps of the historic building where we are being escorted by one of the national security advisor's assistants.

I glance at the two ladies accompanying me, and quite subjectively reflect to myself about how much the two actually resemble one another. I have already decided that these two women will share the rest of my life with me.

Julia Everest and Jacques Guzman both turn their heads back towards me and smile as I follow them past the Marine Guard and through the front door to the most famous residence in the world.

I think about when I met Warren Turner once, before the man became national security advisor to the President of the United States.

That was the night, I recall, that David Palmer almost forcibly put me into the limo, when I was training at Camp Peary more than two years ago. *It was colder than hell!*

As I follow behind the two gorgeous ladies being led through the impressive residence, I'm quite pleased with myself as I weigh on where I am now.... *Who would have ever predicted? Warren Turner asked me to meet with him. Probably wants to thank me for helping stop Orasco. It was nice of him to invite Julia too . . . even paid her airfare.* I smile to myself, *Actually, it makes me feel important.*

A second assistant waiting in the reception area politely greets us and announces, "The security advisor is on a conference call. He'll be with you in just a few moments. Please make yourselves comfortable." She smiles and motions toward the tastefully decorated arrangement of chairs and sofas.

Julia and Jacques decide on the over-size couch while I select a plush sofa chair.

"This is all so beautiful," Julia exclaims with a smile. "Look at this fabric!"

Jacques is also impressed. She smooths her hand over the material, while wondering if they'll get to meet the president.

The two ladies begin chatting about their surroundings while I relax myself and realize that those aggravating sharp pains that had found their luster in my neck and shoulders for the past two years have moved on, away from my life, hopefully forever. My thoughts drift to Hue. I remember the last time I saw her.

* * *

I was sitting next to her bed. Her hands lay at her side. My hand covered one of hers, and I gently rubbed it and her forearm.

Her breathing became slight . . . more difficult. She struggled for each breath. I knew, somehow, it was almost time, and it scared me. The dimly lighted room in the hospital's medical ICU was slow to noise of any level and was deserted except for the two of us.

I watched her. Her eyes were closed. Her mouth was barely opened, and showed no expression. Except for the shallow breathing, she looked like her soul had already gone from her.

Then, I saw her struggle to open her eyes. I stood and leaned over the bed so that my face was just above hers, and I drew close to her, and she looked at me and smiled, only sightly . . . but I saw it. Her voice was nothing more than jarring breaths bearing staccato tones of an anxious essence, and I listened to her raspy voice whisper with her last breath, "Thank you, Michael."

I watched her eyes close . . . her mouth lost its smile . . . and Hue went to her next life.

I didn't cry . . . I knew I wasn't allowed to. I finally understood . . . I had done everything she had told me to do. She "did" love me. I'll miss her.

* * *

"Mr. Turner will see you now," the middle-aged lady announces as she approaches from the inner office. The assistant leads us through the open office door and graciously steps aside for us to enter.

"Mr. Everest!" Warren Turner says as he approaches from behind his desk and extends his arm. "It's so nice to see you again."

"It's nice to see you again, sir!" I reply as I shake the national security advisor's hand, and then turn toward my two companions. "I would like you to meet my wife, Julia."

"How do you do, Mrs. Everest," Turner gently takes her hand in his as he smiles at her.

"It's an honor to meet you, Mr. Turner." Julia's own smile reveals her excitement and genuine sincerity.

I place my hand behind Jacques . . . presenting her to the statesman. "This is Jacques Guzman, our very dear friend." I beam.

"How do you do, Warren," Jacques smiles as she greets the well known national security advisor, and mischievously thinks to herself while shaking his hand and looking at his gray hair, *He is one good-looking man.*

"So nice to meet you, Jacques!"

Warren leads us to a seating arrangement near the fireplace that has green potted plants substituting for a fire, and motions as he says with a warm smile, "Please, sit down. We have a lot to talk about."

I begin to feel a little uncomfortable even though I know that I've already prepared myself to listen to Warren Turner compliment me on a job well done, and tell Julia and Jacques how incredible I was.

Warren says as he looks directly at me, "I know you've transcended much during the past twenty-four months. And, you've undergone things that you've never experienced before. You don't need me to sit here and tell you what a great job you've done. I believe you already know that, Michael. If I may call you Michael."

"I would like that, sir!"

Warren continues, "I know that some very fine men who were involved in this operation have died. I know some were close to you." Turner's warm eyes are still fixed on mine.

"Yes, sir," I respectfully reply as I recall events of the past two years. "I became very close to Henry Sotello. He was my contact . . . and my friend."

The national security advisor seems to be listening attentively as I continue, "Henry had a family . . . three children and a granddaughter. His wife died ten years ago. He loved his family."

Warren solemnly nods his head as he listens to me, his godson . . . a fact I was not yet aware of. *Hue did a remarkable job raising him,* Warren proudly reflects.

I reminisce about Moon Valley and Walter Barron, and Ted Mills . . . *I'm the reason they're gone.* "I also know that I'm responsible for the deaths of others," I tell the national security advisor. "My friends had no idea I was involved in anything like this. One of them was my best friend. I was playing tennis with them when it happened, and they were in the wrong place . . . innocent bystanders . . . " My voice trails off as their images stamp themselves sharply in my view, and I can't help glancing away from Warren Turner, finally settling my gaze on the plush carpet.

I can sense Julia and Jacques watching me and the elderly statesmen. They know how much I've been hurt, they know I bear the guilt for the deaths of my friends.

"No, Michael," Turner interjects, "they weren't in the wrong place." Turner hesitates before continuing, "Walter Barron and Ted Mills were police officers. They were consulted before you were ever brought into this."

A surprised and confused look smothers my face as I glance up at the national security advisor. "They knew all along?" I gasp.

Warren stands up and walks over to the fireplace, turns toward me, his former spy, and answers, "Yes... they knew. They approved it. They were always briefed on anything we were aware of, while you were undercover.

"They died in the line of duty. They knew as much as we about what you were doing at all times. And, they knew the danger you faced every day. Just like they knew the danger they faced."

Julia rises from the sofa, and walks over to me and stands at my side. She places her hand on my shoulder and gently caresses the back of my neck, and with her touch I need only the fragrance of orange blossoms to perfect my ascent to the heavens.

I feel Jacques curiously watching, and I imagine her thinking to herself that she has never had parents... until now.

Warren strolls back to his chair and sits before saying, "Now, Michael, there's the matter of two of your clients, Mr. Worthington and Mr. Campbell... and a few other things you need to know...."

I, accountant and former spy, sit with my wife standing next to me. I feel the softness of her hand still tenderly brushing the back of my neck. Her touch reminds me that the throbbing pain is no longer there.

I shift my eyes toward Jacques Guzman, the woman I've learned to love like a daughter, and I smile.

And, I listen as National Security Advisor Warren Turner begins telling me about Michael Everest's heritage.

* * *

Brentwood, California... St. Sebastian Parish

"He has gone up into the wilderness somewhere in the area of Mount Shasta in northern California near the Oregon border, Ms. Parks," the bishop informs the young lady at the other end of the line. "I'm afraid I don't know how long Joshua will be up there... probably anywhere from four to six weeks, and I have no way of getting hold of him."

"Thank you, Bishop Carbajal," Lora Parks dejectedly tells him. "I'm sorry to have bothered—"

"Just a moment, Ms. Parks!" Bishop Carbajal interrupts. "There's a hunting guide in Payson, Arizona who may be able to help you find Joshua. He has traveled up in that California and Oregon area with Joshua before. I'll give you his number if you like . . .

"That is," Adolfo Carbajal quickly blurts out with a distinct twinkle in his eye, "if you feel that it is very important . . . "